EXTREME PREY

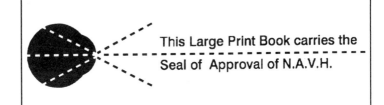

This Large Print Book carries the
Seal of Approval of N.A.V.H.

EXTREME PREY

JOHN SANDFORD

THORNDIKE PRESS
A part of Gale, Cengage Learning

GALE
CENGAGE Learning·

Farmington Hills, Mich • San Francisco • New York • Waterville, Maine
Meriden, Conn • Mason, Ohio • Chicago

LIBRARY OF CONGRESS CATALOGING-IN-PUBLICATION DATA

Names: Sandford, John, 1944 February 23- author.
Title: Extreme prey / John Sandford.
Description: Large print edition. | Waterville, Maine : Thorndike Press, 2016. | © 2016 | Series: Thorndike Press large print basic
Identifiers: LCCN 2016012854 | ISBN 9781410485274 (hardback) | ISBN 1410485277 (hardcover)
Subjects: LCSH: Davenport, Lucas (Fictitious character)—Fiction. | BISAC: FICTION / Thrillers. | GSAFD: Mystery fiction | Suspense fiction.
Classification: LCC PS3569.A516 E88 2016b | DDC 813/.54—dc23
LC record available at http://lccn.loc.gov/2016012854

Published in 2016 by arrangement with G.P. Putnam's Sons, an imprint of Penguin Publishing Group, a division of Penguin Random House LLC

Printed in the United States of America
1 2 3 4 5 6 7 20 19 18 17 16

EXTREME PREY

ONE

Bright-eyed Marlys Purdy carried a steel bucket around the side of the garage to the rabbit hutches, which were stacked up on top of each other like Manhattan walk-ups. She paused there for a moment, considering the possibilities. A dozen New Zealand whites peered through the screened windows, their pink noses twitching and pale eyes watching the intruder, their long ears turning like radar dishes, trying to parse their immediate future: Was this dinner, or death?

A car went by on the gravel road, on the far side of a ditch-line of lavender yarrow and clumps of black-eyed Susans and purple coneflowers, throwing a cloud of dust into the late-afternoon sun. Marlys turned to look. Lori Schaeffer, who lived three more miles out. Didn't bother to wave.

Marlys was a sturdy woman in her fifties, white curls clinging to her scalp like vanilla frosting. She wore rimless glasses, a home-made red-checked gingham dress, and low-topped Nikes. Short-nosed and pale, she had a small pink mouth that habitually pursed in thought, or disapproval.

She popped the door on one of the hutches and pulled the rabbit out by its hind feet.

The animal smelled of rabbit food and rabbit poop and the pine shavings used as bedding. A twelve-inch Craftsman crescent wrench, its working end rusted shut, lay on top of the hutches. Marlys stretched the rabbit over her thigh and held it tight until it stopped wriggling, then picked up the crescent wrench and whacked the rabbit on the back of the head, separating the skull from the spine.

So it was death.

The rabbit went limp, but a few seconds later began twitching as its nerves fired against oxygen starvation. That went on for a bit and then the rabbit went quiet again.

Some years before, Marlys had mounted a plank on the side of the garage, at head height. Before mounting the board, she'd driven two twenty-penny common nails through it, so that an inch of nail protruded, angling upward. Every year or so, she'd use a bastard file to sharpen up the nails.

Now she positioned the bucket, with a used plastic shopping bag on the inside, under the board with the nails. She pushed the dead rabbit's feet onto the nails until the nails stuck through, and, in a minute or so, had stripped the rabbit's fur, pulled off its head, and gutted it, all the unwanted parts and most of the blood draining into the plastic bag in the bucket.

Not all of the blood: a dinner-plate-sized blotch of old black bloodstains marred the wooden side of the garage, supplemented by new red blotches from this last butchery. She carried the bloody meat back to the house, paused to tie up the top of the plastic bag and drop it into the garbage can, and in the kitchen washed the meat.

During the entire five-minute process of killing and butchering the rabbit, she'd never once thought about either the animal or the process. All of that was automatic, like pulling beets or picking wax beans.

Marlys's brain was consumed with other thoughts.

Of murder.

If and when, and where and how, and with what.

Marlys was a woman of ordinary appearance, if seen in a supermarket or a library, dressed in homemade or Walmart dresses or slacks, a little too heavy, but fighting it, white-haired, ruddy-faced.

In her heart, though, she housed a rage that knew no bounds. The rage fully possessed her at times, and she might be seen sitting in her truck at a stoplight, pounding the steering wheel with the palms of her hands, or walking through the noodle aisle at the supermarket with a teeth-baring snarl. She had frightened strangers, who might look at her and catch the flames of rage, quickly extinguished when Marlys realized she was being watched.

The rage was social and political and occasionally personal, based on her hatred of obvious injustice, the crushing of the small and helpless by the steel wheels of American plutocracy.

Jesse walked into the kitchen, running a hand over his close-cropped hair. He peered over her shoulder into the sink. "What are we having?"

"Rabbit fettuccine Alfredo," Marlys said to her blue-eyed son. "We're eating early, 'cause I got to get over to Mount Pleasant. You go on out and get me some broccoli and a tomato. Where's your brother?"

"Messin' around with that .22," Jesse said.

He put a hand to his left cheek, a gesture of thought or weariness in others, but in Jesse, an unconscious move to cover the port-wine stain that marked his neck and the bottom of his cheek. "He says there's nothing wrong with it that a good cleaning won't fix."

"Well, he knows his guns. Go get me that broccoli. We'll eat in an hour."

Marlys and her younger son, Cole, lived on a nine-acre place north of Pella, Iowa, in a weathered clapboard farmhouse with three bedrooms and a bathroom up, a living room, parlor, half bath, and kitchen down, and a rock-walled basement under all of that.

The basement held the mechanical equipment for the house, and a twenty-one-cubic-foot Whirlpool freezer that Marlys filled with corn, green and wax beans, peas, carrots, cauliflower, and broccoli, which kept them eating all winter. Applesauce from a half-dozen apple trees went in Ball jars, stored on dusty wooden shelves next to the freezer.

Her older son, Jesse, until recently had lived in an apartment in town with his wife and daughter, and sold Purdy produce at most of the big farmers' markets between Cedar Rapids and Des Moines.

Cole worked in the truck gardens and ran the mower at the country club during golf season. The two sons would jacklight four to six deer during the various hunting seasons, and the venison steaks and sausage, supplemented by the rabbits, filled out their meat requirements. They'd once had a chicken yard, but a midwinter spate of accounting several years earlier had convinced Marlys that chickens were cheaper to buy at the supermarket than to raise at home, even given the bonus eggs.

In the winter, to raise cash, Marlys made hand-stitched quilts that she sold through an Amish store in Des Moines. She wasn't Amish, but nobody much cared, as long as the quilts moved.

The Purdys weren't rich, but they did all right, not counting the possibly inherited tendency to psychosis.

Jesse walked down to the closest garden, cut a few broccoli heads — they were big and tough, being the last harvest of the first season, but good enough when chopped — and got a nice ripe tomato. All of that took only a minute, but by the time he started back to the house, he was sweating.

There'd been a lot of rain that spring and everything was looking lush and fine. At the moment, the sun was shining and the temperature was in the low nineties, with the humidity close to eighty percent.

The local farmers, of course, were bitching because the bean and corn harvests were going to be huge and the prices depressed. Of course, if it hadn't rained, they'd be bitching because their crops were small, even if the prices were high. You couldn't win with farmers.

For Marlys and her sons, the frequent rain was nothing but a blessing: more food than they could eat, so many apples that they'd have to cull them before they were mature to keep the apple tree branches from breaking; enough raspberries and Concord grapes to make jam for five years of toast. Marlys had been talking of buying an upright freezer for the kitchen. She could freeze a year's worth of cinnamon apple slices and they all *did* like apple pie.

As Jesse walked back to the house, he noticed a pale haziness on the western horizon, above the afterglow left by the sun, hinting of a new weather system moving in, even more rain. All right with him. Looking up at the top floor of the house, he saw Cole sitting behind the bedroom window screen with his rifle, which he had reassembled.

"You don't go shooting nobody," he called

13

up to his brother.

Cole didn't say anything, but lifted a hand.

Gray-eyed Cole sat in his bedroom window, looking out over the road, a scoped Ruger 10/22 in his hands. Squirrel rifle. Below him, a quilt hung on the wire clothesline, airing out. Before the end of the day, the quilt would smell like early-summer fields, with a little gravel dust mixed in. A wonderful smell, a smell like home.

An aging green pickup was motoring over the hill to the south, about to take the curve in front of the house. Cole tracked it with the scope, watching David Souther horse the truck around the curve heading south toward Pella. He whispered to himself, "Bang!"

One dead Souther.

Souther was a hippie kind of guy and had a hundred and twenty acres given over to sheep, which he'd shear so his wife could wash, spin, dye, and weave the fleece into blankets and wall hangings, which they sold at a store at the Amana Colonies. Souther was also a poet and sometimes had a book published. The Purdys had two of his books, which Souther had given them, but Cole had never read any of the poems.

Cole had nothing at all against Souther or

his wife. They worked hard and they didn't get rich, but they did all right, he supposed. Janette Souther was the shyest woman Cole had ever met: she couldn't even *look* at another human being. How she and Souther had ever gotten together, he had no idea. Of course, they had no kids, so maybe they hadn't exactly gotten together, Souther being a poet and all.

Another truck came over the hill to the south.

Cole put his scope on it . . .

Cole had been to Iraq twice with the National Guard. He'd been a truck driver, not a combat troop, but in Iraq, even the truck drivers were on the front lines. He'd been in his truck on two occasions when IEDs went off at the side of the road, once a short distance ahead of him, once behind him, artillery shells fired with cell phones.

He hadn't exactly been wounded either time, but he'd been hurt. He couldn't hear anything for a while after the second explosion and never could hear as well as he had when he enlisted. Right after the IEDs, he'd been too dizzy to drive for a bit, and nauseated for a couple of days, but the Army told him that he was okay, and the VA had waved him off — they had more important things to do.

He wasn't entirely sure about how okay he really was. Hadn't been able to sleep since he got back, and that was nine years now; and he'd had a bell-like ringing in his ears since the first explosion, sometimes so loud that he thought it would drive him crazy.

And maybe it had.

The approaching truck went into the turn: Sherm Miller, who had a farm up the road, nine hundred and sixty acres, one of the richer people around, his land alone probably worth seven or eight million.

Cole whispered, "Bang!"

Jesse dropped the broccoli and tomato with his mother and said, "I'm running down to Henry's to get some cigs. You want anything?"

"Mmm, get me a box of those hundred-calorie fudge bars. You stay away from Willie." Willie was Jesse's estranged wife.

"We gotta get that sorted out soon," Jesse said. "I can't be living here for the rest of my life."

Marlys paused in her dinner prep: "Well, you *could*. You could have your old bedroom back permanently. You know you're welcome."

"Gotta get away from here sooner or later,

16

Ma," Jesse said. "Then I won't have to listen to any more of that political bullshit from you and Cole. That Michaela Bowden bullshit. You guys are a little fucked up on the subject."

"Quiet! You be quiet!" Marlys said. "I don't want to hear anything about her."

"Nobody here but us," Jesse said.

Marlys pointed toward the ceiling: the NSA satellites were watching everything and everybody, and sorting, sorting, sorting. She was on forums that said so. The feds would be listening for the name "Michaela Bowden." Mention it the wrong way and the black helicopters would be all *over* your butt.

"You go on, but be back for dinner," Marlys said. And, "Stay away from Willie."

Jesse said, "Yeah," and "Cole's up in his window again," and walked out.

When Jesse was gone, Marlys went back to thinking about what she'd been thinking about for the past year: getting the right man in the White House.

That would mean killing Michaela Bowden, the leading candidate on the Democratic side. Bowden was a sure thing, everybody thought. Sure to get the nomination, sure to win the election.

17

She might already have some Secret Service protection, but the convention was still a year off. Bowden was running around the countryside, pumping up the base, trying to brick up the nomination, trying to fend off any possible competition, stretching to win Iowa's political caucuses, now only eight months away. She was out in the open and the Secret Service protection would be light, compared to what it'd be after the convention.

If they were going to get her, now was the time.

Right now. They couldn't wait.

Jesse got back to the house with the cigarettes, and two minutes later his wife showed up with the kid. His wife, whose name was Wilma but whom everybody called Willie, was dropping off their daughter, Caralee, for the weekend.

Marlys heard Willie and Jesse collide at the front door and thought, *Uh-oh,* and hurried that way, in time to hear Jesse saying, "I ain't payin' to support that asshole no way. You want to suck his lazy cock, you go right ahead, but you ain't seeing no more money from me . . ."

"I'll get the court after you again, you ugly piece of shit," Willie said.

18

Marlys called, "Hey, hey, you all shut up. Both of you. Willie, you get the hell out of here, you aren't welcome inside the house. You know that."

Caralee was sucking on a Binky and had the dried remnants of green baby food dribbled down her shirt. A small, round-headed blonde, she looked frightened, her eyes switching nervously between her parents, and Marlys got down on one knee and said, "Come on to Grandma, honey, come on, it's okay."

Willie left, banging the screen door behind her and shouting, "Fuck all you Purdys," and Jesse shouted back, "Suck on it, bitch," and Willie threw a finger over her shoulder. Upstairs, Cole put the scope's crosshairs on Willie's back and said to himself, "Bang."

That evening, after dinner, as Jesse, Cole, and Caralee settled down to watch a Cubs game on television, Marlys drove to Mount Pleasant. On the way, she felt the anger burning through her, as it always did when she got together with the other members of the Lost Tribes of Iowa.

Found herself hunched over the steering wheel, her knuckles white, remembering.

It had been thirty years since the Purdys lost the farm. Four hundred and eighty

19

acres of good black soil, gone with low crop prices and high interest rates. Gone with it was the three hundred thousand dollars that her parents had loaned to the newlyweds as a down payment on the mortgage loan, and to buy basic equipment. The loss of the three hundred thousand had crippled her father's retirement. He'd planned to travel, to do great things in his final years; maybe even buy a February time-share down in Fort Myers. He'd been left as an old man staring at a TV screen, sitting out the Iowa winters.

Two years after the disaster, Marlys's husband, Wilt, left their rented house, climbed in the rust-bucket Chevy, wound it up to ninety miles an hour, and pointed it into a concrete pillar on a railroad underpass. He'd been killed instantly, or, at least, that's what the cops said.

Marlys had never remarried, had never gone with another man: no time, no inclination, and not many offers. Maybe a few, turned away before they had a chance to become real. She still flashed to the day of Wilt's death, the sight of the sheriff and the Baptist minister coming up the flagstone path on the rental house . . . Sometimes at night she could roll over in bed and see the back of Wilt's head on the next pillow, silhouetted in the silvery moonlight, and she'd reach out and touch an empty pillow and whisper, "Wilt."

All she had left of Wilt was Cole's wide gray eyes.

The highway patrol kindly ruled Wilt's death an accident and the insurance company had been forced to fork over the money that bought the current house and the acreage outside of Pella.

When they bought it, the house had essentially been abandoned, inhabited by bats and mice and even a raccoon that had nested in the thin attic insulation. Marlys put the kids in school and worked two part-time jobs during the day and then worked half the night fixing up the house and barn, planting her trees and berries and grapes, paying for the compact John Deere tractor she needed to work her gardens.

The kids worked with her: they'd had to.

She'd almost gotten straight with herself and with Wilt's death, when Cole went off to Iraq in '05 and '07 and came back funny. The next year, the economy collapsed and friends and neighbors began losing jobs and homes again.

She could see so clearly that it was not their fault.

The system was rotten. The Administration was rotten, the Congress was rotten, the banks were rotten, the oil companies were rotten, the media were liars and thieves. Michaela Bowden was their instrument, mixed right in there with them.

Something had to be done to save America. The country needed a strong president whose heart was in the right place, who'd take care of the struggling folks at the bottom of the economic heap.

Somebody like Minnesota's governor, Elmer Henderson.

The Mount Pleasant meeting was in the home of Joseph Likely, an aging activist and gasbag who nevertheless knew a lot of history, and how history seemed to work through certain small moments — the assassination of John Kennedy or the 9/11 attacks. Moments that changed the world, usually for the worse.

But not always. Not always, Marlys thought.

At Likely's house Marlys got out of the car and took the insulated pizza-delivery bag, left from one of her part-time jobs, from the passenger seat. The bag was still warm. She climbed the porch and knocked on the door. She could see a dozen or so people already sitting in the living room and then Joe Likely threading his way through them. Likely was a sixties leftover, with a nicotine-stained beard and eyebrows like tumbleweeds.

He opened the door and smiled and said, "I hope to hell that's apple pie you're carrying."

"Two of them. How are you, Joe?"

"Getting older," Likely said. "Hoping to make it until Christmas."

She followed him into the living room, where ten other people were sitting on metal folding chairs. She knew them all. Joe said, "Marlys has brought pie."

A few people said, "Yay," and "Thanks, Marlys," and Joe took the pies into the kitchen, then came back and stood at the front of the room.

"Like I was saying before Marlys got here, the news isn't real good, but I guess you all know that. Right now, politically, we've got nowhere to go. The Republicans, as usual, are batshit crazy, and with the Democrats, well, choose your poison. Dan Grady has filed papers to run for governor . . ." There was a smattering of applause. ". . . but even those of us who like Dan know that he won't get even two percent of the vote.

We're back in survival mode. I have to admit that our network is getting thinner, not stronger. So, the question is, what do we do? We need fresh ideas."

Fresh ideas from this group was virtually an oxymoron, Marlys thought, wriggling her butt against the comfortless chair.

She heard the same old things about organizing, about reaching out to young people, about getting in touch with the unions, about starting a website. The ideas were mostly inane; a few were actively goofy. None of them had even a touch of realism about them. Given what happened to her pies during the break, she began to wonder how many people still came to the meetings only for the free dessert.

She looked around: longtime acquaintances and friends now grown shabby, tired, broken. Cinders. In the old days, they'd all burned with righteous fire.

Anson Palmer stood up and said that he was talking to a press in Iowa City about publishing his book. His book was three thousand pages long now. Palmer suffered from an *idée fixe,* that is, that the Jews controlled everything. Everything. He was writing down every single human process he could think of, and tracing it back to Jewish control, like tracing every human being through six degrees to Kevin Bacon.

His three thousand pages only scratched the surface. His talks with the press were not far advanced, he admitted. He really needed an agent, but guess-what about most agents?

Marlys hadn't met many Jews and those she had seemed ordinary enough — but it was clear to her who ran the banks, the media, the corporations. Or for that matter, the literary agencies. But with Jews, there was no leverage. Sure, you could go around blaming the Jews if you wanted, but they were so dispersed, there was nothing you could really do about them. They weren't a fulcrum that you use to move the world.

Michaela Bowden was.

If she were elected president, it would be the same-ol' same-ol': sucking up to, and taking care of, the powers-that-be, the banks, Wall Street, the corporations, the foundations. Nothing but crumbs for the little people.

With Elmer Henderson, things would be a whole lot different. Henderson was independently wealthy and didn't have to suck up to anyone. He came from a farm state, and even owned a farm, she'd learned. He knew what had happened to the average folks back in the eighties, and then in the

2000s. His heart was in the right place. If he became president, there was a chance for change.

Among the whole bunch, Marlys knew, she was the only one who had a real practical idea that might actually move the world. No way she could talk about it, not even here.

She let Anson Palmer's words flow around her, eyes half closed. The people here, in this room, were right enough in their thinking, in their hopeless way. They knew something had to be done — but they didn't know what, and they wouldn't do it if they did know.

She knew.

And she would.

TWO

August, with the late-afternoon sun glittering off the ripples in the lake outside the double doors; a pleasant silence after the whine of the table saw.

Lucas Davenport sat in a battered office chair with a bottle of Leinie's, looking at the unfinished interior of the room he was adding to his Wisconsin cabin. The place smelled of sawdust and coffee, with a hint of the piney woods that surrounded the house, and the beer in his hand. Through the plastic sheet that separated the new room from the rest of the cabin, he could hear Delbert McClinton singing "Two More Bottles of Wine" over the computer speakers.

The carpenter had left, taking her coffee with her, after installing the tongue-in-groove pine planks on the wall facing the lake. Lucas had been doing the cutting, on the table saw, while the carpenter did the final fitting and nailing. Another two days and the walls would all be in, and then they'd start on the finish work. Jesus don't tarry and the creek don't rise, the room would be done before winter, with weeks to spare.

Of course, he'd heard that story before. In his experience with house construction, the creek did rise, or Jesus did tarry, or both. So far, though, they were on schedule.

Delbert had finished "Two More Bottles" and had gone to work on "Gold Plated Fool," when Lucas's phone rang. His wife, he thought, checking in after work. He dug his phone out of his pocket and looked at the screen.

A single word hung there: *Mitford.*

Neil Mitford was chief weasel for the governor of Minnesota. A finger of pure pleasure touched Lucas's heart: something was up. Mitford never called unless he had to.

Lucas clicked on *Answer* and asked, "What happened?"

"The governor needs to see you," Mitford said. "Soon as possible."

"He get caught with a teenager?"

"Don't even think that," Mitford said, as if thinking it might make it happen.

"Yeah, well, in case you hadn't noticed, I

no longer work for the state," Lucas said.

"He needs to see you anyway."

"I'm up at my cabin. I could probably make it down tomorrow afternoon."

"Unfortunately, we're in Iowa. We just left Fort Madison . . ." Lucas heard somebody in the background call, "Fort Dodge," and Mitford said, ". . . Fort Dodge, on our way to Ames. We've got a noon speech there, tomorrow, followed by a reception at the student union. That'll go on 'til two o'clock. We'd like you to be there by the end of the reception."

"What's the problem?" Lucas asked, because there *would* be a problem.

"I can't tell you that because we're talking on radios," Mitford said. "Be here at two."

"I'm a private citizen now and I don't necessarily jump when the governor —"

"Two o'clock," Mitford said, and he was gone.

Lucas smiled at the phone: something *was* up.

"Good," said his wife, Weather, when she called to check in. "He's got something for you to do. You'll stop driving Jimi nuts and I'll get to see you tonight."

"Treat me right, I might even throw you a quickie," Lucas said.

"As opposed to what?"

"Very funny," Lucas said. "And I'm not driving Jimi nuts."

Jimi was the carpenter. "Yes, you are. Nuts. Like you did when you drove the contractor nuts on this house. Then you spend all day looking at Jimi's ass, up on that scaffold. Which might explain the quickie-ness."

"She does have an exceptionally nice scaffold," Lucas said. "Anyway, see you about seven o'clock. Maybe we can sneak out for a bite."

"Before or after the quickie?" Weather asked.

"In between."

"Big talk, big guy."

Lucas *was* a big guy, but not a lunk.

He was a few pounds under two hundred, now, after much of a summer working on the cabin for three days each week. He'd had no easy access to restaurant food, the big killer, and so had been cooking on his own, mostly microwave stuff. He'd been running twice a day and doing early-morning weight work. Although he was a natural clotheshorse, he'd spent the summer in jeans, T-shirts, and lace-up boots, and was beginning to miss the feel of high-end Italian wool and silk and English shoes.

Lucas was a dark-haired man, with a long thin scar tracking down from his hairline, across his tanned forehead, and over one eye to his cheek; not, as some people thought, cop-related, but an artifact from a fishing misadventure. Another pink/white scar showed on his throat, left over from the day a young girl shot him in the throat. A surgeon — who was not yet his wife — saved his life by cutting open an airway with a borrowed jackknife.

He was no longer a cop. He'd quit Minnesota's Bureau of Criminal Apprehension when a combination of personality conflict and paperwork had finally done what street work hadn't been able to do: push him out.

When he was a cop, still working with the BCA, he'd done a number of quiet jobs for the governor and they'd grown to somewhat trust each other. Only somewhat: politicians could rationalize the Crucifixion of Christ. And had.

The governor, Elmer Henderson, was currently campaigning for the Democratic vice presidential nomination, though that's not what he said he was doing. He claimed to be campaigning for the presidency, but he knew quite well that rumors about his early interest in three- and four-way sex with young Seven Sisters coeds and fellow Ivy Leaguers, as well as in the life-enhancing effects of cocaine, would eventually get out and keep him from the nomination.

However, he was liberal enough that he could nail down the lefty fringe of the party for a candidate who ran more toward the middle; and he had a half-billion dollars, which would come in handy during a national campaign. The sex-and-drugs thing wouldn't keep him from something as insignificant as the vice presidency.

He had a shot.

After the call from Weather, Lucas showered and shaved, put a Band-Aid and some antiseptic on his index finger, above the knuckle, where he'd picked up a splinter earlier in the day, and put on some fresh clothes. He took ten minutes to vacuum up an accumulation of Asian ladybugs that had found their way through the windowless addition, and bagged up the garbage and trash. He called Jimi to tell her he'd be gone for a short time, no more than a few days.

"Thank God," she'd said.

"What?"

"I mean . . . that the time'll be short," the carpenter said.

Closing down the cabin took fifteen minutes. He hauled the garbage bag to his Mercedes SUV, locked up the cabin, and was on the dirt road out.

That night Lucas's friend Del Capslock and his wife came over for barbecued steaks and salad, and they sat around speculating on the governor's problem. "It better not involve a woman," Weather said. "If he's been caught with his hand in the wrong pair of pants, that's not a problem I want you to solve."

"A hand wouldn't be such a big problem — a pregnancy would be," Del said. "But Elmer's not that dumb."

"His penis might be," Del's wife said.

"He has a well-schooled cock, he only impregnates what he wants to impregnate," Del said.

"Hope you're right," Lucas said. "If it's that kind of problem, he's on his own. I'll turn the truck around and go back to the cabin."

Lucas's youngest kid, Gabrielle, was now old enough to sit in her own chair at the table. She pointed a spoon at Del and said, "Cock."

"Oh my God," Weather said.

Lucas's son, Sam, now in third grade, said

to Weather, "Mom, Gabby said 'cock.'"

Del's wife rapped Del on the head with a soup spoon.

And the next morning, leaving behind a wife and two small children — Lucas had an older adoptive daughter going to college at Stanford, and another daughter who lived with the family of an ex-girlfriend — he put the Benz on I-35 and pointed it south for Iowa.

Weather waved from the doorstep. She was smiling.

Quickie, my ass, he thought, as he rolled out of the driveway.

From St. Paul to Des Moines was three hours, more or less straight down I-35. Ames was a half hour short of Des Moines, and a college town — Iowa State. A few miles out of St. Paul, Lucas was into the corn and soybeans, and corn and beans it would remain, all the way to Ames, the grain fields punctuated by snaky lines of junk trees along the flatland creeks, the windbreaks around farmhouses, and the occasional cow.

After he'd quit the Bureau of Criminal Apprehension, Lucas and Weather had taken a vacation trip to France. They'd spent most of their time in Paris, with a one-day run by train to London, but had also spent a week driving around the South of France, where they'd encountered a fundamental difference between European and American farmlands.

In Europe, it seemed, farmers mostly lived in villages, and during the day, went out to their farms. In America, they lived on their farms and during the day, went into the villages.

The European way seemed more . . . congenial. There'd always be somebody to talk to at night. Especially on long winter nights. When you were as far north as St. Paul or Paris, the nights began at four o'clock in the afternoon and ended at eight in the morning; Lucas had been surprised to learn that Paris was farther north than the Minnesota-Canada border. Looking at some of the old farmsteads out on the prairie, Lucas thought he might well have died if forced to sit through a winter in one of those isolated farmhouses, back in pre-TV days, nothing for companionship except the wind and a woodstove and a Sears Roebuck catalog . . .

Halfway down to Ames, Virgil Flowers, a former BCA subordinate, called: "Me'n

Johnson Johnson are going over to Vilas County to rape the lakes of all their muskies," Flowers said. "You want to come along? You might learn something."

"I've done more fishing this summer than any summer in my life," Lucas said. "So no. Besides, I'm on my way to Ames to meet the governor. He might have an errand for me."

"You got your gun?" Flowers asked.

"In the car, not on me," Lucas said.

"Stay in touch, I want to hear about it," Flowers said. "Especially if it involves a woman."

Ames was a different kind of college town from those of Lucas's experience. The University of Minnesota, where he'd played four years of hockey, not counting a fifth year as a rare hockey redshirt, was built on the banks of the Mississippi, and was a thoroughly urban campus, within walking distance of downtown Minneapolis and the strip of bars and music clubs on Hennepin Avenue.

The other college towns he'd visited as part of the hockey team, or on Big-Ten related sports trips, were also pretty interesting, even when small: often a little shabby, with old-line bars and riverside or lakeside walks, and long-haired hipsters and lots of girls reading Khalil Gibran. The presence of *The Prophet* had always, in his experience, boosted the potential for hasty romances. He even knew a few handy lines: *Fill each other's cup, but drink not from one cup.* And you could take that any way you wanted . . .

Ames, on the other hand, was flat and dry, or almost so; and the main street facing the campus looked like it had been built by recent refugees from the old Soviet Union, who'd been allowed to use bricks instead of concrete. The coeds — not too many, in the dead of summer — all looked like they were majoring in something that required math or rubber gloves and weren't carrying copies of *The Prophet.* There wasn't a hipster in sight.

Lucas followed the truck's nav system down Lincoln, spotted the student union, drove around for a couple of minutes and found a parking spot outside a Jimmy John's sub restaurant, which was a good thing. He plugged the meter and ambled on over to the student union.

Checked his watch: 1:45.

He could see Henderson's political rally from the far side of the street, a crowd of brightly dressed young people overflowing down the steps of a concrete terrace off the left side of the student union. He crossed the street and climbed the steps to the terrace, where he found Neil Mitford, a pale, balding man with a sun-pinked face, in a blue-and-white-striped seersucker suit, leaning against a terrace wall, a drink in one hand. The terrace was packed, a hundred and fifty people pounding on a drinks-and-snacks table like ravenous wolves.

Mitford nodded at Lucas and said, "Right on time."

From where he was standing, Lucas could see another, higher level to the terrace, as crowded as the one they were on, with the governor standing in the center of it, surrounded by the coeds that Lucas hadn't seen on the streets.

"You needed a bigger space," Lucas said.

"Which tells me how much you know about politics," Mitford said. "If you think five people are going to show up, you hold the rally in a phone booth. If it's twenty-five, you hold it in a garage. If it's five hundred, it's this place — it's a place where not quite everybody can get in, so the press says you're attracting overflow crowds."

"You've mentioned that before," Lucas said. "I forgot it because it wasn't important."

"And because you're not a political influential, like me."

"I gotta admit, I didn't think the crowd would be this big, this early in the campaign," Lucas said. There were probably a hundred young women in royal-blue-and-gold T-shirts, Henderson's campaign colors.

Mitford said, "Four words: college campus, free food."

"Ah. What does Elmer want me to do?" Lucas asked. "Something criminal?"

Mitford shrugged: "Maybe, but I'll let him tell you about it. It'll take some of your time, though, so you better cancel everything else."

"I'm not going to do it if it involves Elmer's sex life," Lucas said.

"It doesn't."

"Good. Anyway, I charge four hundred bucks an hour," Lucas said. "Eight hundred if it involves something criminal."

Mitford made a farting noise with his lips, then said, "The governor expects you to contribute your time, since you're already richer than Croesus." He paused, then said, "Croesus was —"

"I know who Croesus was," Lucas said. "I was a hockey player, not a moron."

"Sorry. But you know, get hit in the head by too many pucks . . . By the way, we haven't actually seen your name on our donors' list."

"Must have missed it," Lucas said.

On the lawn below the terrace, a fight had broken out. Lucas felt no compulsion to do anything about it, other than to look past Mitford's shoulder and say, "Fight."

Mitford turned to look, where two middle-aged men were rolling around on the grass next to a pond and a fallen political sign.

"Oh, that guy," Mitford said, leaning over the terrace wall, watching with interest. "The one in the white shirt. He's got these big signs that bounce up and down on a spring, on top of a pole that's about fifteen feet high. One says, 'The Henderson Hoagie, Two Girls Better Than One,' and the other one says, 'Henderson Equals Godless Comminism.' That's c-o-m-m-*l*-n-i-s-m."

"Must be one of your right-wing intellectuals," Lucas said.

A crowd encircled the two fighting men, but nobody seemed about to intervene, except a woman in a yellow blouse who kept pleading, "Is this the way to settle anything? Is this the way adults . . ." She stopped and dabbed at a spot of blood that spattered on her blouse.

Lucas wondered briefly if she were intellectually challenged: in his experience, fights settled all sorts of things. Some of them permanently.

"He's been following us around the state. He's harmless, but embarrassing," Mitford said. Now four men were trying to pull the fighters apart, but the guy on top got in a last three or four good-looking shots to the face, and Mitford shouted, "Hit him again, Walt."

Lucas: "Walt? You hired that guy?"

"Of course not. That would be wrong. But we're pretty sure Bowden hired the guy with the sign." Mitford went back to his drink.

The fighters were dragged apart, the winner disappearing with professional discretion into the crowd, while the loser tried to sop up the blood from his nose with a blue cowboy handkerchief.

A woman's arm slipped around Lucas's waist and he looked down at a redhead who was slender in all the right places.

"How are you?" he asked.

Alice Green looked up at him and smiled, her green eyes a little tired. He could feel the gun on her hip.

"Not bad."

"Having a good time?" Lucas asked.

Her eyes slipped away. "I guess. Working

pretty hard."

Lucas looked at her for a moment and she never looked back, and he pulled her a few steps away from Mitford and said, "Don't tell me . . ."

"I don't want to hear a fuckin' word about it, Lucas," she said. "I knew you'd figure it out, right away, and I don't want to hear a single fuckin' word."

"Does Neil know?"

"I'm sure he does," she said.

"How long?" he asked.

"Couple months."

"It's not going anywhere," Lucas said.

"Depends on what you mean by 'going.' He's not going to marry me, but I could come out of it with a hell of a job in Washington."

"Ah, man . . . I hope you know what you're doing," Lucas said.

"I don't, entirely," she said. "I really like him and he really likes me. Trouble is, there are a lot of women who really like him and he really likes them back. And his wife is basically Darth Vader in an Oscar de la Renta dress."

"Really? I always thought she looked like a decorator lamp with a twenty-five-watt bulb."

"The lamp part is right, the dim bulb not

so much," Green said. "She's at least half the brains in the family and she's not going anywhere."

Green headed Henderson's security detail. Lucas had introduced them at the end of a U.S. Senate campaign in which Green, a former Secret Service agent, had been working for a psychopathic Senate candidate named Taryn Grant. Lucas was positive that Grant had orchestrated the murders of several people during a Senate campaign in Minnesota.

Lucas asked, "You hear anything from Taryn?"

"No. She was unhappy when I quit, so I don't think I will," Green said. "You still thinking about her?"

"From time to time," Lucas said. "I know goddamn well that she was behind those killings."

"Won't get her, not after all this time," Green said.

"Not for those," Lucas said. "She'll go after somebody else, though — freaks like her do it for the thrill of it and they get addicted to the risk. She'll screw up somewhere along the line. I'd like to be there when she does."

"You'd need a new cop job," Green said.

"I could see myself coming back, under the right circumstances," Lucas said. "I just haven't figured out exactly what the job would be."

"Nobody likes a freelancer," she said.

"Including me. I wouldn't go freelance. I'd like a real badge, but it's got to be the right one," he said. And, "Do you have any idea what Elmer wants?"

"Yes, but I'll let him tell you. The governor speaks for himself." A group of young women dressed all in black were picking up the leftover food and dumping it into garbage sacks and stacking up unused paper plates, signaling the end of the party. Green said, "Let's go talk to the guy."

Henderson, a tall, slender man with blond hair, was still surrounded by coeds and the kind of soft-faced young men who walked around with policy manuals under their elbows. They'd all wind up in Washington where, even if they never did good, they'd certainly do well.

The governor saw Lucas and lifted a hand and said to the people around him, "My muscle has arrived. We've got to go talk. I'll be back. I'd like somebody to show me those pool tables."

Several young things volunteered and the

44

governor, babbling a variety of assurances and clichés, waded through the crowd, shook hands with Lucas, and said, "Come on, let's go across the street."

He led the way down the steps to the street level, Mitford, Green, and another security guy running interference for them. They crossed the street and Henderson waved back at the crowd, then took Lucas's elbow and led him onto a sidewalk that bordered a large winding pond.

"So what's up?" Lucas asked, as they walked along.

"Let me turn my music on," Henderson said. He took an iPhone from his pocket, pushed some buttons, and JD McPherson started singing "Let the Good Times Roll."

Lucas looked around. "Boom mikes?"

"Can never tell," Henderson said. He held the rockin' iPhone between them. "Better to not take a chance."

"It's that bad?"

"Don't know," Henderson said. "But it's got a nasty vibe."

"Tell me."

Henderson outlined some background that Lucas already knew: that he wasn't really running for the presidency, but for the vice presidency, and that most political insiders knew that.

"I'd like to be president someday and this is my only chance — I can't get to it without getting the vice presidency first. That whole Henderson Hoagie business, and too many people know that I fooled around with some cocaine . . . well. Since 1901, seven vice presidents — Teddy Roosevelt, Calvin Coolidge, Harry Truman, Richard Nixon, Lyndon Johnson, Gerald Ford, and George Bush the First — got to be president, for a whole variety of different reasons. There's no sure thing, but if I can get there, get to be the VP, I've got a fair chance at the top job. Bowden has almost got the nomination sewn up. Jack Gardner's still hanging around, but he's well back in third place and he's too wimpy for any major job. I'm a perfect fit for the vice presidency. I'm popular in the Midwest, where Bowden's weak, I'm a Catholic and she's a Protestant . . ."

"Male and female, tall and short, blond and brunette, left-wing crazy and moderate centrist . . ." Lucas added.

"Exactly," said the left-wing crazy. "We've gotten some strong signals from her camp that if I don't say anything too rude, I'm at the top of the list. If I beat her here in Iowa and ease up and let her take New Hampshire, it's a done deal."

"But. There's gotta be a 'but.' "

"There is." He paused, then, "I was working the rope line down at the Des Moines airport and this chubby white-haired middle-aged lady took my hand and held on to it, walked along with me for a way, and she said, 'Governor, you've got to move to the center. You have to be ready for the nomination, in case Bowden doesn't make it, in case something happens to her.' She was quite intense, very sincere, and I think a little unhinged."

"Uh-huh. What'd you say?"

"I rolled out a cliché or two and kept trying to get my hand back. Eventually I did, but the incident was odd enough that I remembered it, because she had this scary intensity about her. A few days later, I was in Waterloo and this farm kinda guy took my hand and said, 'Governor, you gotta move to the center. We know where your heart is, but you've got to pretend to move to the center if you want the nomination. You gotta be ready if Bowden goes down.' The thing is, this guy had these pale gray eyes, you really felt them. Creepy. And he *looked* like the chubby lady, except he had a thin face and the gray eyes . . . The *features* were hers, you know what I mean? The mouth and the nose . . . And he said the same thing she had, almost exactly the same words. And when *he* said it, I had the feeling that something bad might happen to Bowden. He had that look about him — like somebody had slapped him on the side of the head with a flatiron."

"That's pretty serious," Lucas said. "You talk to Bowden's security people?"

"I didn't myself. What I did was, I called Bowden directly and told her I was worried. She said she'd talk to her security. One of her guys came over to talk to me and I couldn't give him anything but those gray eyes, that curly white hair on the old lady — she wore rimless glasses — and the dates of the encounters."

"Did they take you seriously?"

"Sure, but I didn't give them much to work with," Henderson said. "These guys really aren't investigators. They're security people, bodyguards."

"You want me to find the chubby lady . . ."

"Wait one," Henderson said. He waved at a couple walking along the sidewalk, and they cooed at him, and they went on their way. "Bowden and I had that little get-together in Sioux City, along with the also-rans. I'm looking out at the crowd, and here's this farmy-looking guy again. He looks like those pictures you see of Confederate soldiers. Those flat gray eyes, shaggy hair, too skinny. He was *staring* at Bowden, fixing on her, then he glances at me and sees that I'm fixed on him. Alice was right off the stage and I excused myself for a minute and I grabbed her and told her about him and she tried to get a picture of the guy with her cell phone, but he was moving away, fast. The photo she got is less than half-assed. Anyway, we passed it all along to Bowden."

"What'd she do?" Lucas asked.

"Got more security, I hope — but she's got this weasel working for her, Norman Clay, and he comes by and he says, 'You're not trying to push Secretary Bowden out of Iowa, are you, Elmer?' "

"And you said?"

"I said, 'Go fuck yourself, Norm. I wouldn't pull that kind of bullshit on you.' He went away, but she's still here, and I wouldn't be surprised if they thought I was trying to get her out of the state. We're dealing with some serious skepticism over there."

"One chubby lady with curly white hair and glasses and a guy with gray eyes who looks like a Confederate soldier, and one bad cell phone photo. That's all you've got?"

49

"There's a little more," Henderson said. "Our website is inundated with e-mail. We have a few guys going through it looking for two things: possible donors and possible threats. There have been four e-mails from somebody named 'Babs.' They read like nutty political position papers and they also urge me to move toward the center. One of them says that the author knows my heart's in the right place, but I can't get the nomination unless I pretend to move to the center."

"Exactly what the chubby lady told you," Lucas said.

"Precisely the same words. But, instead of a momentary contact, there are also these position papers. It's the position papers that tell you these people may be crazy and may be dangerous. You'll have to read them. They want a revolution. If a few eggs have to be broken, that's the only way to make an omelet."

"Okay. What do you want me to do?" Lucas asked.

"I want you to find these people and find out what they're up to," Henderson said. "And do it fast. I'm really afraid something could happen here. When you find them, we'll get the Iowa cops to sit on them."

"If something did happen to Bowden, how

would that affect your chances?" Lucas asked.

"What a rotten, cynical question to ask. I'm proud of you," Henderson said.

"What's the answer?"

Henderson shook his head. "I'd be done. I can't take the nomination straight out. I'm too far left. There's no way I could pretend to move to the center and Minnesota isn't a swing state. If Bowden went down, Carl Bartley from Ohio would jump into the middle of it, and maybe Doug Jensen from Missouri. If either one of them got the nomination, neither one would offer me the vice presidency, because I don't match up so well with them. They're both Midwesterners, for one thing. They'd go for a woman or a big-state guy, somebody from one of the coasts. North Carolina or Florida or Washington."

"All right. I'll go talk to Alice, see what she has to say, and see if I can figure something out," Lucas said.

"Alice . . ." Henderson said. He glanced at Lucas.

"Did you really have to do that, Governor?" Lucas asked.

Henderson spread his hands. "You know I've always had trouble with pretty women. Especially redheads. And blondes."

"And brunettes and Hispanics and Asians and a few long-legged African-Americans . . ."

"I know. I feel bad about Alice when we're not actually . . . you know," Henderson said.

"When you get to Washington, you'll take care of her?" Lucas asked.

"Oh, yeah. Even if I don't make VP. I've already started talking to her about it. You know she comes from Virginia?"

"I guess."

"There's a weak-ass Republican congressman, right from her hometown, who needs to be replaced," Henderson said. "Three years out, our Alice could be looking at a major promotion."

"Think she's up to it?"

"I know it," Henderson said. He stopped to look back at Green, who flashed him a smile. "She's smart, got great red hair, great green eyes, great smile . . ."

"Great ass."

"Don't give me any shit about that, Lucas — not with your history," Henderson said, irritated. "No matter what happens with me, I'll get her an impressive-sounding staff job in Washington, something involving Virginia agriculture and natural resources," Henderson said. "I'll buy her some top-end TV training, some good threads, lean on my friends for donations. A hot, female, law-and-order Democrat who carries a gun and has major experience in D.C.? Are you kiddin' me? That Tea Party asshole won't know what hit him. He'll be like Toto in the fuckin' tornado."

They wandered back to the party and the governor lied about how he wished he were doing something simple and earthy, maybe working on his cabin, like Lucas was — Lucas didn't believe a word of it, as Henderson's main cabin was the size of a downtown Holiday Inn and he owned the lake it was sitting on. Then they were back, and Henderson left him to wrap up the lingering coeds.

Lucas stepped over to Green and Mitford and said, "Okay, I got it. I need that photo, Alice, and copies of those e-mails."

"Give me your cell phone number and I'll get it all to you in one minute, though the photo is virtually useless," she said, taking her phone out of her shoulder bag.

Lucas gave her the number, and one minute later the photo popped up on his phone. It wasn't as bad as Lucas had feared — she'd taken it from behind the farm-looking guy, and he'd glanced back at her as she took the picture. Only a slice of his face was visible, but his haircut, the way he dressed in a high-collared, hunting-style shirt, and the way he carried himself, was all there. Lucas thought he might recognize him if he saw him.

She sent the texts as e-mails; he'd look at them later.

"I've only got one question," Green said.

"Would that be 'Why does the governor have his hand on that girl's ass?' " Mitford asked.

Lucas and Green turned to look.

Sure enough.

"He's completely unaware of it and she loves it," Mitford marveled. "If I did that, I'd be imprisoned for aggravated lubricity."

The governor took his hand off the girl's ass and continued talking to her enthusiastically about something they couldn't hear. "He really *doesn't know*," Green said.

"He can't do that — we've got to get him trained," Mitford said. "Maybe we could get one of those electric dog collars and every time he does it, we spark him up. 'Cause that's not gonna work once the voting starts. Once the TV gets heavy, and they start looking for it."

They watched for a moment as the governor kept working the remaining crowd, then Green turned back to Lucas and said, "That wasn't my question. My question is, since you aren't a cop anymore, where are you going to start on this? You've got no resources. You got nothin'."

THREE

Kidd was standing on a golf driving range in St. Paul, a five-iron on his shoulder, looking down the range to where his ball was happily slicing hard to the right.

"Holy cats, that's the biggest slice I've ever seen," said his wife, Lauren, the possibly retired jewel thief. She was giving him a lesson.

"Can't really be the biggest one," Kidd ventured.

But it was big.

"Yes, it is. Because you're so strong and you've got those fast hands, and because you're leading with your right elbow. You can't do that, lead with the elbow, the ball rolls right off the face of your club . . ." Lauren was a scratch golfer and had won the club's women's championship the last three years running.

Kidd's phone rang. He stepped back from the pile of practice balls, pulled the phone out of his jeans pocket and looked at it. "It's Lucas," he said to Lauren. He poked *Answer.* "Yeah?"

Lucas was sitting on a bench next to the pond in Ames, facing what might have been a mid-lake sculpture. He was uncertain about that. "I'm working for Governor Henderson down in Iowa," he said. "He's gotten some questionable e-mails that I'd like you to look at. I need to know where they come from, who sent them, everything you can tell me about them."

"Do I get paid?" Kidd asked. A golf shop guy had driven up in a cart and was walking toward them.

"Of course not. Nor will you ever get any credit for helping out," Lucas said.

"All right, send them to me," Kidd said. "Put a note on them that tells me what it's all about. I'll take a look and call you back tonight."

Lucas rang off and the golf shop guy said, "Uh, Mr. Kidd, some of the members have asked me to talk to you about our dress code. You're not allowed to wear jeans and you need to wear a shirt with a collar."

"Are you kiddin' me?" Kidd asked. He looked down at his T-shirt and jeans; the T-shirt had only the smallest of tears and the jeans, only a few flecks of dried paint.

He handed the five-iron to Lauren. "That's it. I'm outa here. Fuck a bunch of golf. And country clubs."

Lauren said to the golf shop guy, as Kidd stalked away, "Thanks a lot, Dick. It only took me four years to get him out here."

"Uh, my name's Ralph."

"Yes, I know," Lauren said, as she went after Kidd.

The e-mail from Davenport was waiting when Kidd and Lauren got back to their condo. Their son was still at band camp, so Kidd pulled up the e-mails and the note:

Kidd: These are copies of e-mails sent to the governor's campaign site. Elmer thinks there are some pretty serious implications in the letters — not threats, exactly, but a suggestion that he should move to the center in case "something happens" to Bowden, so he'd have a better chance at election. He's also had two different people (who may be related) approach him at election rallies, and tell him more or less the same thing, in the same words. Elmer's informed Bowden's people of all this, but they apparently haven't done much. He's worried and asked me to look into it. Can you dig anything out of these things?

— Lucas.

The forwarded e-mails were tight and well-edited, and while the sentences made sense, the overall content was confusing. Most of the complaints embedded in the e-mails seemed to refer to the Midwestern farming crisis of the mid-1980s, now thirty years in the past. That crisis was tangled up with the Internet market bust of 1999–2000, and the 2008 housing crisis. "Inequality" was often cited, the cost of medical insurance, the lack of prosecution of bankers implicated in the economic crises, the loss of American values, along with rising rates of murder and rape and the Jewish influence on American culture, through the Jews' "control" of the banks and the media.

Lauren read the e-mails over Kidd's shoulder and when they'd both finished, he asked, "What do you think?"

"I can see why Henderson's worried," she said. "These people are nuts. That whole 'Jew banker' thing, the 'Jew media.' I mean, who uses 'Jew' that way, as an adjective, instead of 'Jewish'? Whoever wrote that has been listening to some far-out shit."

"Yeah," Kidd said. "The question is, is it right-wing or left-wing? They don't like corporations, banks, the Fed, or the one-percent, but they also don't like government regulation, Jews, immigrants, abortion, or gay marriage."

"That's why I said the writer's nuts. It's a mash-up of all the various hates," Lauren said. "You gonna be able to figure out anything?"

"I'll have to go deep. I can probably tell him where the e-mails were sent from and if they were all sent from the same machine," Kidd said. "If I can get into that Google text-matching program, I might be able to tell him who wrote them."

"I've heard you say that Google's got really good protection," Lauren said.

"They do, for some value of 'good.' A teeny hack won't get in there, but I can," Kidd said. "Probably."

Kidd had been hacking computers forever. He had access to so many systems that a few knowledgeable people thought he might actually control the world, and the NSA had been trying to find him for fifteen years. Lucas didn't know that. Lucas *did* know, or at least believe, that Lauren was a professional jewel thief, though he hadn't the slightest shred of evidence to prove it.

Kidd and Davenport had been jocks at

the University of Minnesota at the same time. Kidd had been a wrestler who became locally famous — and lost his scholarship at the same time — when he pushed the head of an abusive wrestling coach through two iron uprights in a field house railing. The fire department had to be called to free the man. Although he lost his athletic scholarship, he was almost instantly offered a full ride by the computer sciences department, which he took.

And never looked back.

"Are you going to get us in trouble?" Lauren asked.

"No," he said.

"Really no? For some value of 'no'?"

"If those schnooks at Google catch me, I deserve everything I get."

Sister Mary Joseph, whose civilian name was Elle Kruger, was in her office at St. Mary's University when Lucas's e-mail arrived. A friend of Lucas's since early childhood, she had a PhD in psychology and had consulted on a number of Lucas's criminal cases.

She read through the e-mails sent by Lucas, sighed and kicked back in her chair. The anger that was coursing through America deeply worried her. Although she was too young to remember the beginnings of the civil rights, anti–Vietnam War, and feminist movements, she was also a student of history. Her sense was that as bad as things had been in the sixties, people of goodwill still dominated.

The civil rights and feminist movements had been about gender equality and freedom; and the anti-war movement about the blind stupidity among certain parts of the political class that wound up killing sixty thousand Americans, mostly young draftees, and wounding another hundred and fifty thousand, to say nothing of a million or more Vietnamese. The leaders of all those protest movements had been optimists, trying to pull people together.

Now the echoes of those movements seemed mostly about hate — about hating your opponents, on either side of any of the questions.

The forwarded e-mails she'd gotten from Lucas were a reflection of that.

Hating was one thing, action was something else. There were any number of gun lovers who never in their lives would pull the trigger on another human being, and maybe not even an animal; they were simply living in a fantasy world that was captured by the physical reality of a gun, the implicit power of a bullet.

The e-mails from whoever had sent them to Henderson, though, contained a disquieting thread. The bitterness was too thick and unleavened, the anger too sharp and unrelenting.

She picked up her phone and called Lucas, who was sitting in his motel room, eating a Jimmy John's sub and had signed on to his bank's investment site to see how much shirt he had left.

Quite a lot, as it happened.

Lucas's phone rang. He glanced at the screen, clicked *Answer,* and asked, "Get a chance to read them yet?"

"Yes. You know how in the past we've talked about 'trigger' moments?" Elle asked. "About how a deranged person will progress through a series of stages and finally arrive at the trigger moment?"

"Yeah. Sometimes they don't pull the trigger and the whole issue goes away and maybe nobody ever knows about it. Sometimes they do pull the trigger."

"Reading the letters, it seems apparent to me that the writer has gone through a series of these stages and is close to the trigger moment," Elle said. "Whether or not she pulls the trigger is another question. I believe she's capable of it."

"She?"

"Almost certainly. I can't give you chapter and verse, but I sense that the writer is a woman."

Lucas said, "The governor told me that one of the people who approached him is a middle-aged woman, that the other was male, and younger, and that there was a physical similarity between them, like a mother and son."

"Family members — that works for me," Elle said. "Family members can devolve into something like a cult, with a cult leader and obedient followers. This is usually driven by severe disappointments and failures that are often not the fault of the victims."

"Give me an example," Lucas said.

"Well, using a woman as the leader, as the case here might be . . . suppose you have a divorced mother whose children are badly injured in a school bus accident," Elle said. "She is abruptly thrust into the role of a full-time caregiver, which might badly affect her ability to earn a decent living. The children are thrust into roles of helpless dependents, who would be a burden on anyone . . . I'm talking about friends who might be expected to help, but the problem is so deep and intractable that people turn away from them. The whole family is driven closer and closer by their misfortune. You wind up with an embittered mother with her hopelessly devoted and psychologically and physically dependent children."

"That's what you get when the mother kills the kids," Lucas suggested.

"Yes, that can happen when the anger is turned inward," Elle said. "It can also turn outward. The form it takes depends on the intellect and emotional status of the leader. It can be quite diffuse, as in this case, where the leader wants to change the whole way the world works. It can also be quite specific — the leader gets a gun and kills the person who caused the accident, or the insurance agent who wouldn't pay her what she thought she deserved. Or even the doctor who treated the kids who never entirely recovered."

"What do I look for? 'Embittered mother' won't help much."

"I probably can't give you any more, other than to tell you to take these things very seriously. She's out there and she's angry and she seems ready to act. She's smart, but not brilliant — she's accepted a specific but limited ideology as the source of answers to her problem," Elle said. "She's smart enough to hold these ideals, but not smart enough to see through them. She could be a teacher of some kind, but probably not a lawyer or a minister or a cop or a reporter. She's not cynical and she's not really a skeptic, either. She doesn't have a lot of experience with nuances, or with situations in which there are no good answers. She believes in good and evil, and good actions and evil actions, with a sharp dividing line between them. If she were to do something to Bowden . . . I really hate to even consider that idea . . . she'd think it was a positive good. Not evil in any way. She no longer thinks of Bowden as a human being — she sees her as a mannequin being manipulated by sinister corporate and governmental powers."

"She's crazy."

Elle smiled at the phone. Lucas tended to cut through a lot of theory. "That would be my professional assessment. Yes."

Kidd called back late that night.

Lucas had gone to bed, after his evening chat with Weather, when the phone rang again and he groped for it in the dark.

"Sorry it took so long, but I had to do some sneaking around to get the software tools I needed," Kidd said.

"You find out anything?" Lucas asked.

"Couple things. The messages were all sent from coffee shops, all during the early evening, from Des Moines, Oskaloosa, and Ottumwa," Kidd said. "If you look at a map of Iowa, you'll see that's almost a cluster with Oskaloosa in the center —"

"Wait, wait, let me call this up on the iPad." Kidd waited while Lucas got a map up, and located the three cities. "They're almost in a line. A diagonal line down a highway."

"Yeah. The distance from Des Moines, on the northwest, to Ottumwa, on the southeast, is seventy-five miles in a straight line, with Oskaloosa roughly in the middle. The guy —"

"Probably a woman," Lucas interrupted.

"Okay. I'd be interested to know why you think that," Kidd said. "Anyway, she seems to have this basic Internet security idea that she shouldn't send the e-mail from any one place. She's not just running out to the local Wi-Fi hub and sending it. That suggests to me that none of those places are her home, but that her home is nearby."

"Another possibility," Lucas said, "is that she doesn't have an Internet connection at home and she sent the messages from wherever it was convenient. Wherever she was passing through."

"That's another possibility, though she does own a laptop and uses it consistently, which would suggest an Internet connection."

"Okay. Go ahead."

"I can tell you that she composes the e-mail carefully, on an Apple brand laptop using an older version of Word for Mac. When she's finished, she copies out the message and pastes it into her e-mail program. I can't get a positive identifier on a specific machine."

"Still, Apple laptop and Word, that's all a help," Lucas said.

"There's more," said Kidd.

"All right."

"Here we may be slipping into something that stick-in-the-mud prosecutors might characterize as *illegal . . .*"

"I'm not a stick-in-the-mud prosecutor. I'm not even a cop."

"Okay. Google is developing a text identification program that will allow them to look at messages streaming through Google mail and other places, and match texts with a high degree of accuracy," Kidd said. "Ultimately, they hope that if John Doe is a gun nut and a chess player and a boat owner, they'll be able to pick out every time he sends a message to any website, from any computer, anywhere, anytime, and quickly paste in advertisements for guns, chess sets, and boats."

"Gotta love that," Lucas said. "It's the American way."

"Yeah, well, I . . . borrowed their program for a while this evening and ran it against the e-mails you sent me. I didn't come up with a name, but I did come up with a group of organizations this woman may belong to. They're scattered all over the Midwest and the plains states — farm country — and use her ideological language," Kidd said. "Three of them are in Iowa and it seems likely that they overlap. There's the Progressive People's Party of Iowa, the Isaac Alfred Patriot League, and a group called Prairie Storm. I couldn't find a membership list for any of them, but I've got contacts for all three. They're small organizations, they hit their peak back in the eighties and early nineties."

"Who's Isaac Alfred?"

"He was a kid from Mason City who applied for a religious exemption from the Vietnam War, but was denied the exemption by the draft board. He was drafted and sent to Vietnam as a company clerk, where he was in constant trouble for talking up war resistance. Shortly before the Army was going to arrest him and ship him home, he was killed in a rocket attack on his base. The group was started by his father. That was basically an anti-war group that evolved into a more general populist political-action organization, then got weird and sort of petered out."

"Kidd, I owe you," Lucas said. "If you could put the names and contacts in an e-mail and ship it to me, I'd owe you more."

"I'll collect someday," Kidd said.

"I suspect you will," Lucas said. "Call me if you think of anything new."

Just before he went to sleep, Lucas thought of Alice Green, when she'd said, "You got nothin'."

He smiled to himself: she had no idea what he had.

He still had his friends.

FOUR

At one o'clock in the morning, with broken clouds hanging low in the sky, the scent of rain in the air: a blacktopped highway a half-mile out of Westile, home of the National Guard's D Company, 34th Engineers. The white pickup's lights were the only ones to be seen, other than a distant yard light or two.

"This is it," Marlys Purdy said over her shoulder, through the window to the pickup's truck bed. Cole was in the back, lying flat on a plastic air mattress, a pack between his feet. "Wait 'til I've stopped rolling."

Marlys didn't want to touch the brakes, because she didn't want the brake lights flashing in the dark. The pickup rolled to a halt and she said, "Go now," and Cole bailed out the back, pulled on the pack, and humped down into the roadside ditch. At the bottom, he sank knee-deep in muck and, cursing, plowed through to the other side, the foul-smelling water soaking through his boots and into his socks.

Cole was wearing bow-hunter's camo, with the matching camo backpack, and carrying a StrongArm cutter. Out of the swampy water, he climbed the far side of the ditch and rolled across the fence and into the cornfield beyond, where he instantly became invisible.

With the truck gone, he for the first time realized exactly how dark it was. He could not see his own hands.

Marlys moved on to the next stop sign, looked both ways down a gravel road, and continued through town, out to Interstate 80 and a cluster of cheap motels and two gas stations. She didn't want anyone to see her face, so she parked at an empty motel space and slid down in the driver's seat.

Nothing for her to do but wait.

Cole moved a few rows back into the cornfield and pulled up his face mask, not so much for concealment — not yet — as to keep the corn leaves from cutting his face as he walked through them. He tried to be as quiet as he could be, but he was not quiet, to his own ears, as the saw-edged corn leaves dragged across the camo jacket and pants. The corn rows ran parallel to the road, and acted as guides: he followed two rows straight north, emerging at the gravel road that Marlys had crossed.

He waited inside the screen of corn, listening for motors, watching for lights, then climbed the fence and plodded through the ditch, feeling his way — this one was dry at the bottom — and across the road. He had to grope for the next fence, found it, dropped into another cornfield. That field ran right up to the edge of town and to the edge of the blacktop pad around the National Guard building.

When he got to the pad, he sat again, and listened for a while. He could hear some sound from the sleeping town, but not much — the hiss of a car going by on the main road, some sort of motor noise from far away, maybe at the grain elevator, and the muted rumble of traffic on the distant interstate highway. He could also see a little better in the thin reflected light from the other side of the Guard building.

Cole was apprehensive: not frightened, but tense. A lot could go wrong here: the story of his life.

In trouble through most of his school years, he'd been sitting in an assistant principal's office, in seventh grade, and he heard the guy say to a secretary, "Him again. Something seriously wrong with that boy. He's had more fights than Muhammad Ali."

The secretary had said, "Shhh . . . he's right outside."

Cole pretended he hadn't heard, to everyone's relief; but he *had* heard. And he'd heard that stuff all the time, from the minute he walked into kindergarten and another kid asked, "What you lookin' at?" and Cole punched him in the face.

The only place he'd felt at all at home, besides when he *was* at home, had been in the Army. Army rules had been stupid, but simple, and following them hadn't been a problem. He was athletic enough that basic training had been a snap, and he'd driven a truck for years before the Army sent him to truck driving school.

Iraq had been different. After growing up in the fertile fields of Iowa, he'd looked down at the deserts surrounding Baghdad, and only one word came to mind: "Shithole."

Iraq was a shithole, and in his whole time there, he'd seen nothing to change his opinion. Well, one thing, maybe. He'd come and gone through Kuwait, and if anything, Kuwait was even more of a shithole than Iraq. Was it possible to have a shithole lite?

If so, then maybe that's what Iraq was.

Though Iraq had left him injured, there was one aspect about the place that fascinated him. The snipers. There'd been four of them at the FOB where he'd spent most of his time, and it wasn't so much the non-standard guns that had fascinated him, but the attitude.

Whatever else you might say about them, the snipers were stone killers.

Told to kill, they would do it. They were cool: just do it.

He admired that. Liked it.

Cole pushed the speed dial button on the cell phone, said, "Going in."

Marlys came back: "Don't get hurt."

Cole picked up the Hurst StrongArm cutter he'd surreptitiously borrowed from the volunteer fire department. He was a volunteer, had a key to the building, and would have the cutter back before dawn.

He pulled on a pair of plastic gloves and sat for a few more seconds, letting the electricity flow through him. He was out there, he was operating, fighting the good fight. He'd driven tankers full of high-test gas through towns controlled by Al Qaeda fighters, and here he was again.

Well: more or less. Anyway, the action

seemed to quell the headaches, clear the cobwebs from his brain, bring the world into focus. More than the VA had ever done for him.

The National Guard parking lot was illuminated by two pole lights, both on the other side of the building, near the parking lot entrance. He crossed the fence, not to the National Guard building itself, but to a steel shed at the edge of the parking lot. He was somewhat concealed by parked Humvees, but not entirely. If anyone were to unexpectedly drive past, he might be seen, even with the camo.

The shed was locked with a fat-shanked padlock. Cole turned on the StrongArm and cut through the shank. He pulled the door open and stepped inside, where there was barely enough room to stand, pulled the door shut again, and turned on his flashlight. Now he was invisible again, from the outside. If somebody had seen him going in . . . nothing to do about that.

"You're sweating like a dog," Cole muttered to himself. "You stink."

His boots were even worse, reeking of the muck from the roadside marsh.

The shed was empty, but on the floor, set in

a foot-high circle of concrete designed to keep water out, was a steel manhole cover, with another fat padlock on it. The Strong-Arm cut that one, too, but it took a minute, and a few tries. When it was done, with a loud *clunk,* Cole froze, and listened. Heard nothing — and realized that while the *clunk* was loud in his ears, it probably wouldn't have been heard ten feet away.

"Move," he whispered.

The manhole cover had two steel loop handles, and he lifted it out of the circle of concrete. Beneath it was an eight-foot-deep hole, with poured concrete walls and a concrete floor, and a ladder going down.

Cole went down.

Marlys's cell phone rang. Jesse. She answered, "Yeah? Jesse?"

"Where are you guys?"

"Went out to the all-night Walmart, thought we'd stop and get a bite. We're off I-80."

"Well, I'm home. See you when you get here."

"Don't wait up," Marlys said. She hurriedly clicked off: couldn't have the phone tied up, if Cole called.

Cole shone the flashlight around the underground concrete box. The box was lined with wooden shelves, on which he found two wooden boxes of plastic explosive and smaller boxes of blasting caps. Candy store!

If it all went off at once, he thought, it might blow the manhole cover to the moon, but that deep in the ground, with bunker-weight concrete all around, probably wouldn't hurt much else. Except him, if he were still there. The cops might not even find the raspberry-jelly stains he'd leave behind . . .

Cole carried a whole box of explosive up the ladder, left the box on the ground-level floor, went back down for a box of blasting caps and four electronic detonators. Back up the ladder, he stuffed the blasting caps and detonators in his backpack, picked up the StrongArm. He listened for a minute, in the steel shed, then turned the flashlight off, put it in his jacket pocket, and picked up the box of explosive, which probably weighed twenty pounds.

As he did that, he saw lights swing across the hairline crack where the door wasn't quite closed tight: his heart jumped and he touched the holster at his hip. Then the lights dimmed and he heard a car accelerating away. Somebody had used the parking lot to turn around.

He hoped.

He waited another minute, then another. He reached toward the door to ease it open . . .

Scotch tape! He'd almost forgotten. He got a roll of it out of the side pocket of his camo cargo pants, put it in his mouth, picked up the box of explosive again, and pushed the shed door open.

Outside, in the dark again, Cole lingered just a minute, fitting the broken padlock back on the shed's door latch, fastening the broken ends with a strip of Magic Mending tape. He and Marlys thought it unlikely that the engineers would go into the explosives dump with any regularity. If you could see the padlock hanging there, in place . . . it could be days or even weeks before anybody discovered that the C4 was gone.

With the padlock in place, Cole picked up the box of explosive and the StrongArm, humped them into the cornfield, back the way he'd come in. He crossed the gravel road and then, instead of going back into the second field, he jogged down the road to the corner, where he sank behind a clump of weeds. No point walking through that swamp again.

A mile away, Marlys was getting nervous: then the cell phone lit up, and the call came in.

"I'm out. We're good. Pick me up at that corner."

"Coming," she said. No identifiers.

As Marlys started the truck, she felt as though somebody had stuck an icicle in her heart.

Until this moment, they'd done nothing illegal. With all the reconnaissance they'd done, with all the research, they'd really had no way to get at Bowden — nothing that wasn't purely suicidal. She wasn't suicidal.

She had worked out an idea of how they might kill Bowden and get away with it, but she didn't have what she needed to do that: now they did.

Marlys was a fatalist: if she had a perfect plan, but if something were to stop her from doing that, by denying her the materials . . . well, then, Fate had spoken, hadn't it?

Bowden would walk away from Iowa, get elected, and the whole ugly system would grind on.

But so far, Fate was telling her that she was right on course.

FIVE

At eight in the morning, Lucas called Bell Wood, a friend who headed the major crimes section of the Iowa Division of Criminal Investigation. Wood said, "I was talking to that fuckin' Flowers a few days ago and he said you're being a hangdog about it all and you still don't have a job."

"Yup."

"What are you doing? You gotta work, man."

"Well, I'm putting an addition on my cabin up in Wisconsin. I've been doing that all summer," Lucas said. "Right at this very moment, I'm making an inquiry . . . for Governor Henderson. I'm down here in Iowa, in Ames."

"Uh-oh. What's going on?" Wood asked.

Lucas explained about the e-mails and the woman and the man who'd spoken directly to Henderson, and the problem with getting someone to take the threat seriously.

81

"We've got a security team dealing with the campaigns. Send me the e-mails, and everything else you've got, and I'll run it past the team," Wood said. "Will you keep looking at it?"

"Yeah, unless somebody tells me different," Lucas said.

"I say keep going. You got a gun with you?" Wood asked.

"In the car, I'm not carrying," Lucas said.

"Listen, down here we've got a professional weapons permit deal that would allow you to carry," Wood said. "I'll talk to my guy at Weapons Permits and I'll get you one."

"That'd be nice. I don't think I'll need it, but . . . I'll take it," Lucas said. "And I'll ship you those e-mails in one minute. I've already done some checking around, and I'd like to see if you could get me phone numbers and addresses for three different people. None of them are suspects, but they run political groups that might give me a lead on this woman and the other guy."

"Send them," Wood said. "I'll get back to you as quick as I can, with the information and the permit."

Lucas sent the e-mails to Wood, then called Mitford, the governor's weasel. "When are you leaving?"

"Fifteen minutes. Well, that's when we're scheduled to leave. Probably be more like half an hour."

"I'd like to stop by and talk to the governor for a minute," Lucas said.

"Better hurry," Mitford said.

The Governor's campaign party was in another interstate motel, less than a block away. The campaign bus was idling in the parking lot, belching out diesel exhaust, and a group of underlings was loading luggage and office equipment onto it. Lucas found Alice Green getting a cup of coffee in the front lobby.

"Got breakfast in the campaign suite, if you want a bagel and cream cheese," she said. "Coffee and Cokes and Pepsi for caffeine freaks."

Together they walked back to the campaign suite, and Lucas said, "It occurs to me that once I start digging around, somebody could get pissed off at Henderson . . ."

"Thought of that. The governor knows what these people look like and we've got a safe word. Rumpelstiltskin. He says that, we close around him."

"Best you can do, I guess," Lucas said. "Anybody talk to the Gardner campaign?"

"I don't think he's important enough to shoot, but yeah, I talked to his head security guy and sent him the photo and Elmer's descriptions."

At the campaign suite, Lucas got a toasted bagel with jam and a Diet Coke, and followed Green to Henderson's suite, where Mitford and Henderson were on hardwired phones, dealing with political business back in Minnesota.

As Lucas waited, his phone rang: Bell Wood.

"That was easy," Wood said. "All three of those guys are in our database, they've all been involved in various marches and sit-ins, they've all gone to jail at one time or another. Two of them are nonviolent, more or less, but the other one has a problem. I'm dropping it all to your e-mail right . . . *now.*"

"How big is the guy's problem?" Lucas asked.

"He's getting a little old for it now, but he liked to beat people up, back in the day," Wood said. "Details in the e-mail."

"Thanks. I'll keep you up to date," Lucas said.

Mitford and Henderson were still yammering away on the phones, so Lucas called up the e-mail on his phone, then called up Google Maps. There were three names, with three addresses and phone numbers. Switching between the map and the addresses, he located a David Leonard in Atlantic, Iowa, a small town south of I-80 between Des Moines and Omaha; a Joseph Likely, from Mount Pleasant, Iowa, in the southeastern part of the state; and a Clark Alfred from Mason City, off I-35, near the Iowa-Minnesota border.

Checking the map a final time, he found that Mount Pleasant wasn't too far from Ottumwa, one of the towns from which the suspicious e-mails had been sent, and the drive between the two towns was fast and straightforward, on U.S. Highway 34.

Likely, though, was supposedly a committed pacifist, and his group, the Progressive People's Party of Iowa, had always been of the nonviolent drop-and-drag type, more of a pain in the ass for cops than an active challenge.

Leonard, on the other hand, had done three years at Anamosa State Penitentiary for aggravated assault after trying to break up a foreclosure auction with a baseball bat. Before forming his Prairie Storm group, in the mid-1980s, he'd done two short prison terms for assault and armed robbery, and after the three-year term had been arrested twice more for assault and acquitted once on a burglary charge. To Lucas's eye, he looked like a criminal who'd moved himself into politics.

His group, Prairie Storm, had been involved in violent incidents at foreclosure auctions, loan companies, and banks.

Clark Alfred's anti-war group had started out protesting the Vietnam War, had gotten involved in populist politics after the farm crash of the eighties, had short, local revivals during the first and second Gulf wars. At the moment, it seemed to have only one member: Alfred himself. Alfred, according to Wood's information, was ninety-four years old.

After a moment's consideration, Lucas decided to look at Leonard first, and then Likely. Given his age and history, Alfred didn't seem like much of a candidate for a violent conspiracy.

When everybody was off their respective phones, Henderson asked Lucas, "You got them yet?"

"No, but I've got some things to work with," Lucas said. He gave them a quick recap of the information he'd scraped up, then said, "I'm going to Atlantic first, then over to Mount Pleasant. I'll need your travel schedule and some phone numbers, to stay in touch."

"We're going down to Des Moines for a picnic with Catholic Social Services and a cocktail party for possible donors, and then to Iowa City," Mitford said. "We've got a private event there tonight, then a rally tomorrow morning. Then we go to Cedar Rapids and Cedar Falls. That's the University of Iowa, Kirkwood Community College, University of Northern Iowa, all tomorrow."

"Hitting a lot of colleges," Lucas said.

"I'm a lefty," Henderson said. "If a lefty needs a crowd, he goes to colleges."

"If you're going to Mount Pleasant this afternoon, that's close to Iowa City. If you want a room in Iowa City, call me and I'll have our travel planner get one for you," Mitford said to Lucas.

"Thanks. Right now . . . do you know where Bowden is?"

"She's in Chicago right now, a fast day trip to talk to her money people this morning. She flies to Burlington, that's here in Iowa, this afternoon, for a speech, then she heads up to Davenport by car," Mitford said. "She has a fund-raiser on a riverboat out of Davenport at five o'clock and will be back in town for a speech at six-thirty."

"Where exactly is Burlington?" Lucas asked.

"On the Mississippi, down in the southeast corner of the state," Mitford said. "As a matter of fact, it's only about thirty-two miles from Mount Pleasant and about forty minutes by campaign bus. You could probably drive it in twenty-five."

"Really? You know that off the top of your head?" Lucas asked.

"Yeah, really," Mitford said. "I have a map of Iowa, with all the mileages and travel times, tattooed on my chest and stomach. That little teeny bit of the state that dangles down to Keokuk? That's on my dick."

Henderson said, "Jesus, Neil," and tipped his head toward Green.

"That's all right," Green said. "It's only a little teeny bit."

The governor smiled and turned back to Lucas. "You're going to talk with Bowden?"

"Well, with her weasel, anyway, if you can get your weasel to set it up," Lucas said.

Henderson nodded at Mitford, who said, "I think of myself more as a wolverine."

"A wolverine's a weasel," Green said.

"Yeah, but it's the biggest, meanest one," Mitford said. To Lucas: "I'll call Norm, tell him you're coming."

■ ■ ■ ■

A woman with a clipboard hustled into the room and said, "Governor, I know it's not on the schedule, but a WHO van's outside, they'd like one minute with you, if you could. Jack Gardner says you're an unrealistic dreamer and that Congress wouldn't pass any of your policies —"

"One minute? I've got one minute," Henderson said.

They all drifted through the motel to the parking lot, where a TV cameraman was pointing his camera at the HENDERSON banner on the side of the campaign bus. The woman with the clipboard stopped Henderson before he got to the cameras, opened a lunch box and took out a powder puff, dabbed at his nose and the thin rings under his eyes, did a final touch-up with a tissue, and said, "Go."

While they waited for the governor to finish with the camera and get on the bus, Lucas took Green aside. "Is it possible that there's somebody on Bowden's bus who might be a problem? Anybody I should be worried about?"

"I doubt it. They're thoroughly vetted. I

talked to the Secret Service campaign liaison guy in Washington, an old friend of mine, had him run all the names in depth. That's us, Bowden's and Gardner's campaigns. Everybody seems to be clean, a few pot busts, a couple of cocaines, four DWIs. Most of the bus people are political, but more on the technical side of things, rather than, you know, policy."

"Not nuts, then," Lucas said.

"No. There are a few crazies around, but not on the buses. Why are you worried about the buses?"

"If there was somebody feeding information, or support, or money, or whatever, to these stalkers, if there are stalkers, I need to know who I should look at," Lucas said. "It's like Neil — Neil wouldn't betray Henderson, they're joined at the hip, but he knows everything about Bowden, too. Where she's going, what time she's going there . . . That'd be pretty useful if you were planning an attack."

"Most of that you could find out on her website," Green said. "You wouldn't need Neil to tell you."

Lucas grinned and rubbed his nose. "Okay. I'm the new guy. I didn't think of that. The website gets updated every day?"

"Not just every day, but every hour,"

Green said. "We've got a Web tech on the bus with us. Bowden does, too. Right now, our guy is posting to people in Des Moines that we'll be fifteen minutes late."

"And Bowden does the same thing?"

"Sure. Minute-by-minute," Green said.

"Okay . . . so if you know all this stuff, where's the most uncontrolled spot Bowden will be in the next couple of weeks? Or the governor?"

"That's easy — the Iowa State Fair in Des Moines," Green said. "Every candidate goes there. It's the major event of the summer, as far as the campaigns go. There's between ninety and a hundred and ten thousand people going through the fair every day. There are no effective security controls, as far as I can tell."

"Holy shit."

"Yeah."

"All right. That gives me a deadline," Lucas said.

"But — this is all just a *feeling* on Elmer's part," Green said. "That something's wrong. I kind of agree with him, but when I was with the Secret Service, we dealt with all kinds of perceived threats and virtually none of them were real. Or realistic. Mostly they were goofs who wanted some attention."

"And got it."

"Yes, but the critical thing was, they'd never be a real threat to the president," Green said. "They just didn't have the planning ability, the . . . foresight . . . to be a real threat."

Lucas thought about that as the bus pulled out of the parking lot. He thought Green was interested in what he was doing, but protecting Bowden wasn't part of her job description. While he'd told her of Elle Kruger's psychological analysis of the e-mails, he had the feeling that she hadn't taken that as seriously as he had — because Elle was a nun, and Green didn't know her. Where did a nun get off peddling advice on possible psychotic assassins?

But Lucas *did* know Elle Kruger and she'd left him with a bad feeling about the whole situation. Somebody, he thought, was stalking Bowden. Whether or not they'd pull the trigger on her was another matter. The problem was to get to them, before they had the chance to act, before they had to make that final decision.

After seeing the bus off, Lucas went back to his motel, used the Wi-Fi to send a short note to Weather, who was probably in an operating room and wouldn't see it until the afternoon. He found another short e-mail from Bell Wood that asked, "Do you know where you're staying tonight?"

Lucas sent back: "Don't know for sure, but probably in Iowa City, with Henderson's campaign crew."

With the e-mail out of the way, he got cleaned up, went out to the car, and at nine o'clock headed south and west.

Six

From Ames to Atlantic was a two-hour drive
— a skim across the north side of the Des
Moines metro area, then west on I-80, cutting the edges of a succession of small
towns, with more endless acres of dark
green corn and beans sprawling across the
rolling prairie. Lucas stopped once, to buy
gas and fill the cooler with Diet Cokes. He
was at the gas station, scraping bugs off the
windshield, when Mitford called.

"You're good to talk to Norm Clay this
afternoon. Best to do it in Burlington,
because after that you'd have to chase them
up to Davenport. You don't want to get
stuck on that boat ride." He gave Lucas a
phone number and said, "Good luck."

Atlantic was ten or twelve minutes south of
I-80, a neatly kept town of a few thousand
people, Lucas supposed, a service satellite
for the surrounding farm country. He did a

quick run through the business district to get a sense of the place — it looked like a lot of small towns in the Midwestern countryside, harkening back to the late nineteenth to middle twentieth century, brick, concrete block, low and sprawling — and then punched Leonard's address into his nav system. The nav took him to a trailer park east of the business district. Leonard lived in a dilapidated beige single-wide, with a dusty Jeep Patriot sitting in front of the stoop.

Lucas got out of the Benz, looked around, saw no one, climbed the stoop, heard a television playing, and knocked on the screen door. A moment later a heavyset, sleepy-eyed woman in a quilted housecoat opened the inside door, looked at him through the screen, and asked, "You the police?"

"No. Should I be?" The odor of toast and eggs filtered through the screen, and reminded Lucas that he was hungry.

She said, "I dunno. If you're the police, you gotta say so."

"I'm not the police. I work for Governor Henderson. I want to talk politics with Mr. Leonard. You know, the Prairie Storm thing," Lucas said.

She blinked, then looked past him at the

Benz. "I guess you're not the cops, unless the cops inherited a lot of money. Not much going on with Prairie Storm, not anymore. Anyway, Dave's not here. He's usually down at Winn's this time of day."

"What's Winn's?" Lucas asked.

"Bar. Roadhouse out 83, 'bout a mile past the Mormon church."

Lucas thanked her, prompted her for better directions to the bar — "Go straight out to 83 and hook a left, it's three or four miles out there, look for the eyesore."

He checked the car clock: not yet eleven in the morning. Five minutes later, he was looking at Winn's, a low rambling place that was a few asbestos shingles short of a full set of siding, that might once have been a motel, and maybe still rented out a few rooms. A yellow plastic roller-sign in the gravel parking lot said "Happy Hour, 4–6" and in smaller letters, "Free First D ink For Ladies."

A dive, Lucas thought. Not a dive-themed bar, but the real thing, and as the woman had said, a genuine eyesore. He took a moment to hope that "D ink" was simply "Drink" with a missing letter.

He got out of the truck and went inside.

■ ■ ■ ■

The place was dark and smelled like spilled beer and microwaved cheese and beans and was smaller than it had seemed from the outside. A bartender was watching a rerun of a Cubs game on a TV hung in a corner, next to a stuffed deer head, and a dozen guys were scattered around the interior in booths, one, two, and three at a booth. A few were drinking coffee and eating microwave tacos, the rest were looking at beers. A coin-op pool table sat at the back, but nobody was playing. The customers all wore work clothes, T-shirts and jeans and boots and baseball caps. The bartender took in Lucas's suit as he walked up to the bar and asked, "You lost?"

"Not if this is Winn's," Lucas said.

"Then you're not lost," the bartender said. "What can I do you for?"

"I was told that Dave Leonard might be here," Lucas said.

"Why you looking for Dave?"

"I'm doing some campaign research for Governor Henderson and I was hoping Mr. Leonard could help me out," Lucas said.

A man in a booth said, "I'm Dave Leonard."

■ ■ ■ ■

Leonard was a thick, dark-haired man, Lucas's height but heavier, both in the arms and the gut. He was wearing a plaid shirt, jeans, and yellow work boots. The scars around his pale, suspicious eyes and a withered nose made him into a brawler.

He was sitting in a booth across from two other men, one tall and thin in matching gray work shirt and pants, with a clump of brown hair on top of his head, while the sides were shaved bare; and the other shorter and fat, wearing an orange sweatshirt with cut-off sleeves that said, on the chest, "Party Patrol." A mostly empty pitcher of beer sat in the middle of the table.

"Who told you I was here?" Leonard asked. He slurred some of the words, and Lucas realized he'd been drinking for a while.

"Guy in town," Lucas said. None of the men had gray eyes. "I'd like to talk to you privately, if I could."

"About what?"

"Prairie Storm . . . and some people who might belong to it," Lucas said.

"You smell like a cop," Leonard said. "Not a campaign aide."

"Used to be a cop, but I quit," Lucas said. "You got a minute?"

Leonard looked at the other two men, then said, "These guys are my friends. We can talk right here."

"Okay." Lucas dragged a chair over from a nearby table, sat down at the end of the booth, and looked at Leonard. "Governor Henderson has gotten letters from anonymous people down here in Iowa that seem to threaten Mrs. Bowden. We're taking them seriously. We're looking for an older woman and a younger guy, who might be a family, mother and son. The only thing I can tell you is that the son has pretty distinctive gray eyes. I have a photo . . ."

Lucas began fishing his cell phone out of his pocket, but Leonard broke in to say, "You're not a cop anymore, but you're doing cop work. Investigating."

"Well, I'm checking on these people, to see if they're serious and we need to be worried, or if they're bullshitters and we don't need to worry," Lucas said.

"What does that have to do with me?" Leonard asked.

"The letters use certain kinds of language and talk about certain kinds of political positions that are like the ones in Prairie Storm literature. We're not suggesting that you have anything to do with it, but we thought you might know these people," Lucas said. He scanned the few pictures he had saved in his cell phone, found the one taken by Alice Green, and turned it to Leonard. "This is one of the guys . . . not too good a picture."

Leonard glanced at it, for no more than a fraction of a second, and said, "Never seen him."

"You're sure?"

"Positive."

Lucas peered at him for a moment, then said, "Look, you've got to take this seriously, man. If anything were to happen to one of the candidates and it turned out the shooter was a member of Prairie Storm . . . you could find yourself in big trouble, even if you had nothing to do with it."

"That sounds like a threat," Leonard drawled.

"Not a threat, it's the reality of a bad situation," Lucas said.

"We don't much take to threats," Leonard said.

He'd included his two friends with the "We," but neither the thin man nor the fat man looked like they were much interested in a fight.

"Look, I don't want a hassle, I'm just trying to track down these two —"

"For what? For saying what they think?" Leonard asked.

"I don't care what they *think,* but I'd like to find out what they mean when they talk about, you know, 'What if something *happened* to Mrs. Bowden.' If it's nothing but thinking and talking, they're welcome to it."

"Yeah, you're shuttin' them up, is what you're doing. Shuttin' them up, that's what you're all about."

Lucas pushed away from the table. "All right, you don't want to talk. You don't have to. You may regret it later."

"Tell you what," Leonard said. "What if I kicked your ass? Cops have given me years and years of shit and you're an ex-cop, so I kick your ass, it makes me feel good, and nothing you can do about it, 'cause you're an ex."

"Nothing I can do except fight back," Lucas said. "I promise you, you don't want that."

"You that tough?" Leonard started to slide out of the booth.

"I'm tough and you're drunk," Lucas said. He shoved the chair over to block Leonard's way out of the booth. "And I'm working with the Iowa Division of Criminal Investigation. You take a swing at me, they'll be around to talk to you."

"If they can find me," Leonard said. He tried to kick the chair aside.

"Oh, they'll find you," Lucas said. "Not that hard to find the local hospital, which is where you'll be."

Leonard smiled at that, took it as regular prefight posturing, kicked at the chair again. Lucas pushed it back and said, "I don't want to fight you, Dave. I'm going now. But — you think about what I said. If you change your mind about any of it, you send an e-mail to Governor Henderson's campaign —"

"Fuck you. I'm gonna kick your ass."

Leonard tried to clamber over the chair as Lucas stepped away and turned toward the door. The chair tipped and Leonard fell down, tangled up in the chair legs. Somebody in the bar laughed, the laughter suddenly cut off as Leonard got back to his feet and looked around. The bartender called, "You boys take it outside."

Leonard was coming for him, Lucas realized, and he said to the bartender, "You want to call the sheriff? This guy's about to assault me in your place."

"Not my problem," the bartender said.

"Will be when I file a lawsuit against you," Lucas said.

Leonard said, "Fuck a lawsuit . . ."

The bartender had a sudden change of heart: "Dave, don't do it, goddamnit. I'm calling the sheriff . . ."

"Yeah, and fuck you, Jim," Leonard said.

Lucas was backing toward the door when Leonard rushed him, fists held high. Lucas let him come. The common belief among brawlers was that you didn't let anyone come down on you from the top, which was why they held their fists high. But real boxers didn't.

Lucas was two feet from the door when Leonard got to him. Lucas did a very quick side step and moved slightly forward, when Leonard was expecting him to go back. That took Leonard's left fist out of the fight, and Lucas blocked Leonard's awkward right-hand punch with his own right, and hooked a hard left into Leonard's rib cage, leading with his knuckles, and felt Leonard shudder from the blow and simultaneously make a dog-like *yip*.

The other two men had gotten out of Leonard's booth, and Lucas backed toward them and said, "Stay out of it or I'll break your legs," and they stayed out of it while Leonard, his face red as a ripe apple, came after him again. Lucas sidestepped again, this time to his right, partially blocked

Leonard's left arm with his own left, took a skimming shot to his left cheekbone, and hooked a hard right into the other side of Leonard's rib cage. Leonard yipped again, took several steps backward, crashed into a table, then dropped into a chair.

"Busted my ribs," he groaned. He bent over, head on his knees, holding his sides with his hands.

"Tough shit." Lucas touched his cheekbone, came away with spots of blood on his fingertips. The bartender said, "I called the deputies," and Lucas nodded and walked around behind the bar and checked his face in the mirror. He'd have a bad bruise where he'd been hit, and Leonard's knuckles had scraped a couple of shallow cuts across the bone.

Lucas walked back around the bar and said to the bartender, "Gimme a Coke," and to Leonard, "You sit right there until the cops get here."

"I need to get to a doctor," Leonard moaned.

"You get out of that chair, you'll need two doctors," Lucas said.

Lucas sat on a stool and drank the Coke while Leonard groaned every time he took a breath. Five minutes later, a deputy walked in, looked around, and asked, "What happened?"

"He beat me up," Leonard said, jabbing a finger at Lucas.

The deputy turned to Lucas and Lucas said, "I'm a former Minnesota cop working for Elmer Henderson's presidential campaign. We've gotten some threatening letters . . ."

He told the story and another deputy arrived, and the first one looked at Leonard and asked, "You have anything to do with those letters, Dave?"

"Don't know anything about any fuckin' letters," Leonard said. He had his arms pressing his ribs together, his fingers linked over his stomach.

"Then why'd you jump me?" Lucas asked. "There was no reason for a fight, unless you were trying to intimidate me, trying to keep me from asking questions."

" 'Cause I don't fuckin' like cops, that's why. I don't like guys in suits, either."

"That's all true," said the second deputy. He'd heard what sounded like a confession and asked Lucas, "What do you want to do about this? Looks like you took a hit, you're bleeding."

"Up to you," Lucas said. "You want me to file a complaint, I will, but I'm okay with calling it even, if Mr. Leonard will give me one honest answer."

The first deputy asked Leonard, "What do you think, Dave?"

"What's the question?" Leonard asked.

"Did you know the man in the photo I showed you? Do you know a middle-aged lady with a son who has distinctive gray eyes?"

"No. That's nobody in Prairie Storm," Leonard said. "I know them all, them's that's left."

Leonard's friends said they'd take him to the hospital to get his ribs checked, and on the way out, Leonard said to Lucas, "I'd kick your ass if I wasn't drunk."

Lucas said, "Of course you would."

The deputies hung around while Leonard was helped out to a friend's pickup, and then as Lucas got the first aid kit out of his truck and smeared some Neosporin on his facial cuts.

"What do you think about Leonard?" Lucas asked them, as he peered at his cheek in the truck's wing mirror. "You think this Prairie Storm's got people we should look at?"

"Hell, as far as I know, there're only about three members left and not one of them could organize a decent goat fuck," said the older of the two deputies.

They both knew the other members of Prairie Storm, they said, which was mostly a Cass County group. The members were all fairly old and mostly wrote letters to the editor. "Don't think you're gonna find an assassin here. Maybe some assholes, no assassins," said the younger one.

They said they'd ask around about a white-haired lady with a gray-eyed son, who'd been tied into Prairie Storm. "But I'll tell you what you need — you need a better description."

Lucas remembered the photo on his phone and showed it to them. The younger one looked at it for a moment, then said, "You know who that looks like? Who was that guy, maybe . . . five years ago . . . grew all that weed in the Wilsons' cornfield?"

"Not him," said the older guy. "That's the guy who ran off with Bob Hake's wife. They're long gone to California and they ain't coming back if they know what's good for them."

"Oh, yeah. Boy, she was one hot kitty, huh?"

"Okay," Lucas said. He got out two business cards, wrote his phone number on the back of them, gave them to the deputies, said, "Call anytime, day or night," and got back on the road.

Lucas didn't have many feelings about the fight, one way or the other, because it hadn't been much of a fight. Leonard wouldn't want to cough or laugh for a few weeks, and Lucas would have a black eye. He'd had a number of them over the years; it was an occupational hazard you put up with.

He hadn't even gotten much of a shot of adrenaline; it'd been more a matter of taking care of business than a desperate struggle. Which was fine.

From Atlantic to Mount Pleasant, Iowa, was a drive of roughly three and a half hours, or three hours if you were behind the wheel of a turbo-charged 4.6-liter V8.

Lucas drove back across the top of Des Moines, then southwest through Oskaloosa and Ottumwa, the towns from which the e-mails had been sent. He didn't stop in either place, even to look around, because after he got out of the Des Moines traffic, he called Norman Clay, Michaela Bowden's weasel, on the number that Mitford had given him. Clay told him that Bowden would be speaking until about three-thirty in Burlington, and Lucas could stop by any time after three o'clock to talk.

He'd get to Mount Pleasant a little after two, he thought, which gave him an hour to find and interview Joseph Likely, and then move on to Burlington to talk with Clay.

More beans and corn. Lots more.

Lucas crossed the Skunk River into Mount Pleasant at two-thirty. He hadn't had anything to eat except some peanut-butter crackers at a pee stop on I-80, but ignored a café, which made him feel virtuous, and went looking for Joseph Likely's place. Mount Pleasant was an older town, where no two houses, standing side by side, seemed to come out of the same architectural style, with nineteenth-century Victorians up against pastel-colored postwar ramblers. Most of the houses had traditional flower gardens with marigolds and zinnias, and some with head-high sunflowers.

Likely lived in one of the ramblers; he wasn't home. A neighbor, a chunky, shirtless sunburned man, was lying in a canvas hammock, reading a battered copy of *The Sun Also Rises,* and he called, "If you're looking for Joe, he got out of here early with his canoe up on his car roof. Probably out on the river. The Iowa River, not the Skunk."

Lucas ambled over. "You need a shirt," he said.

"Probably," the neighbor said, looking at his chest. "I don't mind toasting the shoulders, but it does hurt when your tits get singed. But I feel too good to get up and go inside. Say, you look like you ran into a door."

"Yeah, it's embarrassing," Lucas said. He touched his cheekbone and winced. "You know when Joe's getting back?"

"Usually about dark," the neighbor said. "He tries to get off the river before the bugs get bad. You want me to tell him you were here?"

"That'd be great," Lucas said. He took the card case out of his jacket pocket and took out a card. Weather had gotten them for him and the card said nothing but "Lucas Davenport" on an expensive-looking cream-colored stock. He wrote his cell phone number on the back and said, "I'll stop back again this evening. If he gets here earlier than that, tell him to give me a ring."

The man looked at the card, apparently puzzled by the lack of information on it, and asked, "Can I tell him what you want?"

Lucas thought it over for a few seconds, then said, "Yes. Tell him I'm a political researcher."

"I'll tell him," the man said. Before Lucas could go, he asked, "Say, could you step inside that back door there? That's the kitchen and the refrigerator is right there. Get me a beer. Get one for yourself, if you want. And there's a shirt on the counter — toss me that."

Not a man who got nervous about strangers in his yard, Lucas thought, as he handed him the beer and T-shirt.

Before leaving town, Lucas had a few minutes, so he stopped one more time, at the Dairy Queen, got a chocolate-dipped vanilla cone, which didn't do much for his virtue but a lot for his sense of well-being, found his way back to Highway 34, and headed southeast to Burlington.

Burlington was a hard-core Mississippi River town, the best kind, to Lucas's mind. Bowden's event was at the Burlington Municipal Auditorium, which was located on the banks of the Mississippi and looked quite a lot like Uncle Scrooge's Money Bin, for those whose comic-book memories went back that far.

After a quick phone call, he found Norman Clay sitting on the wall that wrapped around a fountain at the back corner of the building, eating a Popsicle and looking out at the river and one of the prettiest bridges to cross it. Clay was a fleshy, square-shouldered man about Lucas's size and age, but blond, and tired-looking, and wearing a non-wrinkle blue knit suit, with a striped tie, the knot pulled open.

He stood up when Lucas approached, held out his hand and said, "Davenport?" and sat back down. "What's up?"

"Did Neil tell you what I'm doing?"

"Yeah, yeah. We've got solid security and I don't know exactly what Henderson's doing, hiring you," Clay said. "We looked you up, by the way. You're the cop who got tangled up with Taryn Grant."

"Yeah, that was me," Lucas said.

"And she's now a respected senator from our very own party," Clay said.

"A psychopath, but don't tell anybody I told you so," Lucas said.

"You don't really have to tell me," Clay said. "I met her a couple of times, around town, and I got that distinct impression."

"That doesn't worry you?"

"In D.C.? Hell, psychopaths are a dime a dozen inside the Beltway, and about a quarter a dozen outside," Clay said. "Gotta be more than rich and crazy to raise an eyebrow in Washington."

Lucas sat down, looked out at the river. "I don't often use the word, but she's the bitch from hell," he said. "Believe me, you don't want to get on her wrong side. She could send somebody after you with a gun."

"That seems a little extreme," Clay said.

"She *is* a little extreme," Lucas said.

"I meant your statement, not the senator," Clay said.

"Yeah, well, you don't know what I know. She's a murderer," Lucas said. After a few seconds of silence, he added, "Anyway, you know I'm not a cop anymore."

"Yes. Neil said that."

"I still have some pretty good resources," Lucas said. "I ran those e-mails past the best psychologist I know, who has quite a lot of experience with criminal psychology, and she's afraid that something serious may be happening here."

He told Clay about Elle Kruger's opinion and about tracking the e-mail language to some radical political groups. He concluded with, "Since you put every single move Bowden is going to make on your web-site . . . she's always easy to find."

"The thing is, we're not going to go away," Clay said. He walked over to the river and threw his Popsicle stick in, then came back. "After talking to Mitford, I kinda thought we should. Maybe spend a few extra days in New Hampshire and then the South, but Mike doesn't want to hear it. She wants Iowa and she doesn't want to be run off it."

"Tough to win an election if you're dead," Lucas said.

"You're right — but you have to understand, Mike has lived with this . . . with the vague threats and so on . . . for half her life. She's been in and out of Iraq, in and out of Afghanistan. Nothing's ever happened, so she doesn't tend to give these threats much credence."

"Is your security going after the threat? Or is the security static?" Lucas asked.

"Not going after it. We have to rely on the Iowa cops for that — we passed Henderson's concerns along to their election security team. Haven't heard much back," Clay said.

He stretched, yawned, and sat down again. A door must have opened on the side of the auditorium, because they heard a burst of cheering, which quickly faded. He said, "I'm not dumb. I'm worried. But Henderson told me you're the best possible guy to be chasing down the threat. If there is one. So . . . God bless you. Mike ain't going away."

"Ah, boy."

114

People began streaming out of the auditorium.

"Had a good crowd," Clay said, standing up. "How's the governor doing? Hitting a lot of colleges?"

"Up at the University of Iowa tonight and more of them tomorrow," Lucas said.

Clay flashed a grin. "Well, if you're a lefty . . ."

". . . you hit a lot of colleges," Lucas finished.

Clay said, "C'mon. I'll introduce you to God."

Michaela Bowden was a tall woman, thin, ramrod-straight, brown hair with copper highlights, attractive in a front-office way. She was talking to a small group of fawning locals, called a couple of them by name. Lucas picked out a half-dozen security people, four men, two women, within twenty feet of her. Every one of them eye-clicked Lucas, maybe smelling a guy with a gun, though he wasn't wearing one. When they saw Clay pulling him along, they looked elsewhere.

Bowden was backing away from the group around her and one of the security women was edging between the locals and the candidate, separating them, and then

Bowden said, "Well, I'm late for a river-boat . . ." and somebody said, "We got a riverboat right here, Mike," and everybody laughed as though that were hilarious, and then Bowden was moving away toward the back of the auditorium with the security screen building both in front and behind her.

Clay pulled Lucas along and as they were approaching the back door, he called, "Madam Secretary . . . I need you to meet this guy."

She stopped and turned and looked at Lucas and then Clay, did a quick price check on Lucas's suit, and asked, "How do you do?"

Before Lucas could answer, Clay said, "This is Lucas Davenport. He's the former cop hired by Henderson to try to dig out those supposed threats. I wanted you to see him, so you'll know who he is, if you see him again, in a crowd."

Bowden nodded at Lucas and showed a half-inch smile: "I understand you're close to Taryn Grant."

Lucas smiled back. Bowden projected an effortless charisma and he had to resist the urge to tug at his forelock: "Not close enough. A little closer and she wouldn't be in the Senate — she'd be in a different federal institution altogether."

"Interesting," she said. And, "Good luck with your investigation. Are you seeing Elmer soon?"

"Maybe tonight."

"Tell him I'm not leaving Iowa," she said.

She started to maneuver away, but Lucas said, "Ms. Bowden — I don't know how well you really know the governor, but he's a good guy. The last thing in the world he'd want is for you to get hurt. He wouldn't pull anything like this threat thing to bullshit you out of the state. This is a serious matter."

Bowden took a longer look at him, and then said, "Okay. So it's up to you to save my butt, Lucas. I'm not leaving."

As Bowden, her security force, advisers, and hangers-on streamed out to a line of Chevy Suburbans and a bus, Clay said to Lucas, "We're running late. I don't have time right now, but I'd like to introduce you to all our security people. What are the chances you could make it to Davenport this evening?"

"Maybe," Lucas said. "I've got to talk to a guy in Mount Pleasant first."

"Mount Pleasant . . . is what, a half hour from here? You could make it to Davenport,

if you don't take too long in Mount Pleasant."

"I'll try," Lucas said.

"See you then," Clay said, and he hurried
after his candidate, who had disappeared
into a silver Suburban.

SEVEN

Lucas headed back to Mount Pleasant, knocked on Joseph Likely's door, got no answer, went back to the café he'd seen earlier in the day, and ordered the open-faced roast beef sandwich, fries, and a Diet Coke.

The whole restaurant smelled of grease and Campbell's mushroom soup, which was about right. Lucas had eaten open-faced roast beef sandwiches all over the Midwest, the kind that came soaked in brown gravy and little bits of things you didn't want to know about and rated this one at about sixty-nine percent.

He added a slice of coconut cream pie after he finished the sandwich, and the waitress, when she dropped the pie plate on his table, asked, "Who won?"

"What?"

"The fight. Who won the fight?"

"I did," Lucas said, catching on. He

119

touched his face, and it hurt.

The waitress smiled and said, "You got a heck of a shiner, that's for sure. Shoulda put a beefsteak on it. Too late now."

Lucas left a few dollars on the table, and went looking for Likely.

Joseph Likely's Ford Taurus was parked in his side yard, a red canoe still up on the roof, the bottom white with cuts and scratches. Lucas knocked on the screen door, and a moment later Likely came to the door.

He was a tall, thin man with a scraggly black beard on his cheeks and a down-curving mustache on his upper lip. He was older, somewhere in his middle to late sixties, Lucas thought, tough-looking, in the way of Abraham Lincoln. He was wearing jeans, a long-sleeved blue cotton shirt, and a rain-faded gold Iowa Hawkeyes Football cap. His hands were gnarled, either from arthritis or work, or both.

Lucas introduced himself and explained what he was doing. Likely said, "You told my neighbor that you were a political researcher."

"I am. I'm looking into who might be a threat to Mrs. Bowden," Lucas said.

"But you're basically a cop."

"I was. I quit a while back," Lucas said. "Right now I'm working for Governor Henderson."

"Yeah, but I really don't talk to cops of any kind, actual or pro tem," Likely said. "I wouldn't inform on my worst enemy."

Lucas looked at him for a second, then said, "Listen, Joe. I don't give a rat's ass about your political inclinations. I believe there's a serious threat against Mrs. Bowden. If it turns out it comes from you or one of your political people, and you know about it, and something happens, you'll be looking at the inside of a really ugly prison for the rest of your life. That ain't bullshit — that's the fact of the matter."

"I don't respond very well to threats, either," Likely said.

"Joe, you're thinking in slogans," Lucas said. "You don't talk to cops, you don't inform on anybody, you don't respond to threats. You've got to *listen* to what I'm saying. This isn't make-believe. This isn't political bullshit, or a TV show — this is a real thing."

"Yeah, well, I suggest you talk to my attorney," Likely said.

"What for?"

"She can tell you about the ins and outs

of the law on this, and all about illegal harassment."

"Hey, I'm not trying to harass you. I'll talk to your attorney and I'll tell you now what she's going to say — if you know anything, speak up."

"I don't believe she'll do that." Likely rubbed the back of his hand across his nose, then said, "No, sir, I don't think she'll say that. She doesn't like oppressive police actions any more than I do."

"Ah, Jesus . . ." Lucas shook his head. "Give me the attorney's name. I'll call her right now."

"Not while you're trespassing on my sidewalk. I'll give you her name and then you go somewhere else to call her."

Lucas's SUV had been sitting in the sun and was uncomfortably hot, so he started it, and jacked up the air-conditioning. The attorney's number that Likely had given him turned out to be a state public defender named Carmen Wyatt, whose office was back in Burlington.

Lucas talked his way past a secretary to get to Wyatt. He explained what he was doing, including his brief conversation with Bowden in Burlington. Wyatt replied that she didn't represent Likely in any current criminal case, though she had represented him in the past, in several protest-related arrests. She would not be representing him in any negotiations about a private inquiry involving a possible election problem.

"I don't want to seem like a jerk, but this doesn't fall under our purview," Wyatt said, "especially since you're not a police officer conducting an official investigation."

"What would you suggest?"

"I'd suggest you stop bothering Joe," she said. "If you, as a private citizen, have a specific complaint, bring it to the attention of an Iowa law enforcement authority. If a crime has been committed, or if it's found that a conspiracy is under way —"

"You do understand what I'm saying, right? That I'm trying to figure out —"

"Not my problem," Wyatt interrupted.

Lucas said, "Look, I've explained this wrong. Let me try again. If there's a conspiracy and if Mrs. Bowden is shot, or even shot at, and if Likely is involved, in the investigation afterwards you'll almost certainly lose your job because you wouldn't help me."

"I don't take threats any more than Joe does," Wyatt snapped.

"I'm not threatening you," Lucas said, getting even more exasperated. He was starting to sound like a broken record. "I'm providing you with information. I'm not trying to oppress Likely. I'm not threatening to arrest him — I'm not a cop. I'm looking for a little information. He's refusing to give it to me out of a knee-jerk anti-cop attitude, or maybe because he does know something and he's covering up. If that's what's going on . . . if Mrs. Bowden gets shot or even shot at and missed, and you failed to co-operate with any inquiry, including mine, you're done. That's not a threat. That's what's going to happen. If you spend more than ten seconds thinking about it, instead of hiding behind a lot of bureaucratic BS, you'll understand what I'm telling you. Doesn't make any difference if you get fired for real obstruction or because you're a scapegoat, you'll still get fired. Believe me, if something happens, there'll be a full-on scapegoat hunt. What do you think the job prospects will be for a lawyer on the wrong side of an assassination?"

"I'm done talking here," Wyatt said. "You have to understand that we hear a lot of vague threats —"

"These aren't vague. And I'm not crazy — check with the Bureau of Criminal Apprehension in St. Paul. Or hell, check my name on the Internet."

"I'll look," Wyatt said. "Now I'm going to

hang up."

Lucas was sitting across the street from Likely's house. He'd seen the curtain move a couple of times in a front window as he was talking to Wyatt — Likely checking to see if he was still there, he thought. Frustrating, not being a cop, and not having that weight behind his questions. What to do?

One possibility: he called Bell Wood at the Iowa Division of Criminal Investigation. Wood had left for the day, but the duty officer said he'd give him a ring on his personal cell and pass Lucas's number along if Wood wanted to call back.

Wood called a minute later: "What's up?"

Lucas explained what had happened, and then asked, "I was wondering if push came to shove, if one of your election security people could have a chat with Likely?"

"I'd have to check with the guys on that team, see if they could have somebody run down there. I could do that in the morning."

"That'd be good. When you don't have a badge, getting anything done is like wading through mud," Lucas said.

"Then you oughta get a badge," Wood said. "By the way, I called Henderson's campaign people and got their hotel for the night. You'll be getting a FedEx there first thing in the morning, with a carry permit."

"Excellent."

"I expect some kind of under-the-table payoff. I've got a steak house in mind," Wood said.

"Count on it," Lucas said.

After thinking about it for a moment, Lucas pulled the iPad out of its seatback pocket, brought up Michaela Bowden's website. After a fund-raising riverboat ride, she'd be at the Hotel Blackhawk, in Davenport, for a public speech and then a fund-raising cocktail party.

He brought up a map program and checked distances and times. He could be in Davenport in an hour and a half, check out the meeting and party, look for gray eyes and long hair, introduce himself to all the Bowden security, and still make it back to Iowa City for the night.

He punched the Blackhawk hotel location into his nav system and was about to pull out, when the phone rang: unknown, from Burlington, Iowa.

"Lucas Davenport."

"This is Carmen Wyatt. I talked to Joe. I told him that you were unofficial, but that you were probably right about his getting in trouble if something serious happened," the lawyer said. "I told him that he didn't *have* to talk to you, but he could listen. Then if he *wanted* to respond, it might save him some trouble later. He said he'd listen. Go knock on his door."

"I appreciate it. I'll do that," Lucas said.

"Do not threaten him. That's a violation of Iowa law and you have no status here," she said. "I don't want to wind up defending you, because I don't think I'd like you."

Likely was already standing at the door when Lucas came up the front walk. He pushed open the screen and said, "I'll listen."

They went into the parlor. The house smelled of old plaster, wallpaper, and cooked vegetables; the late-afternoon light sifted through yellowed-lace curtains, reflecting off framed modernist woodblock prints that crowded the plaster walls. Lucas told him the story, the same one he'd already told several times that day, with Likely sitting in a wooden rocking chair, nodding as he rocked.

When Lucas was finished, Likely said, "I personally can't help you. I'll talk to some other folks in the party, but I know everybody associated with it. This doesn't sound like anybody I know."

"If you could do that, I'd appreciate it," Lucas said. "I have to tell you, I don't have much interest in your kind of politics, but if you were to pick out any one person who you folks might vote for, it's the guy who hired me. Governor Henderson takes your position on a number of issues and you might keep that in mind. We're not trying to oppress anyone or mess with you guys in any way. We're trying to prevent what could be a tragedy."

"You don't even know for sure if there is a plot," Likely said. "If there isn't, and you find this gray-eyed man you're looking for, and given the way the world works now, he'll be slapped in jail whether or not he's up to something. He'll be lucky if they don't get renditioned to some CIA hellhole, and tortured, just in case."

"That doesn't happen —"

"Bullshit. You need to open your eyes and look around, Mr. Davenport. This country isn't what it used to be, even twenty years ago. People are herded around like sheep, and willingly go, because the government's got everybody scared to death about terrorism. Three thousand people died at nine-one-one fourteen years ago. That's terrible, but we've way overreacted. We've hired tens of thousands of anti-terrorism secret agents and fought two major wars and all kinds of brushfires because of it, and we've gotten to the point where we actually torture people, *torture people,* in the United States of America, and in the meantime, more than thirty thousand people die every year in highway accidents and we can't even lower the speed limit to fifty-five. Open your eyes — there's some real terrorism, of course there is, but the government's using it as an excuse to put its thumb down on everybody."

"I can't tell you how little interest I have in politics," Lucas said. "Fixing things is up to people like you. All I'm doing is trying to stop a potential assassination."

"But don't you see, you're part of the whole problem . . ."

Lucas stood up. "If you could talk to your friends and see if anyone knows this lady and her gray-eyed son, I'd greatly appreciate it."

"I'll do that, but you should spend some time looking into your own soul, and thinking about your part in this vast conspiracy that's coming down on us all," Likely said.

"I'll do that," Lucas said. "Use my card, though, and call me if you hear anything, even if it doesn't seem like much."

■ ■ ■ ■

Likely took him to the door and watched as Lucas pulled away from the curb, then touched the cell phone in his pocket. He didn't really believe in cell phones, but he'd gotten old, and he still liked to ramble around in the woods on his own. If he had a heart attack out in the woods, or on the river, having a cell phone was a practical kind of comfort.

Even as he touched it, though, the thought occurred that he shouldn't use it to make the call to the mother of the gray-eyed boy. Davenport was certainly a government agent of some kind and they'd be watching his phone. What he needed was a pay phone.

Where, he wondered, would he find a pay phone in this day and age?

Something a person like himself should know . . .

The pay phone was hanging on the wall at Walmart.

Likely walked half the aisles in the store, looking for anybody who might be watching, and saw nothing suspicious. Of course, there were cameras. He'd have to take the chance, he decided.

He'd found Marlys Purdy's phone number in his files, hoped it would still work. After one last look around, he dropped some quarters in the phone and dialed. Marlys said, "Hello?"

"I don't want to say my name or your name, but you come to my house every three months with pies. You know who this is?"

"Yes?"

"There was a man here looking for you and a gray-eyed son," Likely said. "All he had was a description and a poor picture of the man. He thinks you may be conspiring to . . . do something to a . . . lady candidate. I've got to be careful here, no names."

"I understand. Does he have names?"

"No. All he has is some basic descriptions. He said the candidate from the North saw you and a fellow he believed was related to you, and passed along the description. If he starts asking around among our people, he's going to find you. I won't ask if . . . you know . . . you're planning something. I'm already in enough trouble, lying about not knowing you."

"I appreciate that," Marlys said.

"You better more than appreciate it. Your action isn't . . . appropriate. That's not a strong enough word, but you know what I mean. I won't ask if you're planning something, but I'll tell you, if you are, you better quit it."

"Things are getting desperate. Everything is out of control," Marlys said, a pleading note in her voice. "If we don't do something now . . . four years from now may be too late. We can already see how things are going this year, and we have to do something this year."

"Mar . . . I'm sorry, that's crazy talk. You have to stop and think," Likely said.

"You think I haven't thought about this? I'm more scared and more worried than you are, Joe, but not about myself. About the whole country —"

"Careful about names . . ."

"I'm sorry. But look — we need to talk about this. Maybe I'm too isolated out here," Marlys said. "The only place I get to talk serious politics is the beauty salon."

"I'll talk anytime you want — but you know what my position has to be. No violence. No violence. Violence is the true root of all evil, worse even than money. If John Kennedy hadn't been killed, if Lyndon Johnson hadn't taken us into Vietnam, can you imagine what this country could be? If Reagan —"

"Old fights, old fights," Marlys said.

"But . . . let's talk. There's time. I'll talk to my boy, see what he thinks. Maybe even come by tonight, if I can find a babysitter for my granddaughter."

"Okay. Let me know, soon. I think . . . this is all very troubling."

Likely got off the phone and felt himself creeping around the store, waiting for a hand on the shoulder. Nothing happened. He bought a roll of Bounty paper towels and a pack of paper plates and slunk out the doors, heading back home.

Checked around the parking lot for watching faces; scanned the rearview mirror in the car. At home, walked from window to window . . . Nothing. That didn't mean they weren't out there.

EIGHT

The Hotel Blackhawk was an older building in downtown Davenport — excellent name for a city, Lucas thought as he parked the truck — with a political bustle going on in the streets around it, cars and buses jamming things up, the sound of a band somewhere nearby, a police siren off in the deepening twilight. He'd come up along the Mississippi, and could still feel the presence of the river as he walked across Third Street to the hotel.

He'd called Norm Clay on the way north and Clay said that a woman named Sally Rodriguez would be waiting for him in the lobby with a campaign badge. "She's short, brunette, gorgeous, and unavailable," Clay said.

"I've heard rumors of a thing called campaign sex, which doesn't count," Lucas said.

"So have I, but I don't get any," Clay said.

"Anyway, I told her to look for the big guy in an expensive suit with a black eye. Call her five minutes before you get here. She'll meet you in the lobby."

Lucas did that and found Rodriguez sitting in the lobby, talking on a cell phone: she held a hand up to him and pointed at the chair next to hers. Lucas sat and Rodriguez said into the phone, ". . . can tell Mary Lou that she can go fuck herself, that Mike's going to win the election and the presidency and the next time she'll get an interview is in the late 2040s. I'm going now."

She clicked off without saying good-bye and smiled at Lucas and said, "Straightening out a TV station's priorities." She was as good-looking as advertised, wore a deep-red dress with matching shoes, lipstick, and nails.

"Does it do any good?" Lucas asked.

"Oh, yeah. TV people love it when politicians treat them like they're important and respected. I'd told them that we'd give them an exclusive five minutes with Mike, but she didn't want to talk about the gun issue, because it had been done to death. What's the first question they asked? 'Will you require gun registration if you're elected?' I catch a raft of shit from Mike, and now the producer catches a raft of shit from me."

As she spoke, she was digging into a leather bag and produced a laminated card with a neck loop that said, at the top, "The Mike Campaign, 2016," and at the bottom, in small green letters, "All Venues," with a smiling shot of Bowden in between.

"Norm told me to give you this and I'll ask you not to abuse it — it gets you into everything and there aren't many like it. Don't loan it to anyone."

"I'll use it carefully," Lucas said. "And probably not much."

"Good," she said. Her phone rang and she looked at it and said, "I've got to take this. Mike's up in the main ballroom right now . . ."

"Gotcha," Lucas said. He held up a hand to say good-bye as she clicked on the new call, walked over to the main desk, got directions to the ballroom. On the way, he hung the laminated card around his neck, spotted one of Bowden's security guys, and went that way, to introduce himself.

"Norm told us about you," the guy said. He grinned, gestured at Lucas's black eye, and said, "Looks like you walked into a door."

"Yeah. Door. Lots of doors around. I want to look at the crowd, see how you do things.

I'd like to talk to your other guys, too."

"You go on. I'll call Dan Jubek, he's the boss, and tell him you're coming. He'll be standing at the bottom of the stairs up to the stage. He's a big black guy, wearing a tan suit, looks like an NFL lineman because he used to be one."

Bowden's speech was in a large ballroom with arches and a shaky-looking temporary stage; there were metal detectors at the doorways and security people standing by them, but the audience was already inside. The place was jammed, with standing people crowded around the chairs that took up the center of the room, which smelled of sweat, perfume, and hair spray. Three television crews were shooting from one side, a fourth from the other side. Lucas worked his way around the edge of the crowd until he came to a rope that kept him from continuing behind the platform. A security man saw him, crooked a finger at him, and lifted the rope so he could cross the line.

"Dan's waiting for you . . ."

Bowden was saying, ". . . need to care for the less advantaged among us. The Republicans and even some of my fellow Democrats would have you believe that these people are nothing but lazy . . ."

Her eyes touched Lucas's and she gave him a minute nod and kept talking.

Lucas worked his way to the side of the stage, where Jubek was standing. He was four inches taller than Lucas and six inches wider. He was wearing round-toed shoes that almost passed for dress, but would have a solid steel cap under the toe. He had a bug in his ear and a microphone button on one collar. He leaned toward Lucas and said, "She's about four minutes from finishing and then we're off to the cocktail party down the hall. Be best if we talked then."

"Okay."

Lucas backed off and scanned the crowd. Lots of middle-aged women, but no farm boys with distinctive gray eyes. Everybody seemed well-groomed, even when long-haired. Nothing for him here, he thought; the crowd was too well-watched and chosen and metal-detected. The cocktail party would probably be even more selected. A problem, if there ever was one, would come from the outside, while Bowden was moving from one place to another.

Bowden finished her talk with comments about all the great old friends she had in Davenport and how much she enjoyed seeing them again, which seemed unlikely to Lucas, but then she was off the stage and Jubek escorted her down a side hall and through a couple of back rooms and out into another hallway, to another event space already populated by a couple dozen people holding drinks.

When she was securely inside, Jubek dropped back to speak with Lucas.

"Give me the odds that this is something real and not a false alarm," he said.

Lucas said, "Maybe fifty-fifty."

Jubek's eyebrows went up, and he said, "That bad? Fifty-fifty makes me seriously nervous."

"Mrs. Bowden and Norm Clay suspect that Governor Henderson may be trying to discourage her from campaigning here in Iowa, but that's not true," Lucas said. "Henderson doesn't really believe he can get the nomination, but he thinks if Bowden is nominated, she could pick him as a running mate, and nobody else would. What I'm saying is, he *wants* her to get the nomination."

"Interesting. That's not what I'm hearing from Norm — the governor's doing a little better than we'd expected. Anyway, what I need here is specifics, who and what and mostly when."

Lucas shook his head. "Don't have any of

that yet. I'll feed you everything I get. The thing that worries me the most is the fact that she's going to the state fair. That's gonna be a mess."

"We know that," Jubek said, going grim. "I've tried to talk her out of it, but it's the biggest event on the schedule, and *not* going would be considered an insult to the entire state of Iowa. She's going."

"All right. I'll try to track these guys down before then . . ."

As Bowden worked the room, Jubek took Lucas around to all the other security people and told them to take a good look. "If this guy tells you something, you listen," he told them. He gave Lucas his cell phone number, and said, as Lucas was leaving, "I sincerely hope you're a self-aggrandizing bullshitter who's trying to get attention for himself, but I looked you up and I've got the bad feeling you're not."

" 'Self-aggrandizing.' Pretty big words for a former lineman," Lucas said.

Jubek grinned and slapped him on the shoulder and said, "See ya."

Lucas checked his watch: he'd gotten done what he'd wanted to get done — met Bowden's security, which he hadn't had time to do in Burlington — and he still had time to make it to Iowa City. He pushed through the front door into the street . . .

And saw Cole Purdy leaning against a wall across the street.

Didn't know the name, couldn't be certain that it was who he thought it was, couldn't see that distinctive eye color from that distance, but the hair, the leanness of the face, the stance, and even the high-collared shirt were right. Everyone else around was in short sleeves . . . Was the shirt covering a gun? Lucas turned around and walked back into the lobby and found the security guy he'd met when he first walked in.

"You gotta come with me," he said. "C'mon, c'mon . . ."

"What's up?"

"There's a guy across the street, watching the door," Lucas said. "He might be one of the people we're looking for."

The security guy, whose name was Andy, said, "Go!" and started talking into his lapel, and Lucas led him out the door. The guy was gone.

Lucas ran to the middle of the street — it'd been fifteen seconds, no more — and then saw the guy sixty or seventy yards down the street, more than half a football field, walking swiftly away. He glanced back, as he'd done in the photo taken by Alice

Green, and then Lucas was sure.

"That's him," he said to Andy, who'd come up behind him. He started toward Cole, walking fast, but there wasn't enough of a sidewalk crowd to hide him and the guy looked back again and their eyes touched and the guy broke into a full-out run down Third Street.

"Shit!" Andy said, and he was shouting into his lapel as he and Lucas dashed across the street, through and past cars. Lucas realized that he wasn't far from the truck, and shouted at Andy, "Chase him! I'll get my truck!"

Cole was fast and wearing running shoes and was pulling ahead. They crossed Pershing Avenue, losing ground, then Cole turned at Iowa Street and was out of sight. Lucas came up to his truck and opened it with the remote key, climbed inside, fired it up, had to wait for a passing car, did a U-turn, saw Andy disappear around a corner.

Andy turned the corner at Iowa, couldn't see anyone running, but then a white pickup roared out of a parking lot that faced a set of railroad tracks, banged over a curb, and headed away from them, down Iowa, made a screeching turn onto Second Street. By the time he'd run a block to the corner of Second, out of breath, he was in time to see the truck turn left on Pershing.

Then Lucas was coming up behind, pulling over. Andy popped the passenger-side door and shouted, "Next street, take a left."

By the time they got to Pershing, the white truck was gone, and they didn't know which way.

"Goddamnit, goddamnit, he's gone," Andy shouted into his lapel mike. "Probably on the highway, but which way . . . I dunno. White pickup, a Ford, I think, white male with long-sleeve OD shirt worn unbuttoned over T-shirt, jeans, long hair . . . Goddamnit."

Cole had driven only a short block on Pershing, turned down an alley, back the way he'd come. Before leaving the alley, he pulled behind a car and watched Pershing. A few seconds later he saw a black SUV, moving far too quickly, pass the alley, pause at the highway, and take a left.

Cole pulled ahead, took a left himself, back on Iowa, went around a couple of blocks and onto the highway, heading in the opposite direction from the black SUV. A few minutes later he was on I-74 heading north; and five minutes later, on I-80, going west.

Lucas and Andy never saw him again, though they'd seen a lot of white pickup trucks. They drove around for a while, in case he'd stopped to hide, then went back to the hotel.

At the hotel, Jubek asked Lucas, "How sure?"

"Pretty sure," Lucas said.

Andy said, "I'm pretty sure, too. When he saw us, he started running. No reason to, if he was innocent. He was looking right at us and he took off like a big-assed bird."

"Most of the city cops were here, on crowd control, none of them in cars," Jubek said. "Probably didn't get rolling until a couple minutes after I got to them, and I didn't get to them for a couple minutes after you called. He was probably a couple of miles away before the cops started looking. They stopped about fifty white pickups . . ."

"He could have been across the river in Illinois before we even started looking," Andy said.

"C'mon. We're gonna talk to Mike," Jubek said.

"You already told her about it?" Lucas asked.

"First thing. She wanted to know the chances that you were bullshitting us, that this whole incident was set up to scare us. I told her less than one percent. Because our guy was with you during the chase and Andy knows what he's doing, and if you'd set it up, and if either Andy or the local cops had broken it down, that would be the end of Henderson. Henderson is too smart for that, and so are you."

Bowden excused herself from the cocktail party, and when they were together in a side room, she glanced at Lucas and asked Jubek, "What happened?"

Jubek told her, and then said, "Now we have an actual sighting and a reaction, and it's not good, Madam Secretary. We need to talk to the Iowa campaign security and get them to help Davenport. Whoever this guy was, we need to break him out."

"Then do that," she said. She started twisting a ring on her left hand, glanced at Lucas again, then back at Jubek. "I'll want to staff the incident tonight, after the party."

"Yes. We need to do that," Jubek said.

Bowden nodded at Lucas and stepped back toward the party. Before she got to the door she turned to Lucas and said, "You're not invited to the staff meeting. We'll be

145

staffing you, too. And talking with Governor Henderson."

"I'll tell the governor to expect the call," Lucas said.

NINE

Cole called home as soon as he was clear of the city and was sure no cops were trailing behind. Jesse had gone to town and Marlys had put Caralee to bed early, but the kid was restless and heard Marlys talking to Cole on the phone and started calling out for her.

"Got a problem," Cole said. "A couple of Bowden's security people spotted me. I managed to outrun them, but — I don't know how — they recognized me. This one big-looking dude seemed to know who I was."

Marlys was shocked, nearly into silence. "But that, but that . . ."

"Don't know how, but that's the case," Cole said. He glanced down at the speedometer: he was doing almost ninety, purely from the stress; had to rein it in. He took his foot off the gas.

Marlys said, "That's crazy." Caralee had

been asleep on an air mattress in the parlor, and now she toddled into the kitchen, towing her blankie, a child's quilt that Marlys had made for her, and caught hold of Marlys's pant leg. Marlys patted her on the head and said into the phone: "You don't think we've been under surveillance?"

Cole shook his head; that wasn't right. "I've been thinking about it ever since it happened and I can only come up with one thing. You know how I thought that chick took my picture at the Henderson rally? I wonder if they passed that around?"

"They'd only know what you *look* like?" Marlys chewed on her lower lip for a moment, then said, "That's gotta be it. Nobody's come around here, so they don't know who you *are.* You had mud on your license plates?"

"Yeah, nobody read those . . . I'm gonna stop and clean them off when I get a chance, in case they're looking for a white pickup with muddy plates. I haven't seen a cop at all. Not even one. Anyway, I'll be home in an hour or so."

Marlys shook her head as Caralee started crying. Like being nibbled to death by ducks. "Something else has come up. It's bad."

"What?"

She told him about the call from Joseph Likely. "He said this guy Davenport used to be a cop up in Minnesota and he's supposedly working for Henderson. That's where the connection to you comes in. He saw the picture that woman took."

"But this guy was with Bowden tonight, not Henderson —"

"Joe said that he was talking to Bowden, too. Anyway, I looked him up on the Internet. I'm sending you a picture of him . . . *now.* If Joe talks to him again, we're in trouble."

"Why?"

"Because Joe's gonna sleep on this tonight and then tomorrow, sometime, he's going to talk to some other party people about us, and they're gonna panic, and then they're going to give us up," Marlys said.

"Goddamnit. You think . . ." His phone beeped, and he said, "Hang on, your message just came in." Cole thumbed up the message, tapped the photo, and squinted at it. The big guy at the hotel looked back at him.

"I'm looking at your picture and that's the guy from the hotel," Cole said. "Shit, it's him."

Marlys said, "I was afraid of that. There's all kinds of stuff about him online. He's really rough and he's smart — he made a lot of money from the Internet when it was first getting started and he's been involved in a whole bunch of shootings. One of the articles from the Minneapolis newspaper says he was the guy they sent after the worst criminals."

Cole said, "Well, we haven't really done anything yet. Nothing they could get us for. There's no connection to us from the National Guard break-in. We could back off, Bowden will be around all fall and winter . . . We could start all over again."

"No! No! The closer we get to the elections, the harder it'll be to get to her," Marlys said.

"Well, what are we gonna do?"

After a moment of silence, Marlys asked, "How heavy was her security? Still the same? Or has it gotten heavier?"

"From what I could tell, it was the same. She has six guys covering her and maybe a couple of women. I can't tell about the women, whether they're security or assistants, but I'm pretty sure one of them has a gun. Then, there were cops all over the place, from both the city and the county. There were twenty-two cops in uniform that I could count, but it could be more than that. It was confusing, with people coming and going. There were cops all around the building, at every door, and more inside. They made everybody who was going into the hotel go through the front door, and through a metal detector."

"Never gonna get her in a building," Marlys said.

"I told you that a hundred times," Cole said. He had seen various military and civilian big shots visiting in Iraq and the kind of security they'd had. He'd made the point with Marlys that not even the crazy jihadists had gotten close enough to make a run at them. Professional security was good.

"Gonna have to be the fair," Marlys said.

"We could change directions and I could do her with a rifle," Cole said. "If we could ever find a place to shoot from."

"Impossible to figure that out, at this late date," Marlys said. "And you'd get caught. We've got a good plan, let's stick to the plan."

"What about Joe Likely?" Cole asked.

"I told him I needed to talk to him, face-to-face. Tonight," she said.

"Yeah?"

"Yeah." Then Marlys asked, "Did you take your pistol with you?"

"Couple of them."

"Meet me in Mount Pleasant. You'll get

there first, call me and tell me where to hook up."

Another storm front had come through, but it was a thin one, a hundred miles long and ten wide. Marlys tried calling Jesse but got no answer. He'd said he'd be late, and might not make it home at all: he was going drinking with friends. With Caralee trailing behind, Marlys collected the baby bag from the parlor, and noticed that a misty rain was whispering off the windows.

She went out on the Internet to the National Weather Service in Des Moines and checked the radar. The storm would be short-lived and would probably miss Joe Likely's home completely.

She tried Jesse one last time, got no answer, and headed out to her truck, carrying her granddaughter and the baby bag. The girl was wearing footsie pajamas and Marlys left her in them. The night was chilly and dark and her headlights didn't seem to go anywhere, so she took it slow: this was no time to hit a deer. The windshield wipers seemed to sync with her heartbeat. Somebody was going to die tonight, and he was an old friend.

Cole rolled on through the night, thinking

about killing Joe Likely. He'd met Likely a few times, at the party meetings, but had quit going when it became obvious that the party was useless. Cole had never killed anyone, but the prospect didn't bother him. He would have killed some Iraqis, given the chance, but he'd never had the opportunity. The fact is, he'd never had much of a life, and he didn't know why. He simply knew that was a fact, and he saw people all around who did have interesting lives, who did seem to cruise through the world with women and money and friends, and he'd never had that.

He'd thought that might change when he joined the Guard; it hadn't. He was a truck driver, and truck drivers in the Guard had about the same status as truck drivers in civilian life: that is, not much. Infantrymen get dinged up, and the Army couldn't do enough for them: choppers would come in and fly them off to a hospital, the congressmen come through and shake their hands and give them medals and all. A truck driver gets hurt, and nobody gives a rat's ass; they even bitch at you about being lazy, and in the meantime, your brain feels like it's been turned to Jell-O.

And it wasn't going to get any better, not in this life, not with the way the system

153

worked against people like his mom and himself. They'd be out peddling corn and cutting golf-course grass for the rest of their lives; couldn't even afford to *play* golf on the grass he cut every day . . .

Things had to change, some way, somehow. Killing Likely might be necessary . . . though he was unsure of that. There was more to it than pulling a trigger.

Marlys and Caralee made it to Mount Pleasant, driving slow through the rain, in an hour and a half. Cole was waiting for her in the white pickup, parked outside a closed café. Marlys stopped behind him, left Caralee alone in the back, noted the clean license plates as she walked past Cole's truck to the passenger side and got in.

"Here's the thing," Cole said, when she'd shut the door. "Maybe we shouldn't do anything until we do *everything.* If Likely turns us in, we're just farmers and it's all bullshit and lies. If he doesn't, then we go ahead — hit Bowden without any warning. If we kill Likely now, after he's talked to this Davenport dude, the cops will be all over the place."

"If they were chasing you in the streets tonight, they've already been warned,"

Marlys said. "They'll already be all over the place."

"Yeah, but if we kill somebody, then they'll know for sure how serious we are," Cole said. "Right now, we might be a bunch of goof balls like Joe and his friends."

"I'm one of them," Marlys snapped.

"No, you're not, and you know it," Cole said. "We're serious, they're not. They're a bunch of bullshitters and that's all they ever were."

"Doesn't do us any good to kill Bowden and have Joe pick up the phone one minute later and tell Davenport who we are," Marlys said.

Cole thought about that for a moment, then said, "That's true . . . I wish we had a plan for this."

"We don't need a plan. Joe called me from a pay phone. I told him I wanted to come by and talk to him late tonight after I got Jesse back home and the baby to bed," Marlys said. "We go in, find out what Davenport knows, what he told him, do it, and get out. If you *can* do it."

"Oh, I can do it," Cole said. He fished around between his feet, brought out a plastic box, popped it, and took out a pistol. "Loaded with CCI Long Rifle Quiets. No louder than clapping your hands and plenty of penetration. I get behind him and bang! One in the head, no muss, no fuss."

"You sure? You never done it before," Marlys said.

"No, but I read all about it and I got no problem doing it," Cole said. He rolled his eyes up, and checked his heart and his gut. Yes. He could do it. Sniper. Could have been a sniper, instead of a truck driver.

"Then let's go," Marlys said.

They decided against taking Cole's truck because it had been seen by Davenport earlier in the evening. If anybody saw it around Likely's place, and then Likely was found dead, that would only confirm what they thought about Cole and the truck.

They took Marlys's dark blue SuperCrew Ford. Caralee had slept between Pella and Mount Pleasant, and now was stirring around as Marlys and Cole talked sporadically and nervously about how they'd do this and that.

"I brought some kitchen gloves so we won't have to worry about fingerprints, but I don't know about this DNA stuff. Didn't have time to research it," Marlys said.

"We won't touch anything, won't leave anything behind. I'll be ejecting some brass, but we'll pick it up — and anyway, all my guns are loaded with clean rounds. I clean them off with Windex before I load them, just in case."

"So . . . not touch anything."

"Might want to take his wallet so it'll look like a robbery," Cole suggested.

"That's good, but we gotta be sure to be using the kitchen gloves," Marlys said. They were making it up as they went along. She added, "He's a cheap old man and he hates the banks and he's always had some money — I bet if we looked around his house for a few minutes, we could find some cash."

"We can always use the cash," Cole said.

Three blocks from Likely's house, a familiar stench filled the truck cab and Marlys said, "Oh, boy, I think Caralee just pooped."

"I *know* she did," Cole said.

"We better find a place to turn off and clean her up," Marlys said. "We might not get another chance."

They backtracked and wound up all the way out on the edge of town, on the side of the road, Marlys working on the tailgate, out of the baby bag; and Cole walked up and down the road, arranging and rearranging the pistol under his shirt, practicing his move, pulling the gun without hanging it up.

As Marlys was finishing with Caralee, the

girl said, "Star," and pointed up, and sure enough, the clouds were moving off to the north, and the stars were lighting up. Marlys threw the disposable dirty diaper in the ditch, and they got back on the road, the windows open for the first few miles, and then Marlys said, "We might need another diaper."

"Already?" Cole asked.

"For me," Marlys said. "I'm about to pee my pants."

Likely's street was dark and quiet, but his house showed lights behind the drapes. They parked in his side yard and looked around and then got out, and Cole said, "What about Caralee?"

Marlys hesitated and then said, "I guess we better take her."

They bundled Caralee out of her seat and trooped up to the porch; they could smell rain and sidewalk worms as they knocked on the door, and a fresh baby-powder odor from the girl.

Likely let them in, said, "Hello . . . Cole? You're Cole, right? Where's Jesse? Isn't that Jesse's baby?"

"Jesse's off on a toot," Marlys said.

Inside the house, Marlys, with Caralee in

her arms, dropped onto a couch. She sighed and said, "I'm tired. Long day," while Cole prowled around, looking at the old prints and photographs on the wall around the fireplace.

" 'Cause we're old. When we first met up, you could go two days and a night and not think anything of it," Likely said.

"Thirty years ago," Marlys said. Then with honest anxiety, "What did this guy want, Joe? This Davenport. I mean, did you tell them you thought it was us?"

"Of course not," Likely said. "I put him off, but then I got to thinking — it better *not* be you. Sounded like you, though. They're looking for an older woman with curly white hair and rimless glasses and a young man with distinctive gray eyes who might be her son, and they've got a political line that sounds like the party's. I thought of you and your boys, first thing. A few other people might do that, too, if anybody asks."

"Did you tell them that we're not up to anything?" Marlys asked.

"No, because then I'd be admitting that I knew who you were," Likely said. "You're *not* up to anything, are you?"

"Of course not," Marlys said.

Cole stopped prowling for a moment,

looked at Likely. "Is there somebody else here? A dog? I thought I heard . . . There was a noise."

Likely shook his head. "Nope. Nobody else."

Cole said, "Huh," and then, waving a hand at the photographs, asked Likely, "Are these folks your ancestors?"

"Yup. All the way back to my great-great-grandfather. He came over from Aberdeen-shire in Scotland," Likely said, turning to look at the photos. When he turned back, Marlys nodded at Cole.

"Long time ago," Marlys said. "Did he come right straight to Iowa?"

Likely opened his mouth to reply, as Cole pulled the gun and in a single movement, shot Likely in the back of the head. The gunshot was as loud as a hard hand clap, nothing that could be heard outside the house. They all flinched, including Caralee and Likely, who said, "Wut?" and struggled to get to his feet. Cole shot him again, *Whap!* and Likely sat down again and said, "No! No!" Cole shot him a third time, *Whap!* and Likely rolled forward out of his chair and landed facedown on the carpet.

"That got him," Cole said.

"You sure?" Marlys asked. Caralee looked down at the body and whimpered.

"I can make sure," Cole said. He stepped over to Likely's body and *Whap!* shot him in the temple.

"Put on the gloves," Marlys said. She was holding Caralee over her shoulder and half-turned so the girl couldn't see the body. Cole took the kitchen gloves from his hip pocket and was pulling them on when they heard a distinct *clunk* from the kitchen area.

"There it is again," Cole said. "I knew it — there's somebody in there."

Cole had his gloves most of the way on and made a fist and punched open the door between the living room and the kitchen, where they found an elderly woman trying to work the bolt on the back door. She turned and looked at them in fear and said, "No, no, no."

"Who are you? What are you doing here?" Marlys asked.

The woman shrank away from Cole, her back against the door, and she said, "I'm a friend of Joe's. Don't hurt me, don't hurt me, for God's sake, I gotta take care of Pam."

"What are you doing here?" Marlys asked again.

"Joe asked me to listen in . . . He said he might want a witness," the woman said.

"A witness for what?" Marlys asked.

"He was afraid that you were planning to shoot Mike Bowden, he thought you might tell him that. He wanted a witness . . ."

"Oh, for heaven's sakes," Marlys said, and, "I'm so sorry."

She nodded at Cole and Cole snapped the gun up and shot the woman twice in the forehead, *Whap! Whap!* the shots spaced so closely together they sounded like one.

The woman said "Oh!" and slid down the door, then toppled over on her side.

"Make sure," Marlys said.

Cole shot her twice more in the head. Then he and Marlys turned to the living room, at the sound of movement. Cole led the way back to the door, where they found Likely crawling toward them, his head up, streams of blood running through his hair and down his face and neck, his face like a grotesque Halloween mask.

"Well, Jesus," Cole said, and he stepped over to Likely and shot him three more times in the top of the head, and then the gun locked open, out of ammo. Likely went flat on the floor. They stood around looking at the body, to see if he'd move again, but he was finished.

Marlys went back to the kitchen to check on the woman; she was dead as well.

"Didn't exactly go the way you said it

would," she said, giving Cole a look.

"They're dead now," Cole said, as he reloaded with a fresh magazine. He couldn't stop looking at Likely. He'd learned something valuable here: the .22s were quiet, but they might not get the job done.

Cole started picking up the brass from the pistol. Marlys put Caralee down in a corner of the living room, pushed a couple of wooden chairs over to corral her there, went back to Likely's body and pulled the wallet out of his back pocket with her gloved hands. Forty-two dollars. The old woman had an additional thirty dollars in her purse. Marlys went into the home office and took Likely's laptop computer, which he'd used for party business, and all the associated electronic equipment, including a printer.

"He keeps party stuff on this, and maybe membership lists," she told Cole. "We don't want them to know that we took the computer, so we need to trash the place."

Cole tore the office apart, found nothing more, then went through Likely's bedroom, tipping over the bed to look under the mattress. Nothing there. He emptied all the drawers from the bureau, found nothing of value but a gold pocket watch, which they took.

"Can't leave it because a crook would take it, but we can't keep it, because it's evidence. We'll get out in the country and toss it," Marlys said.

Caralee was trying to get past the legs of the blocking chairs, as Marlys watched Cole tear up the place, so she went and sat in one of the chairs, patted Caralee on the head, and said to Cole, "You know where men hide stuff? Where they keep their tools."

She was right. Cole went down into the basement and tossed Likely's workbench and found a steel box for a socket wrench set at the back of a drawer, where it shouldn't have been. He popped the lid and found a neat stack of twenties, fifties, and hundreds, twenty-two hundred dollars in all.

"Got it," he said, climbing the stairs. He showed the roll to Marlys, who'd moved into the kitchen with Caralee. She took the money and said, "Let's go."

The neighborhood was asleep when they pulled out. Two minutes later they were at Cole's truck, and as Cole got out of Marlys's vehicle, she said, "We did good tonight. Now we know we can do Bowden. We got the steel for it."

Cole nodded, and got in his truck, and they headed cross-county in their two-truck caravan. Marlys threw Likely's watch in a cattail swamp halfway back to Pella, and Cole called her to say, "We need to find a place to dump the computer equipment. If they find that on us, we're screwed."

"Bury it out back tomorrow. We have to keep an eye out for that Davenport fella," Marlys said. "You need to start cutting that pipe and grinding that cap."

"I can do that," Cole said. "Start tomorrow morning. Gotta keep Jesse out of the barn, though. Cutting the pipe's no problem, but grinding that cap's gonna take time, and it's gonna make some noise. He'll wonder about it."

"He's got a farmers' market in Oskaloosa tomorrow, if he's not too drunk to get up."

"Don't care how drunk he is — kick his ass out of bed, Mom," Cole said. "We need him out of the way — not much time now."

"We'll handle Jesse when we get home," Marlys said, and she rang off.

From the backseat, Caralee, hearing her father's name, said, "Daddy."

"That's right, baby," Marlys said over her shoulder. "Let's go talk to Daddy."

TEN

Lucas called Alice Green and told her about the chase and that Bowden would be calling the governor later. "They may ask about whether I'm a psycho," Lucas said. "Tell them, 'No.' "

"I'll have to think about it," Green said. "At the very least, I'll tell them that you're *our* psycho."

"Thanks for that," Lucas said.

He made it to Iowa City late, checked into the Sheraton room that the campaign had reserved for him, called room service and Weather, in that order, and talked to her until the food arrived.

"Off the top of my head," Weather said, "I'd say that your description — older woman, a son with distinctive gray eyes, with those particular kinds of weird extreme political views — would be enough to give them away, at least if you asked the right people. I wouldn't be surprised if lots of

166

people knew them, including everybody in those political groups. That Likely man may have been lying to you."

"I've thought about that, but I don't know what to do about it," Lucas said. "This whole chase, tonight, has everybody on edge, so maybe something'll get done. I'll talk to Bell Wood tomorrow, see if he can get his Iowa guys moving on it."

He told her about Wood and his promise to get a carry permit for Lucas. Weather approved of the gun; she had no illusions about Lucas's work.

When the food arrived, he said good-bye, ate the cheeseburger and fries, got his laptop out and tried browsing the political groups he knew about, looking for membership lists. That got him nowhere — all three groups had formed, and then faltered, before the Internet had gotten big. He found a few references and some position papers, but all were unsigned, except for a couple of anti-cop screeds by Dave Leonard. Leonard was out of it — he wouldn't be chasing after Bowden for a couple of weeks, at least not in person, anyway, not with a full set of cracked ribs.

Unable to sleep, Lucas put his shoes back on and went out for a walk in the Iowa City mall. The night was cool and felt damp, with a line of scattered thunderstorms having passed through.

He left the mall for a couple of streets, window-shopping, found himself in front of the Old Capitol, in which — up under the dome, maybe? Was that even possible? — a Minnesota football tackle and long-lost friend named Hymen Scholls had impregnated a young Iowa coed. They'd later gotten married and, the last Lucas heard, still were. Didn't know what to make of that.

In the morning he found a FedEx envelope on the floor by the door, opened it, and found his carry permit; he put it in his wallet. He was in the shower when his phone rang, and then rang again, and then rang a third time. When he got out, he picked up the phone and saw Bell Wood's name on all three calls. He called him back and Wood said, "Lucas?"

"Yeah, I got the permit. Thanks," Lucas said.

"Holy shit, man, you know the cops are looking for you?" Wood sounded excited.

"What?"

"You talked to that Joseph Likely guy yesterday?"

"Yeah, yesterday afternoon. What'd he tell the cops?" Lucas asked.

168

"He didn't tell them anything," Wood said. "Somebody went into his house last night and executed him and his girlfriend. Shot them in the head. The Mount Pleasant cops found them this morning after a tip, and a neighbor gave them your name. Said they never saw Likely after seeing you leave."

"Aw, Jesus. Give me a number, I'll call them and head down there," Lucas said.

"We've got two guys on the way, right now, along with the crime-scene unit. The Mount Pleasant cops made sure Likely and his friend were dead, then sealed the scene and called us. I'll call everybody and tell them you're on the way."

"Bell, you know what this is, right? These are the guys I'm looking for," Lucas said. "They're gonna try to hit Mrs. Bowden, and Likely lied to me when he said he didn't know who they were. He knew and he called them, maybe to tell them not to do it, and they decided he was a risk, and came over and killed him. You gotta look at his cell phone, see who he called."

"I'll do that from here . . ." Wood gave Lucas the names of the two investigators on the way to Mount Pleasant, and promised to call again if anything came up before Lucas got there. Lucas called Neil Mitford,

Henderson's weasel, and told him what had happened.

"Oh, my God. Elmer was right," Mitford said. "These people are gonna try to kill Bowden."

"Yes. It's out in the open now," Lucas said. "Listen, tell Elmer about this. I'll call Bowden's security people. I'm going back to Mount Pleasant."

"Don't get yourself busted," Mitford said.

"I'll try," Lucas said.

Dan Jubek, Bowden's head of security, was as astonished as Mitford. "What would you do, if you were me?" he asked.

"I'd get her out of town. I'm not sure that would be enough, but it might be, depending on how mobile these guys are," Lucas said.

"Probably not gonna happen," Jubek said.

"If she won't go, you could suggest that she jumble up her schedule, and then not post the new days and times on her website — so nobody would know but the locals, wherever she's going, and then, not until the last minute. I don't think these people are real sophisticated. If she does that, they might have a harder time setting something up."

"I'll tell her that," Jubek said. "Jesus, Lucas, find these assholes, huh?"

Lucas got a couple of bagels with cream cheese, in a bag, and a Diet Coke before he left Iowa City, and ate on the way to Mount Pleasant. When he got there, he found five cop cars and a van parked outside Likely's house — a city car, two sheriff's cars, two Division of Criminal Investigation cars, plus the van from the DCI's crime-scene unit. Neighbors were standing around on porches and lawns along the street, looking toward Likely's house, when Lucas pulled to the curb.

A uniformed cop was peering at him, so Lucas checked the phone numbers given him by Bell Wood, called the lead investigator, Randy Ford, and identified himself. "I'm parked down the street, but you've got a guy in the yard keeping people away."

"I'll be right out," Ford said. "C'mon over."

Not a good time to use the carry permit, Lucas thought. He got out of the truck and walked twenty yards down to the cop and said, before the cop could ask, "Randy Ford's coming out to see me."

The cop nodded and said, "Okay . . ." and looked back at the door, where a thin, white-haired man had stepped out on the

171

porch, still talking to somebody inside the house. "That's Randy."

"Tough scene inside?" Lucas asked.

The cop frowned. "You media?"

"No. I'm an . . . investigator . . . from Minnesota, looking into a threat against Michaela Bowden. I talked to Likely yesterday."

The cop ticked a finger at him: "Davenport, right? Like the city."

"That's me."

Ford was walking over, stuck out a hand and said, "Glad you could stop by." Ford was a short, thin man, wearing tan slacks and a blue short-sleeved dress shirt; he had the knobby, shiny-skinned look of a college wrestler in one of the lower weight classes.

"I got the feeling it was either that or run for the border," Lucas said, as they shook.

"We do need to talk to you about that," Ford said. "What time did you leave here last night?"

Lucas gave him a timeline, from the first moment he'd seen Likely through his trip to Burlington, the return to Mount Pleasant, the drive to Davenport, the chase in Davenport, and the night in Iowa City.

"What you're saying is, your only alibi for last night between ten and eleven is two presidential candidates and their campaign security staffs, a bunch of city cops in Davenport, and the hotel people in Iowa City. Plus you're a personal friend of Bell Wood and that fuckin' Flowers, and they'll vouch for you."

"That's about it," Lucas said.

"Good enough for me," Ford said. "C'mon, take a look at this. You've probably seen a lot more of them than I have."

Lucas had, but it was never a pleasure. The crime-scene crew was working the house and had marked a walking path through the rooms with masking tape. Likely, gray-faced and cold, was lying facedown at the end of a blood trail across his living room carpet; his mouth was open, as though he were trying to bite into the fabric.

"Looking at the holes in his scalp, we think he was shot with a .22 or possibly a .17, but a .17 is unlikely. We haven't been able to find any neighbors who heard any shots, but it's been hot and doors are closed and air conditioners are running, so they wouldn't, unless they were outside. We haven't finished processing, so the bodies are right where they fell. We'll need a medical examiner to tell us for sure, but it looks to me like Likely was shot at least six or seven times, and three different places in his head. Mrs. Baker, that's his friend, she's in the kitchen, she was shot three times in the head."

"You find any shells?"

"No. But that many shots . . . probably an automatic, unless it was a rifle, but that's unlikely. We think they probably picked up the shells, then tossed the house."

Lucas took a long, close look at Likely, then followed Ford into the kitchen, where the other investigator, Jerome Robertson, was sitting in a canvas folding chair, making notes on the scene. A woman was kneeling next to the body, her nose about an inch from Baker's shoulder.

Ford asked, "What?"

The woman looked up and said, "She fell on a cartridge casing. Found it one second ago — it's a .22, all right."

"Good," Ford said. "That's something."

"Not much," she said. "No print — whoever loaded it cleaned it up first."

"Any prints anywhere?" Lucas asked.

"Millions of them," the woman said. "Whoever killed Mr. Likely also took his wallet out of his hip pocket — we think — and took the money out of it and then dropped it back on the floor. I can see the outline of a finger, because the outline is made with a trace of powder. There're no papillary ridges inside the outline. I'm thinking they wore rubber gloves."

"They came prepared," Ford said.

"I think so," the woman said. "I looked around and didn't find any rubber gloves here, or boxes for them."

Ford introduced Lucas to Robertson, who said, "We don't have a single exit wound, so I'm thinking, low-power, solid-lead .22s. We'll get some intact slugs from inside their skulls. And we've got the shell, now. Katie can see the firing pin impression, so we'll get a decent tool mark."

"Gotta hope they didn't throw the gun in the river," Ford said.

Ford and Robertson gave Lucas a quick verbal overview of what they'd found — Likely and Patricia Baker were probably killed sometime between ten and eleven o'clock by persons driving a dark pickup of unknown make, but American. They'd gotten that information from neighbors.

One of the neighbors got off work at a pizza parlor at ten o'clock. He hadn't stopped anywhere, and so had gotten home around five or six minutes after ten. He'd seen the unfamiliar pickup, but hadn't paid any real attention to it. Another neighbor had hurried off to a convenience store for cigarettes and was sure that no pickup had been parked at Likely's. He'd been hurrying because the store closed at eleven and he'd barely made it in time.

"So they were here sometime before ten, but we don't know how long before, and they were gone before eleven," Robertson said. Robertson was sartorially distinct from his partner, wearing a blue-striped Façonnable long-sleeved dress shirt, dark blue slender jeans with the cuffs rolled up a half inch, and tan lace-up shoes; Lucas envied him the shoes. "We have a call on Likely's phone, to Baker, at nine o'clock, so he was alive then."

"I was told somebody got a tip about the killings," Lucas said.

"Not about the killings, exactly," Ford said. "Baker lived with a friend named Pamela Carney. They share a house a couple of blocks from here. Baker and Likely had a sexual relationship, but Baker never stayed the night. Miz Carney is old and doesn't get around so well, she depended on Baker for help getting in and out of the shower and so on. When Baker hadn't gotten back by this morning and didn't answer her cell phone, she called the Mount Pleasant cops and asked them to check over here. One of their cops came around and looked in the back door and saw Baker on the floor. That set it all off."

"Do you know if Bell checked Likely's cell phone for calls?" Lucas asked.

"Yeah, he did, and we have a list, but there was only one after you left, and that was the nine o'clock call to Baker," Ford said. "He apparently asked her to come over. Call only lasted for twenty-three seconds."

"Do you know if Baker or Miz . . . Carney? . . . were involved in this Progressive People's Party of Likely's?"

"Don't know yet," Robertson said. "We do have one really weird thing, though." He looked back to the crime-scene tech. "Katie, tell him about the chairs."

The woman was still squatting next to Baker's body. She looked up and said, "There were a couple of wooden chairs shoved into a corner of the living room. Like when you're trying to temporarily pen up a pet, or a child. A toddler. I took a close look and I could see small fingerprints down the legs, about where a toddler would take hold of them. I pulled the prints, but . . . I have no idea what it means."

"One of the neighbors the locals talked to said they'd never seen a toddler here," Robertson said. "I don't know what it means, either, but it's weird."

Ford: "It's like a cold-blooded assassin

couldn't get last-minute child care."

Lucas asked permission to walk through the scene and Ford and Robertson left him to do it. He spent five minutes looking at the living room, and at Likely's body, and the chairs in the corner, trying to imagine exactly what had happened there.

When he was satisfied, he went to look at the front and back doors, which were intact and unmarked. Returning to the living room, he got down on the floor and looked carefully at Likely's face and his hands. He spent a few more minutes looking at Baker's body, then followed the tape trail through the house, up into the bedrooms, down into the basement.

When he came back up the stairs, Ford asked, "What do you think?"

Lucas shrugged. "Same as you do, I guess. I think Likely knew the people who killed him and didn't expect them to kill him. They were friends and he let them in the house — the doors are intact. He'd spent yesterday canoeing on the Iowa River and loaded a canoe up on the roof of his car, and got it back off, all by himself. So he was a tough old bird, and strong — but his hands and face are clean. No fight or defensive wounds on his hands, no fight marks on his face as far as I can see it. It looks to me like he was sitting in his chair and somebody stepped up behind him and shot him in the head and didn't do a very good job with it, so they continued to shoot him until he went down, which is that big blotch of blood in front of his chair. That's where his head landed.

"Then, they went into the kitchen and shot Baker. She saw it coming, they shot her right in the forehead, then shot her some more to make sure she was dead. She didn't resist, she has no other wounds, either. Likely wasn't dead. He pulled himself together, probably dying but not quite gone, and crawled toward the kitchen door, where they saw him and finished him off. Whoever did the shooting had never done it before, and didn't really know what he was do-ing . . ."

"Brutal," Ford said. "Why didn't the killer run as soon as he shot him? I mean, assum-ing that he ransacked the place afterwards."

"It was definitely afterwards," Lucas said. "There are clean papers on top of blood spatter. They — I think it was more than one person — didn't run because they needed something in the house and didn't know where it was. He might have hidden it, hoping to keep it away from the police raid he thought was inevitable. He was paranoid — he thought he was being watched, and that the police would eventually come after him for political crimes."

"Why more than one person?" Ford asked.

"Because it looks to me like he didn't see the bullets coming and they are all in the back of his head, or the side toward the back. I think he was talking to somebody else when he was shot. The second person distracted him so the shooter could get close."

"Okay," Ford said.

"What were they looking for?" Robertson asked.

"I suspect it was a journal, or a list, or something, that identified the various members of the Progressive People's Party," Lucas said. "They didn't want to be found on that list."

"Probably not a paper list," Ford said.

"Why not?" Lucas asked.

"Because Likely had an Internet hookup, with Wi-Fi, behind the TV. We asked Miz Carney if he had a computer and she said yes, he had a laptop, kept it in the home office, and a printer, too. Nothing there — but when we actually looked at a lot of the paper in his files, it was printed on an inkjet printer. They took all that. All the computer gear. If he was keeping a list, that's where it probably was."

"Okay, so . . . shit, I don't know why they took the place apart, then," Lucas said. "Maybe they thought there was more."

"They didn't take the paper files," Robertson said.

"Maybe it was somebody looking for money and nothing else," Ford said. "Maybe they took the computer stuff so they could sell it."

"They may have torn the place up so we'd think they were looking for money, but these are the people gunning for Bowden," Lucas said. He looked around the kitchen, with the woman's body frozen in death. "This is a hell of a lot bigger than a couple of murders for pocket money."

Ford wasn't sure of that, though Robertson agreed with Lucas. Lucas and Robertson walked two blocks down the street and around the corner to talk with Pamela Carney, a white-haired, wrinkled-face old lady they found huddled in an easy chair next to a walker and, despite the heat, wrapped in a shawl. Her sister was with her.

She was not a member of the Progressive People's Party, nor was Baker, she said. "She and Joe were fuck-buddies," she said.

Her sister was shocked: "Pam!"

"Well, they were," Carney said. "They didn't socialize, or anything, but once a week, old Joe would pop a Viagra and call her up and she'd go over and they'd jump in bed and when they were done, she'd jump right back out. That's why I knew something was wrong when she didn't come home last night."

"We need to find out who's in this political party," Lucas said. "Any ideas?"

"I only know what Pat would tell me, and that wasn't much. She thought Joe was a little goofy when it came to politics, but a nice man otherwise," Carney said. "She did tell me about one old man who was sort of a joke with everybody. I don't know his name, but he lives in Iowa City. He's written a book that's three thousand pages long. That's what Joe told Pat. Joe said he's been to every publisher in Iowa City and is always sending his manuscript out to New York or Los Angeles, but nobody wants it because it's crazy. It's all about how the Jews are in league with the devil. As I understand, he goes back years with the party."

"That's the guy we need to talk to," Lucas told Robertson. "I'm heading back to Iowa City."

■ ■ ■ ■

But not alone.

When they told Ford about it, he said, "I'm all for you digging this guy out, but I want Jerry to go with you. He's got the badge. We'll finish up and get the bodies off to the medical examiner and I'll interview whatever friends of Likely I can find. I'll call up everybody in his cell phone directory."

"Ask everybody about the party," Lucas said.

"I will," Ford said. "Hell, if this is really all about Bowden, I could get a book out of it. 'I Saved Bowden's Butt,' the true story of how a humble Iowa police officer saved the president's life, and she made him the director of the FBI."

They all laughed, for what the joke was worth, which wasn't much, and then a woman's voice from the other room, the voice of the crime-scene tech, said, "I don't think laughter is appropriate."

"Suck on it," Robertson muttered under his breath. Then, calling brightly, "You're right, Katie. Sorry. We lost track of where we were."

They all looked down at Baker's body, and

Lucas said to Robertson, "You're following me up? Let's go."

"I got lights," Robertson said. "If you follow *me,* we can go at a hundred miles an hour. With a siren."

"Lead the way," Lucas said.

ELEVEN

As they were walking out to their vehicles, Lucas asked Robertson if he had access to a researcher at the Division of Criminal Investigation. Robertson said, "We've got the group assistant, she can do some research if we need it."

"It can be anybody, but it'd be nice if somebody could look up publishers in Iowa City, and call us, so we'd have a list when we get there."

"She could do that," Robertson said.

Iowa City.

Their first stop was at New Nexus Press, which occupied half of the second floor of a house on North Linn Street, on the edge of the downtown area. Lucas led the way up the stairs, to a landing and short hallway leading to two office doors. One belonged to an architect, the other to New Nexus. The New Nexus door was standing open, and a woman was working at a desk inside, tapping on a keyboard.

She looked up as they walked in, and Robertson showed her his ID and said, "We're working on a murder investigation. The murder happened down in Mount Pleasant, and the murdered man had a writer friend we're trying to find . . . but we don't know his name. Supposedly he has a very, very long political book, something like three thousand pages, that he keeps trying to get published up here."

The woman had thick plastic glasses and looked up at them, eyes large as eggs behind the lenses, and asked, "Jeez, who got murdered?"

"There were actually two people murdered," Robertson said. "They were involved in a progressive political group."

"You think the writer did it?" she asked.

"No, we're trying to find out who the other members of the party were, who the victim's friends were, and we're having trouble getting that done," Robertson said.

The woman leaned back in her chair and shouted, "Barney? Barney?"

A man yelled from a side room, "Yeah?"

"What's the name of that goofy guy with the big book about the evil Jews?"

The man shouted back, "Anson Palmer.

Is he here?"

"No. The police are here and they're asking about him."

A short wide man dressed in jeans and a kayaking T-shirt, with his red hair pulled back in a bun, came out of the side room, carrying a sheath of paper, looked at them and said, "Who'd he kill?"

"Not funny, Barney. There's been a murder," the woman said.

"Ah, jeez. I'm sorry. Anson did it?"

"Not that we know of," Robertson said. "We're contacting the victim's friends, to see if anybody might know anything."

"Any reason to think Palmer might have done it?" Lucas asked.

"No, not really," the red-haired man said. "I can't say he's harmless because he's a rabid anti-Semite, but I've got no reason to think he'd murder anyone. If anything, I'd say he's another ineffectual kook."

"But he's a local guy?"

"Yeah, he lives here in town," Barney said. "I see him hanging at the Prairie Lights bookstore in the evening. Try to avoid him, when I can. We should have an address or a phone number in our files, if that'll help."

"That would," Robertson said. And, "This might be the first time I had a list of people to talk to, and the very first person knew

187

the guy I was looking for."

"Would have been the same with whatever publisher you went to," the red-haired man said. "He's been to all of us. Repeatedly." He was thumbing through an old-style paper Rolodex, and then pulled a card. "Here we go. Anson Palmer. No address, but a phone number, if that helps."

It did. Robertson had an assistant in Des Moines track the number down, and get the billing address. Palmer lived in an older neighborhood of pastel ranch houses and mature trees, not far from the high school. And he was home.

"Murdered? Somebody murdered him?" Palmer was agog. A thin, soft man with a pitted nose and a bald, bumpy egg-shaped head dotted with dime-sized freckles, he was wearing jeans and a T-shirt that said, "NSA, Our Customer Service Pledge: You Talk, We Listen."

"Murdered both Mr. Likely and his lady friend," Lucas said. They were in Palmer's living room. "We have reason to believe it's related to members of the Progressive People's Party, which is why we need to talk to you."

"I . . . I . . . When were they murdered?" Palmer took three steps backward and sank into a well-used red crushed-velvet-covered easy chair.

"Last night, sometime before eleven o'clock," Robertson said.

"I was down at the bookstore until it closed, I'm sure people will remember," Palmer said. "I had a long debate with —"

"We don't actually suspect anyone in particular of killing Mr. Likely," Lucas interrupted. "We're trying to get together a list of people who might know some other people we're trying to reach."

Palmer was willing to cooperate.

The party, he said, had originally consisted of political radicals who had gathered around the university, but had eventually drifted away from the academic radicals to land-based activism.

"Since we're a farm state, a lot of the concerned people here . . . well, some of them, anyway . . . began to go in different directions during the farm crisis back in the eighties," he said. "Away from concentrating on civil rights and the peace movement. Quite a few party members came from farm families themselves. This is when Willie Nelson's Farm Aid thing started . . . the benefit concerts. Everything was going to hell out in the countryside."

He trailed away, thinking, then continued:

"A lot of the members were couples. Then we all got old and more of the men died than women, so now the party's more women than men, I guess. We still talk politics, but there hasn't been a march in years. We sometimes leaflet for sympathetic candidates."

"We're particularly interested in the women members," Lucas said. "A middle-aged woman, a bit heavyset, chubby, I guess, with curly white hair. She wears rimless glasses and may have an adult son. The son's in his late twenties or early thirties, we think, with distinctive gray eyes."

Palmer considered for a moment, then shook his head and said, "I couldn't tell you who that might be. Some of the women might know. Most of the members had children and we were all about the same age, give or take a few years, because we were at the university. The kids, you know, started coming along about then. Nineteen eighty-five was the heart of the farm troubles and that was thirty years ago, now. So that's how old the kids will be, give or take a few years."

"How many members did the party have?"

"Well, the core membership, maybe a couple of hundred back at the beginning," Palmer said. "Joe used to say eight thousand or some number like that, but that included everybody who came to events, or marched, or even showed up at concerts and so on. Most of those people were never official members. So, maybe two hundred, at the peak. Now . . . maybe thirty or forty who would really call themselves members."

"Would you have a membership list?" Robertson asked.

"No. I'm sure there is one, though, because we get e-mails about items of interest — political events, position papers, and so on. Grace Lawrence has been the secretary for years. She lives in Hills, south of town. She puts all that stuff on the Net — I'm pretty sure she'd have a current list."

Lucas said, "Mr. Palmer, we understand that you're working on a book whose central feature is Jewish involvement in politics —"

"Not just politics! Everything! They run everything!" His eyes were alight now. He looked back and forth between Lucas and Robertson and said, "Are you Jews?"

They both shook their heads and Lucas said, "We thought the woman might be closer to you than to Mr. Likely, because she seems to share some of your . . . concerns . . . about Jews."

"We all share my concerns! We all do! I mean, I've fully documented . . ." Palmer set off on a rant about Jewish conspiracy unlike anything Lucas had ever heard. They managed to slow him down after two minutes of it and get an address for Grace Lawrence, the party secretary.

Palmer was still talking when they walked out, to himself, his voice rising even as they left. On the sidewalk, Robertson looked back and said, "Jesus, that guy needs to be in the fuckin' loony bin. You know, we may be dealing with a whole collection of fruitcakes here. People who *could* pull a trigger."

"Let's go see Grace Lawrence," Lucas said.

Palmer had a brass pot on the floor next to the bedroom radiator, into which he threw unused coins at the end of every day. When Lucas and Robertson were gone, he fished a handful of quarters out of the pot, pulled on a sport coat, drove as fast as he safely could to the university, found a parking spot, hurried down the hill to the student union, went to a pay phone, and called Marlys Purdy.

When Marlys answered, he demanded, "Goddamnit, did you and your boys kill Joe Likely and his girlfriend?"

"What? What are you talking about?"

Marlys was so startled by the question that her reply sounded phony even to her own ears. "Are you calling me on your cell?"

"Goddamnit, you did," Palmer said. "And of course not, I'm calling you on a pay phone."

"Small favors . . ."

"Oh, boy. Listen, I don't want you coming around here trying to kill me," Palmer said. "If you come around here, I'll be shooting back. I've *got* a gun."

"Anson, I have no idea of what you're talking about," Marlys said, still with the phony note. She was in the kitchen and the kitchen window was open, and through the screen she could hear Cole pounding on something in the barn.

"Yes, you do. I can hear it in your voice, Marlys," Palmer said. "Now listen, I'm on your side here. Two cops came to interrogate me. They say they're not Jews, but I'm not so sure. They know you're gunning for Bowden and they are hot on your trail. They've got a good description of you and your gray-eyed boy and sooner or later, they'll be coming around. I sent them over to see Grace Lawrence. I'll call Grace and warn her and she'll cover for you. I'll tell her to give them a list, but to leave you off."

Five seconds of silence, then: "I'd appreciate it," Marlys said. Good as a confession.

"And don't mess with me," Palmer said.

"We won't. Anson, I can't tell you how much we . . . appreciate this. We'll be done in a couple of days, we have to keep them off our backs that long."

"I'll call Grace," Palmer said.

"You think we can trust her?" Marlys asked.

"Oh, yeah. We can trust her." Then, "I gotta tell you, Marlys, this has really got me pumped. I never thought this would happen — we finally move from bullshit to direct action. We've needed to do that for years. Good on you! Good on you! Grace will feel the same way. I know some people already suspect this, but I'm sure of it, and you're the first person I've told — Grace was behind the Lennett Valley Dairy bomb. She'll be with you, on direct action. I can tell you that, for sure."

"I had no idea that she was involved with that," Marlys said, thinking back to the Lennett Valley disaster. She asked, "How long you think we've got?"

"I've no idea. The people who talked to me claimed they were an Iowa state cop and a guy from Minnesota who used to be a cop, named Davenport, like the city. He seems to be the one who's driving the hunt, but it was my real impression that they're not state agents at all. They come from somewhere higher up in the federal government. God only knows what kind of operation they're *really* running. Anyway, I've got to go. I've got to call Grace. You've got to figure out your next move and do it right quick."

His heart still pounding with adrenaline, Palmer called Lawrence, who was monitoring lunch hour at Hills Elementary School as a volunteer. He gave her a quick summary and said, "Marlys is going to direct action. Best you don't know what, for the time being, but it's big. It's huge. We've been talking about something like this for years and now it's moving. She only needs a few days. If you could cut her name off the roll, that would help."

"How long before they get here? The police?" Lawrence asked.

"Could be anytime — they left here fifteen minutes ago. If they don't stop anywhere . . ."

"I'll have to move," she said.

"Go."

"I never did like Joe," she said. "You think he would have talked?"

"Yeah, he would have given them up, sooner or later," Palmer said. "He was a talker, not an actor, and he never did like the idea of direct action. Hey, listen, I'm calling you from a pay phone. If you need to call me about anything, find a pay phone so they can't connect cell phone calls. These guys claim to be state agents, but they're not. They're from one of the federal alphabets, or I'll eat my shorts."

"Smart about the phone," she said. "Gotta run."

Lawrence walked out of the lunchroom, past the office, told the secretary that she was feeling ill, and then scurried home, on foot, two blocks down the street. She lived in an old house, built in 1927, and not well maintained; but she was sixty-two and had suffered from three episodes of breast cancer. She'd only need the house, she often thought, for a few more years.

A bay window, looking out at an arbor thickly covered with Concord grapes, served as her home office. There'd once been a semicircular seat in the bay area, but she'd had a local carpenter replace it with a work surface, with four file cabinets fitted beneath the wooden surface. A laptop, a Canon printer, and a box with miscellaneous office supplies sat on top of it.

Anson said the cops had left fifteen minutes before his call, so that was now twenty-five minutes: she had little time. She turned on the laptop and as she waited for it to come up, dug a thumb drive from the office supply box. She plugged the drive into the side of the computer, went to look out the front windows, saw no unfamiliar cars, went back to the party mailing list, rolled through it to "Purdy," and deleted the entry for Marlys. She had another list on paper, but they'd have to turn the house over to find that one.

She was about to save the edited list, but then thought for a second, rolled farther down, and deleted the name Betsy Skira.

That done, she saved the edited list, brought it back up to make sure that the references to "Purdy" and "Skira" were truly gone, shut down the computer, pulled the thumb drive and dropped it back in the box.

She checked the front windows again and, still moving quickly, went to the back door, picked up a wicker basket, pushed through the door, and walked out to the side-yard garden, where she hurriedly cut free a cabbage, peeled off the outer leaves, and dropped the head in the basket. Moving to the cucumber patch, she pawed through the wide green leaves and found three good cucumbers, picked them, dropped them in the basket; pulled some carrots, which were getting old and woody but looked and smelled good. In fact, all of it looked and smelled good: she could live out her life growing fresh vegetables.

Then she waited, pulling weeds. Nobody showed. She walked to the back door, got a hat, put it on, went back to the weeds.

Marlys Purdy was going to a direct action. Lawrence wouldn't have seen that coming, though she'd known that Purdy bore an unflinching anger toward America's wealthy overlords, the banks, the military, the media, and all the rest. Something that they shared. She was intensely curious about what Purdy was going to do. Anson said it was huge . . .

She was still pulling weeds when two unfamiliar vehicles, a sedan and an SUV, pulled up to the house.

Lucas and Robertson had stopped at a sandwich shop before heading out to Hills. Following Lucas's navigation system, they'd come into Hills on a back road, over a narrow bridge, and were at Lawrence's house a minute later. Lucas knocked on the door, got no response, so Robertson leaned in and knocked harder, and they were turning away when a woman called, "Hello?" They turned and saw an older woman in a wide straw hat, watching them from a sprawling side-yard vegetable garden.

"Miz Lawrence?" Lucas called back.

"Yes? Who are you?"

Lawrence was once a very good-looking woman, Lucas thought: brown-eyed, still shapely into her sixties, with an engaging smile and a still-dark ponytail threaded with silver hair. She was shocked by the murders: "Joe was such a great man! Everybody liked him. I can't imagine any party members are involved."

"We don't think it's a party thing at all," Lucas said. "We think it's a person who's gone off the tracks. Probably a woman, with a gray-eyed son, distinctively gray-eyed, around thirty . . ."

Lawrence scratched the side of her nose and said, "You know, I don't know all the members by sight — a lot of them dropped out a long time ago — but that description doesn't ring a bell with me. Not at all."

"What we're looking for is a membership list, people we can contact who might know who this woman is," Lucas said. He went on to explain a bit: that there was a possibility of a conspiracy aimed at Michaela

Bowden.

Lawrence was shocked by that and couldn't conceal it. But she could turn her real shock in a different direction . . .

"The party . . ." she sputtered. "The party would never be involved . . . Michaela Bowden, my God . . ."

"About the membership list?" Lucas prompted.

"Of course. Normally, I'd want to see some kind of legal document, a subpoena or something, but since Joe was killed and you think Mike Bowden, my God . . . We, you know, the party, has some well-founded fears of the police, but since it was Joe . . . and besides, I know it wouldn't have been any of our members."

"We're interested in the killings, not the politics," Lucas assured her.

"I'm still going to give Anson a hard time about giving my name to the pigs," she said, now with a quick grin.

"Yeah, well, oink," said Robertson.

"Haven't heard that pig thing for a while," Lucas said, as they went into the house.

"It is kinda sixties," she said.

They watched as she plugged a thumb drive into her computer, brought up the membership list, and printed it out. "If we could get two copies . . ." Lucas said.

"Of course."

Lucas's phone buzzed at him and he found a message from Neil Mitford: "Crash meeting in Iowa City at two p.m. Gov and Mike face-to-face. Can you make it?"

He sent back: "Yes. Fifteen minutes away. See you at two."

Lawrence handed them the printouts and said, "Could I interest you guys in a cabbage and cucumber salad? Fresh as you can get."

"We just had sandwiches," Robertson said. "Some other time."

There were a hundred and eighty names on the list. Robertson knew every town in the state, as Lucas knew every town in Minnesota, and began by sorting them into two geographical groups.

One group was tightly arrayed around Iowa City. The other was more scattered, but generally east of Des Moines and west of Iowa City, and most were not too far north or south of I-80. "Which one do you want?" he asked Lucas.

"You pick."

"If I take the I-80 group, I could go home at night," Robertson said.

"Then take it," Lucas said. "I'll get my

room back at the Sheraton in Iowa City, and work out of there."

They exchanged phone numbers, and as they did, Lawrence came out on the porch, chewing on a carrot, and called, "You guys be careful."

Lucas held up a hand and Robertson said, "Nice old lady."

TWELVE

Lucas found Mitford in a Sheraton suite, talking on a phone and simultaneously tapping on a laptop. He spotted Lucas and pointed at a chair, and a moment later Sally Rodriguez, the Bowden PR woman, came in, twiddled her fingers at Mitford, went to a coffee service, poured herself a cup, and took a phone call.

She dropped into a chair next to Lucas, still talking on the phone — "I told him that there was a good reason to hire the Barkers, and that I didn't want to tell him the reason, but that it was a good one. You tell him I don't want to hear about this other group. I want the fuckin' Barkers. And I better get the fuckin' Barkers. If I don't get the fuckin' Barkers, he doesn't get paid. Okay? Okay. Good-bye."

As she was doing that, she'd dug into her tote for another phone and punched up a number with her thumb. When she said "good-bye" on the first phone, she went to the second and said, "We're good for KCRG at four o'clock, and I spoke to Broderick about the Barkers and he says he'll get them there. Okay? Okay."

She hung up and picked up the cup of coffee, looked at Lucas, who said, "You say 'fuck' a lot."

"Only when it's necessary. In a campaign, it's necessary a lot," Rodriguez said.

"Who are the Barkers?"

"A band. They wear T-shirts with dogs on them. Black Labs, I think, though I actually wouldn't know a black Lab if one bit me on the butt," she said.

"Why wouldn't anybody want to have the Barkers?" Lucas asked.

"If you're the event manager? Because the Barkers suck. You're also fronting your own band that would pick up a quick grand for an hour-long gig and get pictures with the next president," she said.

"Why would *you* want a band that sucks?"

"Because a state senator's brother plays in it," Rodriguez said. "Plays the accordion. Badly. Mostly waltzes. But the senator can deliver Monroe County."

"Ah."

Her phone beeped with a message and Rodriguez glanced at it: "Mike will be here in eight."

Mitford had gotten off the phone and said, "I'll have the gov here in seven."

"Good. We've only got about twenty to get this all sorted out," Rodriguez said. She tipped her head at Lucas: "How far can we trust him?"

"He can be tricky, but ultimately, he can keep his mouth shut. If he wants to," Mitford said.

"If he wants to?"

"Yeah. He gets to decide. Not us, because he no longer works for the state, and because he's ungodly rich. But you can talk to him," Mitford said.

Rodriguez checked Lucas out again, then said, "Okay. As long as you can talk to him. How'd he get rich?"

"In one word, software," Mitford said. "Every nine-one-one system in the country uses it. And when I said ungodly rich, I meant *ungodly.*"

"Thanks for not talking behind my back," Lucas said.

"That's okay," Rodriguez said. "Say, have I mentioned the 'Friends of Mike' opportunity for affluent supporters? I have a brochure in my bag."

"Forget that, I want to hear about the murders," Mitford said. He looked at his watch. "Make it short. The gov will be here —"

"In six, I know," Lucas said.

He told the murder story in three or four minutes. The two weasels took it in without comment, and when he was done, Mitford said, "I'll get the gov," and Rodriguez said, "I need to make a phone call," and they both left.

A minute later Norm Clay walked in with a man and woman that Lucas didn't know. Clay asked Lucas, "Did you see Rodriguez?"

"She went to make a call. You're two minutes early."

The man and woman looked at their watches and Clay opened his mouth to say something, when Henderson walked in the room, trailed by Mitford, Alice Green, and another woman that Lucas didn't know, but had seen, always with a clipboard.

"Norm," Henderson said to Clay, with a smile. They shook hands and Henderson wrapped his arm around Clay's shoulders and asked Lucas, "Did I ever tell you what this ol' boy did one minute after the Obama nomination in —"

"No, no, no, I had nothing to do with that," Clay protested. "I wasn't even there. I was in Amsterdam. Or Rotterdam, one of the two. Completely out of the country."

Rodriguez walked back into the room and muttered, "Five seconds," and they all turned to the door and four seconds later, Jubek, Bowden's security chief, came through the door with Bowden two steps behind. Everybody who was sitting got to their feet. Bowden had had her hair blown and was fluffing it with one hand. She was wearing a blue suit with a silk American flag scarf, and was carrying a cell phone in one hand.

As she stepped through the door, she spotted Henderson and said, "Elmer."

"Mike, good to see you," Henderson said. They air-kissed, so as not to disturb the makeup on either one of them. "Wish the circumstances were different."

"Yeah, well, they aren't. Let's get to it," Bowden said.

At that moment, four men in suits walked in; three Lucas didn't know, but Robertson trailed in behind them. State cops, he thought.

Rodriguez said, "Mrs. Bowden has already met these gentlemen, but Governor Henderson, this is Chuck Stevens, assistant chief of the Iowa campaign security team . . ."

"I've already met Chuck," Henderson

said, and the two men shook hands.

". . . and three of his associates," Rodriguez concluded.

Mitford said, "Lucas was just telling Sally and me about the murders. Why don't we start there, so we're all on the same page."

Bowden looked at Lucas and said, "Let's hear it," then immediately looked down at her phone and began texting.

Lucas recapped the day's events, beginning with the early-morning call from Bell Wood, of the Iowa Division of Criminal Investigation, his interviews with the Iowa cops in Mount Pleasant, his conclusions about the murders, and finally his contacts with Anson Palmer and Grace Lawrence.

"Bottom line is, I believe that we'll be able to track down the shooters. Whether we'll be able to hang the murders on them, I don't know — that would mostly depend on the Iowa criminal investigation — but I think we'll at least be able to identify them and make sure that they're . . . neutralized as threats," Lucas said.

Bowden looked up from her texting long enough to ask, "How long before you get them?"

"I don't know. Could be a couple of days, couple of weeks, depending on what the crime-scene crew in Mount Pleasant finds. If they don't find anything identifying, it'll be a while."

"You're saying you have no solid idea," Bowden said.

"No, I do have a solid idea — within a couple of weeks," Lucas said. "That'd be fairly quick on a murder investigation where you don't pick up the killer immediately. I *don't* have a solid idea of how that will work with your campaign schedule and what you think it's necessary to do in Iowa."

"I think it's necessary to go to the state fair," Bowden said. "We're already slotted in there."

Lucas: "As I see it, the problem breaks down into two areas. First, you're not willing to leave the state. If you did that, you could probably be made almost completely secure and we'll get at the threat and cancel it out. And second, your security is static, designed to protect you from people who try to get close. If these people are serious and intelligent, I don't think your static security will be enough, even if your guys are good, as I know they are. These people won't come after you by jumping out of a crowd with a pistol — it'll be a rifle and it'll be carefully set up."

Bowden looked at Stevens, the assistant

209

chief of the Iowa campaign security team. "Will I be safe at the fair?"

"Safe as we can make you. We plan to flood the walking route with highway patrolmen, both in uniform and plainclothes, plus our security team, and your security team. We've already pre-spotted all the possible shooting platforms and we'll be working the whole area from the time it gets light in the morning, right up to your walk. We'll have plainclothes and uniformed guys both on the street and in the crowd, walking right with you." He hesitated, then said, "I don't know Mr. Davenport, though one of the top people at the division knows him and says he's very good. Given his thoughts, I'd be a fool if I told you that you'd be perfectly safe. If you walk, we'll give you everything we've got, but I'd prefer that you were walking in New Hampshire or Georgia. You're a year away from the nomination — we'll get these guys, and you can walk the state fair next year."

"Thank you," Bowden said. "I assume if I'm shot, you'll catch the shooter."

"Catch, hell. We'll kill him," Stevens said. "One more thing. We believe Davenport is correct in his assessment about the need for investigators to push this. Robertson" — he jerked a thumb at Robertson — "tells me they've got a list of a hundred and eighty contacts to work through, who might identify these people. That'll take some time. We're assigning four more men to it, to help. Any more than that and they'd start stumbling over each other. So we'll have five guys looking for these people, plus Davenport. I have to say, though, our information on this is thin. We don't even know for sure that the threat exists. We've jumped to some extreme conclusions based on Governor Henderson's momentary contact with these people."

Henderson: "We do have two murders in Mount Pleasant. And a car chase in Davenport."

"Yes. We do," Stevens said. "Those would seem to be validating incidents."

"Seem to be," Bowden said. She turned to Henderson: "You're not trying to run me out of the state?"

"No, of course not," Henderson said.

"You could be lying," Bowden said. "You lie well."

"Don't we all?" Henderson asked, with a smile.

Bowden turned away from him and said, "Okay. I think we have enough information. I will have my staff call everybody with my decision on what I'm going to do. I will have them call by . . ."

She looked at Clay, who said, "Five o'clock?"

"Five o'clock," Bowden said. "You can all go home to dinner. Now, I'd like a few minutes to speak privately with Governor Henderson, and Neil — how are you, Neil? — and Mr. Davenport and Norm and Sally. We'll open the room back up for coffee and cookies in a moment."

Those not chosen shuffled out of the room, and when they were gone, and the door closed, Bowden said, "Norm and Sally, I want you to start setting up two appearance tracks, one for here in Iowa, one for New Hampshire. We'll make the final decision on whether to go to the state fair, four days from now. If we decide to call off the state fair walk, we'll need a solid explanation, involving a security threat. Something that people will take seriously, so they'll know I didn't just blow them off. In the meantime, I'll want to be set to go to New Hampshire, if we do call it off here. Everybody got that?"

Everybody nodded and Lucas asked, "Are you going to tell the Iowa cops?"

She shook her head: "Not yet. We'll call them up, tell them I've decided to go to the fair. I want them to keep the pressure up. I expect you all to keep your mouths shut about that. Nobody knows we're ready to call it off, until we do."

Everybody nodded again and Bowden said to Henderson, "Elmer, I greatly appreciate what you've done and we are now taking this with the utmost seriousness. Thank you." She looked at her cell phone. "Okay. We're good on time, but we've got to move along. Let's move along. Let's go."

When they were gone, Henderson said to those who were left, "She's never had any trouble making decisions."

"How often are they the right ones?" Lucas asked.

Henderson flashed him his campaign smile. "That's always a key question, isn't it?"

"When a gun's involved, it is," Lucas said.

THIRTEEN

After Bowden's departure, and when all the others had drifted back into the room, Lucas took Robertson aside and asked about the additional four investigators.

"It won't be in the next five minutes," Robertson said. "There'll be a meeting tomorrow in Des Moines and they'll decide who the four are, and then they'll work out what they're going to do . . . We might see one or two of them the day after tomorrow."

"That's how I had it figured," Lucas said. "Let's hit the lists now. Stay in touch. If you get a likely possibility, call me. I can be anywhere you are in less than two hours, and I don't want you walking up to a bunch of killers on your own."

"You got that, for sure," Robertson said. "If I were you, I'd stick to the ones right here in Iowa City. There are a bunch of them. If we don't get anything from those, we'll be able to get at the scattered ones quicker, when we have help. I've got a cluster out along I-80 and I'll work on those."

"Good," Lucas said. "Every time you get to a place, message me, and every time you leave. All I need is the name and 'Arriving,' and then 'Leaving.' I'll do the same thing. That way, when you're shot to death and your body is dumped in the river, I'll know where it happened."

"You are the bluebird of fuckin' happiness, aren't you?"

Lucas checked out with everyone: it was barely two-thirty, and he had eight names in Iowa City. He plugged an address into his truck's nav system and started knocking them down. By five-thirty he'd been at all eight; but since it was a workday, he'd only gotten five responses, and one of those was to tell him that the person he was looking for had moved — five years earlier.

Three of the other four followed a pattern.

A woman named June Ellis answered the door at the second house he visited — he had no response at the first one. When she asked if he was a police officer, he said, "No," and she said she wouldn't violate anybody's privacy by speaking to him.

"If you send a police officer, I may or may not speak to him, but I'd want an attorney present."

"All I'm trying to do —"

"I know what you're trying to do, and frankly, I don't want to be part of it, in any way," she said. "What if I gave you a name and you took some police officers and went there and killed somebody?"

"We don't —"

"Yes, you do," she said through the crack in the slowly closing door. "Don't you even read the newspapers? The police kill innocent people all the time. I want no part of that."

Click.

Lucas walked away, because he had no choice. He had learned one thing: she wasn't the woman Henderson had seen; she was as tall and thin as a stork.

At the third house, another woman answered the door, but he wasn't looking for a woman, he was looking for a man named Lance R. Mitchell. The woman who answered said she was Mitchell's partner, which Lucas took to mean that they weren't married. She said, "Oh, for cripes sakes. Lance isn't a member of the PPPI. Those people are crazy."

"Can you tell me when he'll be home?" Lucas asked.

"His last seminar ends at five, he'll be home at twenty after," she said. "If you come back, you'll be wasting your time."

"He's a student?"

"No, he's a professor. Well, an adjunct professor."

At the fourth house, he was told that Toby Hopkins had moved.

At the fifth, Barry Wright told him that he really didn't know many of the party members by both first and last name, and he hadn't been a member long enough to know who had kids and who didn't. "I have to tell you, I'm really not happy with the idea of cooperating with an intelligence-gathering op."

"We're not an intelligence-gathering operation, we're looking for a woman who might present a real danger to Mrs. Bowden," Lucas said.

"Well, whatever you get from me will go into a file, won't it? That file will be shared all over the government intelligence agencies. Next thing I know, I'm on the no-fly list."

Lucas was getting pissed: "You overestimate your importance. I'm a guy from Minnesota, trying to find a woman who belongs to the PPPI."

Wright was chewing on a stalk of celery and he didn't stop chewing while talking. "Well, whether or not you're telling the truth, that's what you'd say. I have to tell you, you've got the odor of federal intelligence about you."

"I was a cop in Minnesota, but I'm not even that anymore," Lucas said.

"A cop from Minnesota? In that suit? You need a better act, man."

Wright shut the door.

Nobody answered at the sixth house.

At the seventh house, Cheryl Lane never gave him a chance to speak. She answered the door and said, "A friend of mine said you'd come snooping around. I don't believe anything about your story and so as soon as I saw your Mercedes stop outside, I called nine-one-one and reported you. The police will have a car here in a minute."

"Reported me for what?" Lucas asked.

"Prowling. What right do you have to come to my door and demand information?"

"Miz Lane, I haven't even had a chance

to open my mouth . . ."

At that moment, a police car turned the corner a block away, and she said, looking over his shoulder, "Here they come. You're in trouble now, boy."

Lucas looked, then stepped back and called Bell Wood on his cell phone. Wood picked up and Lucas gave him a ten-second summary of the problem, and Wood laughed and said, "Don't run. You'll only look even more guilty. They might shoot you in the back."

"Can you help me out?" Lucas asked.

"Help's on the way, babe. I got the Iowa City chief on speed dial."

The cop car pulled up behind Lucas's truck and two cops got out and headed across the lawn to Lane's doorstep. She stepped out on the stoop with her arms crossed.

The younger of the two cops, who had a Ranger-style haircut, almost shaved on the side, a half-inch long on top, looked at Lucas and said, "Come down from there." He had his hand on his pistol and had flipped off the retainer strap.

Lucas stepped down and said, "You'll be getting a call from the Division of Criminal Investigation in the next couple of minutes."

"Yeah, right. Assume the position. On the

porch railing," the younger cop said.

"Ah, Jesus," Lucas said.

He turned and put his hands on the railing, and from above them, Lane said, "I believe his story is all a ruse. He's looking for women home alone. When he saw you coming, he called one of his accessories."

The younger of the two cops was giving Lucas a thorough rub, and then the older cop went to his phone, and a few seconds later said, "Knock it off, Rob."

"What?" The younger cop had a hand in Lucas's crotch and didn't stop.

"I said, KNOCK IT OFF."

"What're you talking about?" the younger cop asked, turning to his partner.

"It's the chief. One of the top people in the Division of Criminal Investigation called and said not to mess with this guy."

"You sure it's him they're talking about?"

The older cop held the phone out: "Here. It's the chief. Tell *him* you think he's full of shit."

"No, that's okay," the younger cop said.

"No, you talk to him," the older cop said. He spoke into the phone again. "Hey, Chief, Bud thinks you're full of shit about this, so I'm going to let you talk to him. Yeah. I'm giving him the phone now."

The older cop gave Bud the phone, and

that got straightened out and Lane disappeared inside the house and the older cop asked Lucas, "You really think somebody's going to try to shoot Bowden?"

"I'm not sure what to think," Lucas said. "But that's what I'm afraid of."

"Jesus. Well, good luck, man. Sorry about all of this," he said.

Lucas nodded at him and said to the younger cop, "If you think that haircut makes you look like a Ranger, it doesn't. It makes you look like a fuckin' whorehouse doorknob."

"Yeah, well, fuck you, too," the younger cop said.

The older cop said, "Whorehouse doorknob? That's good. I'll have to remember that."

There was no response at the eighth house, so Lucas circled back to the third house, Lance Mitchell's, where Mitchell was unloading a sack of groceries in the driveway. His partner came out to listen in, as Lucas explained what he was doing.

"Wait a minute — you're telling me that Joe Likely was murdered?" Mitchell asked.

"Yes, last night, along with his girlfriend," Lucas said.

"Aw, shit." Mitchell put the sack of groceries down on the driveway. "Aw, goddamnit." He looked at his partner and said, "There goes the book."

Lucas: "What book?"

Mitchell said, "Look, uh, Luke, I'd actually give you whatever I know, but I don't know much about the general membership. I know about five people in the PPPI — I'm doing a book on radical Midwestern farm organizations and that's the only reason I'm on the membership list. To get access. I only talk to the leadership and the real activists. I don't know about children or anything. I'd help if I could, I'm a Democrat and a Bowden supporter."

"You don't have any membership lists or anything?"

"No, but I could print out my manuscript for you, what there is of it," he said. "Probably seventy pages. There are some names in there. If you've been pushing this, you'll already know most of them."

"If you could do that, I'd appreciate it," Lucas said.

"Come on in."

As they were going in, Mitchell's partner said to him, "You know, this isn't the end of the book. You lose Likely as a source, but you gain a *murder*. A *double murder*. You were worried that the book was a little . . .

dull. This could fix that. You could open with it. Or bookend it — open *and* close."

Mitchell slapped his forehead. "You're right! I hadn't thought of that. Open *and* close!"

"If it bleeds, it leads," she said.

Yeah, that's really great, Lucas thought, as he followed them inside.

That evening, before going back to the no-response houses, Lucas skimmed Mitchell's manuscript. He noted three names that weren't on the PPPI membership list he'd gotten from Grace Lawrence, but that had a relationship with the party.

The most interesting part of the manuscript was the interview with Lawrence, who, when asked about the use of violence by radical members of the various farm movements, had asked, in return, "Do you think violence would be illegitimate if used, say, against Adolf Hitler? We were engaged in warfare against the ruling plutocracy, and I'm sad to say that, all in all, we lost."

From Mitchell's manuscript:

Ms. Lawrence was involved in the protests around the Lennett Valley Dairy controversy. She had been injured in a hiking accident a few days before the dairy was

223

bombed, killing three people, and was not there when the bomb was detonated.

"I'm sorry I wasn't there, maybe I could have helped in some way. I was horrified by what happened. Our protests had been largely peaceful, except when the police would intervene with their fascist military tactics, beating innocent, non-resisting protesters. Although I had nothing to do with the bomb — never would have had anything to do with a bomb — I understand the motives of the people who built it. I have to say, even after all these years, that the real tragedy was not that people died, but that they were the wrong people."

Ms. Lawrence said that from the present perspective, the bombing was both the peak of the farm protest movement and the beginning of the end. "That's the other tragedy. Farm families are peace-loving people. When that bomb went off, they began to withdraw from the protest movement. The bomb was an isolated incident, of no real importance when compared to the overall disaster of the economic collapse. It was apparently intended to galvanize the movement, but it had exactly the opposite effect: it killed it."

Lucas felt a tingle when he read the quote,

because it suggested that some people were legitimate targets for terrorism, which was not an ordinary way of thinking; and Lawrence in some way thought the deaths of three people were "of no real importance." He closed his eyes and remembered the woman's face, and her garden, and a feeling of hippie coquettishness, and couldn't put that together with her comments. Had she fooled them, and had it been deliberate?

He went to his laptop and entered "Lennett Valley Dairy bomb" and found nothing but short references to stories in the *Des Moines Register* and other Iowa newspapers, but there were no links — he couldn't get at the stories themselves.

He sent an e-mail to Bell Wood, asking if he could call the *Register* and get the story e-mailed back to him, if it were available electronically.

Grace Lawrence.

Huh. Did she have children? Sons?

He went to Google Images, searching for Grace Lawrence, and found hundreds of Grace Lawrences. He scanned the images, and on the second page, toward the bottom, found a picture of his Grace Lawrence, a few years younger, with two other women, standing in a school gymnasium, getting citizenship awards.

He called Neil Mitford, who answered on the second ring: "Find them?"

"Not yet. I'm going to send you a photo, by e-mail. Right now. I want you to stick it in front of the governor's nose. Ask him if this is the woman who spoke to him."

"Send it."

Lucas sent it; four or five minutes later, he got an answer: "No. That's definitely not her. Not even close."

He had two more houses to check on his Iowa City list. The first was still unoccupied, no lights, no sign of life, several bills and an advertising circular in the mailbox. Maybe on vacation. Or could be out stalking Bowden — no way to tell.

His last stop was with a Bert Hughes, who told Lucas that he hadn't been to a meeting in a few years and that he'd softened his earlier radicalism. "My folks were farmers and they had a terrible time back in the eighties. They didn't lose the farm, but they could have, and that would have killed them. They're all right now," he said. "I've decided that in a country this big, you're never going to get one big political lurch that will solve everything. The only way to move it is by working with the established organizations, so I'm a regular Democrat now."

"If you knew who this woman was, and her son, you'd give it to me?"

"Yeah. Though I might feel a little bad about it," Hughes said. "But I'll be working for Bowden, and I sure don't want anything to happen to her."

"What if Henderson gets the nomination?" Lucas asked.

"I'd love that! He's better than Bowden on the issues, but I don't see him getting the nomination. To get back to this woman, though, have you talked with Anson Palmer?"

"Yes. This morning," Lucas said.

"And he didn't know her?" Hughes asked.

"No. He says he doesn't."

"Then she's not a member of the PPPI. Anson was there at the creation and he's been to every meeting and every action. He's an old backslapper and gossip — he knows everybody. It's just that he's cracked on the whole Jewish thing."

At the hotel, Lucas called Robertson, who was nearly back home to Des Moines after hitting PPPI members who lived along I-80. He'd gotten nothing from the seven people he'd contacted. "I'm beginning to wonder if we're barking up the wrong tree," he said. "Most of these people say they haven't been active in years. One of them who went to a meeting last year says there were only ten people there. Somebody brought in a couple of pies, and there was enough for everyone."

"Yeah, but Likely got murdered," Lucas said.

"If it turns out that it's unrelated — Ford thinks it is — then the PPPI is a wild-goose chase. Maybe we should be looking at other geese."

"I can't believe it's unrelated — but I worry about the possibility," Lucas said. "Goddamnit, we pissed away a whole day."

That night in the motel, after talking with Weather, he lay on the bed, watching a ball game, and thought about the day. Despite the frustration, he was enjoying the hunt, he realized. Operating without a badge was annoying, though, and even more annoying was operating without bureaucratic backup: there was no clerk or assistant to call, to demand that research be done. He was living off crumbs from the Iowa agencies, and if he got annoying, they might just tell him to fuck off.

They'd live to regret it, though, he thought. The more he worked around the

PPPI, the more he got the feeling that he was onto something. People were lying to him, misdirecting him. He couldn't exactly put a finger on why he thought that, but he'd learned the hard way not to ignore even unsupported intuition.

Maybe he'd circle back to Anson Palmer in the morning, he thought. Put some pressure on him. See if he squeaked.

He drank a caffeine-free Diet Coke and went to bed.

FOURTEEN

At eight o'clock the next morning, about an hour before Lucas planned to get up, Bell Wood called from Des Moines.

"Why are you dredging up the Lennett Valley Dairy bomb?" he asked.

Lucas explained about the manuscript fragment he'd read the night before, and the odd vibration he'd gotten from Grace Lawrence's comment.

"How old is Lawrence?"

"I don't know," Lucas said. "I'd guess early sixties. Why?"

"I really don't have to send you that article on Lennett Valley — I can tell you what happened myself. In detail."

He did. The Lennett Valley Dairy had been foreclosed in 1987 after a long struggle to make mortgage payments.

"A particularly brutal case, for a lot of people. Not only were three people killed, a whole bunch of people, all from that area, were ruined financially," Wood said. "The dairy was set up as a small corporation with all the stock locally owned. The corporation had borrowed money to get the dairy going, during the good days, but then the recession came and prices went to hell. They got behind in payments to the Lennett Valley bank, so the bank restructured the loan, basically lowering the payments but stretching them out longer than was normally allowed. Part of the deal was that the bank would get to audit the dairy's progress, and if it looked like the dairy was faltering, they could call the loan at any time. Well, the dairy looked like it was digging itself out of that hole, when the *bank* failed."

"The bank."

Wood explained that when a bank fails, its assets are usually taken over by another bank, as directed by the Federal Deposit Insurance Corporation. The failed bank's stockholders are wiped out — and the new bank has no responsibility for the old bank's debts.

"The new bank came out of Council Bluffs, and it called the loan on the dairy. The dairy didn't have the money to pay the loan, so the bank foreclosed, as they had the legal right to. Wiped out the dairy's stockholders, too, some of the same people who were wiped out as the bank's share-holders."

The dairy operators made an argument that the dairy was only a year or so from becoming very profitable, but the new bank didn't want to hear it, Wood said. "The dairy wasn't very old, and had a lot of equipment and young stock, cows, and any money the bank got was pure profit. Anyway, they foreclosed and scheduled a land and equipment sale. A whole bunch of people showed up for the sale, including quite a few protesters, because the whole thing was so unfair. Partway through the auction, a bomb exploded in the barn. Three people were killed, all from the same family, a father and his two sons. We never identified the bombers. The whole thing plagues us to this day."

"And that made you wonder about Grace Lawrence?" Lucas asked.

"Yeah. There's a motel in Amazing Grace, the town, not the song, which isn't far from Lennett Valley, maybe fifteen miles. Two unknown couples checked in there, two rooms, one couple in each room, paid cash. The motel owner said they looked scruffy — the men both had beards and the women had long hippie hair, no makeup. They weren't local and they weren't apparently in

Amazing Grace for anything in particular. The night before the auction, they were out late — the owner lived in the motel and said they came back at four o'clock in the morning. There's nothing open at four o'clock in the morning in Amazing Grace, or anywhere close. They left the next morning before eight o'clock and were never seen again. Never could track any of the names they checked in with."

"You looked for them?"

"Not me personally, but you bet the DCI did," Wood said. "That's where it gets interesting. When we got the tip — by we, I mean the investigators on the case, I was still in high school — we sent in our fingerprint guy. Guess what, number one? They'd wiped the rooms. Either that or they were housekeeping freaks."

"Interesting."

"Yeah. But guess what, number two? We found traces of a waxy substance on the carpet in one of the rooms. Not much, but enough to match it to a kind of leak-proofing used on dynamite. Unsealed dynamite tends to weep nitroglycerin, so the manufacturer puts the coating on to help contain it."

"That put dynamite in the room," Lucas said.

"And guess what, number three? The man and the woman in that room had sex sometime during their stay. We found traces of semen and a couple dots of menstrual fluid on the sheets."

"Really," Lucas said. "This being Iowa, where everybody is thrifty and sanitary, you naturally sent those sheets right out to the local laundry so they could be dry-cleaned and reused."

"*Au contraire, mon cher,*" Wood said. "We actually sealed them up in a plastic evidence bag, then threw the bag in the back of the evidence room. I drove down here without shaving to see if we still have it. We do. Never been processed for DNA, but that doesn't mean that we can't do that right now."

"You'll have to get some DNA from Lawrence," Lucas said.

"Do you have any reason to go back there? I mean, get invited in?"

"I could do that," Lucas said. "She's only ten miles from here."

"Then ask if you can take a leak before you go," Wood said. "You'll find some hair in the bathroom . . . Bring it in, we'll run it. If it matches, we'll find some reason to do a formal search."

"If I were in the United States of America,

a federal court would say what I'm about to do is an illegal search and everything that comes out of it would be inadmissible," Lucas said. "You guys must have some interesting laws down here in Iowegia."

"Wrong. Wrong even for the federal courts, even in Minnesota. Lucas, you forget, *you're not a cop anymore.* You're not even working for us, you're working for Henderson. You are invited into her house and take a few strands of hair, that's not the government violating her rights. You're a private citizen. You can get away with all kinds of shit that we can't."

"Huh. You could be right."

"Really. Get the hair," Wood said.

"Okay, but I've got other things to do," Lucas said. "You guys are supposed to put some more people on the Bowden thing. If you could hook one up with me, I could pass the hair on to him."

"We'll do that," Wood said. "Lucas, if you solve the Lennett Valley case . . . I mean, this is a pretty goddamn big deal in Iowa."

"Big as it would be if Bowden is shot?" Lucas asked.

"Well . . . no, probably not. But right up there."

"Then I'll stick with Bowden, and let you worry about the bombing. At least for the time being."

"After you get me the hair," Wood said.

"Yeah. After I get the hair," Lucas said.

Lucas had twelve more people to interview, all of them now outside Iowa City — a few to the east, but more to the south and west, and south of the group that Robertson was looking at. None were in Hills, other than Grace Lawrence, but he decided to start with her. He had some legitimate questions for her and he could collect a hair sample at the same time.

He called ahead and Lawrence told him that she was due at the elementary school at eleven o'clock for cafeteria and recess supervision, so he'd have to come out before then.

"I'll be there by ten."

"I'll be out in the garden."

"See you then," Lucas said.

Lucas ate breakfast in a hurry, then drove over to Anson Palmer's house. He parked in the street, walked up the driveway, and through a window saw Palmer poking at his computer keyboard. Palmer saw Lucas, too, and met him at the door.

"I'm not going to invite you in," he said.

"Wanted to tell you that I've spoken to a

bunch of people from the PPPI, and they've told me that you know everybody — so you were lying to me the other day," Lucas said. "That makes you part of the conspiracy, Anson. A guy your age, you'll have trouble in a federal prison."

"I wasn't lying to you! I never said a thing that wasn't true!" Palmer shouted, spittle flying at the screen door. "You're accusing me because of my book, aren't you? Who are you really working for?"

Lucas shuffled backward, away from the spit, and said, "All I want from you are a few names of women who might resemble the person I'm looking for."

"I don't know that person! I don't know her!" Palmer shouted. "You know what I do know? I looked up English surnames for Jews, and you know what I found on the lists? Davenport! Davenport! Who are you working for, Davenport?"

Lucas couldn't think of what to say, so what he said was, "Ah, fuck it. Go to prison."

On the way out to Lawrence's, he thought about Palmer's wild reaction. Was there a little fear there? Hard to tell, with all the other possibilities — anger, bigotry, psychosis.

He got to Lawrence's place ten minutes early. She was already out in her garden, wearing a straw sun bonnet and a faded, long-sleeved peasant's blouse against the sun. "Come on inside," she said, getting off her knees. "I've got a pitcher of raspberry Kool-Aid."

"Gotta be kiddin' me," Lucas said. "I haven't had Kool-Aid since grade school."

They went inside and she got the pitcher of icy Kool-Aid out of the refrigerator. As she poured a glassful and pushed it across the kitchen table to Lucas, she asked, "So . . . what else can I tell you?"

"I know Mrs. Bowden's politics aren't the same as yours, but I'm really desperate to find these people who might be trying to harm her. The people who probably killed Joe Likely and his girlfriend . . ." He took a sip and the Kool-Aid was improbably good on his tongue.

"You said all that in the last visit," Lawrence said, pulling out a kitchen chair and sitting down with her own glass.

"Yeah, but what I'm going to ask you . . . this is important stuff, Grace. I interviewed a bunch of people yesterday, all party members from the list. Some of them simply refused to talk, even after I told them what was going on. They felt no responsibility for . . . for . . . helping me out. For stopping what could be a tragedy."

"Yeah, yeah, yeah, so you're about to ask me to betray somebody, right?" Her eyes were cool and sharp behind the glass.

"See, there *you* go," Lucas said. He took another long sip of the Kool-Aid, peered into the glass and said, "You know, this is the best Kool-Aid I've ever had. What'd you do to it?"

"Used two packages. It's a big secret, don't tell anyone."

"Huh. Okay. Now. One thing I *did* find out was that Anson Palmer knows everybody, knows everything that's ever happened with the party. He *must* know these people, if they're in the party. He says he doesn't. I'm asking you — would he lie to me, even if Mrs. Bowden's life was on the line? I know about the anti-Semitic stuff he's written, but . . . how nuts is he? Could he be part of a conspiracy? If I go back to him and really squeeze him, will he tell me the truth? Or is he telling me the truth already?"

She shrugged. "I don't know what he'd do if you put enough pressure on him. He can be a stubborn old goat. Whoever told you that Anson knows everybody in the party, that's pretty close to the truth. I'm not sure he'd know about everybody's kids, though."

Lucas nodded and said, "What about you? You're the secretary, you must know about everybody . . ."

"Mostly on paper," she said. She leaned across the table and added, "Here's the thing, Lucas, what I believe — if there really is an assassination conspiracy out there, and if it involves a party member, it probably isn't one of the core members. That's why you can't find them. It might be somebody who knew Joe Likely from years ago, and went to him to see if they could get help. Joe wouldn't kill anybody. He wouldn't co-operate in killing anyone. He just wouldn't."

Lucas said, "You think it might be some-body who knew Joe as a radical, thought he might help them, and when he wouldn't . . ."

"They killed him."

After a moment of thought, Lucas said, "I could almost buy that, except that he was murdered the night I visited him."

"So what?"

"The coincidence . . ."

"It wasn't a coincidence, dummy. Look, I

put that a little wrong. They didn't come for his help and kill him right then, on the spot. They came for his help some other time, and he turned them away. After you visited, he called them. Either to warn them or to try to talk them out of doing anything — to tell them that the cops were hot on their trail. *Then* they came over and killed him. It's exactly the way you told me you thought it happened, but instead of being somebody in the core party, it was somebody out on the edge."

"Huh. That's a possibility, I guess."

"You want more Kool-Aid?" she asked.

"One more would be good," he said.

They sat and chatted for a couple more minutes, as Lucas finished the second glass, and then he said, "You know, Grace, I do like you. I hope that you're not involved in this thing, in any little way. Because if it's real, it doesn't matter whether they shoot Mrs. Bowden or not, they're all going to prison. Or worse, if they kill Mrs. Bowden or anyone else. The feds still have the needle, and they use it."

"I would tell you if I knew anything," Lawrence insisted. "Look, Lucas. I don't particularly care for Mike Bowden's politics, it's the same old bullshit we've been fed for fifty years now. But Republican politics are even worse, from my point of view, and Bowden does have one strong thing going for her — she's a woman. I want a woman to be elected president. I really do. It almost makes up for the bullshit she's shoveling us."

"Okay."

"It seems to me that if there really is a plot, it's probably one person, holding it really tight. Us radicals . . . we leak like crazy. We can't organize a picnic without somebody leaking to somebody who didn't get invited. The plotter — if there is one — is holding it pretty tight. You know it's not me, because the plotter killed Joe Likely, and like I told you the first time you were here, I was at parents' night at the school. I assume you checked that . . ."

"No, actually, I believed you."

"Hmm. I'd appreciate it if you'd check, because it makes me nervous not to be cleared," she said.

"Okay. Maybe I will — but I do believe you. I've still got to think about Anson, though," Lucas said.

She nodded. "Of course you do. Because, you know, you're a cop."

"Not really. Not anymore," Lucas said.

"Yeah, you are. Still."

■ ■ ■ ■

Lucas got up to go, told her that he'd had a Diet Coke on the way out. "With this Kool-Aid . . . if I could use your bathroom for a second."

She pointed him to it. He went in, closed the door, flipped the toilet lid up, and spotted a hairbrush on the back of the sink. He peed, flushed, and under the cover of the noise by the toilet, pulled a couple of pieces of toilet paper off the roll, pinched some hair in toilet paper, being careful not to touch it, folded it over several times, and put it in his pocket.

He felt a little guilty about it, because he liked her, but he did it anyway.

When Lucas had pulled away from her house, Lawrence showered, changed clothes, and walked to the school, looking for out-of-place vehicles. She didn't see any, but then, she thought, she probably wouldn't. If they were tracking her, they'd be good at it.

After her spell of volunteer work, she walked back to her house, got into her car, and drove to Iowa City. The road in from Hills was long and almost empty and she didn't see anyone trailing her. After poking around for a while in town, she found an actual pay phone at a 76 gas station.

"Hello?"

"Is this Marlys Purdy?" Lawrence asked.

"Yes, who is this?"

"A friend of yours. Let's not use names. We spoke at a meeting in June, about our gardens and rhubarb pies. You know who I am?"

"Yes. What happened?"

"Nothing, yet. That man from the Henderson campaign, Lucas Davenport, is going to find you. Maybe today or maybe tomorrow, but soon," she said. "All he knows is that you have a son with distinctive gray eyes and that you have curly white hair. I would suggest that you get your hair colored and straightened. Right away. If you have a gray-eyed son, get him out of sight."

"Okay," Marlys said.

"When he does find you, you have to be very careful. He is smart, good-looking, and very charming. And, I suspect, treacherous. So . . ."

Silence. Then Marlys said, "Thank you. Take care of yourself. With all these cops around."

"The cops aren't interested in me. They're only interested in you," Lawrence said.

"Iowa cops will always be interested in the Lennett Valley thing," Marlys said.

Lawrence was stunned: "Lennett Valley? Why would I be worried about Lennett Valley?"

"Anson told me you would be," Marlys said. "He was pretty . . . definite about it."

"Anson! That man is such a fantasist. And a gossip! I . . ." She trailed away, struggling with the thought. She had no idea that Anson suspected anything about Lennett Valley.

"Take care of yourself," Marlys said.

When she'd broken off the call with Marlys, Lawrence walked back to her car, thinking about Anson Palmer and the question that Davenport had asked about him: about whether Palmer might crack under pressure.

He would. He was a radical, a rabid anti-Semite, and at the same time, a man who wouldn't go to jail if there was any way to avoid it. Any way at all. Davenport was clearly a man hard enough and smart enough to crack a twit like Palmer.

After the bomb went off, her group had learned that they had a problem. They'd been more than a hundred miles away, eating breakfast in their favorite diner, where they'd be recognized and remembered for at least a few days, when the bomb exploded. They hadn't intended to kill anyone, and so had hidden the bomb, with its timing device, in the empty barn, while the auction itself would be going on out in the dairy parking lot.

They'd been scared to death when they found out what had happened, and had followed the stories in the papers, which had gone on for weeks. It was from news reports that they'd learned that the motel where they'd stayed had been searched by the police and apparently some evidence had been found.

They'd been careful about fingerprints, but who knew what might have been found? They had no way to ask, so the four of them had spent their lives being careful, avoiding anything where a fingerprint might be sought or required. Her former boyfriend told her years later that he'd never again smoked dope, in case he should be caught and printed.

Lawrence thought about all of that as she sat in her car, then did an illegal U-turn and headed for Palmer's house.

FIFTEEN

Marlys punched *End* on her cell phone and walked out to the barn, where Cole was running a grinder, sparks flying from the iron piece he was working; the place stank of burning metal. The grinder was loud and he didn't hear her coming and he jumped when she touched his arm.

He shut the grinder down and said through his face mask, "Jesus, you scared the shit out of me. Don't do that."

"We gotta talk. Let's go back in the house."

When she told him about the call from Lawrence, Cole said, "We're so close. How did this happen?"

"Don't know. Grace said Davenport was poking at a bunch of different radical groups, but when Joe was killed, that convinced him he was on the right track."

"Told you at the time —"

"Well, we don't know what Joe would have done. I think he would have turned on us, so we had no choice," Marlys said. "Anyway, Grace thinks Davenport is going to find us soon. I'm going into town to get my hair colored. The way Grace was talking, he's interviewing a lot of people, so he might not even get here today. He might not find us at all."

"I could keep working for another hour, then, and if some strange car pulls into the yard, go out the back."

Marlys considered for a moment, then asked, "How much more do you have to do?"

"In an hour, I'll be fitting it together. Or I'll be close to that. Then I got to paint it."

"That can wait a bit, though, the paint. Okay. All they know about you is that you've got gray eyes. Distinctive gray eyes, which you do. I don't want them to see you, but it'd be nice if they got a look at Jesse, with his blue eyes."

"Where is he?" Cole asked.

"Half-day farmers' market in Des Moines," Marlys said. "He should be back by two o'clock."

"Jesse could let something out," Cole said. "I hate to say it about my own brother, but we can't trust him."

"I know that," Marlys said. "I worry about it. You do what you can with your grinding and be ready to run for it. I'm going to call Jean Mint and get my hair done."

"Sure you can get in?"

"If I can't, it'd be the only time in the last decade that somebody got turned away," Marlys said. "I gotta go. You keep a sharp eye out."

Marlys drove into town, found Jean Mint sitting under a hair dryer, smoking a cigarette. She wasn't drying her hair; the chair was just her most comfortable, and she sat around a lot, doing nothing. She was surprised when Marlys told her what she wanted — "You've got a beau, don't you? Don't lie to me, Marlys, I'll hear about it sooner or later . . ."

Marlys was back at the house in three hours with straight light brown hair and matching eyebrows, all of it well-threaded with strands of white. Cole was still in the barn, but saw her car turn into the yard and, when she got out, yelled at her: "Come in here."

She walked back to the barn and he said, "Oh, my God."

"What do you think?" she asked.

"You don't look like you, but . . . I can

remember when you looked like that," he said. "You looked like that when I was in high school. What, twelve or thirteen years ago?"

"About that," she said, touching her hair. "I might keep it this way. Nobody showed up?"

"Not yet. Jesse ought to be home anytime now," Cole said. "You figure out what we're going to do about him?"

"Not yet, but I'll think of something," she said. "How are you doing here?"

"Everything fits perfect," Cole said. "I could do some more grinding. I've got to be careful, I don't want to ruin it, but the thinner it is, the better."

"All right, but stop for today and take off. Go over to the golf course or something in case this Davenport guy shows up today."

Anson Palmer's street was a working persons' street, not many people around midday. Lawrence had pushed her hair up under a baseball cap, walked up the driveway, around Palmer's car to the back door. She knocked on it, and waited.

Palmer came to the window in the door, peered out at her, and opened it up. "Grace?"

"What in the heck are you telling Marlys

about Lennett Valley?" she hissed, looking around, wanting to shout but afraid she'd be heard.

Palmer stuck his head out for a quick look around, then pushed the door open and said, "You'd better come in."

When she was inside, he closed the door behind her, threw the bolt, and led the way through the kitchen to his home office.

"What did Marlys tell you?" he asked, as he sat down in an office chair, leaving her standing.

"That you told her I was involved in the Lennett Valley bombing," Lawrence said.

"Well, weren't you?"

"Of course not," she said. "I wasn't even near there."

"Time bomb," he said. He smiled, an unattractive, knowing rictus. "I know you were there with it."

"Like how you know all about Jews?" she screeched. "Make up whatever shit your tiny brain can come up with and pretend it's real?"

He was instantly angry, and stuttered, "That — that — that . . ." and then pulled himself back together. Then, "I'll tell you how I know, Grace. Harry told me. The whole thing."

"Harry would never —"

"This was fifteen years ago when he was drinking. I picked him up lying on the sidewalk outside McCoy's and took him home and told him he had to quit or he was going to die. He said he couldn't. We got in a long argument, and at the end he told me he was drinking because of Lennett Valley, but it didn't work — he couldn't forget it, and he couldn't stand remembering it. Told me how you got the dynamite from that farm over in Wisconsin where they'd been blowing up stumps. Over by Siren, right?"

Grace stepped away, both hands going to her forehead. He actually knew. He even knew where the dynamite came from. The people they'd stolen it from knew them — one of them was an old friend of Betsy's, from college at Stout, and they'd stayed at the farm for a few days the summer before the bombing.

They'd spotted the explosive, and later, knew where to get it when they came up for the plan for the bomb. Thirty years later, the farm people were still out there, they'd remember the theft of the dynamite, and they'd remember Betsy and her friends . . .

Palmer was going on, but she couldn't make out what he was saying, because her thoughts were screaming at her, and then she managed to ask, "Who else knows about this?"

Palmer threw up his hands. "How would I know? Nobody, I suppose. I mean other than you and Betsy and Harry and Russ and me. I didn't give Marlys any details, I sort of hinted at it. That you could be made to keep your mouth shut, even if you couldn't be entirely trusted. Because if you talked about Marlys, Marlys could threaten to talk about Lennett Valley."

"Ah, shit, Anson, you're an idiot!" Grace cried.

"I'm not an idiot —"

"What did you tell Davenport?"

"Nothing. I stonewalled him. I didn't even let him in the house," he said, his voice shrill with pride. "You know, I doubt Harry ever told anyone, either. Because not long after I picked him up, he crashed his car on 218 and he was in the hospital for two months and when he got out, he was dried out. I don't think he's had a drink since."

"Oh, boy . . ."

Palmer shook his finger at her. "I'll tell you something else, my little chickadee. That goddamned Davenport — did I tell you I suspect he's a Jew? — if Marlys pulls this off and they come back at me, you better figure out a way you can help me out.

You goddamned well better. You can tell them that we talked about it, and couldn't figure out who it could be —"

"You're threatening me?"

"I'm not threatening, I'm articulating," Palmer said.

"Damn you . . ." He'd swiveled toward her, and now she stepped around him to his desk. He had a rock on his desk, round and speckled, a little smaller than a softball, with some lettering carved into it. She picked it up in one hand and when he swiveled to see what she was doing, she smashed him on the top of the head with it.

She actually felt his skull break, almost like feeling an eggshell crack when you hit it on the side of a cup. She hit him again, and again, and then backed away as he toppled onto the floor.

"Oh, my God," she said.

His head was misshapen, but he was still breathing. She looked around, saw a sport coat hanging on a doorknob, still in the plastic bag from a dry cleaner's. She reached toward it, thought, *Fingerprints.* Still with the rock in her hand, she hurried back into the kitchen, saw the paper towel roll. She dropped the rock in the kitchen sink, un-rolled some towels, carried the towels into the office, pulled the plastic sack off the sport coat, pinching the plastic between the towels and her fingers.

Palmer was still breathing, blood draining out of his ears. She knelt next to him and pulled the bag over his head, careful not to touch anything but the protective towels, and knotted it around his neck.

Still breathing.

She went back to the kitchen, washed the rock with soap, and then left it there.

Back in the office, she looked at Palmer.

No more breathing. She put her knuckles against his chest. No heartbeat. She collected all the paper towels and stuffed them under her blouse.

At the back door, she peered out, saw no one. Had to go.

She went, hair up under her hat, ambling down the street, her face covered with a cold sweat. Two blocks away, she climbed into her car.

"Please God, don't let them find me," she prayed, though she'd never been a believer. *"Please, please, please."*

Lucas spent the day walking up to small houses in small towns, getting nowhere perceptible. At two o'clock, he'd taken a break at a café in Oskaloosa, one of the towns from which Henderson had gotten an e-mail. An investigator named Perry Means, from the Division of Criminal Investigation, was waiting for him at the café. Lucas handed over the sample of Lawrence's hair, which Means put in a plastic evidence envelope.

"Bell Wood called me up and said a hairball was waiting for me in Oskaloosa. I said, 'Story of my life,' and he said, 'No, no, a real hairball,' " Means said, over the remnants of a grilled cheese sandwich. "I gotta tell you, if this turns out to be something, I plan to take full credit for driving it to Des Moines."

"I'd hoped to get half-credit for driving it this far," Lucas said.

"Uh-uh, not the way it works," Means said. He was a fleshy man, with nicotine-stained teeth and drooping cheeks. And, "Say, didn't you work for Virgil Flowers for a while, up in Minnesota?"

Lucas laughed and said, "Yeah, I guess I did. Does everybody in Iowa know Virgil?"

"We've traded quite a bit of information over the years," Means said. "I worked out of Mason City for six years, so we got to know each other. He's sort of a hound when it comes to women."

"Not sort of," Lucas said. "He's the fuckin' Hound of the Baskervilles when it comes to women. Every time he gets around my daughter, I make sure I've got my gun."

Means headed for Des Moines with the hair sample and Lucas called Robertson, who was working north of I-80. "I got nothing, nothing, and nothing. I thought I had something for a minute, but it turned out to be nothing," he said.

"More'n I got," Lucas said. "I never even *thought* I had something. What'd you think you had?"

Robertson said, "I pulled into this farmyard — Hendrick Fischer on your list — and there was this older lady in the yard, chubby with white curls. Turned out she was a neighbor, picking up some farm-fresh eggs. Or as Fischer put it, aigs. I checked and she was who she said she was. Never heard of the PPPI."

"Too bad . . ."

"Yeah. I'm doing two more, then I'm heading home, with my farm-fresh aigs," Robertson said. "I'll stay in touch."

Lucas's next stop was in the town of What Cheer, where he spoke to Tom and Mary Moller. Tom Moller said, "Wait, wait . . . Joe Likely was *murdered*?"

"You hadn't heard?"

"No . . . we haven't talked to Joe in five

years, I guess," Tom Moller said. "Somebody should have called us. Is it on the Internet?"

"Probably," Lucas said.

Mary asked her husband, "I wonder if Marlys knows? They were pretty tight at one time."

"Long time ago," he said.

"Who's Marlys?" Lucas asked. He knew without looking that there was nobody named Marlys on the list.

"She's an old party member, lives over in Pella," Mary said. "She was always real active with the party."

"Got curly white hair? A little on the heavy side?"

"Haven't seen her in years," Mary said. "Hair could be white, by now. Wasn't *that* heavy, maybe carried a few extra pounds. Like most of us."

"I'd like to talk to her, if I could," Lucas said. "Where exactly is she?"

They didn't know exactly where Marlys Purdy lived, though they knew it was somewhere near the town of Pella. Lucas checked the geography on his iPhone, cut across country to Pella, and at Pella, made inquiries at the city hall. Nobody knew her there, but it was a slow day and a clerk called to the county courthouse in Knoxville, got an address out in the rural countryside. With that, she called the county land assessor's office, asked them to look at their plat map. They did, and the clerk drew a turn-by-turn map to the Purdy place from downtown Pella.

Lucas followed the map out to the Purdy place, knowing that Marlys might have white hair and that she had a son.

Marlys had lied to Jesse: "Cole might be in some trouble. He went to Davenport a couple days ago to protest at the Bowden rally and he threw a rock at her car. The thing is, it broke the glass on the door. The Bowden security people are looking for him, and one of them has a list of names from the party. He might be coming here."

"What? Why here?"

"Because the party people have been protesting, and the Bowden people know who we are, and they got a list from somewhere," Marlys lied. "Like I've told you, they watch us. All this guy's got is a description — gray eyes, long hair. If you run into him, let him see your eyes and don't mention a brother and then get out of here. You got that?"

"For Christ's sakes, Mom, what are you

259

guys doing?" Jesse asked. "You *can't* go throwing rocks at politicians. Not in Iowa. They catch him, they'll put his ass in prison. I don't think Cole would do real good in prison."

"You don't think I'm worried? That's why I'm telling you this," Marlys said. "Cole's gone over to the golf course. He'll stay there until it's dark, and he'll work there tomorrow until we know whether this guy is going to show up or not."

"Ah, God, I knew your politics would get us in trouble, sooner or later," Jesse said.

"Look, I'm not asking you to go along with hiding him — let the guy see you, and I'll do all the lyin' from there."

Jesse looked her over for a moment, then said, "Yeah. You're good at it."

Jesse had an early farmers' market in Cedar Rapids the next day, taking in a couple hundred ears of perfect sweet corn, which had to be picked and cleaned up. He got gunnysacks out of the shed and walked down to the cornfield and started picking.

He kept an old mattress in the back of his truck for corn deliveries, to keep the ears from bruising as he drove up to I-80 on the back roads, and had just dropped the second sack on the mattress when a black Mercedes SUV nosed into the driveway. Jesse stood watching it, and the truck pulled up to him and a tough-looking dark-haired guy ran the window down and asked, "Is this the Purdy place?"

Jesse said, "Yeah. Who're you?"

"I'm looking for Marlys Purdy."

"That's my mom," Jesse said. "She's in the house." He tipped his head toward the side door.

Lucas looked at Jesse, taking in the blue eyes and the short hair, which, though short, was ragged, and hadn't been recently cut. Not the guy who ran from him in Davenport — and his truck wasn't the truck they'd seen. "We're looking for some people who've been talking with Governor Henderson . . ."

"Don't know nothing about politics, but Mom does," the man said. "I think she's for Bowden. Or maybe Henderson. One of them. I just sell the corn around here. You better talk to her."

As he said it, he was backing away from Lucas's Mercedes, the last gunnysack in his hands. Lucas said, "Okay," and got out of the truck as Jesse walked down the slope to the sweet corn field.

Like most of the other members of the PPPI, Marlys Purdy didn't like cops and wasn't afraid to say so. "What I want to know is, where were the cops when the banks were robbing us of our farms? How come Wall Street is making billions and not a single big-time banker went to prison after they tore down the whole damn economy in '08? Have you even read *The Big Short*? Where were you cops then? That's what I want to know."

"That would be worth knowing," Lucas said, "but that's not what I'm looking into. I'm trying to find a woman who has made some implicit threats aimed at Mrs. Bowden and may be involved in the murder of Joseph Likely."

Something seemed to retract in her eyes, and she said, "Joe Likely? Joe Likely was murdered?"

"And his girlfriend with him," Lucas said.

They'd been standing in the kitchen, where the eyeglasses-free Purdy had been washing apples. Now she took a chair and said, "I haven't seen him for a while, but the last time I did, he was happy, he didn't seem threatened. If he felt threatened, I think he would have told us."

"Was there anybody who you think might have been . . . angry with him? Or opposed to him? Anybody who might have confided in him and then decided they'd made a mistake?"

She shook her head. "Nothing like that. The PPPI doesn't hurt people."

"What about Anson Palmer?" Lucas asked.

"Anson wouldn't hurt anyone. I promise you that."

"He seems a little . . . off balance."

"You mean because of the Jew thing? His book?"

"That, and his general attitude toward police. It's like he's almost eager to get up in their faces . . . I'm not a cop anymore, but he got up in mine, because I used to be," Lucas said.

"He's got his reasons," Marlys said. She massaged her forehead with her fingers, and Lucas took in the brown hair with the white streaks. Her hair was shortish, but not the curly white lamb-like hair described by Henderson. She said, "I hate to give up anybody who's done good work, but I don't want anything to happen to Mike Bowden, either. Have you ever heard of a group called Prairie Storm?"

"As a matter of fact, I have — I ran into their leader the other day, over in Atlantic." He touched his black eye, which was still tender.

"Really? He did that? Did you get back at him?" Marlys asked.

"I handled it," Lucas said. "He won't be breathing easy for a couple of months."

"You beat him up?"

"I defended myself," Lucas said.

She took him in, a moment of silent appraisal, then she said, "I believe that. I don't intend to be rude, Mr. Davenport, but you look kinda mean."

Lucas left ten minutes later. Marlys Purdy fit the bill in some ways, and in more ways, did not. He was thinking about checking her with the neighbors, when Bell Wood called.

"I haven't found them," he said, without saying hello. "I'm down in the town of Pella, heading your way."

"You might want to turn around," Wood said. "Your friends on the Iowa City police force called. Somebody murdered a guy named Anson Palmer."

264

Sixteen

Lucas was starting to feel like a yo-yo, and Iowa City was the finger.

When he got back, off I-80, he threaded his way through town to Anson Palmer's house and found a half-dozen cop cars coagulated in the street outside. Randy Ford's state sedan was among them.

He had Ford's number on his cell phone, called it, and Ford said, "Yeah?"

"I'm outside."

"Come on in," Ford said.

Ford was standing in Palmer's living room, looking disgusted. "I don't know," he said, when Lucas appeared in the doorway. "It's like amateur night at the slaughterhouse, but we can't find the goddamn amateur who's doing the killing."

"You're sure it's a murder . . ."

"Unless he hit himself on the head about three times with a rock, and after crushing his own skull, put the rock in a sink, washed it, and then tied a plastic bag around his head."

"Okay. When do you think it happened?"

One of the crime-scene people said, "No scientific estimate, but looking at the blood when we got here . . . we're thinking maybe between one and two o'clock, give or take."

Lucas went to look. Two crime-scene technicians were working Palmer's office, collecting samples of everything the killer might have touched. One of them was working over a visitor's chair with tape, pulling off any residue.

Lucas had once gone to a murder scene at a fishing cabin in northern Minnesota where a man had been beaten to death with a souvenir cribbage board, which had been shaped like a short canoe paddle. The heavy oaken board had been swung edge-on, like an ax, a half-dozen times, and the victim's skull had been crushed.

Anson Palmer was lying facedown in his home office, his head cocked back, propped against the bottom drawer of a filing cabinet. His bladder had released as he was dying, and the room still stank of urine. His head was wrapped with a transparent plastic bag, but was misshapen in the same way the cribbage-board victim's had been. The bag had been tied around his neck and a pint of blood had collected below his chin.

No sign of a weapon near the body.

"You said he was hit with a rock?"

"We think so," Ford said. "There's a rock in the kitchen sink, it's been washed with soap. But some of the victim's hair, with a couple flakes of scalp, were caught in the sink drainer. The killer didn't notice."

Lucas went to look. The bun-shaped chunk of speckled granite was a bit larger than a baseball, but smaller than a softball, and had a laser-cut slogan carved in the surface: *Molon Labe.*

"Come and take it," Lucas said.

"Yeah, I looked it up on the Internet, it's pretty famous," Ford said. "A lot of the pro-gun guys use it and radical political groups. The Texans used it during the Texas revolution. The Greeks supposedly said that to the Persians before a battle when the Persians told them to surrender."

"I knew about the gun guys and the Greeks," Lucas said. "I didn't know about the Texans. You think the rock belonged to Palmer?"

"Yeah, it did. There's a picture of him with another guy, that was taken in the office, looks like a few years ago, and you can see the rock on his desk."

Lucas went back and looked at the body again. "You know where the plastic bag came from?"

One of the techs said, "We think it's a plastic bag from a dry cleaner. There's a sport coat hanging from a doorknob in the living room, and the hanger's from a dry cleaner, but there's no bag around it."

"Then the killer didn't bring it with him."

"We don't think so — we're thinking that the murder was spontaneous — an argument, weapon of opportunity, whacks him on the head when he's not looking," Ford said.

Lucas agreed, but added, "Whack a guy a few times with a rock, you turn his head to mush . . . It takes a cold guy to find a bag to wrap around his head to finish the job, and then go wash the rock."

"Nobody said he was a sweetheart," Ford said.

"Makes me think it was a spontaneous use of the weapon, but the killer might have come here thinking about the possibility of killing him. With a really hot spontaneous murder, there's usually more . . . trashing of the place. Evidence of a fight or an argument. The killer leaves some blood around, the victim has a little bit of a chance to fight.

This guy killed Palmer and then took some time to tidy up. Not rushed, not frightened, not panicked. Cold."

"Like Joseph Likely and his girlfriend," Ford said. "That was cold."

"Yeah, but why not bring the gun with you?" Lucas asked.

"Maybe you already threw it in a river?" Ford suggested. "Or maybe because it didn't work so well the first time."

"Maybe. Or maybe you were thinking you wouldn't need it again, so you didn't bring it," Lucas said. "Anybody talk to the Bowden people about this?"

"Not as far as I know," Ford said. "You're basically the guy talking about Bowden — the rest of us are not so sure it's all connected."

"Well, it is," Lucas said. And after a minute, "Talk to all the neighbors?"

"Yeah. There was a red truck parked across the street and down the block from Palmer's, for maybe an hour and a half. A woman on the next street up saw a man getting in and out of the truck, but we've got no real description. Might have been wearing a blue uniform shirt, like a repairman or something, but maybe it was just a short-sleeved shirt. Probably brown hair. Haven't found anybody yet who knows who it might be. A woman at the other end of the block saw two unfamiliar women on the street, looked Hispanic or maybe Filipino, but they were carrying pamphlets and she thought they may have been religious people. Nobody seen going in or out of Palmer's."

Lucas spent another fifteen minutes looking at the murder scene — he'd found the longer you looked, the more likely it was that you'd pick up some small thing that would become more interesting as you got deeper into the investigation. Not this time: it was what it was. Pick up the stone, whack, whack, whack. Game over.

A cold mind, but you couldn't see a mind.

After fifteen minutes, he'd seen enough.

Lucas asked Ford to send him whatever he could, said good-bye, went out to his truck and called Mitford, told him about the second murder, and then called Bowden's security guy, Jubek. That done, he went off to find some dinner and check back into the Sheraton. As he ate, he thought about Grace Lawrence: a possible bomber, the possible creator or accessory in a murder that took planning and efficient execution. A cold mind.

The problem was, he had no idea what

could have caused Lawrence to have gone after Palmer, and Lawrence in no way resembled the woman that Henderson had spoken to. When they were talking, Lawrence had mentioned that she worked at the elementary school as a volunteer, "sometimes I think because I never had kids of my own."

If she were telling the truth about that, there'd be no gray-eyed country son.

He tucked her away in the back of his mind, in case the DNA from the dairy bombing came back with a match.

He also thought of the people he'd interviewed that afternoon: they could be ruled out of the Palmer murder, simply because they wouldn't have had time to drive back home after the killing, before talking to him. Those he'd interviewed late in the afternoon might have had time to drive back — barely — but he didn't believe they could have been involved. The number of people who could murder someone, and then have a cop unexpectedly arrive at the house, and still show no signs of stress or agitation, would be vanishingly rare. That would take a kind of psychosis that would show in other ways, and he would have sensed it.

He hadn't.

Still, they'd all been members of the PPPI and the party was connected to the two murders, and so was whoever was stalking Bowden.

He finished dinner, drove to the hotel, and checked in. He had been in the room long enough to wash his face when the phone rang.

Randy Ford calling.

"Davenport," Lucas said. "What's up?"

Ford said, "Lucas, this is really embarrassing . . ."

"What?"

"The director called because he wanted to know about the two murders," Ford said. "When I told him about you coming by the scene, he hit the roof."

"Aw, shit."

"Yeah. He's told me that you can't be involved," Ford said. "Told me to keep you away from the scenes and I'm not allowed to give you any reports."

"Gives me an ice cream headache," Lucas said.

"Yeah, well, I told him he's making a bad call and he reamed me a new one. So . . . now you know."

"I'm out."

"You're out of the police picture," Ford

said. "There's nothing to keep you from asking questions on your own. If you do that, I hope you'll call me up if you find anything."

"I will," Lucas said. "This doesn't make it easier, though."

"I know, but that's the way it is. Call me if you get anything."

Lucas called Neil Mitford, who didn't seem impressed by the fact that Lucas had been kicked out of the police case. "They'll change their minds. You be thinking about what you should be doing next."

"Neil, this is exactly the kind of bureaucratic bullshit that pushed me out of the BCA," Lucas said. "It's a guy protecting his territory. Actually it's not even as bad as the BCA deal. I kind of understand why the Iowa guys wouldn't want an outsider sticking his nose in, especially a civilian."

"You think about your next move," Mitford repeated. "Assume you'll have full police cooperation. I'll talk to the governor about this Anson Palmer guy and we'll figure out what *we* want to do next."

Lucas talked to Weather, told her that he might be on the way home. When he got off the phone, he looked at his watch: he had enough time to walk down to a bookstore he'd passed on the street and pick up something to read. He did that, found a Joseph Kanon spy novel, propped some hotel pillows behind his back, and settled down to read until bedtime.

Took a call from an unrecognized number at eleven o'clock. A man asked, "Davenport?"

"Yes?"

"Hold for Mike Bowden."

Bowden came up a few seconds later: "I've been briefed on the second murder and your investigation. I understand that you had already interviewed the dead man, Mr. Palmer."

"Yes. Twice. He was killed probably four or five hours after I last talked to him," Lucas said.

"Then you must be close to the main thread of this conspiracy, if there is a conspiracy," she said.

"I think so, but I haven't gotten very far with it," Lucas said.

"Keep pushing — the police will cooperate," Bowden said.

"I was told otherwise, about an hour ago."

"The director of the Division of Criminal Investigation is having a conversation with the governor of Iowa right now, and his mind is being changed about that," Bowden said, her voice cool and undramatic. "I spoke to the governor, and as he put it, 'Who in God's name wouldn't take all the help he could get if one of the presidential candidates is threatened?' He seemed quite perturbed."

"I'm starting to feel squeezed by all you big-time politicians," Lucas said.

"Can't help you there. I'm a squeezer myself and I don't much identify with the squeezed," Bowden said. "Get back to work tomorrow. Or even tonight, if you have something to do."

He didn't, so he went to bed.

Feeling squeezed.

SEVENTEEN

Sometime during the night, Lucas, in a half-waking, half-dream state, thought about/dreamed about *connections,* and woke the next morning thinking about the web that connected the Joseph Likely and the Anson Palmer killings.

Connections.

All kinds of connections, in time and space and in personal relationships.

He'd realized the day before that the people he'd interviewed that afternoon couldn't have killed Anson Palmer, because they wouldn't have had *time* to drive home afterward. Didn't matter about motive or personal feelings or any of that, because they were physically disconnected by distance.

The times between Lucas's visits to Likely and to Palmer, and their murders, were very short.

Connections also involved personal aspects. Tom and Mary Moller, the What Cheer couple who'd turned him on to Marlys Purdy, said that they hadn't talked to Purdy in years. Lucas could probably check that if he wished to, but, basically, he believed them: that meant that the personal connection between them and Purdy was tenuous. They didn't talk, didn't run into each other in town, didn't visit, didn't maintain a tight, intimate relationship.

The same would be true of the Mollers and Likely and Palmer — they'd never run into each other, unless they intended to, didn't chat, wouldn't know much about their respective psychological makeups. Wouldn't have a feel for whether their counterparts were really trustworthy.

That wouldn't work for the killer, Lucas thought. The killer or killers would have fairly intimate ties with their victims: there should be phone calls, e-mails, traces of face-to-face encounters between them.

If Joseph Likely's murder was tied into Lucas's interview with Likely, and he thought it was, then somebody had found out about the interview almost immediately after it happened and had quickly acted on that. How had they learned about the interview? Probably because Likely told them, or Likely had told someone who'd immediately passed the word along.

The killer had seen some kind of risk in Likely, and so eliminated him . . . had gotten the word, thought it over, planned the killing, and carried it out, all within a few hours. Conversely, Likely probably hadn't seen the risk and had considered the killer a friend, someone he trusted. He'd let the killer in the house, hadn't tried to defend himself, probably hadn't even seen the murder coming.

The same thing applied to Anson Palmer. Somebody had seen a risk in Palmer and had moved quickly and decisively to eliminate him after Lucas's visit. How had they learned about that visit? Probably because Palmer had told them. Palmer, like Likely, had let the killer in the house, hadn't tried to defend himself.

The killer was somebody near the core of the PPPI, and, Lucas suspected, probably lived close enough to Likely and Palmer that he/she encountered them frequently and had some degree of intimacy with them both. Someone that Palmer and Likely would both confide in.

That mostly applied to people who lived around Iowa City.

Again, he thought about Grace Lawrence.

But *time and distance:* Lawrence said she'd been at a school activity the night Likely was killed that would have totally covered the time between Lucas's visit and the murders. She couldn't have done it . . . if she were telling the truth.

He could check that and would. Once he'd eliminated the people who couldn't have done the murders, he'd be close to the one who did.

Bell Wood called while he was shaving:

"Jesus, you really set off a shit-storm this morning," he said. He sounded amused. "The director sent out a memo to everyone yesterday afternoon, telling us that we weren't cooperating with you, no way, no how. This morning I get a clarifying memo saying we *are* cooperating with you, in every way possible. The rumor is, he got his ass handed to him by the governor, in person."

"I don't know," Lucas lied, "but I'm happy I'm working with you guys again."

"Shoot, you're not working with *us,* we're working with *you,*" Wood said. "Robertson got the word, he'll be calling. The question is, what do you want us to do?"

Lucas told him about his calculation of the night before and his conclusion that the killer was tied tightly to the small core of

PPPI members between Iowa City and Mount Pleasant. "That includes Grace Lawrence, who lives in between the two places. Speaking of Grace, what's happening with the DNA analysis on her hair?"

"Under way. Pissed off some lab people because there's a hell of a backlog and we jumped the line," Wood said. "But we're working it around the clock. We should have something back the day after tomorrow, roughly seventy-two hours after it came through the door."

"Great. Anyway, my feeling is that we should forget about that whole long membership list — most of them aren't all that active — and focus on Iowa City. It'd be good if we could pull your other guys in here and make multiple visits to the people we know. Ask the same questions over and over. Put on the squeeze. Sweat them."

"I'll talk to Robertson right now and we'll have two more investigators there this afternoon," Wood said.

"Somebody said we'd have four more . . ."

"That was before the bureaucratic shit hit the fan," Wood said. "The director is showing that he still has some clout in this and has decided that four total should be enough . . . that's counting you."

"Figures," Lucas grumbled. "All right. I

280

want to spend some time at the two crime scenes we have. I need access to Likely's and Palmer's telephones and e-mail. I might need somebody to break passwords and get me into hard drives."

"Okay. I'll check around about the computer, the Iowa City cops should know somebody who could handle that. Can't send one of our own computer people without inflaming the red-ass."

"Stay in touch," Lucas said.

"I will — and listen. From what I'm hearing around here, the governor was almost on his knees, pleading with Bowden to go to the fair. He doesn't want her people telling the media that she's skipping the fair because she's been told she might be assassinated," Wood said. "The gov would consider that a blot on the whole state. He supposedly told Bowden that he could guarantee her safety. Half the highway patrol will be there and they're talking about shortening the candidate walk . . . Anyway, she's going to the fair."

Lucas ate a quiet breakfast of pancakes and sausage, read the *Press-Citizen*'s account of Palmer's murder — *known to have controversial views of Jewish culture and life* — got his truck, and drove back to Hills and stopped

281

at the school where Lawrence worked as a volunteer. After explaining to the principal what he was doing, and who he was working with, he asked about the night Likely was murdered.

The principal made a call to Bell Wood to verify Lucas's identity, got the okay to talk, and then told Lucas, "I was there and so was Grace. It was a meeting for the parents of prospective kindergartners. She was there the whole time. I talked to her before we started, I talked to her during it, and after we finished. Basically, she was there from six to ten o'clock."

"Thank you," Lucas said, and it surprised him a bit that he felt something like relief. He drove past Lawrence's house on the way back out of town: she may have blown up that dairy, he thought, but she hadn't killed Likely.

An Iowa City cop car was parked outside Anson Palmer's house and a sleepy young cop told him that the state crime-scene crew had left, as had the Iowa City detectives who were investigating the homicide; Palmer's body was at the medical examiner's for the autopsy. "We're keeping an eye on the place until the investigators are sure they don't need it anymore. Then we'll turn it over to the heirs, I guess."

He'd been told that a computer guy was coming over, along with one of the city detectives. "Should be here any minute."

They were.

The detective introduced himself as Russell Monroe and the computer jock as Jim Whalen. Monroe was a tall, fleshy blond in a decent suit but a too-wide tie and heavy shoes, the kind you used to kick people with in a fight. Whalen was a white-haired older man in jeans and a short-sleeved white shirt, who might have been a digitally recycled TV repairman. He was carrying a leather tool case the size of a child's lunch box. "We've been talking with Bell Wood and we're fine with you going over the place, as long as we get what you get," Monroe told Lucas. "If you get anything."

"I'm just trying to solve a problem," Lucas said. "If somebody else solves it first, I'm fine with that."

"We heard that you think somebody might try to hit Mrs. Bowden. Is that right?" Monroe asked, as he unlocked Palmer's front door.

"We don't know the exact situation, but it's worrisome," Lucas said.

"Why don't you tell her to go somewhere else until it's settled?" Monroe asked.

"Tried that, but she's a stubborn woman. She's got it in her head that the people of Iowa will be insulted if she doesn't show up for the state fair."

"That's silly," Monroe said.

"Well, I've been told that she doesn't worry that *all* the people will be insulted . . . but the Iowa caucuses could be a close-run thing and a couple extra percentage points going to Henderson could make a difference."

"Okay, so maybe two percent of the Iowa population would be insulted if she didn't go to the fair," Monroe conceded. They pushed through the door, and Monroe said to Whalen, "The home office is through the living room on the left."

Lucas and Monroe followed Whalen into the home office, which included a desk made out of two-by-twelve boards laid over four two-drawer filing cabinets, with an old-style tower computer sitting in the middle of it. Whalen thumbed through a scratch pad on Palmer's desk, turned it over and looked at the back, checked the first and last pages of a calendar, opened both drawers on the filing cabinets on either side of the leg-hole under the desk. No poorly hidden password.

"Probably something easy to remember and he never wrote it down," Whalen said. To Monroe: "You didn't find anything in his wallet or cell phone?"

"Nothing that looked like a password," Monroe said.

"Did his phone have a password?"

"Nope."

"Gonna have to do this the hard way, I guess," he said. He turned the computer on. "Machine's so old it might not even have password capability."

"Really?" Monroe asked.

"No, not really."

"How long's this gonna take?" Lucas asked.

Whalen was taking a USB thumb drive from his tool kit. "Mmm, probably . . . eight to ten minutes."

Lucas and Monroe looked at each other, and Monroe said to Whalen, "Hell, I thought you were going to call up the CIA or something."

While Whalen worked with the computer, Lucas pulled the drawers on the file cabinets and began thumbing through the folders inside. He found careful files for Vanguard Investments, Wells Fargo, income tax statements, appliance warranties. One drawer was full of bills marked *Paid.*

The bills went back years. The phone bills listed long-distance calls, but no local calls. Lucas gave a clutch of the bills to Monroe and said, "If you guys have a clerk who could run down these numbers . . . we're trying to figure out who he might have been talking to. We need to get his local calls, too."

"He's with Verizon, Vernon's already on it."

"Vernon?"

"Ed Vernon, he's the other guy on the case," Monroe said.

"I'd like to see the names he comes up with . . ."

"Sure."

"My work here is done," Whalen announced. "His password is Zarathustra."

"What the fuck is that?" Monroe asked.

"Fuck if I know," Whalen said. "If only we had some easily accessed, widely distributed source of information that we could tap into . . . Oh, wait! We have the Internet." He rattled a few computer keys, brought up a Wikipedia entry, peered at the screen, and said, "It's part of a title of a book by Nietzsche."

"Shit," Monroe said. "I gotta read Nietzsche?"

"It's only a password, not a clue," Whalen said. To Lucas: "Anyway, it's all there. What do you want?"

"I need to sift through it. Get the e-mail up, if you can. I'll look at that first."

Whalen rattled a few more keys, stood up, and said, "Good luck. He has six thousand in-box e-mails, and twenty-two hundred replies."

"Better you than me," Monroe said to Lucas. He looked around the room, back at the list of e-mails on the screen, the tip of the iceberg, and then said, "Tell you what. I wouldn't do this with any other civilian, but I'm going to leave you here. I gotta talk to a woman about an assault. When you're ready to go, give me a call, leave the key under the downspout by the porch, and I'll come back and lock up."

"See ya," Lucas said. He dragged a chair in from the kitchen — Palmer's office chair was still being processed — and settled in to read for a while.

One of Palmer's file cabinet drawers included a stock of office supplies, and Lucas requisitioned a yellow legal pad on which to make notes. He began with the outgoing mail, noting the names of the correspondents. The first thing he noticed was that most of the people with whom Palmer had been talking were not PPPI members from Iowa City — they were mostly people who wanted to discuss his views on Jews: a sprawling web of anti-Semites that reached across North America and Europe.

Rather than note names, he realized he'd have to actually read the subject lines, and often part of the messages, to separate out the PPPI people. He'd begun doing that when Robertson called: "Hey, man, we're partners again. What do you want me to do?"

Lucas explained his theory that the killer was probably from the Iowa City area, and an intimate of both Palmer and Likely. "I've hit them all, but you need to hit them again. Be unpleasant. Suggest that they know more than they're telling. Push them around."

"I can do that," Robertson said. "We've got two more guys coming this afternoon, we oughta get dinner together and work everything out."

"Call me when they get here, we'll meet downtown," Lucas said.

"Sounds good."

Lucas went back to the e-mails. After an

hour of work, he had noted on the legal pad the names of thirty-one people involved with the PPPI, most of them already on the list he'd gotten from Lawrence. He found a few more by Googling their names, but there wasn't much you could do with a name like Gregory Wilson — 87,200,000 Google results.

When he was finished, he'd gotten the most PPPI hits on the names of Grace Lawrence and Joseph Likely. Of the thirty-one names he'd uncovered, there'd been only a single contact with twelve of them, and all twelve had been recipients of an old press release about an upcoming party "convention" in Cedar Rapids. Eight hadn't bothered to reply, while the four replies were perfunctory: I'll be there, or I won't.

Of the nineteen with more than one hit, other than Lawrence and Likely, twelve had more than six contacts, and one had thirty. The killer, he thought, was very likely on that list of nineteen. He'd already talked to five of them, including Marlys Purdy, one of nine women on the list, and Robertson had talked to six more.

Lucas kicked back in his chair, and thought, *Let's go to Sherlock Holmes. When you've eliminated the impossible, whatever was left, however improbable, must be the truth. Or something like that.*

There were only three logical possibilities:

(1) The killings were carried out by one person he hadn't found yet.
(2) The killings were carried out by conspirators who were talking to each other, which meant that he may have wrongly eliminated somebody as a suspect because that person couldn't have carried out both of the murders, but could well have carried out one of them, while another conspirator carried out the other.
(3) The killings were basically not connected to each other.

He was reluctant to consider the third possibility. The willingness to commit murder was extremely rare. The possibility that two people who were closely connected should be killed within a day of each other by different people for separate reasons would be more than unusual. He'd never encountered anything like it. (The third murder, of Patricia Baker, he believed to be a consequence of the murder of Joe Likely, so was probably unrelated to the motives for the other two.)

290

It was much, much more likely that he simply hadn't yet located the killer, or that he had spoken to the killer but had eliminated him/her because he/she couldn't have committed both of them. That could have been his mistake.

Most probable, he thought, was that he simply hadn't yet found the killer.

Then, more reluctantly: Was it possible that there were two killers? Well, yes, of course it was possible — Henderson himself had seen two candidates, the white-haired woman and her gray-eyed son, if the gray-eyed man was the woman's son.

The problem with that was, nobody close to the center of the PPPI seemed to fit their descriptions — he'd yet to find a white-haired, chubby older woman with a gray-eyed son, or anyone who knew who they might be, or, at least, who would admit to it.

He thought about it for a moment, then picked up the phone and called Grace Lawrence. Lawrence was at the school and answered on the second ring. Lucas explained what he was doing, and asked, "First, I've got this new list of names . . . do you have any idea where these people live?"

He read the names of the people for whom he had no location. Lawrence gave him general locations for several of them, from memory — the towns they lived in, or the towns they lived nearest to, but said that none of them were really closely involved with the machinery of the PPPI, and only a couple of them lived within an hour's drive of Likely or Palmer. A few she didn't know at all.

"Sounds like you're kind of stuck," Lawrence said.

"Well, I'm going to crack Joe Likely's computer and see what I can find there . . . I can tell you, Grace, I'm right on top of the killer. I just can't see him yet."

"Is Mrs. Bowden still going to the fair?" she asked.

"At this point, yes. She could change her mind, though."

"Then you better find this killer, or change her mind."

EIGHTEEN

Two hours later.

Grace Lawrence was angry and frightened: she sat in her country kitchen, which smelled of bread and herbs and a glass of dill tops she'd picked early that morning, curling into herself, staring at her half-empty coffee cup. Robertson, the DCI agent, had been rough, threatening, a coarse slap in the face after Davenport's charming touch.

He'd been waiting on her stoop when she arrived home from school, and had invited himself in: "C'mon, Grace, you're not gonna do real fuckin' well up at Mitchellville, you're too goddamn old for prison," Robertson had said. "Talk to me now and maybe we can do something for you. Don't talk, then fuck ya. If *Bowden* gets hurt, the feds will probably ship you off to Alderson, and some days, like once a month, they might even let you see some fuckin' sunlight . . ."

Davenport had been so friendly, both in person and that afternoon on the phone; Robertson had been just the opposite. Now, she realized, Davenport had been nothing more than the good guy in a good-cop/bad-cop hustle. She'd figured that out when the school principal called to tell her about Davenport's visit, and to ask . . . "Is there something we should know, Grace?"

The principal even pretended not to know that Lawrence had been involved with the Progressive People's Party, though of course she *had* known. Grace had never made a secret of it, though she'd been careful not to preach.

Lawrence watched Robertson pull away in his state car, walked to a window and watched him disappear around the block. Would they be watching her? Had they somehow bugged her? Davenport had been alone in the bathroom . . .

She went to the bathroom and looked around, saw nothing unusual. Got down on her knees and looked behind the toilet, searching for a bug. But what would a bug even look like? And why would he put it in a bathroom, where she'd be by herself? Suddenly feeling dopey, she got up, washed her hands, looked at herself in the mirror, and said, "Dummy."

She went out and worked in the garden for an hour, pulling weeds. She threw the weeds in a mulch pile out along the back fence line, then got in her car and drove around the town, up one street, down another. The town was small enough that the unfamiliar was obvious, and she looked for lingering cars, unfamiliar faces. Saw none, and set out for Iowa City. Back to the 76 station, where she used the pay phone to call Marlys Purdy.

"This is the rhubarb woman again. We have a large problem," she said. "This Davenport man is coordinating a harassment attack on the party. He's going to find you."

"He already did," Purdy said. "We pulled the wool over his eyes and sent him on his way."

"Good. That's good. I've got to warn you, though, they've changed their tactics. No more Mister Nice Guy. A state investigator was here and he was very, very threatening. It's obvious to me what they're doing — they're trying to break down resistance. Pretty soon, people will be implicating anyone they can, because they'll be scared.

This man took a picture of me with his cell phone, to show around."

Purdy thought about that for a few seconds, then said, "I appreciate the call. You sit tight, deny everything. We will figure out how to reach this Davenport person, and . . . Say, do you have his phone number? Did he leave it with you?"

"Yes, he did. He left me a card," Lawrence said.

"Okay. Give me the number," Marlys said.

"What are you going to do?"

"I had an idea pop into my head. Best not to talk about it on a telephone."

Lawrence went back to her house, and her garden, picked a butternut squash for dinner, then simply sat down among the vines and began to weep. She was frightened, she was appalled by the unfairness of it. After all this time, after all these years of being a good and decent person, trying to make amends for the accident at Lennett Valley.

She didn't think of Anson Palmer at all. He'd gotten what was coming to him.

At three o'clock Lucas left Anson Palmer's house with a list of names and a list of local calls he'd made in the past two months. He'd made a couple of dozen calls to Joe

Likely in the past two months and a few to Grace Lawrence. The calls were usually only a couple of minutes long. He'd made a couple other short calls to local PPPI members; that'd have to be checked.

From Palmer's house, he headed south to Mount Pleasant and Likely's place, where he would hook up with Robertson, who had a key to the house. He found Robertson waiting for him with another investigator named Tom Robb, who would join them in interviewing PPPI members. Robertson and Robb were eating sack lunches.

"How'd it go with Lawrence?" Lucas asked.

"I scared her," Robertson said. "I took a picture of her with my cell phone, told her we were going to put it on our network."

"You got a network?"

"Yeah. It's called the Internet," Robertson said. "You want a dill pickle? I don't do pickles."

"Sure, I'll take a pickle . . ."

Robertson gave the house key to Lucas and he and Robb left to continue interviewing party members. Lucas ate the pickle and began combing through Likely's file cabinets. The house pushed against him as he worked: it hadn't yet been cleaned, and the blood on the floor added a hostile stink to the place; and the ghosts of recent death hovered around, in the small reminders of an unfinished life: dull pencils tossed next to a pencil sharpener, food-encrusted plates in the kitchen, a coffee cup with a quarter-inch of coffee in it, sitting on a bookshelf.

Lucas worked through it, and when he was finished, without finding anything of interest — Likely apparently did most of his work on his missing computer — he headed back to Iowa City to meet with Robertson, Robb, and the last of the two new investigators assigned to the case. Halfway there, he took an incoming call from an unknown number.

"Officer Davenport?" A male voice; more young than old.

"Lucas Davenport, yes. Who is this?"

"Don't worry about that. I'm a member of the Progressive People's Party. Or, I was, but I quit. Anyway, the party people have been talking about you and I got your phone number from one of them. I know the people you're looking for. This white-haired lady."

"Hang on, I'm going to pull over so I can write this down," Lucas said. He did that, pulling onto the shoulder of the highway.

When he'd stopped, he said, "It'd be really good if we could get your name."

"I'm sorry, I can't be involved. My parents . . . Anyway, I can't. But. The woman you're looking for is named Sandra Burton. She has two sons and both of them have those gray eyes you're looking for. The other thing is, they told me they had a project that they wanted help with. This was the last time I saw them . . . They said they were keeping track of Mrs. Bowden so they'd know where she hadn't been, and those might be soft spots in her vote, places that Governor Henderson could exploit. That seemed pretty weak to me. They were acting funny, so I said I had to concentrate on my classes. Anyway, they sound like the people you're looking for."

"Sandra Burton. Is there a Mr. Burton?"

"Yeah, he's a truck driver, he's gone most of the time. His name is Don. Anyway, it's kinda hard to find their place, it's out in the country. If you start exactly at the corner of E Street and Sixth Avenue in Grinnell, and then go exactly six-point-one miles on your car odometer from that corner out Sixth Avenue East — that turns into Highway 6. They're on the north side of the road in a white house with a four-car red garage on the left side of the house."

Lucas repeated the directions, and said, "I appreciate all of this, but please — we really need your name."

"Can't do that. I don't want to get in trouble with my dad. You got the directions. Good-bye."

Lucas thought he remembered a Burton on his list of e-mails sent or received by Anson Palmer. He checked, and found an e-mail from Palmer to Burton, but it was short, a few lines about an upcoming event in Iowa City sponsored by another group called Left Coast. Lucas hadn't heard of Left Coast and didn't have time to do the research. There was no Burton on Grace Lawrence's list of members. The Burton residence was reasonably close to the line of towns from which e-mails had been sent to Henderson.

Lucas dug an iPad out of the seatback pocket, found that he had a good cell connection, and called up a map of Iowa. From where he was, the fastest route to Grinnell was through Iowa City, and then west along I-80. A map of Grinnell showed E Street and Sixth Avenue intersecting near Grinnell College — probably the "classes" that the caller had referred to. The Burton place would be about an hour from Iowa City, running just at the speed limit. For somebody who knew the roads and the habits of the highway patrol, probably less than an hour.

Lucas tossed the iPad on the backseat, pulled onto the highway, called Robertson and told him about the phone call.

"I want to go there right now and I'd like you or Robb to come with me, because you guys got the badges," Lucas said. "If I pick you up in Iowa City, we'd get there before dark."

"I'm coming — Robb's got an interview at seven o'clock," Robertson said. "This could be a break."

"Pick you up in half an hour in front of the hotel," Lucas said.

Robertson was waiting when Lucas arrived. "Grinnell's an hour from here, or less, so we should be good on daylight," he said, when he got in the truck. He adjusted the bucket seat to his long legs and added, "Nice ride."

"We gotta be careful when we get there," Lucas said. "They don't know we're coming, but if they're as goofy as we think they might be . . . The other possibility is, we're being set up."

"Huh. Why would you think that?"

301

"Because in my experience, tips like this don't fall on your head, not unless the guy wants something. This guy didn't want anything. Wouldn't even tell me who he is."

"What do we do about that?" Robertson asked.

"I'm open to ideas," Lucas said.

"Do you have phone numbers for the Burtons?"

"Can't your DCI guys get them? I know where she lives . . ."

Three minutes later, they had two cell phone numbers, one for a Donald Burton, one for a Sandra. "Watch this," Robertson said.

He put his phone on speaker and dialed the number for Donald Burton. Burton picked it up immediately: "Yeah?"

Robertson: "Don! This is Chick Weber from State . . . Is this my boy Don Burton who once fought three strippers in the parking lot outside Iowa Bush Country and lost?"

Burton: "Hey, Chick, that sounds like me, but you got the wrong guy."

"Ah, hell. Sorry to bother you, man. I'm going on Internet searches and I thought I had my guy. Say, what's that buzzing sound? You in a plane?"

"I wish. I'm in an eighteen-wheeler going

into Shaky Town," Burton said.

"Well, take it easy," Robertson said. "Sorry to bother you."

He rang off and Lucas said, "Sounded like a truck to me — I think Shaky Town is L.A."

"Which means we're calling Sandra and her gang," Robertson said.

He dialed Sandra Burton's number. She picked up and they could barely hear her over the background noise, and then the noise quit, and she said, "Sorry, I couldn't hear you. I'm out mowing the lawn."

"Okay. I think I might have the wrong number. I'm trying to get Don Burton about picking up a load in L.A."

"That's my husband," she said. "I can give you that number."

"That'd be great."

Burton gave Robertson the number, he thanked her, and rang off. "What do you think?" he asked Lucas.

"If we're being set up, I don't think the Burtons are doing it. If they're the ones . . . I don't know. I still don't like the idea of a tip like this, coming out of nowhere, falling on my head. But we gotta check."

"I'm with you," Robertson said. "This could be a big deal. You got a weapon?"

"In the back. Bell Wood got me a carry permit, so I'm legal," Lucas said.

"Might want to get it out, then, before we get there."

"I'll do that," Lucas said. "In fact, when we get to Grinnell, I might want to run into a McDonald's and get a sandwich. I'm starving to death. I can gun-up then."

Lucas and Robertson hadn't had any real chance for casual conversation, and when they got out of town, Robertson asked about the BCA, the salaries and retirement. "You quit there, right? Bell told me that you don't get along with bureaucrats all that well."

"Not exactly right," Lucas said. "Bureaucrats have their uses and a good bureaucrat is worth his weight in gold. The particular one I ran into, though, wasn't a good one. His idea of his job was to make the empire bigger, and not get in trouble. Not necessarily to get anything done, unless it's convenient and noncontroversial. The last straw was when we got in a fight over an assignment to investigate a noncrime on behalf of a particularly stupid state senator."

"Not good. I'm interested because I've been with the DCI for three years and I've done pretty well. Our organization is flat, though — not much vertical rise. I could be there for thirty years and not move up much," Robertson said. "I'm looking around to see what else is out there. I like the Twin Cities. I'd move there in a minute."

"Cold up there," Lucas said. "Though I like it."

"I was born and raised in Okoboji. How much colder is Minneapolis than that?"

"Not much," Lucas said. "Tell you what: the bureaucrat that I ran into isn't long for the political world. Henderson will fire his ass right after the next elections, a year from November. If you came in as a new agent, you wouldn't be dealing with him anyway. A year from now, he's outa there and maybe sooner than that."

"You're not a candidate for the job? You're supposed to be asshole buddies with Henderson."

"I'm not interested in administration," Lucas said. "I'm not good at it, either."

"Bell said you're rich, that you've shot a whole bunch of people, and that you live for the hunt," Robertson said.

Lucas glanced at him and said, with a grin, "Bell is sometimes too social . . . if you know what I mean."

"He talks too much," Robertson said.

"But he's a good guy," Lucas said.

"Yeah, he is," Robertson said. He leaned

back in the seat and put his feet up on the dash, caught himself and said, "Whoops. Sorry about that."

"Not a problem, put them back up there," Lucas said. "I like those shoes. Where'd you get them?"

"Vegas . . ." They talked about fashion for a while, then Robertson asked, "You're straight, right? You seem really straight."

"Yeah, of course. Straight guys can't talk about fashion? Clothes? Shoes?" Lucas said.

"Of course. FYI, I'm as gay as a fuckin' Christmas tree," Robertson said.

"Yeah?"

"What? I don't seem gay?" Robertson asked.

"I hadn't thought about it," Lucas said. "Maybe the turned-up jean cuffs should have been a clue."

Robertson laughed and said, "Or tan shoes with blue jeans."

"I wear cordovan shoes with navy suits all the time," Lucas said.

"There you go. I totally approve. But you know what the British say, 'No brown in town.' "

"That's why we threw their asses out of here in 1776," Lucas said. "Not a moment too soon, as far as I'm concerned."

■ ■ ■ ■

They bullshitted their way down the highway to Grinnell, which was a few miles north of I-80, and when they turned off, Robertson retrieved Lucas's iPad from the backseat, did a search for fast-food restaurants, and said, "Subway, McDonald's, and Jimmy John's, all on the way."

"Jimmy John's. Had a good one over in Ames."

They made the turn onto Highway 6, made a quick stop at Jimmy John's. Lucas got his .45 and a holster out of the back, pulled his shirt out over his slacks to cover the gun, then took the passenger seat so he could eat while Robertson drove.

"Your guy said it was six-point-one miles from the turn . . . Got about five miles to go," Robertson said, as they left town, heading east on Highway 6.

"Drive slow. I want to enjoy the sandwich," Lucas said.

Lucas could see the sun in the right wing mirror. Twenty minutes or a half hour to sunset, he thought. Plenty of time before it got dark.

NINETEEN

Highway 6 was flat, heavily patched, and nearly dead straight as it ran east between cornfields and farmhouses. The air was clear and soft with humidity from the frequent rains, with occasional creeks trickling under the highway to the south, and islands of trees, elms and cottonwoods and box elders, sometimes woodlots but mostly windbreaks, dotting the landscape.

Robertson kept his eye on the odometer as Lucas finished the sandwich. At six miles he slowed and they spotted the red four-door garage and the two-story white house. A weathered white barn with a sagging ridgeline sat in back, with weeds growing up around it. A car was parked outside the house, and there were lights on, so most likely there was somebody home.

"How do you want to do it?" Robertson asked. There was no traffic behind them, and he'd slowed, then stopped the truck in the middle of the highway.

"Your state. I'm not as comfortable on farms as I am in the city," Lucas said.

"All right. On houses like this, people are gonna use the side doors, not the front doors so much," Robertson said. "I'll crowd the side door with the car, one of us stays behind it, the other one knocks, until we see what the situation is."

"Sounds right," Lucas said. "Who knocks?"

"I do. I've got the badge. There's a good chance we won't have to knock at all," Robertson said. "If there's somebody home, they'll probably come to the door to see who we are. If that happens, I'll pull them out into the yard."

Lucas nodded. Robertson was doing it the way he would have. "Watch for dogs," Lucas said.

Cole Purdy was invisible in the cornfield.

He'd arrived an hour earlier, after parking his truck off a side road to the east, behind trees that had grown up along a creek. He'd counted his paces after leaving the truck and jumping a fence into the cornfield and figured he was about three-quarters of a mile from the truck.

He wouldn't have to worry about concealment when he was running back to the vehicle, because it was corn all the way, twenty-inch rows with the stalks probably averaging ten or eleven feet in height. It was easier to see somebody in a rain forest than in a mature cornfield. He figured it would take about ten minutes to get back, carrying his bag and the rifle.

The rifle was a new one — new to him, anyway — purchased six months earlier at a Missouri gun show, a Colt in 5.56 NATO, shooting military ammo and equipped with an Aimpoint Pro red-dot optic. He'd picked it up back when they'd thought they might shoot Bowden. He'd hidden the gun carefully, had never let anyone see him shoot it, not even Jesse. Deep in the woods, he'd sighted it in dead-on at fifty yards, a bit high at a hundred, dead-on again at one-fifty, a bit low at two hundred yards — but none of the lows or highs would take the slug out of the kill zone. Here, he'd be shooting at fifty to sixty yards, depending on where Davenport put his vehicle, and with the two-minute-of-angle red dot, accuracy shouldn't be a problem.

He'd taken some granola bars with him, because that seemed to be the thing to do, along with a couple of bottles of water. He was wearing the full bow-hunter camouflage, including a face net to keep the bugs off.

He settled into a screen of low weeds right next to the edge of the corn. His mother had seen Davenport's truck, a black Mercedes-Benz.

Not something you often see pulling into random Iowa farmyards.

As the sun dropped down to the horizon, he saw a black SUV coming in from the west, slowing. Then it stopped in the middle of the highway, and despite his sense that he was cool, even calm, he felt a clutch at his heart. What were they doing? Did they know he was there?

"All set?" Robertson asked.

"Sure. Let's go."

The farmhouse's side door was on the left side of the house as they looked at it, across the driveway from the garage. A line of flagstones ran from the bottom of the stoop to the driveway, and Robertson turned down the drive and put the truck close enough to the edge of the driveway that Lucas would be stepping out on the flagstone.

They both popped their doors before the truck was fully stopped. Lucas got out a half-second before Robertson, turning to shut the door and to step to the back of the truck, where he'd be out of the line of fire if somebody came to the door with a gun. Simply by chance, he was looking toward the cornfield when he got out of the truck, and he saw the orange wink of the muzzle flash when Cole Purdy pulled the trigger.

A split second later, he heard the blast from the shot and Robertson cried out and went down. Lucas leaped backward, trying to get behind the truck, when a second shot knocked the wing mirror off the passenger side of the truck, glass flying everywhere, and he felt a stinging in his cheek, then he fell on his ass, behind the truck, rolled back to his feet, crouching. He was behind the hood, his gun already coming up, his eyes fixed on the spot where he'd seen the muzzle flash. He unloaded the .45 as quickly as he could with rough accuracy: he had no illusions about hitting anything at fifty yards, but it should keep the shooter occupied.

The gun locked open and he slammed another magazine in. As he did it, he either saw or imagined he saw a ripple moving through the cornfield and fired four more shots at it, then stopped, crouched, and stepped sideways across the nose of the truck, saw Robertson facedown in the driveway gravel. He was alive, pushing up with his hands, getting nowhere.

Lucas took the chance, jumped into the open, grabbed Robertson by his shirt collar, and dragged him behind the truck, and then heard another *bang!* coming from behind him, jerked around and nearly shot the woman who'd just let the screen door slam shut.

She was middle-aged, wearing a dress and an apron, but with nothing like kinky white hair. She had dark blond hair to the middle of her back and her mouth was open, and she was shouting something as the .45's front sight crossed the line of her eyes, but Lucas couldn't make it out immediately, what she was screaming, and fought the automatic trigger pull, and then realized what she was saying was, "Don't shoot me! Don't shoot me!"

Her hands were up and empty: no gun there.

He turned and looked back toward the cornfield, saw no movement, and the woman was screaming at him, "What happened? What did you do?"

Robertson was at Lucas's feet, looking up to him, seemed to be choking, and Lucas shouted at the woman, "Is there a hospital?"

She shouted back, "Yes, yes, in town . . ."

They were shouting, five feet apart. Lucas: "Help me, get the truck door."

"You're bleeding . . ."

"Get the goddamned door!"

Lucas picked up Robertson, and when the woman yanked the passenger door open, Lucas put him in the front passenger seat, strapped him in; Robertson's head was rolling on his neck like a ball bearing, no control at all, a guttural growl coming from his throat. The Iowa cop was bleeding heavily from a chest exit wound and also from the entry wound on his shoulder blade.

Lucas shouted at the woman, "Get in the backseat, take me to the hospital," and as she got in the backseat, he ran around to the driver's side. The engine was still running — Robertson hadn't killed it — and he made a quick U-turn, his head low behind the steering wheel in case the shooter was still out there, yelling at the woman, "Get down, get low!" and then they hit the highway, throwing gravel and dirt, got back on the hard surface and he dropped the hammer, rattling over the patched pavement at a hundred miles an hour, then a hundred and fifteen, and a hundred and twenty-five.

Robertson groaned and bubbled blood down his chin, made a choking sound like *huh-huh-huh.*

As a cop, Lucas had had emergency lights on the truck: no more. He was running naked, and blew past a pickup that was probably doing eighty, the other driver's stunned white moon face looking over at him through the window.

The woman in the back hadn't belted in, but was half-standing, leaning over the seat at Robertson, who was now sputtering blood, and she shouted, "I'm going to tip him right, so he doesn't drown in his blood," and Lucas shouted back, "Yes, yes . . ."

She did that and then grabbed Robertson's shirt and ripped it away from the wound, and as Lucas watched, she said, her voice down a notch, "Not a huge hole, but he's bleeding bad, I'm gonna stick my finger in it."

Lucas: "Press your palm to it, press your palm to it, seal it up."

They got to the edge of town in less than three minutes. The woman had one hand over Robertson's chest, and with the other she was on her cell phone, and then she was saying, shouting, "We're bringing in a man with a gunshot wound, he's hurt bad, he's shot in the chest, he's bleeding bad, we'll be there in one minute, call the police, call the police . . ."

She directed Lucas through Grinnell, Lucas barely slowing through the business district, leaning on his horn the whole way, running stop signs, and then around the hospital and up a ramp to the emergency entrance.

The woman was out of the vehicle as soon as it stopped, tugging open the passenger door as two nurses, an orderly, and a doctor ran out to the car with a gurney. The orderly and the nurses lifted Robertson onto the gurney and rolled him inside. As Lucas followed behind, a cop came out the entrance and the woman pointed at Lucas and blurted, "This man has a gun."

The cop put his hand on his pistol and Lucas put up his empty hands and said, "State police. That's Jerry Robertson of the Division of Criminal Investigation. He was shot by a sniper at this woman's farm. We were going to interview her."

The cop looked at the two of them uncertainly, then Lucas lifted his shirt to show him the empty holster and said, "The gun's in the car. It's loaded and cocked but the safety is engaged. It's been fired, so you'd be better off not to touch it until this is all sorted out."

The cop: "That's a DCI guy in there?"

"Yes. We need to get some people out to

this woman's farm," Lucas said. "There was a sniper waiting for us across the road. I fired a magazine and a half into the cornfield where he was hiding, but I was probably too far away to hit anything."

The cop said, "All right. Back inside. I'll get some help here . . ."

The woman said to Lucas, "I didn't do anything. Why did you come to my house?"

Lucas looked at her shocked, reddened face and said, "You're right. You didn't do anything."

"But why . . . ?"

"They set us up to kill us and they used you for bait. They must have known about your farm. I'm sorry. I can't tell you how grateful I am for helping Jerry like you did. You were . . . wonderful. You're Sandra Burton?"

"Yes."

In ten minutes, the emergency room was swarming with Grinnell cops, Poweshiek County sheriff's deputies, and one highway patrolman who'd come to the hospital after being alerted by the 911 operator that a truck had gone through Grinnell at a hundred miles an hour.

As the cops were arriving, Lucas got on the phone to Bell Wood, who freaked.

"Sniper? Sniper? Jesus, God, Lucas, what have we got here? Is Jerry gonna be okay?"

"I don't know. He was hit hard. Bleeding out his mouth, bright red blood, so he probably took a hit to his lung. He was alive when they took him into the operating room . . ." Lucas gave him the details he had, then gave the phone to the highway patrolman, who knew Wood, and Wood confirmed Lucas's status.

Robertson was in the operating room and no word on his condition was coming out. A bloody-handed nurse, who'd taken him in, stood washing her hands, and when Lucas asked, she said, "I've seen worse who lived. But then, I've seen better who died."

No help there.

A nurse practitioner approached him and said, "You're bleeding, your face is cut . . ."

Lucas spotted a mirror, checked himself: four or five cuts on the side of his face opposite the black eye. Nothing serious, damage done when the sniper's shot had hit his wing mirror, but if one of those shards had hit him in the eye, he'd have been blinded.

The nurse said, "Here . . ." and touched Lucas's face with a sterile pad wetted with something that smelled like alcohol. When he pressed on the cuts, Lucas felt nothing but the pain from the alcohol on three of the cuts, but the fourth cut delivered a sharp cutting jolt, and he flinched. The nurse took him to a side room, sat him down, and a few seconds later fished a tiny sliver of mirror glass out of the cut. He covered the cuts with tape and Lucas went back out the door.

The sheriff showed up, checked his black eye and the taped cuts, and said, "We've got to go back out to Miz Burton's place, see what there is to see. Maybe you hit that sucker and we'll get some DNA. Or a body."

"Have you heard any more about Jerry?" Lucas asked.

"They're pumping blood and oxygen into him, that's all I know. He's alive, his heart's okay."

"Let's go then. It's almost dark."

Lucas's .45 was retrieved from the floor of the truck, unloaded, decocked, and put in an evidence bag.

The sheriff asked him to leave the truck where it was, so it could be processed, and they went back to Burton's farm in the sheriff's personal car, which he'd been driving when he got the call. Sandra Burton rode with them, in the backseat. Lucas told them his story, and when he was finished, the sheriff said, "You were set up, all right. That'd be you in the emergency room, if you hadn't stopped at Jimmy John's and switched to the passenger side."

"Why me?" Sandra Burton asked. "Why'd they pick me?"

"Because somebody in the Progressive People's Party knew you and knew it would be a good place to ambush us," Lucas said. "You probably know whoever set us up. Might even be a friend. You have any ideas about that? Somebody seriously off balance, a Bowden-hater?"

"No, no. Most of my friends are Bowden lovers," she said.

Four sheriff's deputies had followed them to the farm; when they all had pulled into the farmyard and parked, the sheriff called back to the hospital. Still no word on Robertson.

Lucas wasn't precisely sure where he'd seen the muzzle flash — the weeds along the edge of the field all looked about the same — but he remembered he'd stepped out of the truck onto a flagstone. He went back to the end stone, and looked toward the field, and that gave him an angle.

Staying focused on the spot, he led the sheriff and his deputies across the road, spread in a long skirmish line. Everyone had a powerful LED flashlight, three deputies had shotguns, one had a rifle. They found the sniper's nest in a minute. The sheriff didn't want to let anyone get right on it, not until they could set up a formal crime-scene perimeter, but they spent a few minutes looking for an expended shell, and for blood, but found neither.

Lucas could see where the sniper had run through the field, knocking down or breaking some of the closely spaced cornstalks, and one of the deputies got a roll of blue tape and they marked out the trail as they followed it through the corn to a creek, and then along the creek to a side road. The trail disappeared at the road, but one of the deputies walked across the road, down into the roadside ditch and up the other side, and found vehicle-crushed weeds behind a stand of creek-side trees.

"Parked here, walked back to his spot, and waited. He knew you were coming, and he probably knew what your truck looked like," the sheriff said. "Shot the guy who got out of the driver's side. Thought he shot you."

They walked back through the field, staying clear of the sniper's path. The sheriff said, "We'll be back in daylight, we'll go over every inch of it. In the meantime, we'll talk to the neighbors, see if anybody saw a vehicle back there."

Back at Burton's house, Sandra Burton said her husband and his partner were truckers on a West Coast run, out on I-80, and wouldn't be back for three to five days, depending on their loads and destinations. They had three daughters, no sons. The daughters were all grown, two moved away, one living in Grinnell.

She'd been a member of the PPPI since the eighties, she said, but had had little direct contact with other members for a long time.

"Don never was a member. In fact, he was never a farmer. He's my second husband. My first husband *was* a farmer, until we lost the farm. That's when I got involved in the PPPI, but after, you know, twenty years, it started to seem pointless."

"Why pointless?"

She shrugged and said, "Farmers, the ones that survived, were getting rich when the Chinese came online, and the fire died out. I wasn't going to get the old farm back no matter what I did. Me'n Don have a quarter section here, a hundred and sixty acres, we rent it out, but we only paid two hundred and forty thousand for it back in the nineties. Now, it might be worth a million-five.

So, I don't feel like I got that much of a complaint anymore. But there are some people who never did get back — like my ex-husband. He's still working in Des Moines, at the air-conditioner factory."

The sheriff sent his deputies to knock on doors and Lucas showed his list of names to Burton, who recognized many of them. "I haven't seen any of them in years, though, you know, I'm still on some e-mail lists. We had a PPPI party here one summer, oh, a long time ago. A lot of people came — I couldn't tell you who they all were."

"But a lot of the people on the list knew where you lived. Had seen the place," Lucas said.

"Yeah, but the garage is new, that's only five or six years old. You said he mentioned the garage, and they wouldn't know about that."

"He'd cruised the place, setting it up," Lucas said. "He might already have been in the field when he called. He might have been looking at it."

Bell Wood and another man were getting out of an SUV when Lucas got back to the hospital. Lucas went to shake hands and Wood introduced the other man as Anthony

Pole, head of the DCI. Pole was a blocky, crew-cut man in a brown suit, with tortoise-shell glasses, and he wasn't interested in shaking hands. He snarled, "I knew having you interfere was a bad idea. Now you got one of our guys shot."

"Hey, fuck you," Lucas said.

"What!" Pole started to move at Lucas, but saw something in Lucas's eyes that made him take a step back. Bell Wood got between them and Lucas growled, "Stay away from me, asshole."

He brushed by Pole and went into the hospital, where he saw the nurse practitioner who'd patched up his face. "What do you hear?"

"They're still working on him. We took in a couple of Pepsis a few minutes ago, for the surgeons. They said they're gonna be a while. I think he's going to make it, the way they were talking. Unless, you know, he has a stroke. I think that's the big danger now."

Lucas left the emergency suite and found an empty conference room, shut the door, got on the phone to Mitford, told him about the shooting, asked him to pass the word on to Henderson and to Bowden's people, then called Weather to tell her.

"You should come home — this really

isn't your business anymore," she said.

"Can't now. Not with Robertson down," Lucas said.

"How bad are your cuts?" she asked.

"Nothing. Little dings," Lucas said. Weather did plastic surgery. "No scars, you won't have to get involved."

"Lucas . . ."

"I'll call you again tonight."

Robertson was in the operating room for three and a half hours. Lucas sat in a corner of the emergency area, doodling on his legal pad, trying to think how they could have been set up. Somebody he talked to must have done it, or somehow enabled it, either consciously or not: the shooter had his phone number. He'd given his card and phone number to twenty people and somebody must have passed it on. He had a good ear for voices and he hadn't recognized the caller who sent him to the Burton place.

He kept coming back to Grace Lawrence. He'd spoken to her several times now, and she was close to the center of the whole PPPI group. In fact, she *was* the center, now that Likely had been killed. He knew two things for sure about Lawrence: (1) she wasn't the woman Henderson had spoken to, who'd set off the whole investigation, and (2) she hadn't killed Likely. Those two things seemed to take her out of the loop.

Of course, he thought, she could be guiding the other group, the shooters; she could have sent them to Likely's place, and then to Anson Palmer's. Or she could have sent them to Likely's, while she took care of Palmer herself. She could be the ringmaster in the whole conspiracy.

He'd have to think about that, when he had time. She'd seemed far too mellow for a killer, a leftover hippie working her garden and volunteering at the elementary school. The school principal said she'd been volunteering for years, so it wasn't an act.

Bell Wood came over, a big bluff man with a mustache and a gap between his two square front teeth; he wore round gold-rimmed glasses like Teddy Roosevelt. He had a cup of coffee in his hand and nudged the leg of Lucas's chair. "Sorry about Pole. He can be an asshole."

"I picked up on that," Lucas said, looking up. "You in decent shape with him?"

"Oh, yeah. I'm just a cop. If you're just a cop, he won't fuck with you too much. He's more engaged with the politics of it all."

"I feel pretty bad about Robertson," Lucas said. "They shot him because they thought he was me."

"Can't feel bad about not getting shot," Wood said. "Shit just happens."

Robertson came out of the operating room after eleven o'clock and was taken to an intensive care unit. "We'll keep him here until we're sure he's stable, then we'll move him to Mercy in Des Moines," the lead surgeon told the waiting cops. "He's obviously in critical condition, but unless we have some new event — we're most concerned about blood clots resulting in a stroke — we think he'll make it. If he'd gotten here five minutes later, he would have died."

He wouldn't be talking for a while, the surgeon said — they'd need to keep him sedated. When Robertson was plugged into the ICU, Lucas said good-bye to Bell Wood and told the sheriff he'd like to watch the site search the next morning.

The sheriff said he'd be welcome, and when Lucas walked out, he found two TV vans waiting outside, and saw Pole talking to one of the reporters, under the lights. Lucas went by without looking at any of them. He'd checked out of the hotel that morning, so he had his clothes with him, and went to find a room.

He'd begun to settle into a Comfort Inn when he took a late call from Governor Henderson. "I spoke to Bowden. She spoke to some guy named Pole . . ."

"He's the DCI director. He's here in Grinnell because of the shooting," Lucas said.

"Yeah. Well, he told her that she should go ahead and do the walk at the fair, but plan to cut it down to four blocks. He says there's a stretch where there's no long sight lines that she could be shot from — they'll have it all covered. It's not the whole traditional parade-route walk, but it's long enough that they can do all the media shots."

"Not a good idea," Lucas said.

"I agree, but that's what she's going to do. This Pole guy told her that he holds you responsible for the shooting of his agent."

"Right."

"Wanna know what she said?" Henderson asked.

"Sure."

"She said, and I quote, 'You'd probably be better off holding the sniper responsible, don't you think? I certainly would.' "

"Good for her," Lucas said.

"But this short-walk thing . . . I dunno."

"Better than a long one," Lucas said.

328

"I guess. I'll be right behind her," Henderson said. "If she called it off, that'd give cover for the rest of us to call it off. But if she goes, I gotta go."

"That's, uh . . ."

"Stupid, I know. You wouldn't have a spare bulletproof vest in your truck, would you? And maybe a helmet?"

"No, I . . . Goddamnit, I gotta get these guys," Lucas said. "I don't think anyone else will."

"That's why I called you in the first place," Henderson said. "I don't think they will, either. But I think you will."

TWENTY

On any normal day, Marlys and Cole went to bed between nine and ten o'clock and got up with first light, but that night they sat in front of the TV, waiting for KCCI in Des Moines to come up on the satellite. The shooting led the news, with a live report from Grinnell. The report said that an agent of the Division of Criminal Investigation had been shot in an ambush at a farm home east of Grinnell, but didn't name the agent.

A severe-looking guy in a brown suit, whose name was Pole, came up and said it was a tragedy, that they would get the shooter whatever the cost. "This was an attempt at cold-blooded murder and we have ordered every available law enforcement officer to the scene."

"Shit, I got the wrong guy," Cole said, leaning toward the TV. "It was the right truck, a black Benz, he got out of the driver's side . . ." Cole felt nothing in particular about the shooting. It was just something he'd done.

Marlys looked over at her son and asked, "What does it mean that they ordered every available law enforcement officer to the scene?"

Cole thought about it for a minute, then said, "It's bullshit. I don't even know why you'd say something like that. If they said, 'We ordered every available law enforcement officer to the Purdy farm,' then it'd make some sense."

"Well, even if it was the wrong man, it should keep Davenport out of our hair for a while. All we have to do is make it through tomorrow."

"You know, we could load up and go tonight. Check into a motel . . ."

Marlys turned back to the television: "Let's stick with the program. One more day."

"Davenport might have seen my truck. Or maybe it was the other guy, but one of them did. I'll move it out behind the cornfield, in case he shows up here," Cole said.

"Not a bad idea. Don't do it until tomorrow, after Jesse leaves for the farmers' market. Davenport won't be here tonight, they'll be investigating the shooting scene tomorrow."

"How do you know that?"

"From watching *CSI* reruns," Marlys said. "You say you didn't leave anything behind, but they don't know that and they'll be going over that field inch by inch tomorrow. That'll take time. All we need is one more day. All you have to do is stay out of sight."

"I can do that."

Coverage of the shooting took up the first ten minutes of the newscast and then moved on to the killing of Anson Palmer in Iowa City, which Marlys hadn't heard about.

"What? What in God's name has happened?" she blurted.

"Don't know . . ."

They watched the news report on Palmer, and the weather, then during the sports, Marlys said, "Grace. I betcha Grace killed him, or one of her bomber pals. They don't like the idea of him talking to me about Lennett Valley. I told Grace about that."

"What if she doesn't like the idea of us knowing?" Cole asked.

Marlys considered that, then said, "I don't think she'd come after us. But keep your gun handy."

"One more day," Cole said. "All day tomorrow, I'm gonna be itchin' like I got poison ivy."

When the news was done, and they'd turned off the TV, Marlys said to Cole, "One thing we've never talked about is what Jesse might do if Davenport and a bunch of cops come down on us. Jesse's seen you working in the barn, getting ready."

"You think he might give us up?" Cole asked.

"He might think he's doing us a favor, protecting us from ourselves," Marlys said.

"That's bullshit."

"I know, but what can we do about it?" Marlys asked. "I'm not going to do something that would hurt him."

Cole stared at the blank-screen TV for a moment, then said to Marlys, "I know how to handle Jesse . . . but I'd have to get going."

"What do you have in mind?"

He told her, and she thought about it, then said, "It's mean, but it could work."

Jesse had been drinking about every night — not a lot to do in town if you didn't drink — and Cole found him, a little after eleven o'clock, in Gabbert's Bar and Grill, chalking up a cue tip while waiting his turn at the coin-op pool table.

"What're you doing up this late?" Jesse asked, when Cole slouched over with his beer.

Cole didn't answer, took a tug at the bottle, shrugged, and his eyes flicked away.

Jesse looked at him with curiosity: "Had a fight with Ma?"

"No." Cole turned to his brother and said, "I don't want you to get in no trouble."

"What?" Jesse asked. "What happened?"

"I was talking to Charlie Watts. He said Clark Berg was over to Russo's with a couple of other guys, Stout and Merritt, and they were going over to Willie's and see if she'd pull a train."

Jesse stared at him for a moment, then said, "Sonofabitch," and put the pool cue he was holding back on the wall rack.

"I thought you ought to know, because, you know, Caralee's in the next bedroom over," Cole said. "If she really does pull a train, it'll get noisy, and with Caralee right there . . . I don't know that Willie would do that, you'd know better than me."

"I know that bitch would fuck Merritt if she had a chance, and she's already fuckin' Berg," Jesse said. "There's no way she can do it around Caralee. No way that's gonna happen."

Jesse went steaming out of the bar and Cole followed, calling, "Don't do nothin' crazy, Jesse," and Jesse got in his truck and roared away. Cole went back into the bar, to the bartender, and said, "Gotta use your phone, Jim."

The bartender pulled a phone out from under the bar and Cole called the cops: "He doesn't have a gun or anything, but he's drunk, and there's gonna be a hell of a fight. I don't want nobody to get hurt. Naw, I'm not gonna give you my name, but you better get somebody over there in a hurry."

Jesse was flying blind. He knew he was drunk, at least a little, but the idea of his daughter listening . . . he was flying blind. When he got to Willie's place, his old apartment, there were a few trucks in the small parking lot, but none that he recognized as belonging to Berg, Stout, or Merritt.

He parked and jogged around to the front door, twice stumbling over his own feet. There was a security pad there, but it didn't work and he pushed the door open, jogged up the stairs and down the hall to the apartment. He banged on the door, and a few seconds later, heard Willie: "Who's that?"

"It's me. Jesse."

"Get the fuck away from here," she

screamed.

"Open the door, goddamnit, or I'll kick the fuckin' thing down," Jesse yelled.

"I'm calling the cops."

Two seconds later, he heard footsteps on the stairs, more than one guy. Berg, Stout, and Merritt, he thought, and he turned to face them.

Two cops came around the corner. In the back of his drunk mind, Jesse thought, *Jesus, that was quick.*

Cole walked out to his truck, took his time driving over to Willie's place. When he was a block away, he saw two cops leading Jesse, handcuffed, to a cop car. Willie was at the front door of the apartment house, screaming at all of them. A few neighbors had come out on their lawns to watch. Willie, Jesse, and the cops were all caught in the high-beam headlights of the two cop cars, like people on a stage. Cole hung back: he didn't want the cops — or Jesse or Willie — to pick him out. When the cops got Jesse to the first car, one of them gave him a straw to blow on.

Drunk driving test.

The cop checked the straw, talked some more to Jesse, and then put him in the backseat. Then both cops went to talk with

Willie, and Caralee came out of the house and took hold of her mother's leg. One of the cops patted her on the head, and they went back to their cars and drove off.

Perfect.

Cole called Marlys and said, "The cops got him. He's fine, he's not hurt. Willie had that restraining order, so that'll be one thing, and then I think they got him for drunk driving. They did a blow test right out front of the apartment, that'll be another. With us not answering the phone and nobody to bail him out, he'll be in there for a couple days anyway. And with the paper not coming out until Thursday, nobody'll know until then that he was busted."

"Feel bad about it, though," Marlys said. "He's gonna miss the market tomorrow. Those vegetables gonna go bad."

"I feel bad, too, but he's safe and out of the way. I can call John Pugh early tomorrow morning. He'll be running his stand somewhere, I'll see if he'll take our produce with him," Cole said. "I'm on my way back. Got to get going early tomorrow. We got a lot to do."

TWENTY-ONE

At the Grinnell hospital the next morning, Lucas was told that Robertson had been transferred to a medical center in Des Moines two hours earlier, that he was conscious and responding, that his outlook was better, but he was not yet safe. He could move his hands and feet when asked to do so, which meant that there was no unexpected spinal involvement.

That was mostly good news. After leaving the hospital, he drove out to the Burton place, where he found seven law enforcement vehicles parked in the yard, from various jurisdictions, including a state car driven by Randy Ford. A deputy told Lucas that Ford was out in the cornfield with a half dozen other cops, including two state crime-scene people, looking for anything that might point them at the shooter. As far as the deputy knew, they hadn't found anything yet.

Lucas kept a travel pack in the back of his truck, with equipment and clothing he might need but wouldn't normally wear. The pack included jeans, a canvas shirt, and hiking boots, which he'd put on when he got up. Now he tramped across the road from the Burton farm and down through the field, following the path they'd found the previous night. The morning was still cool, with the sweet smell of corn everywhere. He caught up with the search crew about two-thirds of the way down to where the truck had been parked.

They'd found absolutely nothing.

Ford came over, wearing a blue DEA ball cap, shook his head, and said, "You think the guy might belong to some nut group, and I'm thinking, they might be paramilitary or something. He knew what he was doing. Pulled you in, was set up in exactly the right spot for the shot, was gone before anybody could get here, didn't leave as much as a matchstick behind. Even if he had, I suspect he'd have been wearing gloves."

"Has anybody been down to the truck site?"

"Yeah. We started that right away," Ford said. "We did get a foot-long tread imprint, so if we ever find the truck, we'll be able to figure out if it's the same kind of tire."

"If we get to that point, we'll already know who it is," Lucas said.

"I'm thinking about trial evidence," Ford said.

The search crew was literally going through the field inch by inch, and Lucas joined them, moving each of the hundreds of corn plants along the shooter's flight path, looking for anything that might hold DNA or a fingerprint: a scrap of paper, a rifle shell, a wad of gum. Lucas would prefer a fingerprint to DNA, because there'd be some prospect of sending it to the FBI and getting an answer back the same day.

At ten o'clock they emerged onto the side road. After minutely inspecting the roadside ditch, they crossed the road to where two more cops and a crime-scene investigator were finishing a hands-and-knees search around the truck site.

They all wound up walking together back to the Burton place, on the shoulder of the road, and Ford said, "If your theory is right and these people are going after Bowden, and maybe at the state fair, you've got about twenty-six hours from right now to find them."

"Getting tight," Lucas admitted.

■ ■ ■ ■

At the Burton place, they stopped in for a glass of water, and Sandra Burton asked, "If you interviewed everybody in the party, how come you never came to me? I was pretty active in it, back in the eighties."

"The list is more current than that," Lucas said, propping his butt against the kitchen sink. The sink gave off the faint sulfury smell of well water, although the glass of water she'd given him tasted fine. "The problem is, the list still has about a hundred names on it that we haven't gotten to. We haven't been able to dig into anybody, because there're simply too many and we don't have the time. We've been focusing on the Iowa City area. We have three murders and the two dead men are pretty closely linked. We think the third murder was committed to eliminate a witness that the killers didn't know would be there."

"You want me to look at that list? I might have some ideas," Burton said.

"Sure. That'd be great," Lucas said.

Lucas went out to the truck and got the list, returned to the kitchen and handed it to Burton. She scanned it for a moment, smiled once, and said, "Gosh, I'd forgotten

341

some of these people. Are they all still with the party?"

"That's what Grace Lawrence tells us, and so far, everybody we've talked to admits to being a member," Lucas said.

"Grace Lawrence," Burton mused. "She was a crazy one. Her and that girlfriend of hers, Betsy — what was Betsy's name?"

She scanned the list again, and then said, "Betsy's not here. She was a member, though. I mean, she joined *after* some of the people on this list."

"Huh. You think Grace might have left her off deliberately?" Lucas asked.

"What do I know?" Burton asked. "Grace and Betsy hung out a lot, for a long time. We might have thought they were gay, except they kept coming around with these mountain-man boyfriends."

"What does that mean?" Lucas asked. "Mountain man?"

"Oh, you know. Rural hippies," Burton said. "They lived on a farm outside of Hills."

"Grace still lives in Hills," Lucas said.

"I think I heard that," Burton said. "Anyway, she and Betsy were these latter-day hippies, peasant blouses over their perky little boobies and hair down to the cracks of their asses, guys had beards, and you'd go to a party at their place and the guys would be sharpening chain saws in the living room. Like they just happened to need to sharpen the saws during the party. My first husband, who was an actual farmer, you know, he used to laugh at them. Bunch of posers."

"You didn't get along," Lucas said.

"Oh, I got along well enough with Grace and Betsy," Burton said. "Damnit it, what was Betsy's last name? Something unusual — it's right on the tip of my tongue. I know one of the guys was named Harrison. Same as Harrison Ford. We went to see *Return of the Jedi* with them, when that movie came out."

"You say Grace was crazy?" Lucas asked.

"She was always giving speeches about direct action. How we had to go to direct action. Direct action was never defined, but you know, we all had the feeling it was more than singing 'We Shall Overcome.' "

"If I get a chance, I'll ask her about it," Lucas said.

Burton: "Instead of that huge list, you should get the names of the people who'd go to the meetings at Joe Likely's place. That's the real core of the party, what's left of it."

"What meetings?" Lucas asked.

"They have quarterly meetings at Joe's place," Burton said. "I used to get e-mails

343

for them, but I didn't go to the meetings anymore. Always the same thing, we gotta do this or that, and they never do this or that. I think the last one . . . let me check." She led the way out of the kitchen to the front parlor, where an iMac sat on a repurposed dining table. She brought the computer up and went to her e-mail, scanned through it, said, "I never delete anything, I've got like fifteen million e-mails . . ." and then, "Here it is. June fourteenth. That was the last meeting."

"Two months ago."

"Yes. The next meeting would have been in September. If you can get a list of names at the last meeting, you'd have the real hardcore members. They'd all be close to Joe and Anson Palmer. Anson went to all of the meetings — they were the only people who'd talk to him."

"Huh. A list like that could be helpful," Lucas said.

They chatted for a few more minutes, Lucas learned nothing more, gave her a card with a phone number, then went out to his truck and fired it up. Sat for a moment, then called Bell Wood. "What's up?" Wood asked.

"I heard Robertson was moved. You got any more news?"

"Yeah, we talk to his partner every half hour or so," Wood said. "He says Jerry's pretty much out of it, because of the pain medication, but when he does come around, he's coherent enough. He knows he was shot, he knows you were with him, doesn't remember anything after he went down except that he kept getting gravel in his mouth."

"Then he'll make it," Lucas said.

"Remains to be seen. One thing, he was shot with a solid core slug, like military ammo. That isn't the most common thing. If he'd been shot with a hunting bullet, he'd be in a lot worse shape, getting hit in the lung like he was."

"Anything on the DNA from Grace Lawrence?" Lucas asked.

"Yeah, I should have called you before this. We got it back a couple of hours ago, but with Jerry being shot and all, we weren't thinking about it. Not her. No way. And nobody related to her."

"Damnit."

"Yeah. Too bad. I had hopes," Wood said.

"One additional thing on that dairy bomb deal," Lucas said. "I talked to Sandra Burton a few minutes ago, and she said Grace was a little crazy back then, always calling for direct action. She also had a girlfriend named Betsy and the two of them lived with what this woman called 'mountain-man boyfriends.' She said the two women, Grace and Betsy, had hair down to the cracks of their asses and wore peasant blouses over their perky little boobies — her words, not mine — and the two guys had beards. Mountain-man beards. They lived on a farm outside of Hills."

"Damnit, Lucas, that's them! They're the bombers," Wood said. "That's exactly how the motel guy described them. We got DNA from the wrong woman."

"I don't know. Could be," Lucas said.

"Give me a number for Burton. We need to know who this Betsy is."

Lucas gave him Burton's phone number and address, and added, "One of the boyfriends was named Harrison. That's the first name. You might go back and look at arrest records from farm protests at the time. They were apparently pretty big in them."

"I will do that," Wood said.

Lucas went back to the motel where he'd spent the night and asked to check back in. They said the room wasn't ready yet, but he said that since he was the only one who'd stayed there, he was happy to check back in just as if he'd never left, damp towels and all. The motel manager saw the wisdom in that, and five minutes later Lucas was spreading across the second bed all the paper he'd collected during the investigation.

And started drawing on his legal pad.

The drawings wouldn't make sense to anyone else, but Lucas used them to try to integrate geographic information with time data, of who knew what, and when they knew it, and how that might lead to a murder. At noon he went out for Diet Cokes and mini-doughnuts and an Iowa road map.

He simply couldn't put together the information from Kidd, concerning the probable location of the people who sent the messages to Henderson, with the timing of the killings well to the east, around Iowa City. He concluded that Likely and Palmer were on the edge of the conspiracy. They'd either been told about it or had guessed it after talking to Lucas, had refused to cooperate or had threatened to give it up, and had to be killed as a result.

It was probable, he thought, that Palmer and Likely were killed by different members of the conspiracy — if there were two killers, rather than one (or even one with a murderous son, as long as the son was in the same location as the mother), then the time problems became irrelevant. He knew that Lawrence couldn't have killed Likely, but she certainly could have killed Palmer.

If, of course, she'd killed anyone at all. He was leaning in her direction because she'd been fairly close to both Likely and Palmer, and Robertson had been shot shortly after he'd spoken to her.

Was it possible, he wondered, as he got up and stretched his legs, that Robertson really *was* the target of the sniper? He thought about that, but that was another difficult proposition to accept: the first shot had come almost immediately after Robertson had gotten out of the truck. The sniper, in the dying light of day, would hardly have had time to figure out which large sport-coated cop was which, and had shot the one getting out of the driver's side of Lucas's truck.

How did they know it was Lucas's truck? Because somebody had seen it and had either passed the word along or acted on it directly. And Lucas had been the one the sniper called — he'd have had no reason to think that Robertson would be in the truck. Lawrence, even if traumatized by Robertson's tough-guy interrogation, wouldn't have known.

No. Lucas had been the target.

He was working through it when Neil Mitford called.

"Yeah?"

"Where are you?" Mitford asked.

"Grinnell."

"Good. We're headed for Des Moines. The hotel is fifty-two minutes from you, or, given the way you drive, forty-five minutes. Bowden is across the street and Gardner is five minutes away. We'd like you to attend a briefing for all the campaigns, by the Iowa campaign security team."

"Man, I really don't have a lot of time to fuck around."

"You're not fucking around. Tomorrow's D-Day," Mitford said. "We need to make sure that all our shit is coordinated, and I need the Iowa security people to see your face."

"All right, I get that. What time?" Lucas asked.

"Ten o'clock tonight."

Lucas went back to his paper. Bell Wood called: "Betsy Rose Skira and Harrison John Williams the Third."

"How'd you find them?"

"After telling everybody to search every known radical database, I decided to run Betsy *and* Harrison as a unit through the vital records. They got married in '91, moved to Cedar Rapids, divorced in '97. Betsy changed her name back to Skira and remarried in 2000. Harrison Williams is still single as far as we know — nothing in the records about another marriage, but he could have gotten married again in Vegas or something. Skira's still in Cedar Rapids, Williams is in Stone City, which is a tiny place northeast of Cedar Rapids."

"Not so close to Iowa City," Lucas said, as he wrote the names on his drawing charts.

"An hour or so, I suppose. Not right on top of it, though," Wood said.

"Randy Ford is still around here somewhere, right?"

"Yeah. He should still be out at Sandra Burton's place," Wood said.

"Listen, I got this idea . . ."

Lucas outlined the idea and there was a moment's silence, then Wood laughed and said, "Man, I got a feeling that the lawyers might have a problem or two or eight with that."

"Why?"

" 'Cause we're tricking her, we're leading her along, we're setting her up . . ."

"Bell?"

"Yeah?"

"I'm not a cop. You told me so yourself," Lucas said.

"Yeah, but —"

"You won't need anything I get from her, to get her, or Skira, or Harrison, or the fourth guy, on the dairy bombing. I won't record anything, so it can't be thrown out. Everything you'd use against her, you've already got. What I'd be getting from her goes only to the conspiracy against Bowden. All I want to do is break the conspiracy, and I don't care if we get her on that, because you'll have her on the dairy bombing . . . if she did it."

"Well, hell . . . go for it. But Jesus, be careful."

"Oh, boy," Ford said, when Lucas found him at Burton's. "You're sure you want to do this?"

"Yup. I want you to witness the phone call and hear what she has to say to me," Lucas said. "Come on out to the truck, I'll put it on speaker and tell her I'm driving."

Lucas called Lawrence. She said, not bothering to say hello, "Lucas! I had nothing to do with that Robertson shooting. I didn't know where he was going, I had no idea."

"How'd you hear about it?"

"Lucas, this is Iowa," Lawrence said. "We have about one murder a week in the whole state. It's all over the news. It's on every fifteen minutes. State investigators don't get sniped in Iowa."

"Okay. Listen, are you at home?" Lucas asked.

"No, I'm at a supermarket in Iowa City," she said.

"I need you to take a look at some of your older records. You know, whatever you have. I'm looking for a Betsy Skira and a Harrison Williams. Do you know them?"

There was a crashing sound at the other end of the call, and Lucas said, "Hello? Hello?"

Lawrence: "Sorry, I fumbled the phone. Who'd you say?"

"Betsy Skira and a Harrison Williams. I got a tip from a party member that I should take a close look at them. Skira fits the description of the woman we're looking for, and they may have been involved in some violence in the past, too."

"I remember Betsy. I think she lives up in Waterloo. Or Cedar Rapids, it might be Cedar Rapids," Lawrence said.

"I can't find her online, she may have gotten married or something," Lucas said. "I need anything you've got on her."

"What kind of violence was she involved in?" Lawrence asked. "I don't remember anything like that, or anybody saying anything."

"There was some kind of bombing here, a long time ago," Lucas said. "People got killed. My . . . source . . . tells me that Skira might have been involved. The bombers apparently stayed in a motel in a place called Amazing Grace and the state investigators still have the sheets from the motel beds. That means they'll have DNA. If Skira's in on this Bowden thing, I can use that threat of the DNA to break the conspiracy down. I'll tell her that if she doesn't cough up what she knows, I'll talk to the DCI about the sheets."

"Oh my God, I remember that bombing," Lawrence said. "I don't know if I'd have anything on Betsy Skira. When I got the secretary's job, I got about ten boxes of records that I've never looked at. There could be something in there."

"You gotta go home and look," Lucas said. "This could be a really big deal. Skira, Williams . . . if there's anything there, it could help."

"It could take a day or two to go through

that stuff . . . unless you want to come down and help."

"I'm getting short on time. The fair walk is tomorrow," Lucas said.

"Then I might not be able —"

"Listen, I'm on the road right now," Lucas said. "Goddamnit, we need to do this. I can be there in an hour. You get that stuff out, we'll rip through it. We're running out of time, I need to get to Skira."

Lucas got off the phone and Ford said, "Well, she bit. Sorta."

"Yeah." Lucas looked at his watch. "We gotta roll. Time is getting short."

Twenty-Two

Ford had lights on his car, so he led the way back to Lawrence's house in Hills, rolling down I-80 at a hundred-plus, then south on Highway 218, through the sea of beans and corn. Lucas had read somewhere that the acreage of beans, corn, and wheat planted in the American Midwest and plains states was greater than the area of France and Great Britain put together. Iowa was right in the heart of that, and after a week driving around the state, he was a believer.

At Hills, they got off 218 and rodeoed at the Casey's General Store, around to the side, a bit out of sight. Lucas got a pullover nylon rain shell out of the travel pack in the back of the truck and pulled it over his head.

"How do I look?" he asked.

"Like a fuckin' moron," Ford said. The sun was beating down on the side of his face and he was sweating behind his silvered aviators. "It's eighty-eight degrees out here."

"Ah, shit. She's no dummy, either," Lucas said. "I got that hunting shirt . . ."

Lucas dug out the wrinkled olive-drab hunting shirt, pulled it on. "How about now?"

"Still look like a fuckin' moron, but you could say you've been working in a cornfield . . . she might buy that."

"I *was* working in a cornfield," Lucas said.

"Then she might buy it. Maybe. If you get lucky," Ford said.

"Fuck it," Lucas said. "Let's go."

Hills couldn't have been as much as a mile square, with a few hundred people living there. Lucas pulled into Lawrence's house a minute and a half after leaving Casey's. He climbed out, pulled the shirt down, got his yellow pad. He was wearing sunglasses and left them on, to hide his eyes. He planned to lie a lot.

Lawrence met him at the screen door, pushing it open, then closing both the screen and the interior door behind him. She said, "I've got the boxes in the dining room, but I haven't found anything about a Betsy."

"At least it's cool in here," Lucas said. "I spent the whole goddamn morning crawling through a cornfield and didn't find a single thing."

"What happened out there?"

They stood in the kitchen for a moment and he recounted the ambush. "That's awful," she said, a hand at her throat. "Let me tell you something, privately, though. Robertson was terrible to me. Terrible and mean. I thought . . . he might hit me. He's a bully. The point is — did he go to another house after me? Could somebody he bullied, maybe followed him with a gun?"

"No. The shooter was after me, not after Robertson," Lucas said. "Anyway, let's go look at those files."

She'd piled ten or twelve banker's boxes on the living room floor, still with dust on the lids. "They were stored down in the basement. Almost killed me getting them all up here."

Lucas put a box on the dining room table, popped the top, and found a pile of political leaflets and press statements along with printing bills and other miscellaneous paper. "Doesn't look promising," he said.

He put two more boxes on the table and pulled the lids off. The boxes left an imprint of dust on the front of his shirt, and he brushed it off with his fingers. "About wrecked this shirt out in the corn. I must smell like a locker room."

"A little sweaty," she said. She took a chair behind the table and said, "What about this Betsy person? The PPPI has *never* advocated any kind of violence."

Lucas had taken a chair across from her and pulled a stack of paper out of the banker's box. "We think she might have had her own group, inside the PPPI," Lucas said. He thumbed through some of the papers, then looked up at her and added, "I've got to talk to my boys at the DCI yet, but I think there's a good chance she did that dairy bomb, whatever that was. I don't actually give a shit about the dairy bomb, so before I talk to the DCI people, I thought I'd try to run her down and make a side deal with her — I won't ask about the bomb if she talks to me about the Bowden conspiracy. If she doesn't give me something on that, screw her, she goes down for the bomb. If she's a bomber."

"What if she's not?" Lawrence asked.

Lucas shrugged. "Then she's not and I've wasted some time that I don't have to waste. But if she is . . . she's looking at life without parole. With that as a crowbar, we should be able to get anything out of her that we want. You know, offer her a manslaughter deal with a few years inside if she talks, or life in prison if she doesn't."

"That's really . . . brutal."

"Not as brutal as a bomb," Lucas said. He looked at the paper in his hands. "Man, this looks like junk. We need only member lists. Do any of the boxes have like lists of members . . . ?"

He turned back to look at her as the old revolver came up from behind the table and the thought flashed through Lucas's mind that he might have really, really screwed up. She said, "I'm sorry," and shot him in the chest.

She shouldn't have said anything, because by the time she pulled the trigger, Lucas already had the edge of the table in his hands. The muzzle blast, confined in the small room, was terrific, and so was the impact of the bullet, but he hung on to the table and lifted it up and threw it at her, and she and her chair toppled over behind the table.

She was on her butt, legs under the table, still with the pistol in her hand, when he cleared the table and punched her in the forehead and she went flat. The door behind them exploded open and Ford was there, pistol in his hand, and Lucas stepped on her gun hand with his hiking boot and she yelped when he twisted the gun loose.

"Roll her," Ford said. They got her untangled from the table, still stunned by the blow to the head, and Ford cuffed her hands behind her back. He asked Lucas, "You okay?"

"Yeah. Shot me right in the heart," Lucas said.

He peeled off the hunting shirt, then the bulletproof vest beneath it, and pulled up the thin white T-shirt under the vest. A red spot the size of his palm was blooming to the left of his heart.

"That's gonna make a mark," Ford said.

"I've been more bruised up and cut up in a week in Iowa than in ten years in Minnesota," Lucas said, touching his black eye, and the cuts beside it. He still had tape on the glass cuts on the other side. Then, "Let's get her up."

They got Lawrence sitting in a chair, still dazed, and Lucas brought the table upright, and his own chair. Ford said to Lawrence, "You have the right to remain silent . . ."

Lucas watched Lawrence's face as Ford read her rights, saw her eyes clearing out. When he'd finished with the rights, Ford asked her if she understood what he'd read. She nodded and Ford said, "I'm placing you under arrest for attempted murder."

Lucas said to Ford, "Why don't you go outside and call this in — see what Bell Wood wants us to do."

"Good idea," Ford said, and he might as well have winked at Lucas as he stepped away. And to Lawrence: "Hey, Miz Lawrence? You're gonna need a new door."

When he was gone, Lucas said to Lawrence, "I'm not recording this and I'm not a cop."

"You're a lying asshole fascist," she said. Her head was down, her teeth clenched.

"I can't arrest you, I can't do anything to you, Grace. But — I don't care about the dairy that you and Betsy blew up, I don't care too much about the fact that you tried to murder me, since you didn't get it done," Lucas said. "What I care about is, you're part of a conspiracy to kill Michaela Bowden. I need to stop that. Here's the thing — Ford's gonna get you for attempted murder or aggravated assault, which means you're going to do time. How much time you do, though, depends on whether you cooperate now. We can always reduce the charge if you cooperate, if you just tell me —"

"Fuck you," she said. "You . . . you kept coming back to me, and I got you your

361

boxes, and then you tried to sexually assault me, which is why you kept coming back, and why I shot you . . ."

Lucas said, "That's not bad — but nobody'll believe you. I *came* here with Ford. He was right outside the door the whole time, listening. To get back to the dairy bombing — there's menstrual fluid on the motel sheets, along with some semen. When we grab Betsy and Harrison — we know where they are, by the way — the DNA will match, and one of them will give up you and your boyfriend to get a reduced sentence for themselves. Looked at from the other direction, you could give up Betsy and Harrison and your ex-boyfriend, and cut a whole lot of years off your own sentence. We need to know who's hunting Bowden. That'll also give us the sniper who shot Robertson."

"Fuck Robertson," she snarled. "If there'd been a witness here, I'd have sued you for a million dollars for what that fascist faggot did to me."

"I don't think you want to spend time around any kind of court, Grace," Lucas said.

He sat there looking at her for a moment, and she suddenly began to cry, her shoulders shaking against the cuffs behind her back. "My house . . . my garden . . ."

"Shouldn't have shot me," Lucas said. "I suspect you're the one who killed Anson Palmer, too, so we're going to look for any piece of DNA we can find there."

"Fuck you, fuck you . . ."

"Give me the goddamn names, Grace," Lucas said. "C'mon. Please. Talk to me. Save yourself."

"Fuck you."

Ford came back, looked at Lucas, asked, "Get a name?"

"Not unless it's 'Fuck you,' " Lucas said.

They moved a few feet away, past the doorway to the kitchen, where they could watch Lawrence as she sat behind the table on a wooden chair. Ford said quietly, "We've got the Johnson County sheriff on the way and we'll get a crime-scene crew here quick enough. Since she shot you and this is a crime scene, we can tear the place apart. We won't need a search warrant. If you want to take a look around . . ."

"I want to take a look at her computer, for sure. It may be password-protected — if we could get that computer guy down here from Iowa City, he cracked Anson Palmer's password in about five minutes."

"I'll call him. You okay?"

"Yeah. Almost peed my pants when she came up with that old revolver — thought it might be a .357. That wouldn't have been good."

"No kiddin'. We'd be scraping your kidneys off the back of that vest."

The sheriff's deputies came in with lights and sirens and Ford went out to meet them. Lucas stepped over to Lawrence and said, "I'm not gonna plead with you anymore, but I'm curious about one thing. What were you going to do with my body?"

She looked up and said, "I hadn't worked that out." She thought for a moment, then said, "I would have waited until night. I've got a wheelbarrow and I would have had your car and keys. I know a place where I could have parked you by the river. They wouldn't have found you for a week."

"How would you have gotten home?" Lucas asked.

She thought about that for a bit, then said, "Bicycle. I would have thrown my bike in the back of the car."

The back door, what was left of it, scraped open again, and they could hear boot steps on the stoop, and Lucas said, "This is it,

Grace. Who's going after Bowden? Give me something that'll give you a break."

She shook her head. "Fuck you."

The cops took her out, and on the way she cried out again, "My house," and then she was gone. With the silence settling on him, Lucas looked around the sweet-smelling kitchen, the kitchen that smelled of fresh bread and lettuce, and thought about all those "fuck yous." She hadn't, he realized, ever denied knowing about the conspiracy pointed at Bowden. She'd simply said, "Fuck you." And that, Lucas thought, meant that she knew something.

That he'd stepped on one end of the conspiracy thread.

The computer guy from Iowa City arrived an hour later, looked at Lawrence's computer and cracked the password five minutes later.

"Must have sky-high rates if you only get paid for five minutes at a time," Lucas said, as the other man packed up his little tool kit.

"My rates are only middling," the guy said. "But I charge day rates, like photographers. Use me for six hours, day rate. Use me for five minutes, day rate."

"Ah. What happens when somebody refuses to pay a day rate?"

The guy smiled and said, "They don't do that, you know, if they want to stay online."

When Lucas first got a list of the membership from Lawrence, she'd plugged in a thumb drive that she kept in an office supply box on the table. He thought he'd look at it first: plugged in the drive, found the membership list and a hundred files of new releases and PPPI position papers. He scanned them quickly; not much of interest in the position papers, but a quick look at the membership list turned up, to his surprise, Betsy Skira's name, address, e-mail, and phone number. He checked Lawrence's e-mail and found two e-mails to Skira. Neither involved the PPPI — they were merely e-mail visits, plans to get together for lunch.

Skira hadn't been on the list that she'd given him. Lawrence had tried to keep her friend out of any investigation. She hadn't done it while Lucas was watching her print it, though, so she must have done it earlier. Anson Palmer, Lucas thought, had called her to warn her that he was coming.

Lucas set the thumb drive aside and went through Lawrence's e-mail, looking for correspondence involving the June meeting at Likely's house. There was lots of it, but all but two e-mails about the meeting were outgoing, routine notices of time and place.

Of the incoming two, George Spate said he wouldn't be able to attend, because of medical problems. Lucas checked Robertson's interviews, and found Spate's name, but he hadn't yet been interviewed. He lived in the town of Fairfax, a few miles outside Cedar Rapids, and about a half hour away. The other one, a Marcia Boone, lived in New Sharon, a little less than an hour and a half away. Robertson had talked to her.

Lucas called Spate, but there was no answer. Boone, on the other hand, picked up on the first ring. Lucas identified himself and Boone blurted, "I felt so bad about Jerry. I couldn't believe it when I saw it on the news."

"We think he's going to be all right," Lucas said. "Listen, we need some help in finding the sniper who shot him. Did you go to a meeting at Joe Likely's place in June?"

"Yes, I did," she said. "I went every three months. Why?"

"We really need the names of the people who went," Lucas said. "Do you remember who was there?"

"Same people who were there every time,"

she said. "Although, quite a few people have dropped out. More would have come in September, for the annual barbecue."

"Who are those people?" Lucas asked. "Could you give me their names?"

"Well, I guess . . ."

She gave him twelve names. Scanning down the list, Lucas figured that he and Robertson and the others had interviewed all but three of them, because most of the people on the list lived around Iowa City and Mount Pleasant. Of the people on the list, he knew that Grace Lawrence hadn't killed Likely, because she'd been at the school, and Marlys Purdy hadn't killed Anson Palmer, because neither she nor her son would have had time to commit the murder and get home before Lucas arrived to interview her.

But then . . . He scratched his forehead.

If there were two killers — and he now knew that Lawrence could kill — then Purdy, or for that matter, any one of the people who didn't live too far from Likely's, could have been the killer. He went to his map of Iowa, where he'd plotted the PPPI member locations, and drew a circle around those who could have killed Likely between the time Lucas had left and the probable killers had left.

The circle made him grin, but not a happy grin: it included almost everyone.

But he'd missed something. There was something in the papers or on the computer that should have given him a name, or at least an idea. He'd seen it, but it hadn't registered, except subconsciously. What was it?

He dug at it, but nothing came up. Lucas looked at his watch: 4:45.

Ford came back: "We need a quick statement and to start processing the place."

"The statement's gotta be quick," Lucas said, checking his watch again. Now 4:48. Time was slipping away. There were, what, seventeen hours before Bowden started walking down the street at the state fair?

No time.

TWENTY-THREE

Unable to think of anything better to do, Lucas left Hills and headed north and a bit east to the town of West Branch. He wanted to look at Gloria Whitehead, one of the three people, and the only woman, who'd been at the June meeting at Likely's and who had not yet been interviewed. He let the truck's nav system get him there, while he picked at his subconscious, trying to think what he might have seen, and missed, at Lawrence's house.

A half hour after leaving Hills, he was passing a bunch of signs advertising Herbert Hoover's birthplace, which was apparently in West Branch. Even if he had time, he wouldn't have stopped: his interest in Herbert Hoover couldn't be characterized as minuscule, because it wasn't that large, though West Branch itself seemed pleasant enough.

Gloria Whitehead lived in an older, neatly

kept two-story white house on North Fifth Street, almost a duplicate of Lawrence's house in Hills.

He parked in the shade of a curbside maple tree and walked up the front sidewalk to Whitehead's house, stopped to wipe off the sheen of sweat that had instantly appeared on his forehead — nobody likes to talk to a sweaty stranger — and climbed up on the porch and knocked on the screen door. The interior door was open wide and a woman called, "Coming . . ."

She took her time, clumping through the house, and when she got to the door, a dishcloth in her hands, Lucas asked, "Miz Whitehead?"

"Yes?" Whitehead was a plump middle-aged woman with curly white hair, rimless glasses, and a friendly smile, almost precisely as described by Elmer Henderson.

Lucas explained his mission, asked if she could add to the list of people who'd been at Likely's meeting in June. She checked his list, then shook her head. "That's about it, I think that's everybody," she said. "I'm sorry I couldn't help."

"That's okay," Lucas said. "Had to check."

He walked back to the truck, called Neil Mitford. "Where are you?"

"On the bus. Half hour west of Des

371

Moines," Mitford said.

"Is the governor with you? I need to talk to him," Lucas said.

"Yeah, he's right here. Hang on."

Henderson came up a few seconds later: "What's up?"

"This middle-aged woman you saw, with the curly white hair . . . she didn't have an artificial leg, did she?"

"What? An artificial leg?"

"Yeah, you know. A prosthetic. Plastic," Lucas said.

"I probably would have mentioned that if she had," Henderson said, after a long pause.

"Yeah, I thought you probably would have," Lucas said. "Sorry to have bothered you, Governor."

He hung up and pulled away from the curb. As he did, he saw Whitehead standing by the door, watching him go. He twiddled his fingers at her, and she lifted a hand, and he drove to the end of the block.

Where his subconscious poked him.

A couple of years earlier he'd broken a case in which a man was mistakenly identified by several different people as a person of interest. He'd found the right man, a serial killer, by showing a photo of the wrong man to a group of people in a grocery store, and asking, "Who do you know who looks like this?"

He thought for a moment, then turned around and drove back to Whitehead's house, stopped, walked to the door, and knocked again.

"Coming . . ." Whitehead clumped back to the door and said, "Hi, again."

"Hi. Listen, this is going to sound strange, but was there anybody at the Likely meeting who looks like you?" Lucas asked.

"You mean, with a fake leg?"

"No, no, no . . ." Lucas was a little embarrassed, without knowing why, since she wasn't. "I mean, a woman with curly white hair, about your build, about your age."

"Well, Marlys Purdy, of course. I thought you'd interviewed her," Whitehead said.

"I thought . . . I mean, she has brown hair."

"You've got the wrong Purdy, then," Whitehead said. "Marlys's hair is as white as a snowflake. From the waist up, we look like twins."

"Really," Lucas said. "You don't know if she has children, do you?"

"She has two grown boys. I have a couple of grown girls and we joked about getting them together."

Lucas said, "Really," again, and then, "Miz Whitehead, please don't tell anyone about our conversation. It's really important to keep it to yourself."

"I can do that, at least for a while," she said. "How long do I have to keep my mouth shut?"

"Let's say a week," Lucas suggested.

"I can do that," Whitehead said.

Lucas started down the steps, then turned back. "Uh, Miz Whitehead . . . have you ever seen her sons?"

"Yes. Several times. Since they were small."

"Does one of them have distinctive gray eyes?"

"That'd be Cole," she said.

Back in his truck, his subconscious poked him again. That thing about Skira being on Lawrence's computer list, but not on the printed one. That's what he'd seen, but not recognized — and he'd not recognized the implications of that.

Purdy hadn't been on the printed one, either — he'd found her by talking to the couple in What Cheer. He got the original list out and checked it. As he thought, Purdy was missing. The list was alphabetized, and the name above where Purdy's would have been was numbered 66, and the next one down was 68.

Lawrence had edited the paper list before she'd given it to him and had eliminated Purdy. He checked the point on the list where Skira should have been and found the numbers skipped again, from 77 to 79.

Lawrence had time to edit but not to renumber. He checked the rest of the list for skipped numbers and found none.

"Got her," he said aloud.

He called Ford: "I think I got our woman. The white-haired lady."

"Who is it?

"She's named Marlys Purdy and she lives in . . . uh, let me look . . . Pella. Not right in Pella, but a few miles out of town. I suspect our sniper is one of her sons, named Cole."

Lucas explained about the white hair and the change of hair color, and Ford said, "Okay, you maybe got her. I can't leave here yet, but I'll call Bell and get him to ship somebody out there. I assume you're going?"

"Yes. Right now."

Lucas took the truck out to I-80 and headed west.

Fuckin' Purdy.

He was about eighty-seven percent sure she was the right one — Pella was right where Kidd had thought the e-mails to Henderson might have come from — but the hair had fooled him: straight and brown instead of white and curly, but how long, in this day and age, did it take to go from one to the other? Two hours in a beauty parlor? That much?

He'd been chumped: Lawrence had probably told her that he was coming and about his description of the woman they were hunting.

He was ten miles down the road when Bell Wood called. "I'm coming myself and bringing another guy. I've never shot anyone, and what the hell, this might be my chance."

"Happy to have you."

Wood told Lucas to follow his nav system into Pella. "It should bring you right down Main Street. When you get to Franklin, take a right for a block. On the corner of Franklin and First, you'll see a windmill. I'll meet you at the windmill."

"The windmill."

"Yeah. Great big full-sized windmill. There are some restaurants around there, and I missed lunch and now I'm going to miss dinner. Call me when you get close, and I'll be standing under the windmill."

The run from West Branch to Pella took ninety minutes. As soon as Lucas saw the Main Street sign, he called Wood and said, "I'm coming down Main."

"We're on First, getting a Coke. We'll be at the mill in one minute."

Lucas was three minutes away, and when he saw the windmill looming above the street, he saw Wood and another man standing on the corner, hot dogs in one hand, cups of Coke in the other. He pulled into a parking space and got out. Wood came over, put the Coke on the hood of the truck, and shook hands. "Been a while," he said. Wood introduced the other man as Sam Greer.

Greer, a tall, thin man who looked like he might run marathons, shook hands and said, "Your reputation precedes you."

"Well, hell, nothing I can do about that," Lucas said. "I'm in a rush, here, guys, but I need a couple of hot dogs and we gotta talk about how we're gonna do this. If this is the sniper . . ."

"Well, we got the hot dog place," Wood said. "I brought a rifle and some gear for you, in case you didn't have it."

"I used to have a .45," Lucas said. "The

Grinnell cops have it now. I haven't had time to get it back."

"We gotcha covered, then," Wood said.

They got more hot dogs and more Cokes, and talked about how they'd get to the Purdy property. Wood hadn't had time to file for a search warrant, so they'd have to feel their way forward when they got to the farm. "If we think her son was the sniper, we're investigating, not searching," Wood said.

Lucas suggested that they begin by touching base with a neighbor, to ask about the gray-eyed son. "The one I saw was distinctly not gray-eyed."

The sun was still as much as an hour above the horizon, Lucas thought, as they trucked out toward the Purdy place, Lucas in the lead, Wood riding shotgun, Greer following in the state car.

They came over the top of a hill and Lucas said, "That's the Purdy place, straight ahead, above the turn." They were coming up to another house as he said it, and Lucas said, "I thought we could ask here."

They passed a mailbox that said "Souther," with a wooden sheep mounted

above it, and turned down the long driveway.

A woman was crossing the drive, carrying
a couple of buckets. When she saw them
coming, she stopped, looked at them for a
second, then hurried to the side of the
driveway, put the buckets down, and ran
into the house.

"Wonder what that was about?" Wood
asked.

"Don't know, but you might want to be
ready," Lucas said.

Wood slipped his pistol out of its holster,
rolled his window down, and sat with the
gun in his lap as Lucas pulled into the side
yard, Greer behind them.

Then a man came out of the house, wearing coveralls and a Fender hat, and walked
over to them. "Looks friendly enough,"
Wood said.

Lucas got out of the truck and the man
nodded and asked, "Who're you guys?"

Lucas said, "We're with the state Division
of Criminal Investigation."

Wood and Greer got out, Wood's gun back
in its holster, and Wood said, "I hope we
didn't startle your wife."

"She's shy," Souther said. "I mean, *really*
shy. Anyway, what's up?"

Wood told Souther about the investigation, and as he did, the woman eased out of the house, and Souther held a finger up to Wood, stopping him for a moment, and Souther called, "It's okay, Janette. These folks are police officers."

She drifted over, not looking at them, and Souther said, "So go on . . ."

Wood finished telling him about the investigation, and then Lucas said, "We think we need to talk to the Purdys. Marlys Purdy was described to us as a little heavy with white curly hair, which is right, but I saw her son, and he has blue eyes. The man we're looking for was described as having very distinctive gray eyes . . . think it might be another son."

From behind them, Janette Souther said, "Cole."

Souther glanced at her and said, "There are two sons and that sure sounds like him — Cole Purdy. You hardly ever see Cole without his gun, not when he's walking around on their land over there. You hear him shooting all the time. He's not a bad guy, not that I've seen. All the Purdys work hard. They're good neighbors."

"Have you seen them today?" Greer asked.

"I haven't," Souther said.

Janette Souther said, looking away from them all, as though she were talking to a pasture, "I saw them go. Cole and Marlys in her truck."

"White truck?" Lucas asked.

"No, it's blue. Cole has a white truck, though," Janette Souther said.

"When did they leave?" Wood asked.

"An hour ago." Now she was looking at her feet. Then, "Jesse Purdy is in jail."

Souther looked at his wife again and asked, "What? In jail?"

She nodded. "Amy told me."

Souther turned back to Lucas, Wood, and Greer and said, "Amy's the mail lady. She knows everything."

Wood asked, "In jail in Pella? Does Pella have a jail?"

"A small one," Souther said. "Mostly for overnights."

Lucas said to Janette, "You're saying they're not home, Marlys and Cole, and Jesse, the blue-eyed one, is in jail in Pella."

She said, "Yes."

Wood said to Lucas, "Let's run back into town, see what he has to say."

Lucas nodded and asked Souther, "Do you have a phone? If you see them come back, could you call? We're a little worried about Cole and his gun."

"I'll tell you something," Souther said, as he slipped his phone out of his pocket.

381

"Cole is . . . not quite right. He was in the National Guard and got sent to Iraq, and as I understand it, he was nearby when a couple of bombs went off — you know, those devices, whatever they call them."

"Improvised Explosive Devices — IEDs," Wood said. Wood was a major in the National Guard and had done a year in Iraq and another in Afghanistan. "I hate to hear that — that he's hurt."

"Yeah, that's it, IEDs," Souther said. "Anyway, he's had some trouble ever since, with" — he waved his fingers at his brain — "his brain, I guess. I don't know whether it's physical or psychological, but he's had his problems. Probably find out more from the VA."

"We'll check," Wood said.

Souther and Lucas traded phone numbers and names. Lucas cocked an eyebrow and asked, "David Souther? You're not the poet, are you?"

Souther, surprised but pleased, asked, "How'd you know?"

"I got about three of your books, man," Lucas said. "I collect poetry books. University of Chicago Press, right?"

"That's right. Jeez, I never met anyone before, you know, who wasn't on the poetry scene, who heard of me."

"Well, now you have," Lucas said. " 'Bobcats.' That's a great poem there. That's probably my favorite. And 'Winter Water.' "

As they were rolling out of the Southers' driveway, the couple watching them go, Wood said, "You honest to God collect poetry? I didn't know you were a delicate little rosebud."

"I'm pretty delicate," Lucas admitted. "You know, when I'm not beating somebody senseless."

TWENTY-FOUR

They were back in town eight minutes later, and Greer had an idea where the jail was. Lucas followed him, and they did find the jail, which was not much of a jail, more of a closet for people who wouldn't be there long.

A cop ushered them in, where blue-eyed Jesse Purdy was stretched out on a cot, looking not at all uncomfortable. He was reading a battered book called *Chevrolet: Yesterday and Today.*

"What?"

Wood identified himself and said, "We need to talk to your mother and brother, in a hurry . . . but they're not home. You know how we could get in touch?"

"Well, you could call them and ask," Jesse said, not getting up. "What's this all about?"

"We're wondering if they might have involved themselves with the Michaela Bowden campaign," Lucas said, hiding in the weeds of ambiguity.

Jesse sat up now and said, "Awww . . . shit. What'd they do?"

"You think they might have done something?" Wood asked.

"Well, they sure as hell don't like Bowden," Jesse said. "Not that it means much, you know."

"You don't think your brother might . . . try to hurt her? Mrs. Bowden?" Greer asked.

Jesse looked at all of them, then ran his hands through his hair and said, "Look, Cole isn't exactly right. Not since he got back from the war. But I don't think, no way . . ."

Lucas: "Would you be willing to go back out to the house with us, in case they've come back home? So we can talk?"

"Sure, if you could get me out of here. That fuckin' Cole is the guy who got me here in the first place."

"How was that?" Lucas asked.

Jesse gave him a quick summary of his talk with Cole in the bar and his arrest outside Willie's house. "I didn't mean to hurt her, or nothin', and she knows it. That restraining order was her lawyer's idea, to give me a hard time when I want to visit with Caralee."

"Why would your brother do that? I mean,

if it really was bullshit?" Lucas asked.

Jesse said, "I thought about that last night and this morning and . . . why he didn't come and get me out of here. Now . . ." His voice trailed off, and he looked away from them and said, "I don't give a shit about Michaela Bowden, no way. Might even vote for her, depending on who the Republicans put up. But Mom and Cole . . . I mean . . ." He turned back to them. "Were they getting me out of the way? Was there something they didn't want me to see? Get involved in?"

The cop didn't have the authority to release Jesse on his own, and when he tried to call the chief, the chief's wife said he was out running and didn't have a phone. He'd be back in fifteen minutes, if he didn't have a heart attack.

"I'd like to move before it gets dark," Lucas said to Wood. And to the cop, "If you can't release him on his own, could I bail him out?"

The cop brightened and said, "Yeah, I can do that. Five hundred dollars."

"Take a check?" Lucas asked.

Five minutes later they were on the street, and one minute after that, on the way to the Purdy farm, Jesse and Wood riding in Jesse's truck, Lucas following, Greer trailing. They turned off again at the Souther place, and when Souther came out, shadowed by his wife, Wood told them, "We need to leave Lucas's truck for a few minutes."

Souther nodded, and said to Jesse, "Hey, Jesse. Hope this is nothing."

"Yeah, man."

They armored up: SWAT-quality neck-high vests with crotch guards, .223 rifles for all three of the cops.

Jesse: "I don't think you need —"

Wood: "Jesse, you might be an all-right guy, but somebody sniped and almost killed one of my agents last night and tried to shoot Lucas here. We can't take the chance."

Jesse went pale under his farmer tan. "Oh, Jesus . . ."

Jesse led the way to the farm in his truck, Wood riding with him, Lucas and Greer in the state car. Lucas's truck was left behind, because Marlys Purdy had seen it.

The trip down to the house took only a minute. There was a light on in the kitchen area, but Jesse told Wood that the light was always on. "I don't think they're back yet. It's getting dark and Mom always turns the lights on early."

They pulled up to the side of the house, and Jesse got out first, followed by Wood, who left his rifle in the truck and carried a Glock in his hand, while Lucas and Greer carried the long guns, ready to go. Jesse tried the door, found it locked — "If they were here, it wouldn't be."

He unlocked the door and they followed him in, Jesse calling, "Ma? Cole? You here?"

No answer, and the silence had the kind of thick texture that meant that nobody was around. Lucas relaxed an inch and clicked the safety on the rifle, and then Jesse said, "Come on up here. I wanna check something."

He led the way up a narrow stairway to the second floor, and down a short hallway past a bathroom, and pushed a bedroom door open, and looked in. Nobody home. The room was furnished with a bed, a side table, a chest of drawers, and a gun safe. The safe was locked, but Jesse picked up one leg of the side table and scraped out a brass-colored key, and unlocked the safe.

Inside were a Bushmaster .223 with a thirty-round mag, a Ruger .22, a modern muzzle-loading rifle that looked like it could shoot a brick, and three shotguns. They could see a stack of ammo boxes on the interior shelves, and the butts of two pistols, both automatic, and one empty pistol slot.

"All his rifles and shotguns are here, I think," Jesse said, with obvious relief. He touched the empty slot. "This is an old revolver that he keeps in his truck. He's got a carry permit, but he doesn't carry it much, says it's a pain in the ass."

"What kind of revolver?" Wood asked. "Make and caliber?"

"It's a Smith, a .357. But really old."

"That's not good," Lucas said, thinking of that moment when Grace Lawrence brought the revolver up, and shot him. A .357 would have scrambled his guts, vest or no vest.

Wood said, "Jerry was shot with a .223 — they recovered a core. I've got to get a bag out of the car and wrap that rifle, take it with me."

Greer bent toward the safe, then squatted, looking at the trigger guard on the .223. "There's dust on the action and the trigger — I don't think it's been shot in the last couple of days."

"Got to take it anyway," Wood said.

Jesse led them to his own room. He had guns himself, he said, and they should check them: but they were all there, in his bedroom closet, another muzzle-loading rifle and two shotguns.

"Don't have any regular bolt-action deer rifles?" Lucas asked. That was what he most feared: a high-velocity hunting rifle, a .243 or larger.

"Not legal in Iowa," Jesse said. "I mean, they're legal to have, but you can't shoot deer with them. Gotta use a muzzle-loader or a slug gun."

"And Cole doesn't have one, for target practice or shooting around or out-of-state hunting trips?"

"Nope. Anything you can do with a big-caliber rifle, you can do with a muzzle-loader," Jesse said.

Except long-distance sniping, Lucas thought.

Jesse opened up the Purdys' home computer for them. "She doesn't have a laptop?" Lucas asked.

"She does, but she carries it around with her," Jesse said. "This thing's mostly for me and Cole, messing around on the Internet."

"Is the laptop an Apple or PC?" Lucas asked.

"Apple. MacBook," Jesse said.

Lucas glanced at Wood, and gave him a small nod. That fit.

Lucas wanted to take a look at the barn.

They all stripped off their combat gear and stowed it in the trunk of the car, and while Wood got a big evidence bag out of the trunk and went to wrap up the Bushmaster .223, Lucas and Greer got flashlights and walked back to the barn. Jesse turned on the barn lights from inside the house.

Jesse told them that they hadn't raised animals and the barn was mostly for machinery, with a workshop for repair work. Inside they found an older compact John Deere utility tractor, along with an older Deere Gator with a towable cart, and a heavy-duty lawn mower, all in the signature dark corn-green-and-yellow John Deere colors. All of it was bathed in the scent of gasoline and oil.

There was a loft, and they climbed the stairs up to it and found a metal- and woodworking shop. The floor was speckled with sawdust and metal grindings, and marked with a fresh overspray of green and yellow paint. "Looks like they've been refinishing one of the Deeres," Greer said, scuffing up the overspray with the toe of a boot.

"Yeah." A band saw and table saw stood on one side of a long workbench, and a drill press on the other side. A router lay on a side bench, next to a welder, and a handful of half-inch-thread hex nuts. Lucas picked up two of them and rattled them like dice.

A pegboard wall held drills, hammers, pliers, and wrenches, along with a number of tools that Lucas couldn't identify. "Pretty good shop," Lucas said.

"Like a lot of farm shops. Smells good," Greer said.

"Yeah, it does." There was good light over the workbench area, but the corners were dimmer; they shone their flashlights around, probing the edges of the barn.

"See anything interesting?" Greer asked.

"Nothing." Lucas started pulling open drawers in the workbench and found a bunch of paper targets, used; the holes had been punched with a .22. Depending on how they'd been hung, the holes could have been made by a little .22 or a much more powerful .223, the standard American assault-rifle caliber. Cole Purdy had both in his gun safe. The shooting distances weren't marked on the targets, but whoever was shooting had kept the groups the size of a silver dollar. The groups were consistently tight, which meant that the shooter was good, but the gun might not have been; again, depending on distance.

Lucas said that, and Greer said, "But they're old targets. The paper is ready to fall apart."

Lucas nodded. "Let's go."

They went back down the stairs and out of the barn, where they found Jesse and Wood in the side yard, talking under the sodium-vapor yard light. Wood said, "Not much in that computer. Cole and Jesse don't use it much and there was hardly anything in e-mail or documents. Nothing interesting. I did get some pictures of Marlys and Cole, taken in May or June. I sent them on to my office, we can print them there. I'll get copies out to every cop and security guard at the fair."

"Good." Lucas turned to Jesse. "Do you guys go to the state fair?"

"Sure, most years."

"Then your mom and Cole would be familiar with the fairgrounds."

"Sure. We compete in some of the vegetable competitions — you know, best onions, and like that," Jesse said. "We weren't planning to go this year. We've all been pretty busy."

"Think they might have gone anyway?" Greer asked.

"Why go in the middle of the night?" Jesse asked.

Lucas shrugged. "I don't know." He still

393

had the hex nuts he'd picked up in the barn, and rattled them nervously in his fist. "But that missing .357 makes me nervous."

"I'll tell you something about that gun," Jesse said. "Cole bought it at an estate sale, some old farmer over by New Sharon. Paid fifteen dollars. It'd been in a drawer for about fifty years, I think. Shells were corroded up inside the cylinder, I was worried Cole was gonna kill himself, prying 'em out of there. But he got them out and polished everything up and oiled it and all. When it was all done, it looked like it was perfect — but you couldn't put five shots in a dinner plate at ten feet. I saw him try to do it and he couldn't. That gun shoots about the way Willie fucks. All over the place, and not very good."

"Who's Willie again?" Lucas asked.

"My wife."

They talked for a while longer and Jesse told them that he thought that Marlys and Cole, if they were doing anything connected to Michaela Bowden, it was probably leafleting or trying to organize a protest by the PPPI, whom he called "a bunch of old farts."

They were heading toward Greer's car when a battered Toyota pulled into the driveway behind it.

"Ah, shit," Jesse said. "It's Willie."

A chunky young blond woman got out of the car and half-shouted at Jesse, "I ain't talking to you."

"Goddamn good thing after you screwed me over last night," he half-shouted back. "What the fuck you want, anyway?"

"Caralee. What'd you think?"

"She ain't here. She's supposed to be with you," Jesse said.

"I dropped her off with Marlys this afternoon," Willie said. "What're you doing here? Who are these assholes?"

"These assholes are cops," Jesse said. "They're investigating that you filed false charges against me yesterday and they're gonna put your whorin' ass in jail."

"What?"

"No, no," Wood said. "We're trying to talk to Mrs. Purdy, is all."

"What'd she do?" Willie asked.

"As far as we know, nothing," Wood said. "You say your daughter is with her?"

"I had to do some shopping," Willie said, her voice sliding from a shout to a whine.

"Yeah, she was over suckin' Berg's dick again," Jesse said, loud enough for her to hear, but with a confidential tone, as though he were talking privately to the cops.

"Was not," Willie said, starting toward them. "I want my daughter."

Jesse continued, with the confidential tone: "Tell the truth, she could suck a golf ball through a water hose . . . the only reason I married her."

Willie screamed, "You fucker," and had her fingernails out, and Greer and Wood got between them and said, "Hold it, hold it . . ."

"I want my baby . . ."

"She's not here," Wood said. "We've been all through the house. And we got Jesse out of the jail, so we know he doesn't have her. She's probably riding around with her grandma. Maybe you ought to check back later. By phone."

After some more screaming, Willie left.

"I like the way you handled that, Jesse," Greer said. "Classy."

"I lose my shit when I get around her," he said.

Lucas asked Wood, "You want to call Marlys or should I?"

"I'll call," Wood said.

They'd gotten the phone numbers from Jesse, and Wood punched in Marlys's number. They waited for a few seconds, as it started to ring, and then, in the quiet of the side yard, they heard a phone ringing in the house.

"Sonofabitch," Jesse said.

He led the way into the house. The phone had gone to an answering service, so Wood dialed it again. They found two cell phones sitting side by side in a china cabinet.

"Now I'm worried," Jesse said. "That phone is usually welded to Mom's hand. And she left it behind on purpose. That's . . ."

He didn't finish, so Lucas did it for him: "That's not good, number two."

After some more discussion, Lucas told Jesse, "We ought to take you back to jail, but we don't have time. If you've got some way to warn your mother or brother that we're coming for them, don't do it or you'll be right there in prison with them."

"They're not doing nothing," Jesse insisted.

"That's what we all hope," Lucas said. "We can't take the chance, though. So you keep your mouth shut. If they come back tonight, tell them to call me. Tell them that's the safest thing they can do, because tomorrow, we're gonna have a bunch of Neanderthal highway patrolmen hunting them down.

The shoot-first, ask-questions-later guys. Your mom needs to call me."

"I'll tell them," Jesse said. "I'll sit right there in the kitchen until they show up."

"Something else," Lucas said. "Whatever happens, if you don't show up for that court date and get me my five hundred dollars back, I'll take it out of your ass."

They left Jesse standing under the yard light and drove back to the Southers' place, where Lucas picked up his car.

Checking his watch, he realized they'd be a little late getting to the meeting that night.

"Listen," Wood said, "Marlys and Cole know the fair, they left their phones behind, and they're carrying a .357. That's all bad. On the other hand, the gun's a piece of junk and he could have taken a better one with him, and they've got a child with them. That's all good. Given all that, what are they going to do?"

"I don't know," Lucas said. "The phones . . . That worries me more than the gun. It's like they didn't want to be tracked and thought they might be. They're working on something and they know we might be coming for them."

"Maybe they're gonna like hit Bowden in the face with a cream pie, or something," Greer said.

Wood and Lucas frowned at him, and Greer muttered, "Okay. Sorry about that."

TWENTY-FIVE

The Embassy Suites in Des Moines was of
the architectural style known as 20th Century Hotel Unremarkable, a large beige
building apparently designed not to piss
anybody off, except maybe the local aes-
thetes.

Lucas skipped the valet and left his car in
the parking lot across Locust Street. Crossing the street, he could smell the river to his
right, and see a gold dome a few blocks
down to his left, well lit, which he assumed
was the Iowa Capitol; he would forget to
confirm that with anyone.

Running late, he'd called Mitford, and was
met in the hotel lobby by Alice Green. She
was wearing a subdued olive-gray knit
pantsuit that vibrated with her hair and
eyes, and low-heeled black leather boots,
which, if some shit needed kicking, could
get the job done.

She flashed her smile at him when she

came through, then killed it and asked, "What happened to your face? Again?"

"The shooter hit the wing mirror on the side of the truck with his second shot," Lucas said. "I picked up a couple pieces of mirror."

"I couldn't believe it when I heard about it," she said. "By the way, we get half-hour updates from the state guys. Robertson's going to make it, but he's lost a chunk of his lung."

"Two inches to the right and he'd be dead or a quadriplegic," Lucas said. "Bad things happen when you're shot."

As they talked, she led him through the hotel atrium, back to a compact meeting room with security people hanging around to keep the riffraff out. Henderson was already there — he was staying in the hotel — and Bowden was expected at any moment, and would be coming in through the back, along with the Gardner campaign crew.

Twenty people were sitting in a cluster of chairs in the meeting room; Henderson and Mitford were standing in a corner, isolated from the main group, and both were talking on their cell phones. Most of the people in the room seemed to be security officers of one kind or another, and Lucas saw Pole, the DCI director, as Pole spotted him and scowled.

Bowden came into the room in a rush, shook hands with a couple of people that Lucas didn't know, then walked over to Henderson, who got off the phone to shake her hand. Bowden looked tired, Lucas thought, the first time he'd seen that in her. Gardner arrived a minute later and the politicians and their aides milled around for a moment and pretended to like each other, then another man whom Lucas didn't recognize — he turned out to be the governor of Iowa — stood up and said, "All right, folks, let's get this going. Al Brown, why don't you lead off?"

As Bowden, Henderson, and the others found chairs, a tall man in a champagne-colored suit got to his feet, looked around at the group through his scholarly gold-rimmed glasses, wiped his extra-high forehead, and said, "I think I've met most of you, and for the rest, I'm Al Brown, and I head up the Iowa campaign security group. Again, as most of you know, a DCI agent was shot last night by a person or persons who may pose a threat to the candidates. I spoke to one of our senior agents, Bell Wood — Bell, raise your hand, thanks — who tells me that the shooter may have been identified, and that one of the persons involved in that identification, a security agent for Governor Henderson, may be here in the room. Is Lucas Davenport here?"

Lucas raised his hand, and Brown asked, "What have you got for us?"

Lucas stood up and said, "Bell and another DCI agent, Sam Greer, and I interviewed a man named Jesse Purdy at his home near Pella this evening. We believe that his mother, Marlys Purdy, and his brother, Cole Purdy, may have been involved in at least one and possibly three murders, and probably in the sniper shooting of Jerry Robertson last night."

He went on to tell them of the interview with Jesse Purdy, and about the .357 Magnum that Cole Purdy was probably carrying. He also told them that Jesse said all of Cole's rifles were in the gun safe. "Jesse Purdy confirmed that his mother and brother have developed a serious animus toward Mrs. Bowden and we fear that they might try to shoot her. We're puzzled about the rifle — why it was still there if it was used to shoot Jerry Robertson — but I think it's possible that Cole Purdy has another rifle unknown to Jesse that he could safely shoot, and then abandon, that couldn't be traced to him. It seemed to Jesse that Cole deliberately led him into a confrontation with his ex-wife, so that he'd be put in jail, and be out of the way, before they moved . . ."

Brown asked, "You don't believe Jesse Purdy was involved?"

"I don't believe he is. He was quite open with us this evening," Lucas said. "That's just a first impression. He provided photos of his mother and brother, which Bell is having reproduced."

Wood spoke up: "We're having a Photoshop guy update them. He's giving Mrs. Purdy straight brown hair instead of her white hair."

Brown said to the group at large, "Bell says he'll have those by dawn tomorrow, a couple thousand of them, and we'll have them plastered all over the fair before the gates open."

Bowden said, "Lucas, I'm desperately sorry about Mr. Robertson and about your face, for that matter . . ."

A ripple of laughter went through the crowd, and Lucas interjected, "I actually thought it gave me a Hollywood glow."

Bowden gave him her Number 2 tolerant smile and continued, ". . . but what I really need is your best guess as to what the

404

Purdys are planning. If it is the Purdys, and if they're planning anything."

Lucas thought for a moment and then said, "You know, I don't have any idea. I thought probably he'd take a long-distance shot, if he could. We've seen paper targets that suggest he's a decent marksman, and if he's the one who shot Jerry, we know he's willing to kill. But I've been told about the security group's plans for tomorrow and I can't see how anybody with a long gun could get anywhere close to your walking route. If Cole can get in the parade route crowd, close enough to rush you . . . that .357 is a killer. His brother says it's wildly inaccurate, but you don't have to be accurate at six inches or two feet. The .357 was originally developed for the highway patrol, to punch through car doors and windshields and to put people down for good with one shot. On the other hand, we know that Cole had the option to use two other modern semiautos if he wanted them, and they're still in his gun locker. Jesse doesn't believe either his mother or his brother is suicidal. You add that up, and it's all very confusing. I don't know what they're doing. I don't know what to tell you."

A cop in the crowd asked, "Is it possible

that the fair is a decoy? That they're planning to attack at a different place altogether?"

Wood said, "Lucas and I have talked about that. It's possible, but Mrs. Bowden has been focusing on small venues these past couple of weeks. Almost any place she's been, a shooter would get caught in a hurry. You don't 'get away' out in the countryside, not that easily. We thought they'd probably want to use the fair, with a hundred thousand people rolling through it, as cover to come and go. Then, they disappeared last night and Mrs. Bowden's supposed to walk tomorrow . . . My feeling is that they're out there, at the fair."

Lucas and Wood answered a couple of additional questions, then Brown came back in and described the security precautions that the Iowa cops were taking. ". . . literally have a highway patrolman every six feet, facing the crowd. Plainclothes guys walking through it, pacing the candidates. The candidates' own security people will be walking with them, so I don't think the idea that she might be rushed would be a viable one. Before the walk starts, we will look at every square inch of every structure where they could get high enough to shoot her and then we will shut down access to those places."

"You're telling me that it'll be safe," Bowden said.

"I can't make any guarantees," Brown said. "I *think* you'll be safe, but we have to assume that these people are not dummies. They may understand what they'll be facing and have plans of their own. Of course, they *may* be dummies and we'll take them down two minutes after the gates open tomorrow."

"That would be helpful," she said.

"Still, I wish you wouldn't do the walk," Brown said. "If you went to Sioux City instead of the fair, I'd be a lot happier."

The Iowa governor stood up and said, "C'mon, guys, we need optimists here. I feel that with the precautions we've taken, Mrs. Bowden will be perfectly safe."

A couple more cops talked about the details of the security ring, and then Bowden said, "This just isn't a matter of my personal safety — it's a kind of test. Do I have the guts to go out there and face some unknown peril, or do I shrink away from it? I don't think the major candidates themselves would blame me for not walking, but there are many, many people in both parties who dislike me and wouldn't hesitate to suggest that I was a coward. That's the reality of it. Unless some new information comes up, I'll walk tomorrow."

That set off a round of muttering and cross-conversation, and Henderson stood up to roll out a few clichés about bravery, as did Gardner, and then Pole stood up and said, "We'll do our best tomorrow and that will be more than good enough. You'll be fine. I have to say, I don't give a whole lot of credence to our more excitable . . . consultants."

As people began to stand and move around and out of the room, Norm Clay, Bowden's ranking weasel, came over and said to Lucas, "Mrs. Bowden's going out the back. She'd appreciate a moment of your time."

Lucas nodded and followed him down a hall, to a cluster of Bowden's people. Bowden saw Lucas coming and stepped away from them and said, "I'm disappointed that you haven't caught them yet."

"Trying hard," Lucas said.

"Try harder," she said. She reached out and touched the bandages on his face, then pulled her hand back. "I had a rather long talk with Elmer about you and he says that if these people, these Purdys, are out there doing something sneaky, you're the one who'll break them down. So, Lucas — I'm counting on you."

He couldn't think of what else to say, so he nodded and said, "Okay."

TWENTY-SIX

Bell Wood was waiting in the hall outside the meeting room, and asked, "What are you going to do?"

"Well, you're planning to hand out all those Purdy photos, so it doesn't seem like there's much point in my milling around the fairgrounds all night, looking at faces. There'll already be a hundred guys doing that," Lucas said. "But Lawrence deleted two people from her party list. If she's part of the conspiracy with Purdy, then maybe that Skira woman is, too. I was thinking I might run back to Cedar Rapids, knock on her door."

Wood looked at his watch and said, "It'll be midnight before you get there."

"So she'll probably be home," Lucas said, "unless she's going to the fair, too."

"Let me see if Greer can go with you," Wood said.

"That'd be good," Lucas said.

"And not to put too fine a point on it, my boy, I get the feeling that the candidate sort of likes your looks. Am I wrong?"

"Ah, Jesus, Bell . . ." Lucas shook his head. "Man . . ."

"Just sayin'."

Greer was willing to go. He offered to lead the way, as Robertson had a few days earlier, because he had lights and sirens. Wood said he'd nail down an address for them, and Lucas said, "Let's go," and they went.

Greer had a heavy foot, and pushed the state car up over a hundred and held it there, flashing through the night, overtaking cars and trucks. Forty minutes out, Greer's taillights flared, and he roared into a rest stop, Lucas right behind.

Something had happened?

Greer slowed but kept rolling until a parked cop car turned on its flashers. Greer pulled up beside it and Lucas stopped behind him. A sheriff's deputy hopped out of the car and ran around to Lucas's driver's-side window and handed him a plastic bag and said, "Bell Wood said you might need this."

His .45.

"Thank you."

411

Greer hauled ass with Lucas right behind him, but now with his pistol on the seat beside him, riding . . . shotgun.

Wood called fifteen minutes later with an address for Skira: "It's Betsy Jacoby now. Betsy and Stan."

They took I-80 all the way to Iowa City, then turned north on I-380 to Cedar Rapids. Lucas took the lead when they got there, having punched the address into his nav system while they waited at a stoplight.

Skira lived in a brown-shingled bungalow-style house on Bever Avenue, on the southeast side of town. There were still two lights on in the house when they arrived, and they parked at the curb.

Greer got out and said, "Fuckin' people don't know how to spell beaver," and, "A Cedar Rapids cop's gonna be here in a minute."

Lucas took the time to dig out his carry holster, clipped it to his belt, and slipped the .45 into it. Felt good.

Two or three minutes later a Cedar Rapids black-and-white slipped into the curb, and a uniformed sergeant got out. Greer went over to identify himself and to shake hands. He introduced Lucas as a consultant; they shook and the cop said, "Mark Soper. We

412

got a problem here, or what? You want more guys?"

"I think we're fine," Greer said. "We mostly wanted a uniform so we don't scare the shit out of these people when we start knocking on the door."

"We want to arrest this chick?" the cop asked.

"Don't know that, either. Mostly, we're looking for information," Greer said.

"Then let's go," Soper said.

They followed him up to the front door. Soper knocked on the door, then hit the doorbell a couple of times. A dog started barking, and Greer said, "Great. They got a wolf."

The dog turned out to be a Labradoodle with smoky gray hair and a deep voice. The dog got to the door first, followed by a barefoot balding man in sweatpants and a short-sleeved sweatshirt, who squinted at them through the door glass, saw Soper, and opened the door. "Can I help you?"

Greer stepped up. "Are you Mr. Jacoby?"

"Yes. What's the problem?"

Greer identified himself and said, "We need to talk to Mrs. Jacoby."

"What about?"

"We probably ought to tell her at the same

time we tell you," Greer said. "Is she home?"

"Yes . . ." Jacoby turned and called, "Betsy? Could you come here?"

A moment later Betsy Jacoby came out of the back, tying a bathrobe over silky pajamas. She peered at the three cops and said, "Yes?"

"We need to talk to you . . . urgently . . . about a friend of yours. Grace Lawrence."

"Grace? Oh my God, is she okay? Is she hurt?"

In that one second, with that answer, Lucas decided that he'd wasted three hours of the little time he had left. He needed to get back to Des Moines, because Betsy Jacoby knew nothing about a conspiracy to kill Michaela Bowden.

"Actually, she's in jail," Greer said. "She's been charged with attempted murder, for trying to shoot this gentleman here." He nodded to Lucas, and then said, "We were talking to her about a conspiracy to assassinate Michaela Bowden."

"Oh my God," Betsy Jacoby said again. "That doesn't sound right. I . . . I . . ."

Stan Jacoby asked, "Who in the hell is Grace Lawrence? What does she have to do with Betsy?"

Betsy half-turned to her husband and said, "She's an old friend, from years ago.

You don't know her."

Stan Jacoby looked at Greer and asked, "Then why do you want to talk to Betsy?"

"If we could come in, we could sit down and talk about that," Greer said.

The Jacobys looked at each other, then Stan Jacoby asked, "Do we need a lawyer?"

Greer glanced at Lucas, who said, "I don't think that Mrs. Jacoby knows about this particular issue." Lucas went back to Betsy Jacoby: "Would you know a Marlys Purdy?"

"Marlys? Well, I've met her . . . I haven't seen her in years. I mean, lots of years, probably the nineties."

"You wouldn't know about her current political leanings?" Lucas asked.

"Well, she was one of the more outspoken people in the Progressives . . ."

Stan Jacoby said, "Let's go in and sit down. I've got some questions of my own."

They all trooped into the front room. The Jacobys sat side by side on a couch with their decorator dog, while Lucas and Greer took two easy chairs across a coffee table. Soper stood by the door, his thumbs hooked over his gun belt.

"First off," Jacoby said, "are you going to read Betsy her rights? Or both of us our rights?"

"Should we?" Greer asked. "We don't

really know —"

"I have nothing to do with any kind of conspiracy against Michaela Bowden, I can tell you that right now," Betsy Jacoby said. "I'm going to vote for her. I'm going to support her at the caucuses."

Her husband said, "I'm not. But Betsy is. We've been talking about it."

Lucas said to Betsy Jacoby, "Okay. The reason we wanted to talk to you is that Grace Lawrence gave us a list of all the main members of the Progressive People's Party, going back quite a few years. But she cut two people out of the list she gave us — you and Marlys Purdy. We know for sure that Purdy's part of the conspiracy. We think Grace is. Do you know any reason why she would have deliberately taken your name off that list?"

Betsy shook her head. "No . . . I mean, we were close friends at one time. Maybe she just wanted to save me the inconvenience."

Greer asked the next question. "Is it possible she cut your name off because she didn't want us questioning somebody who might have been involved with her in the Lennett Valley Dairy bombing?"

Lucas was looking directly at Betsy's face when Greer asked the questions, and the woman's eyes seemed almost to pull back into their sockets: an expression he'd seen before, somebody deciding between flight and fight.

She was, Lucas thought, the bomber.

She cleared her throat and turned to her husband and said, "You know what, Stan? I think we better get a lawyer here."

"What the hell is the Lennett Valley Dairy?" he asked.

Betsy put her hand on his thigh and said, "Stan, we need to call Carl Lane."

"Whaa . . ."

Lucas gestured to Greer. Greer stood up and followed Lucas to the front door, where Lucas said quietly, "She doesn't know about Purdy or the conspiracy, but she's the bomber."

"I agree," Greer said. "I saw her face turning."

"My problem is Purdy, not Jacoby," Lucas said. "I'm gonna head back to Des Moines and leave you here with Soper. I'll call Bell and tell him the situation."

"Okay," Greer said. "Shit, man, I wish you could stay."

"Got no time," Lucas said. "But she's your dairymaid, all right. There's DNA on those sheets. You got her, even if you don't

417

get her tonight."

Back in the car, Lucas called Bell Wood, who was still up. "We got your bomber, I think. I'd bet dollars to doughnuts that she's the one, and you've got the DNA. She doesn't know about Purdy."

"Would have been convenient if she'd known about both," Wood said.

"Yeah. I'm heading back that way. Catch a couple of hours of sleep, then go right out to the fairgrounds in the morning."

"I'll be out there at seven o'clock," Wood said.

"Hey — and thanks for the gun," Lucas said. "It's a comfort."

"Hope to hell you don't need it."

Twenty-Seven

The sun had dipped below the horizon when Cole Purdy paid the price, got his ticket, and walked onto the grounds of the Iowa State Fair. It was a good hike past the grandstand and through the midway, past the Ferris wheels and the Gravitron and the Scorpion, past the ranks of stuffed animals, the offers for henna tattoos and old-timey photos, through the odors of popcorn and dry grass and hot cotton candy, into the heart of the fair.

And it was hot, especially on the back of his neck. He'd been to a chain-store barber, told the lady haircutter to take it all off. She had. The top of his head now felt like a cactus, and every couple of minutes he'd take his hat off and run his hand across it.

Cole was looking for a truck, a particular truck. He didn't know where it was, or what it looked like, but it was out there, somewhere.

In fact, there were trucks all over the place, but generally locked with the windows up, or with people close by. He wandered past the Triangle and down Grand Avenue, cut between some buildings, always looking.

The place was packed with people: no matter where he went, he would never be out of sight of somebody, and usually that person was eating something, and often enough, on a stick. Chicken on a stick. Snickers on a stick. Wiener schnitzel on a stick. On the other hand, there were so many people around that almost nobody was paying attention to anyone else.

Or that's the way it seemed.

A couple of teenage girls went by, laughing about something, cell phones clutched in their hands, ignoring him. A guy with a rodeo belt buckle the size of a dinner plate went by, and a woman with a pink plastic cowboy hat on her head, carrying a cob of sweet corn on a stick, butter running down her fingers.

He spotted his truck by the Pioneer Livestock Pavilion. It was moving slowly along a pedestrian walkway, the guy in the cab talking on a cell phone as he rolled to a stop outside the pavilion. He stopped, talked for another minute or so on the phone, then hopped out of the truck and walked quickly into the building, the phone still pressed to his ear.

A man on a mission. He'd shut the truck door when he got out but hadn't rolled up the window. Cole eased over to the truck, checked the door where the guy had disappeared, then popped the unlocked door and slid into the driver's seat. An employee's pass was taped to the inside of the windshield, down in the far left corner just above the dashboard. Cole carefully pulled it off, folded it, stuck it inside his hat, got out of the truck, and wandered off, never looking back.

He walked past the Triangle and back through the midway, didn't stop to look at a middle-aged man who was vomiting into a trash can after getting off one of the rides, then continued on through the gate to the parking lot.

Marlys and Caralee were waiting on the far side of Des Moines at the Jordan Creek Town Center, well away from the fair. A place to kill time . . .

He found Marlys and the kid staring in a window at a Victoria's Secret.

"Like that, huh, Ma?" he asked.

"It's . . . ridiculous," she said.

"Don't see those women hanging around Pella, not that much," Cole said, inspecting a six-foot-tall photo of a Dream Angel in a red demi-bra.

"Get a card?" Marlys asked.

"Of course. Never was gonna be hard to do," Cole said.

Marlys looked at her watch: "Two hours."

"Let's go get something decent to eat," he said. "I saw a steak house coming in."

"Okay, if it's not too expensive," she said.

"Got to live a little, Ma," Cole said. He added, "I gotta tell you, though, you look strange. Even stranger than you looked with the brown hair."

"I feel bad enough about it," she said. "So shut up."

On the way out to the truck, Cole put his finger on Caralee's nose and wiggled it until she started to laugh, and Marlys said, "This kid . . . it's like carrying around twenty pounds of potatoes."

Caralee said, "Potatoes."

"That's right, honey," Marlys said. "If that goddamned Willie hadn't been flyin' around town . . . We needed her to be at home."

"Willie doesn't like to stay home and she doesn't much like havin' a kid," Cole said. "I believe after the divorce, she'll try to unload Caralee on Jesse."

"Jesse'll be a good dad, if he can quit drinking," Marlys said.

"He'll quit, if it comes down to takin' care of Caralee," Cole said.

"I think he will. He's a good boy," said Marlys, changing arms with the kid. "Here, you carry her for a while. My back's killing me."

They ate steaks and fries, hung out some more, and rolled through the state fair gates just before nine o'clock, Caralee asleep in the child seat. They'd fed her and changed her at the steak house, so she should be good for the evening. The guard glanced at the dashboard pass, at the kid in the back, and then looked into the bed of the pickup and said, "Looks heavy."

"Weighs a ton," Cole said affably. "Dropping it off at the water department."

"Better you than me, buddy," the guard said, losing interest and waving them through.

This would be the first tricky part, they knew. They'd come in on the south side of the fairgrounds, between the swine and sheep barns. There would be cops all over the place — though fewer at night — and they wanted to get to the machinery grounds, where there were always a number of pickups parked. While they had the truck pass, it wouldn't stand a real check. If somebody called in the pass number, it'd show up as lost or stolen.

Marlys had worked out the route from memory, and from an online fair map. They rolled slowly down the street between the animal barns, took a left at the horse barn, paused to let a woman lead a steer across in front of them, rolled past the exhibition center. A couple of cops were standing on the corner, chatting, but paid no attention as they took a right toward the machinery grounds. There were four trucks parked in a row on the grass, with space for a fifth. Cole slipped into that spot.

"Good," Marlys said.

"Want to walk?"

"I guess. Better than sitting in the truck. I'd like to wear out Caralee a little bit, so she doesn't wake up during the night."

They'd brought kid food in a cooler, and Marlys poured a can of apple juice into a sippy cup and gave it to Caralee, and put a plastic bag of Honey-Nut Cheerios in her pocket, in case she needed something to eat to keep her quiet. They walked a loop around the fairgrounds, sometimes carrying the little girl, sometimes letting her walk on her own. She was fascinated by the whirling lights of the midway and the crazy carny music. At a DNR exhibit, they walked around looking at the fish, Caralee tracking a beat-up northern pike with a fingertip on the aquarium glass.

The fairgrounds was emptying out by eleven o'clock, though the midway was open until midnight, and the fair guards wouldn't start running people off until one o'clock.

When they got back to the truck, two of the other four trucks that had been parked next to them had gone. Caralee was exhausted, and when they put her in her baby chair in the backseat, she was asleep almost immediately. Marlys kicked back the passenger seat, for a bed, and Cole pulled a tarp over the truck bed and tied it down, and unrolled a foam camping mattress.

"Least it's cooling off," Cole said. "Like to sleep if I can."

"Empty your head out, you'll sleep," Marlys said. "Wish I had my own phone."

"Yeah. Listen to some tunes."

Marlys fished a phone out of her jacket pocket, checked the time, and the alarm. The phone was a cheap burner, bought at Walmart, using instructions she'd read on the Internet. The alarm was set for three o'clock in the morning.

"Wonder where that Davenport guy is," Cole said.

"Shhh. Don't worry about Davenport. Worry about getting some sleep."

"Night, Ma."

"Night, Cole."

"Hope Jesse's okay."

"He'll be fine."

"Night, Ma."

"Good night, Cole."

The alarm vibrated against Marlys's thigh at three o'clock. Her eyes popped open, and she was disoriented for a moment, looking up at the underside of the truck cab. Her back hurt from sleeping half upright in the truck seat. She groped for the phone, and turned it off. Felt her head. What? Then she remembered. No hair: bald as a cue ball. Caralee was still asleep in the backseat.

She got out of the truck as quietly as she could and rapped on the truck bed. Cole asked in the dark, "Already?"

"Yes." Marlys smacked her lips, dug in her pocket, and came up with a pack of Dentyne. "You get some sleep?"

"Yeah, I did."

"Want a couple sticks of gum?"

"Yeah." Cole pried up one corner of the tarp and got out, took the gum from Marlys, and looked around. It was night, all right, but it was never really going to be dark on the fairgrounds.

"Caralee is still asleep," Marlys whispered. "Let's try to keep it that way."

Cole untied the tarp and pulled it off the truck, and they folded it into a tight square. There were three steel rods lying along the side of the truck bed, and a posthole digger. He pulled the posthole digger out and pushed it under the truck. He was as quiet as possible, but wasn't entirely quiet, and as he pulled the steel rods out, they clanked against the inside of the truck bed. Marlys hissed, "Quiet!" until Cole whispered back, "If anyone hears you saying, 'Quiet!' they're gonna wonder what the hell is going on."

"Well, be quiet," Marlys said.

It wasn't all that easy being totally quiet while carrying three long steel rods through the gloom, past all kinds of metal objects in the machinery grounds, but he managed as best he could, with Marlys trailing behind with the tarp. They slipped past a building and got out to the main drag. A couple of trash trucks were working a block away and a car was turning a corner, and even farther down the street they could see a couple of people walking away from them. Cops? Too far to tell. They could hear music nearby:

an old Robert Palmer song called "Addicted to Love," so somebody was up.

"Don't see anybody," Marlys said.

There were bright globular lights on the shops all along the avenue, but no lights directly overhead, which was why they'd chosen that spot; they weren't exactly in the shadows, but they weren't brilliantly lit, either. Cole walked out to the curb with the three steel rods, forced one of them a foot and a half into the dirt, close to the curb. The other two went out the corners of a wide, shallow triangle.

Marlys unfolded the tarp. They'd practiced back at the farm, but this was for real, and they fumbled around for a minute, and finally got it rigged. When it was up, they were screened from the street, with an open back — but nobody should be walking up behind them.

"Back to the truck," Marlys said.

They hustled back to the truck, got in, slumped in the seats. They'd wait for ten minutes — see if the tarp attracted any attention. The ten minutes crawled past, and while they saw two trucks pass on the street, neither of them slowed for the tarp.

"I'm gonna do it," Cole said.

"Gotta be quiet," Marlys said.

Cole slipped out of the truck, reached

beneath it for the posthole digger, pulled it out and trotted back to the street. This would be his longest exposure and the one that would be hardest to explain. In fact, if caught, or questioned, he wouldn't try to explain it. He'd run.

Behind the tarp, he listened for a minute, then began to dig. The ground was soft from all the rain and the digging went more quickly than he'd expected. The fresh dirt went on a corner of the tarp: when they took the screen down, they'd take the dirt with them. They'd tied a wire around the handle of the posthole digger, so he'd know when he was exactly deep enough . . .

Car. He stopped digging to listen.

Went by, never slowing.

He started down again, pulling out six inches of dirt each time, screwing the posthole digger into the earth. Took five or six minutes to get down four feet, and when the wire marker was even with the mouth of the hole, he gave it a last turn and pulled out the last plug of dirt.

A minute later he was back at the truck, slipped the posthole digger into the truck bed, and got in the passenger seat.

"Get it?" Marlys asked.

"Yeah."

"You want to rest a bit, or do it now?"

Marlys asked.

"Let's do it. Bring the paint," Cole said.

Marlys got an eight-ounce can of paint from under the seat, and a screwdriver. "Okay."

Caralee made a sleepy sound, and they both froze: they didn't want to deal with a crying baby. After a moment, she was sleeping soundly again and Marlys whispered, "Okay."

Out of the truck again, they checked for watchers, took a fat-wheeled dolly out of the truck bed, then pulled the bomb straight out. The bomb was made of wrought iron and was heavy as a safe. They'd practiced carrying it at the farm, but it was a struggle, so they'd gotten the dolly at Home Depot. Now they lifted the bomb down onto the dolly.

Checked around.

Checked around again, when Marlys thought she heard something; with the bomb lying there, they couldn't be stopped, or inspected. Cole had a 9mm Beretta in his hand. He'd bought it at a gun show, for cash. Jesse didn't know about it, as Jesse hadn't known about the new .223 black rifle. All of Cole's guns were accounted for back at the farm and in the gun case in the truck.

"Let's go," Cole said.

They pushed the dolly, bumping across the ground along the side of the building, and up behind the tarp. Marlys could see the hole waiting for them, and the dirt. Looked easy enough, but wasn't; they struggled with the weight, but the pipe at the bottom had to go straight down into the ground, and instead, threatened to collapse the side of the hole.

Cole finally whispered, "I'll pick it up myself, you guide it in."

That's what they did: he got it two inches off the ground, staggered a little, but Marlys fit it in the hole, said, "That's got it," and he let it slide down. Once a foot into the hole, it dropped straight down the rest of the way.

Perfect fit. Cole reached down along the side, feeling for the ring of the wire trigger. It was in place. He stepped back, felt a pulse of pride in his work: better than anything he'd heard about in Iraq.

"Let's get the tarp down, bundle up the dirt," Marlys said. "I'll get the paint."

They checked for vehicles, and then, as Cole pulled the tarp down and over the waste dirt, Marlys pulled the three poles out of the ground and lay them next to the building.

Cole started back to the truck with the dirt. After a last check around, Marlys pried the lid off the paint can, walked into the street, checked herself, and then poured the paint on the pavement.

She strolled back to the curb, picked up the rods next to the building, and carried them with her. Cole was already in the truck.

"All set," she said. "You check the pin?"

"Yeah. It's fine. It's a half-inch below the dirt line, but the dirt's soft. No problem getting at it."

When they'd caught their breath, Cole eased the truck out of the machinery grounds, and they rolled slowly back to the animal barns. They stopped there for a moment and looked around. Nobody in sight. Cole walked around to the back, where a pale green telephone junction box sat next to the perimeter fence. The lid was down, but loose; he lifted it, looked around again, and slipped the pistol under the lid and pushed the lid back down.

A minute later he was back at the truck, and a minute after that they were through the gate. They'd be back at nine o'clock, on foot.

Set to go.

TWENTY-EIGHT

Lucas drove back to Des Moines. He needed at least a few hours of sleep: the next day was going to be intense, no matter what happened. He had a secret stash of amphetamines in the truck, but sleep would be better. Might pop a pill in the morning.

Lucas was barreling through the night on cruise control when Mitford called at one o'clock and asked, "Anything happen?"

"The Iowa cops will eventually get Betsy Skira for that dairy bombing, but she doesn't know anything about Purdy," Lucas said.

"All right. I'm going to bed. There are no hotel rooms left in Des Moines, 'cause of the fair, but we've got one here for you, if you want it."

"Absolutely. I'll be there in an hour."

Lucas got to the hotel at two o'clock, took a fast hot shower and fell into bed, his phone alarm set for six-thirty. At six-thirty-one he was on his feet, in and out of the shower, shaved and dressed in fifteen minutes. As he was scooping change and keys off the nightstand, he noticed he still had the two steel nuts he'd picked up in the Purdys' barn workshop. "Shit," he said aloud, "I'm a shoplifter." But they felt like good-luck tokens now, and he dropped them in his pocket. Maybe he could ask Cole Purdy about them, in person.

He was out of the hotel before seven with a can of Diet Coke in his hand, feeling a little fuzzy. The day would be too hot for the work shirt he'd worn to hide the bulletproof vest when he'd gone to see Grace Lawrence, so he'd pulled on a heavy-weight Duluth Trading long-tail T-shirt, worn loose, to hide the .45; and jeans and running shoes, and a ball cap.

He popped the back hatch on the truck, dug his stash of amphetamines out from under the spare, popped one. The fuzziness had cleared by the time he turned into the north parking lot at the fairgrounds.

The sun was still low but bright, not a cloud in the sky, and the parking lot was rapidly filling up, Chevys and Fords, long streams of Iowans headed for the gate. Lucas fell in with them, slipping on a pair of sunglasses.

He fit in the crowd like a pea in a pod, he thought: the basic difference between Minnesotans and Iowans was a line on a map. Other than that, they were the same bunch, except, of course, for the physical and spiritual superiority of the Minnesota Gophers over the Iowa Hawkeyes, in all ways, and forever. Between the Hawks and the Badgers . . . they'd have to work that out themselves.

When he got to the gate he found himself looking at a metal detector, and remembered the gun. Greer had planned to arrive early and Lucas called him: "I got a .45 and I'm looking at a metal detector."

"Where are you?"

"North parking lot gate," Lucas said.

"Give me five minutes."

A few minutes later Greer arrived, driving a green-and-yellow John Deere Gator, newer but otherwise identical to the Gator at the Purdys' place. Greer walked out through the gate and said, "Before we go through . . . I got a vest for you, if you want it, but you'll need a different shirt."

Lucas said, "Nah, too hot."

"If you say so, dude."

Greer showed his badge to the guard at the gate and they walked around the metal detector. As they did it, Lucas noticed the large printer-paper color photos of Marlys and Cole that Bell Wood had taken from the Purdys' place hanging on the glass wall of the gate. Marlys Purdy's hair looked fake in the Photoshopped reproduction, and maybe a bit too long, but nobody would have any trouble recognizing her.

"Did a good job on that," Lucas said.

Greer yawned. "Yeah, they did."

"You get any sleep? What happened last night?"

"I read Betsy her rights, she refused to talk. I took a hike. I probably got back here ten minutes after you."

"She did it."

"Yeah, but it's all on the DNA now. If we get a match, she falls. If we don't, she walks."

As they rode the Gator into the fairgrounds Greer asked, "What do you want to do?"

"Walk the route that Bowden will take," Lucas said. "And I want to tour the whole place."

Greer looked at his watch: "You got about two and a half hours. You'll need all of it, if you're planning to do a tour."

They drove past the racetrack and stage to the edge of the grandstand and Lucas said, "Why don't you drop me off here? I need to walk it."

Greer pulled over and stopped, produced a map of the fairgrounds and a Sharpie, drew a line down a street called Grand Avenue/Concourse, and said, "That's where Bowden will walk. They'll park the bus over in a handicapped lot by Gate Eleven and head right over to the walking route, which is less than a block. Nobody except law enforcement knows where the buses will be, and the area's roped off and sterilized. The announced time for the walk is ten a.m., but they won't start until ten-thirty. We're hoping that the Purdys will be in the crowd right at the announced time, so we'll have a half hour to pick them out. During the march, Gardner will lead with a band and a bunch of his people — they all have bands — and Bowden will be the middle, Henderson bringing up the rear. It'll be quick: most of it's for the benefit of the TV cameras, not really to shake a lot of hands."

"Good."

Greer went back to the Gator's storage compartment and produced a radio handset, about the length of an iPhone 6 but narrower and thicker, and a plastic folder a bit smaller than a passport. "The alert call is three loud beeps and it'll vibrate. You're on the general emergency channel. The red button is the alert signal — press it if you want everybody to shut up and listen to what you have to say — that's the three beeps button, but you only have to press it once. The rest is obvious. Press the big button to transmit and know that everybody will hear you."

"Got it. Thanks," Lucas said, taking the radio.

"Last thing," Greer said. He handed Lucas the plastic folder. "Bell says if you run into our beloved director, for God's sakes don't let him see this. It's one of our IDs. We took your photo off the Net. You are not deputized or anything else, but if a cop braces you about the gun, show him the ID and the handset. If he's still not happy, call me and I'll be there in one minute."

"I feel almost like an Iowan," Lucas said.

"Whoa, whoa, whoa. Try to control yourself. You got a *lot* of work to do before you get to that place," Greer said. "And listen — call me for anything. Call me if you get a rock in your shoe."

"What about Robertson? You hear any more?"

Greer brightened. "Yeah. He's talking. Mostly about how much he hurts, but he's talking and he's coherent and the docs are happy."

Lucas climbed out of the Gator and slapped it on the back bed, and Greer took off.

Lucas had been to the Minnesota State Fair six times in his adult life, three times as a uniformed Minneapolis cop and, years later, three more times at the insistence of his adoptive daughter, Letty, who brought along three hot female friends in skimpy clothing who ignored Dad. Now, as he walked past the hulking grandstand and through the midway rides, it all began to come back: he really didn't like state fairs.

Small, out-of-the-way county fairs were okay, with their traveling carny shows that might have been taken from a Stephen King short story, and their weird, idiosyncratic events like speed chain saw sculpture — one minute to do a four-foot bear — and snow-mobile water-skipping. A big institutional fair was just that: institutional. Sure, deep-fried ice cream bars might be a good idea, but after you've eaten a few, then what?

As he probed the midway, circling around the rides and the games, he looked at faces. Iowans, on the whole, were probably not any heavier than Minnesotans, but there were a lot of heavy people around and a lot of tall guys. Marlys Purdy would be hard to find in a crowd simply because she was short. As the crowds grew thicker, she'd be submerged in moving flesh. Cole would be easier to spot because he was six feet tall and thin, and would stand out in the crush.

Lucas approved of posting the photos at the gates, but had little faith in the idea that a guard would spot the mother and son. The most he could hope for, he thought, other than a lucky identification, was that they were still outside the fairgrounds, that the photos would warn them away, and they wouldn't try to come inside, so Bowden would be safe. They could always catch the Purdys later.

But they probably knew they were being hunted. If they were the ones who'd killed Joe Likely, they'd have known about Lucas for several days. Even if they'd only known about him since Lucas first talked to Marlys, they would still have been warned. The fact that they'd sent Jesse to jail suggested that they knew that they were going to be identified, and would be prepared for it.

So either they were already inside, or they had a plan to get through the gates. Any reasonable plan, Lucas thought, as he peered at a teenage boy who was tall and thin but wasn't Cole, would probably work.

Lucas had come out of the midway and was crossing the Concourse when the radio in his pocket vibrated and he pulled it out and put the speaker to his ear and a female voice, a little breathless, said, "Possible identification of Cole Purdy walking toward Gate Fourteen, about to enter midway. I'm in pursuit with John Allen. We will stay in touch until we get more people here . . ."

Another woman's voice came up and said that cops were being routed to the area. Lucas pulled the map out of his back pocket and after a few seconds, spotted gates fourteen and fifteen back the way he'd just come. He turned and ran back that way, the radio in his hand. He was maybe three hundred yards away, he thought, a minute or more, having to circle and dodge his way through the crowd pouring in the opposite direction.

The radio buzzed again and he put it to his ear and heard the woman say, "He's right there by the ticket booth, see him? Green long-sleeved shirt and cutoffs . . ."

Another voice. "We got him, okay. We see you and John, we're coming in."

"We'll move on him now," the woman said.

"Careful . . ."

■ ■ ■ ■

Lucas arrived a minute later to find a circle of people around two plainclothes cops and two highway patrolmen, all focused on a thin, long-haired man who was leaning with his hands against the side of a ticket booth while the cops looked through his wallet. He resembled Cole, Lucas thought, but his eyes were brown, and his nose too big.

The man next to him, who was carrying a soft drink cup the size of a bucket, said, "For a minute I thought it was a terrorist attack."

Lucas started to back away as the thin man argued with the cops; Greer was pulling up in his green-and-yellow John Deere Gator and he'd know the man wasn't Cole. A good-looking blonde bumped into Lucas's holstered gun as he tried to extricate himself from the crowd; he glanced down at her and saw in her eyes that she knew what it was, and he grinned, held up the handset, and whispered, "Cop."

And she apparently saw *that* in his eyes, and nodded and said, "Good," and, "What's going on?"

"We're looking for a guy, but that's not the guy."

Then he was in the open again, and having been prompted by the good-looking blonde, noticed that he was surrounded by good-looking blondes: they were everywhere. So many blondes, so little time on earth . . .

He headed back up the midway. At the end of it, he looked down to his right. That was the Concourse. He'd have to walk down that later, anyway, so he turned to his left and followed a much less-crowded street past a miscellany of buildings, and at the end, looked past a gate and over an extensive campground.

The Purdys could have spent the night there, he thought, and have gone through the gate as soon as they opened, with a crowd of other early birds. He had to remember that they came to the fair in most years, according to Jesse, so they'd know the place well . . .

He got close enough to the gate to see the pictures of the Purdys posted on the glass walls, then turned and wandered back the way he came, took the first left, walked under a cable car, past a big barn-like building with a red dome, then stopped to watch some people throwing horseshoes at a horseshoe court. Hadn't seen anyone playing horseshoes in years; maybe decades.

He was still watching when he felt somebody watching him and turned to see two
cops ambling up, but ambling with purpose.
He held up the handset and they stepped
over and one of them asked, "Who you
with?"

Lucas handed him the DCI identification
folder, and the cop glanced at it and handed
it back and said, "Saw the bump under your
shirt."

"I figured," Lucas said.

"I understand there was some excitement
over at the midway," the cop said.

"Wasn't him," Lucas said. "Resembled
him, but wasn't him."

The other cop looked around and then
said, "You know what? Not one guy in a
hundred looks like him. But there are going
to be a hundred thousand people here
today, maybe more. Half of them will be
male. If it's one in a hundred, that's five
hundred guys who'll look like him. How in
the heck are we supposed to pick him out?"

The first cop said, "He'll be the only one
shooting Mrs. Bowden."

Lucas had to laugh, bumped the cop with
his elbow, and said, "I didn't hear that."

The other cop was now looking at the
horseshoe court, and said, "You know, I
could see *playing* horseshoes, but I'll be

damned if I could see *practicing* horseshoes."

Lucas said good-bye to the cops, worked his way past Grandfather's Barn and, fifteen minutes later, walked through the swine barn, which was on the far south edge of the fairgrounds. The swine were looking pretty good, in their maze of pens, all freshly washed and odor-free, some with curly tails, some without, some cheerful, some not, most of them asleep. From there he walked through the cattle barn, watched a woman giving a shower to a steer in a dedicated cow shower; he hadn't seen that before, and found it interesting. He'd heard rumors that in Texas they actually shaved their cattle before showing them at the state fair. He wasn't sure about the credibility of the report, but it sounded like something Texans might do.

As he left the cattle barn he checked his watch. Nine o'clock. He skipped the sheep barn, but spent a few minutes with the horses, and then moved on, past some kind of auctioneering contest, through a lot of machinery, and back to the main drag, where the candidates would be doing their campaign walks. The street was crowded:

more crowded than he'd ever seen a street in New York City. When the candidate-walk started, they'd push everybody off the street, which meant that the sides of the street would be packed, virtually impassable. Yet, looking both ways, he could see cops almost everywhere.

The Purdys were crazy if they thought they could penetrate that. But the Purdys weren't crazy, not in the sense of being stupid. Still, they wouldn't be able to move without being spotted . . .

Unless, he thought suddenly, they didn't look like the Purdys anymore. He turned and looked at the mass of humanity with new eyes. If they didn't look like the Purdys . . . Somebody had mentioned the possibility of disguises the night before, but that had seemed far-fetched; now, not so much.

His phone rang. He checked the screen and saw that Greer was calling.

"What's up?"

"You anywhere near the Varied Industries building?" Greer asked.

"Let me look at my map . . ." He checked, found the building on the map, turned around and looked right at it. "Yeah — in fact, I'm out front."

"Go straight through it to the back, to the Fabrics and Threads Department. I'll be waiting in the door."

"On the way," Lucas said.

The Varied Industries building was full of . . . varied industries. Hot tubs, docks, bundles of socks, microwaves and blenders, barbecue grills and canoe paddles. And it was as crowded as everyplace else. Lucas plodded through the aisles, spotted Greer talking to a uniformed cop. Greer broke away when he saw Lucas.

"We found out that Marlys Purdy has exhibited her quilts here, in other years, and thought we should check," he said. "We wondered if anyone has seen her. No luck so far . . ."

"And?"

"Wanted you to take a look," Greer said.

Lucas followed him into the Fabrics and Threads Department . . . which was full of Marlys Purdys. He could see eight or ten of them from the doorway, slightly plump white-haired women with glasses.

"Ah, Jesus." He remembered the question asked by the cop at the horseshoe courts. How do you spot one in five hundred? With all these Marlys Purdys, it could be one in a thousand, or two thousand . . .

Greer said, "Yeah."

"It's worse than you think," Lucas said. "We're looking for Marlys Purdy and Cole Purdy and I got to thinking, would they really walk in here, knowing that a lot of people might be looking for them? Really? After seeing their pictures at the gates?"

"You think . . ."

"Yeah. They might not look like the Purdys anymore. And we got no idea what they do look like."

The Purdys had walked through the back gate, by the horse barn, a few minutes after Lucas left it. The truck was six blocks away, tucked among non-fair-going vehicles in a corporate parking lot. They'd come in separately and they no longer looked like the Purdys.

Marlys was wearing a pink dress she'd made herself, with a pink sailor hat with a pink breast-cancer ribbon pinned to it. She also wore a white satin sash over the dress, with the words "Race for the Cure."

She was carrying Caralee and a baby bag; as she came up to the gate, she knocked her hat off, apparently accidentally, and bent to pick it up. The guard at the gate saw a pink bald head. He didn't look a second time and she went through.

Cole was wearing his National Guard

fatigues, with his OCP patrol cap. The cap was pulled down over his forehead; the hair on the sides of his head was an eighth of an inch long; white sidewalls. The ticket taker waved him through. A few steps onto the fairgrounds, a heavyset man looked at him, held up a hand, and said, "Thank you for your service."

"Sure. Thank *you*," Cole said.

Marlys led the way to the 4-H building, where they could find a place to sit, and where they were unlikely to run into anyone who knew them — neither of them knew anybody in 4-H. When they got there, Marlys went into the ladies' room to change Caralee's diaper, and Cole went out back to the phone junction box by the barns, lifted the cover, and took out the 9mm he'd left there the night before. It was in a belt-clip holster, and he pushed it under his waistband and walked back to the 4-H center to wait.

"Forty-five minutes," he said to Marlys, when he got back.

She nodded, but said nothing. Caralee was on her lap, working on her sippy cup full of apple juice. Marlys stared out over the room for a long time, then said to Cole, "This is a great and bold thing. This is one of the greatest, boldest things anybody's ever done."

Caralee said, "More apple juice."

Greer listened on his phone for a moment, then said to Lucas, "Bowden's here."

"Let's go walk the street," Lucas said.

The street was more jammed than ever, lots of cardinal-and-gold colors for the Iowa State Cyclones and black-and-gold for the Iowa Hawkeyes, lots of big guys and blond women. They threaded through, fifteen feet apart, eyes hitting the faces of the people around them. They were moving slow, and the walk took twenty minutes — and Lucas was eye-checked by a dozen cops along the way.

More than ever, he was convinced that the Purdys no longer looked like the Purdys — and he found himself looking hard at every face, and people flinched away from him.

At the far end of the street Greer led the way to the handicapped parking area, where the three campaign buses had been sequestered. Campaign people were all over the lot, and more were coming in from outside, most of them carrying food. Greer and Lucas checked through the cops, and Lucas spotted Bell Wood talking with a couple of athletic-looking women, whom he assumed were undercover cops.

They went that way, and Wood said, "Hey, guys," and introduced them to the two women, both DCI agents. Lucas told Wood about his worries: that the Purdys would not look like Purdys.

"Yeah, that idea popped into my head about an hour ago," Wood said. "We've had the patrol checking trucks, and Marlys Purdy's truck isn't in any of the parking lots —"

"And they're checking for Cole's truck, right?" Lucas asked.

Wood said, "Ah. Forgot to tell you. We've had the sheriff out there checking on the Purdys' place. They must've taken it seriously, because they found Cole's truck parked in the cornfield — I mean, *in* the corn. They hid it before they left."

Lucas took off his ball cap and wiped his forehead. "Jesus, it's hot."

Lucas left Wood and went to Henderson's bus, where the top people were sitting in maximum air-conditioning. One of Henderson's security guys let him through, and Lucas climbed on the bus and took an empty seat in a cluster of people that included Henderson, Mitford, Alice Green, and a couple of other aides. Henderson asked, "No luck so far?"

"Not so far," Lucas said. He looked at his watch again. Fifteen minutes to ten. "There's no sign of their truck. If they don't have an inside source, they'll think the walk starts at ten o'clock, so that's when every cop and his brother will be going through the crowd, looking for them. It's a zoo out there."

"You could be wrong — they might not be here at all," Henderson said.

"I believe they are," Lucas said. "It's possible that they have no idea of what's waiting for them. How much security there is. When the Iowa guys said there'd be a cop every six feet, they weren't kidding." He scratched his forehead, then added, "Then again, we've got to remember that the Purdys come to the fair almost every year, so they know this place like the backs of their hands. They've probably even seen the candidate walk before."

"Bottom line, we have no fuckin' idea of what's going to happen," Mitford said.

"I'm going back out there," Lucas said.

He left the bus and started toward the line of cops at the access, when he heard a man calling his name: "Lucas! Lucas!"

He turned and saw Norm Clay, Bowden's weasel, hurrying toward him. When he came up, Clay asked, "What do you think?"

"I don't think Mrs. Bowden should walk," Lucas said.

"I told her that one minute ago, but she's going to do it," he said. "She's got her guts up, and she's going ahead."

"Huge crowd out there," Lucas said, looking down toward the street. "Lotsa cops . . . man, I don't know."

"Come on over to the bus and talk a minute," Clay said.

Lucas followed him to the Bowden bus and climbed aboard. The end of the bus had been partitioned off, and Clay knocked once on a cardboard door, stuck his head in when a woman called, "Come," and said, "I got Davenport."

Clay waved a finger at Lucas and led the way through the door. Bowden was sitting on a stool, being worked on by a makeup artist. She said to Lucas, "If you tell anyone about a makeup artist, and I'm elected president, I'll have the CIA kill you."

Lucas didn't smile. He blurted: "Ma'am, don't do it. There's a mob out there."

"And a million cops. Half the mob is cops."

"The Purdys aren't totally stupid. I have

to think that they're up to something," Lucas said.

"Well. You've got a half hour," Bowden said. "I have to say, I only think it's fifty-fifty that they're out there. If they are, it's about ninety percent that the police get them before they have a chance to get close. If they get close, it's about ninety percent that the police get them before they get to me. So what's that? A tiny chance that they get me? I'll take that. I take that every day."

Caralee was being a pain in the ass. She'd been held, and penned up in the truck, for much of the past eighteen hours, and hadn't been in her bed for more than twenty-four. She'd gotten whiny, and then overactive, and every time she was put down, she'd wait until Cole and Marlys were not paying attention, and then she'd take off and they'd have to chase her down.

Cole caught her after the break for freedom and carried her back to Marlys, who was packing up the baby bag.

"Five minutes to ten," he said. "We have to go."

Marlys didn't look at him, her marble-blue eyes now locked into the thousand-yard stare. "The biggest thing in the world," she said. "The biggest, boldest thing in the world."

TWENTY-NINE

Lucas walked out to the street thinking, *Okay, what would they do?*

As he looked to the east down the Concourse, the grandstand for musical shows and the racetrack was on his left, on the north side of the street. A Kennedy-style assassination would put a sharpshooter up on the grandstand with a rifle. From there, anyone on the street would be a sitting duck.

But the grandstand, he'd been told, was crawling with cops, both in uniform and plainclothes. Not only that, Wood had told him that all the grandstand cops were highway patrolmen who actually knew each other. There'd be no fake cops up there, and there'd be nobody up there *but* cops.

In addition to the grandstand, there were several other buildings on the left side of the street. All of that meant that most people standing on the left side would have their backs to a wall. They might be able to attack Bowden from there, but there'd be no escape. And for practical purposes, the crowd there would be thinner, and the Purdys would be easier to spot, even in disguise.

On the right, south side of the street, there was one large structure, the Varied Industries building, and several smaller ones, but there was much more room for a crowd. In addition, most of the fairgrounds were on that side of the street, and anyone running away would have lots of space to run.

If the Purdys were there, Lucas thought, they'd be on the right side of the street. Unless, of course, they weren't . . . if they had a plan nobody had thought of.

A bomb? Were they that crazy, crazy enough to set off a bomb in a crowd this dense? Wood had said that bomb-sniffing dogs would be working the crowd, but what if Cole Purdy had a hand grenade, smuggled back from Iraq? He would stand way back in the crowd, never even get close to the sidewalk, lob it like a baseball.

Lucas got on the phone to Wood: "Bell? Listen, Cole Purdy was in Iraq. What if he brought back a hand grenade?"

"I don't know what we'd do," Wood said. "See him first, is the only thing I can think of. We gotta see him first."

"If that was the play, then we should be looking for a tall thin guy who hangs back from the crowd, but rushes forward as Mrs. Bowden's about to pass," Lucas said. "He'd need some room to throw it."

"The Army says the lethal radius for a grenade is about five meters, which is . . . sixteen feet or so," Wood said. "Wounding radius is fifteen meters, which is about fifty feet. Mrs. Bowden will be surrounded by a lot of people . . . I don't know. Sounds unlikely. I'll tell you what, I'll call Jesse and ask if there's been any hint of a grenade."

"Call me back."

The crowd was getting thick on the sidewalks, but cops held them on the curbs. Lucas got off the street and moved back into the crowd. The going was slow but he stayed with it, checking every face. More people were flowing into the walking route behind him, though, so he was already missing many of them.

He saw Greer, going by in the green-and-yellow Gator, another man standing in the back, braced against the motion of the vehicle, scanning the crowd. Greer spotted Lucas and shook his head.

They moved on, in opposite directions. The sidewalk was now so crowded that Lucas had to physically squeeze past people, some of whom didn't want to lose their places.

One large man said, "Hey, take it easy, bud." Lucas looked him in the eyes and the guy asked, "Cop?"

He wasn't Cole Purdy and Lucas nodded and went on.

Took a phone call from Bell Wood: "Jesse says there's never been a hint of a hand grenade and it's been years since Cole got back. He thinks he would have known if there was one. I think he's telling the truth."

"Breathing a little easier," Lucas said.

He moved on, got to the Varied Industries building door, went inside, walked the aisles for five minutes. The aisles were nearly as crowded as the sidewalks outside, people poking at racks of sale clothing and piles of Tupperware, checking out billiard and shuffleboard tables, considering offers to take thirty percent off the price of a new roof, demonstrations of every kind of hot tub known to Iowans, displays for several colleges and universities, with loan offers to help you go to them . . .

Lucas took another phone call from Wood. "The Des Moines cops found Marlys Purdy's truck. It's in a parking lot six or eight blocks from here, nobody around. They had a judge on call, for a search warrant. They popped the door and found the .357 under the front seat."

"They're here, then," Lucas said.

"Yeah. I don't know what the gun means, though," Wood said. "Why wouldn't they take it with them?"

"It means that we don't know what's going on, Bell."

"Gonna be goddamned embarrassing if they *are* planning to throw a cream pie at Bowden," Wood said. "After all this."

"Yeah, especially if a cop shoots them to death for doing it," Lucas said.

As Lucas spoke to Wood, Marlys was using the burner phone to talk to Cole. "Davenport's here. Here in the building. I saw him walking down the aisles."

"We knew he probably would be," Cole said. "You've got to stay out of sight."

"There's no way to stay out of sight," she said. "What I need is to stay out of *his* sight. I've got the baby up by my face, so he can't see much of my face. He's tall, I can see the top of his head, I'm trailing him through the building. Anyway, he's here."

"If you can stay with him, keep calling me. I need to know where he is," Cole said.

"I need to know if he leaves the building, and if he does, which way he goes."

"I'll call," she said. "Do you see the candidates?"

"Nothing yet. They might have lied about when they were going to march," Cole said.

"All right. Let me know when you see them, I'll let you know which way Davenport goes," she said.

Marlys was weighed down by Caralee and the baby bag, but followed Lucas until he went out the door, and then turned right. She called Cole back and said, "He's headed east on the Concourse, following the sidewalk."

"Okay. I'm still down with the machinery."

When Marlys got off the phone, she realized that Caralee needed another diaper change. Too much apple juice. She carried her to the women's restroom, changed the diaper. Women were walking in and out, including a woman Marlys recognized from the quilt shows, but the woman looked right through her, blank-faced: the cancer disguise was working.

Still, best that she get totally out of sight, if she could. Not much longer. The handicapped toilet booth was empty, down the way . . .

She said to Caralee, "C'mon. Grandma

needs the potty."

Caralee, stoned on sugar, smiled and nodded.

Lucas left the Varied Industries building, took a right outside the door, and continued up the street, searching the crowd.

Something had changed. He remembered the moment when he'd seen Whitehead, the woman who looked like Marlys Purdy, and it had prodded his unconscious mind with an idea. He'd tracked the idea down in his own head, and it had turned into something.

Now he was struck by the same feeling: he'd seen or heard something important, in the street, in the last minute or so, but he couldn't put his finger on it. He cast his mind back, trying to track it down. Had he seen something in the building he'd just left? He turned and looked back at it, but it didn't seem right. It wasn't in the building . . . Where was it? And it wasn't a face . . . So what was it?

Wasn't the phone calls from Wood. Nothing about a grenade. Was it Greer? Something to do with Greer? Why would it be Greer?

He looked at his watch: ten-twenty. The march would be starting in ten minutes. He was at the end of the route, had seen nothing. He turned back, thought about walking down the other side of the street, but that felt wrong.

The radio in his pocket vibrated, and a man's voice said, "I think we've got Cole Purdy. He's over at the Riley Stage. We need some guys to start moving in that direction, *now.*"

There was more radio chatter, but from his morning tour, Lucas knew where the Riley Stage was, and it wasn't far, maybe a hundred yards away. He began jogging in that direction, saw a uniformed cop doing the same thing. Fifty yards out, he slowed, saw the uniformed cop doing the same thing and then another cop closing from farther down south.

Another vibration from the radio and the man said, "We're moving in now."

There was some kind of presentation going on at the stage, with some kids facing a sparse crowd in a semicircle of seats. As he closed in, Lucas picked out the three cops who were moving in: and saw the target.

Could be Cole Purdy, he thought, but if it was, Marlys was somewhere else.

The target wasn't looking in his direction and he started jogging again, and then as the three cops moved swiftly to get on top of the targeted man, Lucas broke into a full run.

Five seconds later he joined what was now a small crowd of cops surrounding a tall, thin man with long hair, wearing an olive-colored long-sleeved canvas shirt.

"Not him," Lucas said to the cops.

One of the cops asked, "Who are you?"

"Davenport — working with Bell Wood," Lucas said.

"Sure it's not him?" one of the cops asked.

Lucas took another long look at the scared tall man, who said, "Whoever it is, it's not me. My daughter's supposed to go up there for the 4-H awards."

Lucas said, "He looks like him, even the shirt's right — but it's not him. Goddamnit. He's in exactly the right place, too. This is where Purdy should be."

The lead cop got on a radio and talked to Wood, who told them that Lucas would know Purdy, and other cops looked at the tall man's driver's license, which had a good photo and an address near Sioux City. A minute later, the lead cop was apologizing and giving a perfunctory explanation for the stop.

Lucas listened for a minute, then wandered out of the stage area. There were all kinds of cops along the street, so he decided to walk behind the Varied Industries building, which would take him along a line parallel to the street but a hundred yards or so south of it.

Cole Purdy was at the machinery grounds. There were trees around the stage area, but he had a clear view of it when the commotion started, men running toward the back of the seating area.

They gathered around somebody in a seat, a whole bunch of them, and then he saw Davenport join them. Cole stepped behind a John Deere windrower to watch; Davenport said something to the group, and the group suddenly loosened.

Cole got on the phone to Marlys. "Davenport's over by that stage. They thought they caught me, the guy looks just like what I used to look like," Cole said.

"Be careful," Marlys said. "I'm in the diaper-changing room. I keep going in and out. Have they started marching yet?"

"Not yet. I don't know what's holding them up. Maybe we should call it off —"

"No! No! We're right there, and they *will* march. You be ready."

"I'm ready," Cole said. Then Lucas started walking toward him. "Gotta go."

Cole peeked around the windrower and

saw Davenport getting closer. He touched the pistol at his hip, but he really didn't want to get in a shoot-out five minutes before they went after Bowden. That wouldn't work. And Davenport was wearing a loose T-shirt, and Cole had a feeling that it *would* be a shoot-out, not just a one-way bullet . . .

Better to walk away. Now.

Lucas was looking at the John Deere vehicles on the machinery grounds and was again prodded by the feeling that he'd seen something and missed it. Greer had gone by on John Deere equipment, they'd seen John Deere equipment in the Purdys' barn . . .

As he watched, a soldier in fatigues stepped out from behind one of the machines and walked away. Lucas fixed on him. The way he was walking, that self-consciousness . . . The soldier glanced back at him, then kept moving, and Lucas *knew.*

He put the radio to his face, squeezed the alarm button three times, and said, "This is Davenport. I've got Cole Purdy. I'm ninety-nine percent. He's south of all that machinery stuff, the plows and stuff, at the back of the Varied Industries building, and he's walking south. He's dressed as a soldier in camo fatigues and an army hat. I'm a hundred yards behind him and we're walking toward the barns, if we've got anybody down there."

Cole glanced back and saw Davenport on the radio and fixed on him, and then *he* knew, and he started running. If he could get down to the barns, he might get lost in the crowds and the pens . . .

Lucas saw Cole break into a run, and he ran after him, shouting into the radio, "He's running . . . He's running . . . He's going around — Ah shit, I don't know what it is, it's that big brown building with that dome thing, it's down by that zip line, the west side of the barns . . ."

Cole pushed the speed dial button on his phone, about the only luxury the phone had, and when Marlys came up, he shouted, "Davenport spotted me, I'm running, I'm running . . ."

He dropped the phone in a cargo pocket, yanked the jacket open and pulled the pistol out of its holster and shoved it into his belt line, with his hand over it. Davenport had been calling somebody on a phone or radio . . . had to be ready.

He glanced back as he was about to turn a corner behind the exhibition center, saw

Davenport, still a hundred yards back, or more. Cole was naturally faster than Davenport, but he was wearing combat boots. He hadn't thought about the possibility of having to run . . .

He turned the corner and two cops were *right there,* running toward him, thirty feet away and closing fast. Neither had a gun in his hand and when they saw him they both reached for their holsters . . .

Too late! Too late!

Cole yanked the 9 out of his waistband and shot them both. Fearing that they were wearing bulletproof vests under their uniform shirts, he shot them in the legs, one-two, one after another, the second shot from no more than five feet, and they went down screaming and he jumped over the cop on the left and kept going . . .

Heard a shot behind him, must've gone wild . . . and he had the crowd in front of him, if they kept shooting, they'd be shooting into a crowd . . .

Ran as hard as he could. More cops ahead. He dodged into the horse barn, and *ran . . .*

Lucas turned the corner and saw the cops on the ground, a few shocked spectators standing, twisting, trying to see where the danger might be, a man picking up his young son and running away, running in the same direction that Cole had gone, another man, then two, with iPhones overhead, making movies . . . people screaming and running . . .

Lucas dropped to his knees next to the wounded cops and shouted into the radio, "We got two men down, two men down behind the big brown building with the dome, by the barns. We need an ambulance here right now! Right now!"

One of the cops said to him, "I think it busted my leg, but Danny's bleeding bad, bad . . ."

The other cop groaned, "Shot me in the balls, shot me in the balls . . ."

He was holding his groin and Lucas dropped the radio and the .45 and pulled the cop's hands away and said, "Let me look, let me look . . ."

The cop hadn't been shot in the balls, but on an inner thigh and was leaking blood ferociously. Lucas clapped his hand over the wound and with the other hand, picked up the radio and shouted, "We've got an artery here, we've got an artery, we need somebody here right now, goddamnit, get me some help . . ."

To the cop, he said, "Your balls are fine."

A woman came out of the crowd and said, "I'm a nurse, let me look, let me see it . . ."

Lucas pulled his hand off and the woman said, "Okay, we need lots of pressure, lots of pressure . . ."

She jammed her hand against the wound and the cop screamed and said, "Don't, don't," and the woman said, "Got to," and the cop cried, "It hurts bad, it hurts bad . . ."

No ambulance, no siren . . .

Lucas was screaming into the radio, realized that somebody was talking, and another woman broke out of the crowd and dropped next to the other wounded cop and said, "Let me see, let me see . . ."

Lucas: "You a nurse?"

"Yes, physical therapist," and to the cop, "Let me see where you're bleeding."

Lucas stood up and saw an ambulance lurching toward them, moving too slowly, too tentatively, and he waved his arms, and then shouted to the crowd, "Everybody wave, everybody wave, get the ambulance over here . . ."

People started waving and the ambulance veered toward them and Lucas said, "I gotta go, gotta go . . ."

He picked up his .45 and shouted, "Did anyone see which way the soldier went?" and a bearded fat man in a Hawkeye shirt shouted back, "He went in the horse barn. The soldier guy went in the barn . . ."

Lucas ran that way and said into the radio, "He's in the horse barn. He went in the horse barn . . ."

Lucas ran into the entrance to the horse barn, saw people running away from the door, but a few standing, staring, and he shouted, "Which way did the soldier go? Which way . . . He's not a soldier, he's shot some cops . . ."

One man tentatively pointed toward the far end of the barn and Lucas ran that way. He could hear people calling on the radio but had no time to listen.

At the end of the barn he peered across a narrow street. An exit gate was down to his left, the entrance to another barn across the way. No sign of Purdy. He looked down to his left again, saw a guard at the gate peering at him. He ran that way, and the guard shouted, "I'm unarmed, I'm unarmed . . ."

Lucas shouted back, "I'm a cop. Did you see a guy in fatigues?"

"He went there," the guard shouted. "Through there, into the swine barn."

Lucas ran that way, pressed the alert button on the radio, called, "This is Davenport. He's in the swine barn. Get some people

471

here, but be careful, he'll kill you . . . he's a good shot, he'll kill you . . ."

Cole ran into the south side of the swine barn, pulling off his fatigue jacket as he went. People were looking at him, but he didn't care, it was the cops he was worried about, they'd be calling on their radios about a man in fatigues. He threw the jacket and his army hat into a pigpen and ran on, holding the gun next to his thigh.

He looked back, saw nobody after him, stopped, caught his breath, *walked* out the exit and across a narrow street into the cow barn. As he did, he looked to his left and saw three cops running toward the scene of the shooting, running away from him.

Had a chance, had a chance . . .

Kept walking. Had to get out of the fatigue pants . . .

He tucked the gun under one armpit and called Marlys. She came up and said, "I heard shots . . ."

"That was me, I'm okay, I can't come up there, you gotta pull the trigger. I got guys after me. I'm down in the cow barn . . ."

As he said it he was coming up to the exit of the barn and a man in a civilian shirt and tan slacks came through the door, mouth open, breathing hard, checked around . . . gun held chin high, ready to fire. Cole was coming up to him and shot him in the chest and ran on when the man went down, out of the barn, slowed again, walking again now, not running, not catching the eye . . .

Lucas was in the swine barn when he heard the gunshot ahead, but muffled, not in the barn, maybe outside . . .

He shouted into the radio, "Another shot, this is Davenport, got another shot outside the pig barn."

He ran toward the exit and saw people running out of the cow barn, where he'd been earlier that morning, and he shouted into the radio, "This is Davenport, he's in the cow barn, cow barn . . ."

He ran across the street into the cow barn, saw a crowd of people milling around the opposite exit, ran that way, and when people saw him coming, they began to run away: his gun, but he couldn't help that, and as he came up he shouted, "Where did he go? Where did the soldier go?"

Several people pointed and then Lucas saw two men hunched over a figure on the ground with a gun beside him, and he saw that man was shot and he shouted into the radio, "Got another man down in the cow

473

barn, in the cow barn, need an ambulance . . ."

Lucas ran out of the barn and shouted, "Where did the soldier go?" and a man behind him shouted, "Hey, cop! Cop!"

Lucas turned and the man yelled, "He took off his camo shirt and hat. He's wearing a white T-shirt now."

Lucas shouted, "Where did he go?"

The man pointed to his right and Lucas ran that way. And saw, a hundred yards away, a tall, thin man walking fast, white T-shirt and camo pants and yellow desert combat boots, and ran after him, trying to keep only Purdy's head in sight while he hid himself in the twisting running crowds of people at the barns . . .

Into the radio he said, "Davenport — got a cop shot bad in the cow barn, gotta get an ambulance, Purdy is walking east toward the art show place, he's wearing a white T-shirt and fatigue pants, need more guys going that way, he might be heading for the campgrounds, need guys with guns at campground gates."

Lucas was closing in on Cole, but the crowd was thinning out and he wouldn't stay hidden much longer.

Cole was running for the campground

gates. Once there, in the welter of campers and RVs and trucks and cars and tents, he could hide and even hijack a truck out of the place, but first he had to get through the gate before the cops figured out where he was. He glanced back and saw a man in a straw cowboy hat looking at him, pacing him, but fifty yards back, talking into a cell phone, and he realized he'd seen the man near the barn and that the man was following him, probably talking to 911.

Had to run. Not far now.

He began walking faster, looked back again . . .

Saw Davenport, coming fast, still sixty or seventy yards back.

Now he did have to run. He broke into a sprint, running right at the gate, and saw a big man in a dark uniform come through the gate with a gun. The man pointed the gun at him and fired, and missed, and Cole fired a shot at him and the man jumped back, behind a phone pole, and Cole realized he wouldn't be able to force his way out and he turned left and ran across the horseshoe courts along a fence line toward the next gate.

Saw a man in a John Deere Gator pull around the corner of a building, look right at him, jump out of the Gator, pull a gun.

Too far away to take down yet, Cole thought. He swerved . . . and was hit in the hip by a gunshot from behind.

Going down.

Got back up, dragging his leg, into the shelter of some kind of museum. The leg was bleeding bad, the pain was crawling all the way up to his shoulder . . .

Looked back and saw the guard in the dark uniform and Davenport coming, realized he had to move . . . or give up.

He moved, one last spurt: if he could get past the guy with the Gator and get through the gate behind him, still had a chance. He brought the gun up and fired three wild shots at Davenport and the guard, who went down to the turf, not hit, but getting ready to open up on him . . .

If the guy with the Gator was still there, and he could get to him, he could ride the Gator out . . .

He dodged around the corner of the building, away from Davenport and the guard, before they could fire at him . . .

And the guy from the Gator was right there, ten feet away. A half dozen 9mm bullets crashed through Cole's chest, and the world went away, dissolving in a bruised purple light, and then nothing at all . . .

■ ■ ■ ■

Greer was standing over Cole Purdy's body when Lucas and the guard got to them and Greer was looking shaky and Lucas looked down at Purdy, who was lying on his back, gray eyes open to the hot sun, but already gone dull and blank. Blood spotted the front of his T-shirt, which was pulled tight over his chest: Greer had shot him six times, all the shots in the space of two hands, including two through Purdy's heart.

Lucas clapped him on the back and asked, "You okay?"

Greer said, "I think so," but then dropped his gun, muzzle-down, into the dirt, and almost fell when he reached down to pick it up. Lucas picked it up for him, pulled the magazine and ejected a round from the chamber, handed the mag and the cartridge to Greer, and said, "Put these in your pocket," and then passed him the empty gun.

He reached for his radio, but it was gone. He'd dropped it back when Purdy fired at him and it was still there, on the ground. He asked Greer if he had a radio, and Greer nodded and handed it to him, and Lucas said into the radio, "Davenport — Purdy is down. Purdy is shot and down. We're by some gate . . ."

"Behind the museum by Gate Four," the guard said.

Lucas repeated that.

"Gotta get an ambulance," Greer blurted.

"Not right away. He's gone, man," Lucas said. He handed the radio back to Greer. "We need ambulances at the other places, we don't want one here if it pulls it away from somewhere else."

"Okay, okay," Greer said.

"Really, really dead," said the guard. And, "I think I shot him, too."

"You did," Lucas said. "I think you hit him in the butt — that stopped him. Hell of a shot."

Greer had broken into a heavy sweat, looked like he might faint: "How many guys did he hurt?"

Lucas said, "Three. At least three. All cops . . . man, you did so good. Listen, we . . ." He was suddenly aware of the distant sound of a band playing "Happy Days Are Here Again," and said, "Is that the march? Are they marching?"

"Yeah. It was about to start when you spotted Purdy . . ."

More cops were running up and a squad car pulled in. Within a minute or so there were cops everywhere, and Lucas slipped his .45 back in its holster and said, "We've still got to find Marlys."

"I don't think she has a gun," Greer said. "We found that .357 —"

"I better get over there, though," Lucas said. "You gotta stay here and sort this out. If I could borrow your John Deere . . ."

"Sure," Greer said. He waved at the Gator. "It's still running."

Lucas jogged forty or fifty yards over to the vehicle, figured out the shift, and shifted it into gear and turned it around and almost ran into a fire hydrant.

Then he had to figure out how the reverse worked and he backed up, and as he did, noticed that he was sitting on bright corn-kernel-yellow seats with that dark green cornstalk color of the machine itself, and on the other side of the hood was the light pastel green and yellow of the fire hydrant.

And he still had those two big nuts in his pocket that he'd picked up from the Purdys' barn workshop, the one with the green-and-yellow overspray on the floor, a green-and-yellow spray that didn't match the hard green and yellow of the John Deere, but did match the green and yellow of fair fire hydrants . . . and those nuts in his pocket.

Why would you need a whole bag of big nuts, but no bolts?

You wouldn't — unless they were shrapnel.

And that nagging intuition he'd had by the Varied Industries building: he'd been walking by fire hydrants all morning, the same yellow and green as the overspray on the Purdys' barn floor.

A bomb.

The Purdys had built a bomb. The farm kid who'd been brain-injured by IEDs in Iraq had built himself an IED.

A bomb disguised as a fire hydrant that was probably standing on the Concourse, right where the candidates would be marching by, right on the curb.

He no longer had a radio. He turned and looked at Greer, couldn't see him in the cluster of cops . . . He screamed, "Greer! Greer! It's a bomb! It's a bomb!"

And he put the Gator into gear and wheeled it onto the closest street and accelerated down toward the sound of the band, and thanked God he'd done the tour that morning and knew where he was going, in fact right down a feeder street to the Concourse . . .

He fumbled his cell phone out of his pocket as he went, hoping against hope that

Greer had understood him, and he speed-dialed Neil Mitford, who answered, but when Lucas shouted at him, said, barely intelligibly, "I can't hear a fuckin' thing over these bands, Lucas."

Lucas thought, *Shit,* dropped the phone, and tried to make the Gator go faster, but it was going as fast as it could, which wasn't a lot faster than he could run . . .

No time left, no time.

THIRTY

Marlys hurried head-down out of the ladies' room, Caralee clutched to her chest, the girl's arms around her neck, and out the back of the building. The plan had been for Cole to pull the pin on the bomb, but he wouldn't be doing that now: he had to focus on escape.

Marlys was the backup.

"Up to me now," she said aloud.

Caralee: "What, Grandma?"

"We've got to go," Marlys said. "Can you walk with Grandma?"

She could hear the band down the street, getting closer. Caralee said, "Walk," and pointed her finger.

Marlys put her down and said, "Hold Grandma's finger. That's a girl."

The aisles of the Varied Industries building had grown too coagulated, so Marlys led the girl around the building, the girl's legs churning to keep up. They came out directly behind the fire hydrant that they'd planted the night before, separated from it by the dense crowd. Marlys asked a tall man at the back, "Do you see them yet?"

"I see Gardner," he said. "The other ones are behind him."

Marlys began edging through the crowd: "Can my baby see? Can we get through?"

They emerged at the curbside rope, a few feet to the left of a cop, a few feet to the right of the phony fire hydrant. Looking down the street, she could see the first band, still a minute or so away, and behind them, volunteers for Gardner in his jazzy blue and white campaign colors.

There was another band beyond them, and then the Bowden marchers with their "Mike for Pres" signs and banners. They were what, three or four minutes away? Five minutes? Did she have that much time?

Then she heard the shooting from the far east end of the fairgrounds, from the area of the campgrounds, where Cole had been running. Coming from the distance, the rapid-fire shots sounded almost like popcorn being popped in the next room, but she knew what it was, and so did some other people around her — men, mostly, in ball caps and sport shirts, who turned at the sound and lifted their noses to the wind, as they might during deer season.

Marlys pulled the phone out of the baby bag and looked at the screen, willing it to light up. The phone remained silent, and for a moment her vision was dimmed by the tears welling at the corners of her eyes.

Now it *was* up to her. For sure.

Lucas gunned the Gator down the street; it was an ungainly machine and slow, and he tried to steer and call Bell Wood at the same time. Wood answered, but like Mitford, he couldn't hear anything: it sounded like he was actually marching *with* the band.

Lucas thought the bomb — if there was a bomb — would be somewhere near the beginning of the march. They wouldn't want to risk having the march cut short, and there was simply no benefit to having it toward the end of the march.

A cop tried to wave him down, to slow him down, but Lucas waved him off and kept going, and then another cop tried to stop him, and the crowd got so thick in the area where the march was scheduled to end that Lucas finally braked and turned the Gator's key to shut it down and then plunged into the crowd, headed on foot for the roped-off part of the street.

He was still a long way from the marchers

— six or seven hundred yards.

"No time! No time!" he chanted to himself, and pushed harder.

At the end, shouldering his way through the crowd, shouting, "Out of the way! Police! Out of the way!" he emerged at the rope line near two highway patrolmen watching the crowd. He shouted at the closest one, slid under the rope with the ID in his hand, and when the cop asked, "What?" Lucas shouted, "It's a bomb! Get on your radio, find somebody down there, and tell them it's a bomb!"

And he ran.

He could see a band dead ahead, a drum major with a six-foot-long gold baton, high-stepping toward him, but a heartbreakingly long way down the street . . .

He ran harder . . .

Marlys asked the people to her right to trade places with her so Caralee could stand on the fire hydrant and see better. "I'm getting pretty tired of holding her up," she said good-naturedly. They gave way and she perched Caralee atop the fire hydrant.

On the bomb.

Cole had stolen the hydrant from a group of discarded hydrants that lay in deep grass next to the county shed. Nobody would have noticed in a hundred years. The hydrants were rusted, most beyond repair. He'd gotten the best one, used a wire brush to get rid of most of the external rust, and a grinder to thin down the outlet nozzle cap.

Thinning the cap had been the most delicate operation, and had taken him days. When he was done, the cap wall, which pointed toward the street, wasn't much thicker than an aluminum cookie sheet, though that couldn't be seen from the outside.

Into the nozzle he'd fit a four-inch stainless steel pipe, filled with a hundred and thirty-two stainless steel nuts. A fist-sized wad of plastic explosive and a firing cap were packed into the back of the pipe. The firing wires from the detonator were trailed to the base of the hydrant column, where he'd mounted the detonator and switch. The detonator had a timing circuit, currently set to the shortest possible time: fifteen seconds.

Cole had attached an ordinary metal meat skewer to the switch, through a small hole that led outside the hydrant casing. The skewer had a loop on the outside end. To fire the bomb, all Marlys had to do was pull the skewer out, which would trip the timer switch.

She'd actually seen it work, out behind the barn, with a fingernail-sized chunk of plastique.

Once she pulled the pin, she had fifteen seconds to get away from the bomb. They'd designed it to work as an ultra-powerful shotgun, blowing the stainless steel nuts across the street, directly at the splotch of white paint they'd poured on the street's centerline. If everything worked perfectly, she'd time it so that Bowden would be close to, or on, the white paint when the bomb fired.

When it went off, she and Caralee had to be well away from it. They were sure that the nuts would blow across the street in a deadly fan shape, but weren't so sure what would happen with the rest of the cast-iron hydrant. It might also blow like a bomb shell — and she had to be behind the building when that happened.

The marchers were moving right along. The first band went past, and then the Gardner people, waving their placards and trailing their banners, and blowing their horns.

Then another band, this one, Bowden's.

The bands were setting the pace, and Marlys counted the steps as they moved along. Then down the street, she saw

Bowden coming. Mike Bowden was wearing an orange-ish dress, smiling and waving, a TV cameraman running backward in front of her, his soundman facing forward, holding on to the cameraman's belt to guide him.

Thirty seconds out.

Twenty-five seconds.

Twenty.

Marlys dropped the baby bag, reached down to pick it up, counting to herself. Her finger was down in the dirt. She found the loop on the firing pin.

Fifteen. She pulled the pin, stood up, said, "We gotta go, Caralee."

She lifted the child off the bomb and the woman behind her said, "You're gonna miss Mike," and Marlys said, "I'm for Gardner," and pushed her way through the crowd, to the back, and started to run.

Bell Wood was standing at the corner of the Varied Industries building, trying to make some sense out of what some cop was shouting at him on the radio, when he saw the woman in pink, in one of the breast-cancer crusader outfits, running toward him. He didn't recognize Marlys at first, but then he eye-clicked on Caralee, who was openmouthed and bilious, as though she'd been severely put-upon, and there was something really unusual about this bald old lady running so hard, and then he saw the rimless glasses and the small bud-like mouth, and she turned and looked in his eyes . . .

He took a couple of steps toward her and then heard Davenport screaming, and turned his head and saw Davenport go by and finally caught what the cop was saying on the radio and what Davenport was screaming . . . "Bomb . . . it's a bomb, everybody run away, it's a bomb . . ."

Wood said, "Shit!" and looked after Marlys, who was scuttling away into the crowd behind the Varied Industries building . . .

And the bomb blew, a noise so loud, a flash so bright . . .

Like the end of the world . . .

Lucas was running as hard as he ever had in his life. Two cops had tried to slow him but he had the ID in his hand and he screamed at them, "Bomb!" and they let him go and he saw Marlys, from two hundred feet, appear to stand up next to a fire hydrant — he knew it was her, saw the bald head and knew what she'd done — and then saw the white paint on the street and recognized it as a target . . .

He screamed, "Run! Run!" at the band that was marching over the white paint. "There's a bomb, run, run . . ." and he ran on to Bowden where the big black body-guard, what was his name? Jubek! Jubek was staring at him and he shouted, "Bomb! Get her out of here! Get her out of here . . . Go back! Go back!"

Jubek turned and physically picked up Bowden and started to run and Lucas's momentum carried him almost up to them . . .

And the bomb blew.

Lucas didn't know what happened until it was reconstructed later, but a Bowden sup-porter named Randy Pence, not a security man but an organizer from Council Bluffs, had seen him dashing toward Bowden and thought it might be an attack on the presi-dential candidate and attempted to stop him, and in doing that, hooked an arm around Lucas's waist, and was between Lu-cas and the bomb when it blew.

They were fifteen feet short of the blotch of white paint, on the edge of the kill zone, and Pence soaked up three of the stainless steel nuts and bits and pieces of cast iron from the hydrant itself; and together they went down in a heap. Jubek was two or three steps farther down the street and took two of the nuts in the back, and went down, Bowden beneath him.

The crowd across the street from the bomb took a hundred hits, spread over thirty or forty feet of rope line; the TV cameraman who'd been running ahead of Bowden was hit many times and died instantly. His soundman was not hit by nuts, but by a large fragment of the hydrant, and died a few seconds later. More people were torn up by hydrant fragments that cut through the crowd behind the ropes; a cop was nearly decapitated, and lay spread-eagled in the street, the top part of his skull gone.

The band that had been marching over the paint spot had gotten a few feet clear of it, but two of the bass drummers in the back were killed instantly, four more grievously wounded.

A hundred cops were on the scene within a few seconds. Lucas pushed Pence off him, realized that he was relatively unhurt, looked across fifteen feet of concrete at Bowden, who was pushing out from under Jubek. She caught his eyes and seemed to mouth, "Help me," and he crawled over to her and she mouthed something else and he realized that he could barely hear what she was saying, that he'd been partly deafened by the explosion, and he shouted, "How bad?" and she shouted back, "I'm not hurt, but Dan's hurt bad . . ."

Lucas lifted his head to look around and saw that dozens of people were dead or wounded; and that cops were flowing in from everywhere, that fifteen civilians were filming the chaos with their iPhones, that two TV crews were already working it, and that people everywhere were screaming in pain . . . He and Bowden knelt next to Jubek and Jubek's eyes were open and he said, "Hurt," and Lucas could hear more clearly now and said, "Hang on," and Jubek almost laughed and said, "I'm trying, dumbshit. Get me something . . ."

Then two cops were there with first aid kits and they found big entrance wounds on Jubek's back but no exit wounds and they plugged the holes in his back as best they could . . .

Henderson came jogging up, knelt next to Bowden and asked, "How bad?" and she said, "I'm okay," and Henderson said, "We gotta help these people." She said, "Yes," and they duckwalked across the street to a swatch of the wounded people and then Lucas lost track of them as Bell Wood came up and asked, "You hurt?"

Lucas had gotten to his feet and he looked down at Pence, who was being covered by a cop with trauma bandages, and said, "I got lucky again."

Wood said, "I think I saw Marlys Purdy with that kid . . ."

"Pink dress? Bald? I think I saw a woman . . ."

"Yeah, that's her. She was running back behind the building there."

"Let's get her," Lucas said. "They've got enough help here."

There were still cops running toward the bomb scene. Wood and Lucas flagged down four of them, told them that they couldn't help at the scene, and spread them out to sweep toward the south fence, where Wood had seen Marlys Purdy going.

"Don't think she could have gotten out yet," Wood said. "She's not a fast runner and she's got that kid."

"Block the gates. Can you do that?"

"I can have our communications guy do it," Wood said. He called, and ordered the gates sealed immediately, nobody in or out unless they had a cop's ID or were carrying the wounded out. He added that they were looking for a bald woman in a pink dress.

When the bomb blew, Marlys realized that she'd been recognized by at least one cop, and here she was carrying a baby and wearing a pink dress that was like a billboard. Instead of continuing across the fairgrounds she hooked back into the Varied Industries building, which was in chaos, people fleeing through the aisles, some trying to get out the back, some trying to get out the front, some dropping to hide under the display tables.

She went past a heap of women's clothing, a little of everything, under signs that said "S," "M," and "L," and snatched a pair of medium shorts and a blue blouse and crawled under a table with Caralee and told the girl, who'd started crying, "You be quiet just a minute for Grandma." She still had the baby bag, and dug in it for the sippy cup, found it, poured a miniature can of apple juice into it, and gave it to Caralee, who took it and stopped crying.

There wasn't much space under the table, but nobody was looking, and Marlys pulled the pink dress over her head and pulled on the shorts and blue blouse. All she had to cover her head was the giveaway pink hat but that was better than the baldness, and she pulled it back on, got Caralee and the baby bag, and said, "Let's go home."

Out from under the table, she could hear sirens shrieking and people screaming and she wanted in the worst way to know that Bowden was dead, but nobody in the panic-swept building seemed to be doing anything but screaming and running, and she expected that nobody actually yet knew what had happened, let alone the results. She shouldered her way toward the west end of the building, but the mob was so thick that she took a left and pushed back to the quilting area. On the way, she went past a stack of gold University of Iowa ball caps, snatched one off the pile, put it on her head, and threw the pink sailor hat under a table.

Cole, she thought, was probably dead; or at least taken prisoner. When they'd identified him, they'd be coming after her. There was almost no reason to run, she thought, but she ran anyway, purely from instinct to get away.

If she could get back to the truck . . . well, then what?

In the quilts room, she saw a half-dozen women that she knew, crouching behind a heavy table they'd overturned, their white-haired heads poking over the top, looking out through the room entrance toward the front of the building, where the bomb had exploded.

She hurried toward them, said to the nicest one of the women, "Jeanine, please . . . could you hold Caralee for just a minute? My son was out there somewhere, I have to look for my son . . . I'll be right back."

"Then I got her, go, go," Jeanine said.

"Here's the baby bag . . ." Marlys dropped the bag next to Jeanine, who took Caralee around the waist, and Marlys bent and kissed the girl and said, "Grandma loves you."

She turned and ran out of the building.

Lucas, Bell Wood, and the other cops spread out and ran toward the south end of the fairgrounds, back to the area of the animal barns. They swept through them and to the gates, not knowing that Purdy was behind them, not in front of them. More cops joined them, looking for the lady in pink.

They got to the fence, no sign of her; now every cop on the fairgrounds had her description.

"She's hiding someplace," Wood told Lucas. "Matter of time, now. It's a snake hunt."

"No bald women go out the gates, and . . . hell, I don't know what else," Lucas said.

They'd just come out of the front of the

cattle barn, after talking to a guard at the south gate and then walking through the swine and cattle barns. Wood stopped talking for a moment, looking at a heavyset woman jogging past the cultural center, and then he said, "That's her. I think that's her. In the shorts and blue shirt and gold hat. She runs like Purdy . . ."

"No kid," Lucas said. Then he shouted, loud as he could, "Marlys!"

Purdy jerked her head around and looked at them.

"That's her!" Wood said.

They sprinted after her, Lucas outrunning Wood, who was talking into his radio.

Marlys heard her name, and couldn't help it, jerked her head around, saw the two men looking at her, knew she'd given herself away. She cut left around the end of the Cultural Center. She'd been headed for the campgrounds, where she'd hoped to get lost. Wouldn't get there, now. She continued along the Cultural Center, a three-story tan building with lots of glass and curving sides. She'd never outrun the two cops; she had to hide, but not in an obvious way. Not in the Cultural Center, where they'd be sure to look.

She ran past open doors and around the

far corner of the building, and then down the side, and peeked back toward the cattle barn in time to see Lucas disappear behind the other side of the Cultural Center, followed by Wood, who was still on the radio, calling for help.

As soon as Wood went behind the far side of the building, she began jogging again, almost on a line back to the blast area, where she had the inspiration: there'd be hurt people going out, maybe she could become one of them, smear some blood on her chest and arms . . .

Her chest felt like it was full of ice, from the running, she was dragging in each breath, and she ran past a stage and onto Pella Plaza, when she encountered Ricky Vincent.

The thing about Ricky Vincent was this: he'd been a Des Moines cop for four years, and though he'd taken his pistol out of his holster a few times, he'd never fired it. The fact that he'd actually drawn his gun made his partners nervous, because he'd never really had to.

Vincent, they suspected, wanted to kill someone, to see how it felt.

They were right.

Vincent was working the fair on his day

off, and he'd missed the action down by the horse barn, when the two cops had been shot by Cole Purdy. He'd already had a half-dozen waking fantasies that placed him on that spot, and in which he'd shot Cole three times, clean through the heart.

His disappointment became even more intense when he heard the shooting that had killed Purdy. He'd run that way, but was too late to do anything but stand around and look at the body, thumbs hooked over his gun belt for the people filming with their iPhones. Like he'd been there . . .

Then the guy from Minnesota started screaming at them and had roared away in the Gator, and they hadn't been able to make out what he'd been shouting until somebody got to them on the radio, and seconds later, the bomb went. He and the other cops ran toward the bombing scene, and a few minutes later the state cop, Bell Wood, had called for help, looking for the woman in pink. Vincent had run around behind the Varied Industries building, too late again. He could see a line of cops running into the barns all the way to the south.

He stood there for a moment, uncertain what to do, then started drifting back toward the bomb scene, where he'd already been told he wasn't really needed — but the bomb scene might get him on television. He'd been on television twice before, and liked it, and this particular scene would go everywhere in the world. He could be on TV in France, in Russia. Hell, even China.

Then Wood was calling again. Purdy had changed to white shorts and a blue top, he said, and was running around behind the Cultural Center, but they'd lost sight of her.

Vincent started running that way.

He and Purdy collided at Pella Plaza.

He saw her coming, a half-jog, out of breath, hat askew, showing the bald side of her head.

Vincent drew his gun, dropped into the approved stance, and shouted, "Purdy! Purdy!"

Marlys Purdy skidded to a stop thirty feet away, threw her hands up, and shouted at him, "I give up. I give up."

Vincent thought, *Bullshit,* and shot her three times before she fell down.

Wood and Lucas pushed through a gathering crowd to find a uniformed cop standing over a dying Marlys Purdy. The cop looked at Wood and said, "I yelled at her to stop, but she threw up her hands and I thought she'd thrown something at me . . . I was thinking another bomb or a grenade or something."

A half-dozen people were filming the scene with their iPhones, getting it all down, the cop posed there for the iPhone cameras, his pistol pointing in the air, Lucas kneeling beside Purdy.

Her eyes were still clear and she recognized Lucas and he said, "We've got an ambulance coming."

She asked, bubbling blood, "Bowden?"

Lucas said, "Wasn't hurt. A lot of other people are dead."

Marlys Purdy closed her eyes, sighed, her head fell to the side, and she died.

Thirty-One

Lucas stood up and looked at the cop who was posing with his pistol, and said, "Put the fuckin' gun away, dumbass."

Wood nodded at the cop and said, "Put it away."

Somebody in the crowd called out, "She said, 'I give up, I give up,' and she held up her hands and you could see she didn't have anything in them. He shot her anyway. Pure murder."

Wood said, "Let's not go there . . ."

Vincent pointed his finger at the man who'd called out, "You keep talkin' that way and you'll find your ass in jail."

"No, he won't! No, he won't!" Wood said, speaking to the gathering crowd. More quietly to the cop: "Put the goddamn gun away. Now!"

Vincent put the gun away and Lucas said to Wood, "You better stay and handle this or he'll shoot somebody else. It could get ugly if there are any iPhone movies. Get somebody pleasant to ask the crowd about it, and get something to cover Purdy. I'm going to run around to the other side of the building."

Lucas jogged around to the site of the bombing.

There were ambulances, but nowhere near enough of them, and he saw three people being loaded into a single ambulance, and a man bleeding heavily from a leg wound loaded into a private SUV. An enormously fat man — maybe five hundred pounds — was lying on the ground next to his overturned wheelchair. A Mercedes Sprinter van had been backed up next to him, plenty of space inside, but the people on the ground couldn't pick him up. When they tried to lift him by his clothes, the clothes ripped; when they tried to pick him up by his limbs, he screamed with pain, not from his chest and facial wounds, but from the stress on his skin. One man came running with a plastic tarp, which they tried to get beneath him: Lucas moved on before he saw how that worked out.

There was a burst of screaming from the far end of the street and when Lucas looked that way, he saw dozens and maybe hundreds of people running. Then, just as suddenly, the running mob slowed, and turned, and nothing happened.

Across the street a dozen wounded people were still lying on the roadway and along the curb, bleeding, covered with cloths and jackets, next to a dead man with a wadded-up T-shirt covering his face. He had a hole in his chest the size of Lucas's fist; the hole was no longer pumping blood.

And everywhere, people making movies with iPhones.

"Lucas! Lucas!" A woman's voice, and he turned and saw Bowden hunched over the body of a woman. Henderson was kneeling next to the woman, and when Lucas jogged up, she said, "She's pregnant, we've got to get her on an ambulance, but . . ."

Henderson had stripped off his suit coat and asked Mitford for his, and they used the two jackets to make a kind of hammock, and the four of them moved the woman onto it, and then, with each of them holding a corner of the improvised sling, they ran her to the nearest ambulance. The ambulance was nearly full, but when the attendant saw that it was Bowden helping with the woman, they simply loaded her on top of another body and a moment later rolled away.

When the ambulance moved, they saw a dead cop lying on the edge of the street, what was left of his face covered with a dark blue shirt.

Bowden gripped Lucas's arm and said, "I did this. If I hadn't come, they wouldn't have set off the bomb."

Lucas shook his head: "You can't know that. They were crazy. The woman who set off the bomb sacrificed her own son. You're not responsible for crazies."

"Where is she?" Henderson asked. The governor's shirt and Bowden's blouse were soaked with blood.

"She's dead," Lucas said.

Henderson nodded and Bowden said, "Good."

"Maybe not so good, hard to tell," Lucas said. "The guy who shot her, a Des Moines uniform, pretty much executed her. People in the crowd said she was empty-handed and trying to give up when he shot her."

Bowden looked around at the chaos and said, "Liberal as I am, I can't say I feel that bad about it."

It took nearly an hour to move the last of the wounded out of the fairgrounds. There were twelve dead, forty-four wounded, with the wounds varying from grievous and disfiguring lacerations to minor cuts. Twelve of the injured had been hurt by other fair-goers in the stampede that followed the blast of the Purdys' bomb. One of the trampled was among the dead. Other dead included two TV people, two members of the band that had been hired to lead Bowden's party, the cop, three people who'd been standing next to or leaning on the fake fire hydrant, and three people who'd been standing across the street.

None of the cops shot by Cole Purdy died. The one who'd been shot through the right femoral artery had nearly bled out, but in the end, a fast transfusion and emergency surgery had saved him.

After the wounded were gone, the arguments began, about who was to blame. Almost no one blamed Bowden, who had retreated to her bus, as had Henderson, who'd gone to his own bus. Two hours after the explosion, the most noticeable people in the street were police photographers, documenting the scene, and bomb-squad members, who were looking for pieces of the bomb, for a reconstruction. The fairgrounds was mostly deserted, except for cops and people who were related to the dead and wounded, who'd been gathered in the

Varied Industries building for police interviews.

Three hours after the explosion, an FBI anti-terrorism squad showed up.

Lucas found Bell Wood a hundred yards down the street, sitting on the curb. Wood looked like he'd been painted with blood, which was now deepening to a cold umber color. Lucas realized that he looked the same way, and that his fingers were sticking together from the blood smeared between them.

Wood was eating a Wiener schnitzel on a stick.

"Where'd you get that?" Lucas asked.

Wood pointed down the street: "The Wiener-schnitzel-on-a-stick place. They're giving them away free. Bring me a beer."

"You sure? There're still a lot of cameras around."

"Fuck 'em," Wood said.

Lucas walked down to the Wiener schnitzel stand, was given a handful of wet napkins to clean his hands, and as he waited for the food, realized how quiet everything had become. No sirens anymore, no ever-present fair music.

He walked back to Wood with a Wiener schnitzel on a stick and two Diet Cokes. He sat on the curb next to Wood, handed him a Diet Coke, and said, "For your own good."

"Fuck you very much," Wood said. "But I suppose you're right."

At that moment the DCI director, Pole, walked up and sat on the curb on the other side of Wood. He was wearing a brown suit and a tan shirt, all speckled with blood.

"Well, I'm fucked," Pole said. "If I had any sense, I'd be halfway to the Mexican border by now."

"What's gonna happen?" Bell asked.

"We're about to go through the mother of all cluster-fucks and the DCI is gonna be right in the middle of it. Our guys were supposed to provide the security for Mrs. Bowden and she almost got her tits blown off."

"I've thought of all that," Wood said.

Lucas said, "One of the first questions they're going to ask is, 'Why didn't we think of a bomb before it went off?' The answer is, 'We did.' "

Wood: "We did?"

"Yes. We had bomb-sniffing dogs here, but they didn't find a bomb, and the bomb was so cleverly made, by a brain-injured ex-military guy who had experience with IEDs, that there was no way we could have predicted this. When I say 'we,' I mean 'you.'

The DCI."

"Not gonna save my ass," Pole said, the gloom thick in his voice.

"Probably not," Lucas agreed. "If you want to go down fighting, the first thing I'd do is make a hero out of Sam Greer."

"What'd he do?" Pole asked.

"Shot Cole Purdy to death. Heard police calls that Purdy was coming his way and had already shot three police officers. Sam met him head-on and killed him before he could do more harm. It was like the O.K. Corral."

Pole thought about that for a moment, then said, "That's something."

Lucas said, "Bell, here, was in close pursuit of Marlys Purdy when she was shot to death. He'd hoped to capture her alive so that she could testify about her motives and any accessories she might have had."

"Really? That's what I hoped?" Wood asked.

"That's what I'd say," Lucas said. "I'd also point out, if I were you guys, that it was a team led by Bell Wood and Sam Greer that turned up the Purdys in the first place and actually prevented the assassination of Mrs. Bowden. And other DCI agents, investigating the group to which Mrs. Purdy belonged, may have solved the Lennett Valley

Dairy bombing."

Pole took his cell phone out of his pocket, looked at the screen. "Another woman died. That's thirteen. She was standing across the street. They think two more aren't gonna make it." Pole had started to cry, tears running down his cheeks, and said, "This is so fucked up."

"Yes, it is," Lucas said. "You should go get a Wiener schnitzel on a stick, and then find a TV camera to talk to."

Pole asked Lucas, "What about you? You were with Bell and Sam last night."

Lucas shrugged and said, "Nothing about me. I don't need the publicity. Hey — I'm not even a cop."

Pole stood up, wiped his face, and said, "Gotta go find a fuckin' TV camera. Just unreal. Just fuckin' unreal. Thirteen people dead and I gotta find a TV camera to talk to."

He walked away, and when he was gone up the street, Lucas said, "That wasn't so bad. He sounded almost human."

"Fuck him," Wood said, throwing his empty Wiener schnitzel stick into the street. "He's an asshole."

Lucas spent part of the remaining summer and early fall working on his cabin, but felt like half of his life was spent in Iowa. There were hearings, both legislative and judicial, and investigations that he didn't even know about until the results were published.

The explosive in the bomb, it turned out, had come from a National Guard dump, and the Guard hadn't known about the missing C4 until the FBI showed up to ask about it.

The FBI anti-terrorism team had also searched the Purdy property, where they'd discovered a cache built into the back wall of the stone foundation of the barn. They'd found the black rifle there, the one Cole used to shoot Robertson; ballistics had nailed that down.

Betsy Skira was found to have been the source of the menstrual fluid on the sheets from the motel in the town of Amazing Grace, near Lennett Valley. She refused to talk about it, on the advice of her attorney. Her ex-husband, Harrison John Williams III, on the other hand, on the advice of *his* attorney, and in the face of DNA findings that confirmed that the dried semen on the sheets was his, rolled over on everybody, and gave up Grace Lawrence and Russell Madsen, her mountain-man boyfriend from back in the day.

Williams told prosecutors that Lawrence

and Madsen had stolen the dynamite from the farm in Wisconsin, and the farmers, when questioned, agreed that the dynamite had been stolen and that they'd informed the county sheriff of the theft.

That put the dynamite in Grace Lawrence's hands. Lawrence, Skira, and Madsen eventually pled to second-degree murder and got fifteen years in prison, no parole, which would put them all close to eighty before they'd get out. Lawrence got another ten, to be served concurrently, for aggravated assault in the shooting of Lucas. Williams got ten years, with five suspended, in return for his testimony.

The Anson Palmer case remained unsolved, but Lucas and Bell Wood both testified that they believed Grace Lawrence had killed him. She was not charged, as there was essentially no evidence — no fingerprints were ever found, no DNA discovered. But there were three known killers in the case, Lawrence and the two Purdys. Marlys Purdy had been interviewed by Lucas the day of Palmer's killing, and couldn't have done it. A time card at the golf course where Cole worked was found by DCI agents, and the card indicated that Cole had been cutting grass all that afternoon. That left Lawrence.

Jesse Purdy was arrested and charged with conspiracy to commit murder, but there was no evidence that he knew of the plot, and there *was* evidence that he'd cooperated with investigators and that his mother and brother had conspired to get him thrown in jail so he couldn't interfere with the attack on Bowden.

On the advice of *his* attorney, he told the prosecutors to suck on it, although there was some Latin involved in the actual phrasing of his plea, and eventually he was cut loose.

Not to go back to the farm, though.

Every single person wounded in the Purdy attack, and every single survivor of a dead person, sued the Purdy estate. The eventual suits added up to a hundred and thirty-odd million dollars, while the Purdy assets added up to a hundred and ten thousand, after an auction sale of the house, equipment, and land. Of the hundred and ten, the lawyers got ninety-six.

Then everybody sued the state fair for failing to provide adequate security.

Willie Purdy didn't want to have anything to do with Caralee, who'd been recovered from Marlys's quilting friend. Caralee and Jesse eventually moved up the highway to Des Moines, where Jesse got a good-paying job working for an old high-school buddy, selling Colorado marijuana to real estate agents, and started saving for a truck farm of his own. He stopped drinking.

A number of television cameras and dozens of iPhones had captured movies of Bowden and Henderson crawling among the dead and wounded. Bowden was so soaked with blood that she looked like a victim herself. At the end, she cried, and the crying alone moved her up nine points in the polls against likely Republican challengers. Henderson didn't cry, but he moved up with her, while Gardner, who'd run from the explosion, was knocked out of the race altogether.

The DCI agents, and especially Greer, Wood, and Robertson, were anointed as heroes, the glow of which lasted nearly a month. Pole was transferred to a job as assistant director of the Iowa Department of Elder Affairs.

Ricky Vincent, the Des Moines cop who shot Marlys Purdy, was cleared of wrongdoing in the shooting. He remained a hero to some people, and a pariah to others. Wood told Lucas that the Des Moines cops were looking to lose him, as soon as they could do it without too much publicity.

Every time Lucas went to Iowa that summer and fall, he'd stop to talk to Robertson.

"One second in your life, everything changes, and you don't see it coming," Robertson said. "I got out of your truck, and I woke up in the ICU, wondering what the fuck happened. One second. I played football up in Okoboji, you know? I had a date with this chick after a game, a party at a friend's house, and I wound up in a bedroom making out with a guy named Carl. I went back in the bedroom to take a leak, and bumped into Carl, and he gave me a squeeze, and . . . I kissed him. One second in my life, and everything changed, and now it's happened again."

"Thanks for sharing," Lucas said.

Robertson tried to laugh, and failed, because it still hurt. "I owe you big, man," he said. "If you ever come back to Iowa . . ."

Robertson would take nearly a year to recover, and he never recovered fully — he'd lost enough lung that serious running was a challenge. He eventually took a full disability pension from the DCI, and after circulating a résumé, became an investigator for State Farm Insurance.

At ten o'clock in the morning on a cool day in October, after a last walk around the cabin, Lucas helped Jimi the carpenter fold up her table saw, and he and Virgil Flowers carried it out to her pickup. The cabin was done: now it needed a fish on the wall, and maybe a deer head or a bearskin, some decent wildlife art, and it'd all be good.

Lucas and Virgil dropped the table saw into the bed of the pickup. Jimi said, "Thanks," as she settled into the driver's seat, and they waved as she drove away. Virgil said, "I gotta tell you, Jimi probably has the best ass north of Highway 8."

"I never noticed," Lucas said.

Flowers looked at him closely, then said, "You lie like a Persian carpet."

Virgil's friend Johnson Johnson had come out the door carrying a fly rod, in time to hear the Persian carpet comment, and said, "Lies like a Persian carpet? I don't get it."

Virgil said, "Some common, ordinary

people like you, Johnson, lie like a rug. Smart people, see . . ."

". . . lie like Persian carpets," Johnson Johnson said. "Okay, I get it. Are we going fishing, or you guys gonna sit around and bullshit about floor coverings?"

Elle Kruger, the nun, came to the door carrying another fly rod. She asked, "Where should I put my fishing pole?"

Johnson Johnson said, "It's a fly rod, honey, not a fishing pole. Leave it out on the front deck."

Lucas said to Johnson Johnson, "You and Virgil go on out. I'm going to run into town and get the steaks and another case of Leinie's."

"Not as good as fishing, but a worthwhile task," Johnson Johnson said. "I only wish I was still drinking."

Lucas's phone rang and he looked at the screen, where he saw one word: Mitford. He smiled and answered: "Yeah?"

"You need to be at the governor's office at ten o'clock sharp, tomorrow," Mitford said.

"I'm up at my cabin. I'm no longer at the beck and call of —"

"Ten o'clock," Mitford said, and he hung up.

"What was that?" Virgil asked.

"Mitford," Lucas said.

"Ah — something's up," Virgil said.

Lucas had brought up his friends for the inauguration of the enhanced cabin. Virgil and Johnson had come up early with Virgil's girlfriend, Frankie; Elle Kruger, the nun, had been an overnight guest who'd ridden up with Weather, Sam, and Gabrielle; and five minutes after the steaks went on the grill, Kidd and his wife, Lauren, showed up with their son, followed by Del Capslock, wife, and kid.

Good group; and stuffed with meat and fried potatoes and pecan pie, they pestered Lucas about the events in Iowa, about the details. Lucas spun the story out, and finished by adding, "Kidd and Elle pointed me in the right direction. If they hadn't — if Kidd hadn't told me where the Purdys came from, if Elle hadn't convinced me that it was a serious threat, Bowden would be dead. And all the other people, too."

"The history of the United States would be different," Del said. "She's probably going to win. If she'd been killed . . ."

"Glad we could help," Kidd said. "Kinda wish I could have been there."

Elle nodded: "But it was so awful. So awful."

Frankie said, "Sometimes the world does

518

seem like it's going nuts. Then, you go to a party like this one, with your friends, and you realize how wonderful everything really is. With all the bullshit — it's still wonderful."

They drank to that — quite a bit.

Virgil, Frankie, and Johnson left when the stars came out, followed into the dark by Kidd and Lauren and their son, and then by the Capslocks. Elle Kruger was put in the new guest room, the kids in the second bedroom. "Great weekend," Weather said, as she and Lucas headed back to the bedroom. "Hated to see it end."

"It ain't over yet," Lucas said.

All during the sex, Weather kept moaning, "Be quiet, Elle's gonna hear us," and Lucas said, "I'm not making any noise."

They had to leave early in the morning to get back to St. Paul; Lucas took the boat out at six o'clock for a fast ten minutes of throwing musky baits, and by seven they were on their way south. At a little before ten o'clock, Lucas showed up at the governor's office, wearing a medium gray Cesare Attolini sport coat over midnight blue slacks from Brioni, a snappy white shirt and no tie. Black oxfords from Anthony Cleverley.

Henderson was waiting, with Bowden, Mitford, and Norm Clay, Bowden's weasel.

"We thought we ought to chat," Henderson said. "Everything seems to be winding down in Iowa, and since Mike was passing through town . . ."

Lucas took a chair. "Go ahead. Chat." Then he turned to Bowden. "By the way, are you going to ask the governor to be your running mate?"

Henderson held up a finger, as if afraid to hear the answer, but before he could say anything, Bowden said, "Probably. If he doesn't screw up between now and the convention."

Mitford said, "It's also possible that the governor could be asking *you* to be *his* running mate . . ."

"Shut up," Clay said. "It's all over but the shouting."

"Shut up, both of you," Bowden said. She turned to Lucas. "Has anyone given you our invitation to join the Friends of Mike, an opportunity for affluent supporters?"

"Someone tried," Lucas said. "I managed to sneak away."

Bowden smiled and the smile even touched her normally cool eyes. She said, "Lucas. I never had a chance to thank you. You saved my life — you and Dan. You as much as Dan."

"How is he?"

"We hope to get him back to work before Christmas," Bowden said. "He thinks he'll never have all the strength back in his left arm, but I told him that we paid him more for his brain than his muscle. He seemed to like that."

"He made an amazing move to cover you," Lucas said.

"Yes, he did — I've seen it a hundred times on TV. I still can't believe it," she said. "Now, the question is, what does Lucas Davenport want?"

Lucas shrugged. "Why would Lucas Davenport want anything in particular? To tell you the truth, when it's all said and done, I had a pretty good time down there."

Mitford looked at Bowden and said, "It's true. He likes that kind of shit."

"That's fine, but I don't like the feeling of walking around, owing something to somebody," Bowden said. "I mentioned that to the president when I saw him last week."

"The president?" Lucas's eyebrows went up.

"Yes, he doesn't like that feeling, either. Since he owes me, and he wanted to get rid of that particular obligation, we worked something out. Just between him and me, after consultation with Governor Henderson. Would you like to be a U.S. marshal?"

Lucas was caught off-balance: "A marshal? Jeez, I'd like a decent badge, but I don't know. I don't know much about what they do. I know they move prisoners around, and I have zero interest in anything like that —"

"We had something different in mind," Bowden said. "In addition to the courtroom stuff, marshals do some very rough criminal investigations. As we see it, you'd stay here, in St. Paul. You can have an office in the federal building, if you want one, nothing that would attract the eye of the media. You'd get to decide what you want to do — we want you working, but *you'd* decide. We'd give you complete independence. Most of the time, anyway. Investigate whoever you want, chase whoever you want, anywhere in the country. Or the world, for that matter."

"Uh . . . you slipped in that 'most of the time.' What does that mean?" Lucas asked.

"Governor Henderson mentioned to me that he'd found it quite useful to have a smart, hardworking, discreet law enforcement officer available to work on special cases. Like the Taryn Grant case. From time to time, after I'm elected, I may want you to handle a special case for me."

"A special case? Do you have one in mind?" Lucas asked.

"No, but I've been assured by the president that after I'm elected, a few will come up," Bowden said, smiling again.

Lucas looked around the room. Nobody else was smiling. Everyone was intent. A deal was going down and they were all serious about deals. "When do you need an answer?"

Bowden said, "Soon. I'm sure you'll want to look into the idea. But soon."

"Give me a week," he said. "I need to talk to some guys."

"Go ahead," Bowden said. "Keep my name out of it, for both our sakes."

"Okay," Lucas said. He looked around the room again. "Hey, this could be interesting."

"Yes," Bowden said. Then, "The rest of us have some other items on the agenda, and we don't want to delay you."

She was telling him to go away, and he went.

Walked out behind the Capitol to his car, whistling. Couldn't wait to tell Weather. U.S. marshal. Sounded like something he could get used to.

U.S. marshal. He stopped: Was marshal

spelled with one *l,* or two?
He'd have to look it up.

ABOUT THE AUTHOR

John Sandford is the author of thirty-five published novels, including the Prey and Virgil Flowers series, and two works of non-fiction. He is married to journalist and screenwriter Michele Cook.

The employees of Thorndike Press hope you have enjoyed this Large Print book. All our Thorndike, Wheeler, and Kennebec Large Print titles are designed for easy reading, and all our books are made to last. Other Thorndike Press Large Print books are available at your library, through selected bookstores, or directly from us.

For information about titles, please call:
(800) 223-1244

or visit our Web site at:
http://gale.cengage.com/thorndike

To share your comments, please write:
Publisher
Thorndike Press
10 Water St., Suite 310
Waterville, ME 04901